APPETITE

PHILIP KAZAN

An Orion paperback

First published in Great Britain in 2013
by Orion
This updated paperback edition published in 2014
by Orion Books,
an imprint of The Orion Publishing Group Ltd,
Orion House, 5 Upper St Martin's Lane,
London WC2H 9EA

An Hachette UK company

1 3 5 7 9 10 8 6 4 2

A CIP catalogue record for this book
is available from the British Library.

ISBN 978-1-4091-2788-8

Typeset at The Spartan Press Ltd,
Lymington, Hants

Printed in Great Britain by Clays Ltd, St Ives plc

The Orion Publishing Group's policy is to use papers
that are natural, renewable and recyclable products and
made from wood grown in sustainable forests. The logging
and manufacturing processes are expected to conform to
the environmental regulations of the country of origin.

www.orionbooks.co.uk

Praise for *Appetite*

'...h's rich, sensuous prose is always a pleasure'
— *Sunday Times*

'...celebration of the senses: what Patrick Süskind's *Perfume* did for scents, this does for flavours. A love story which will also appeal to fans of Joanne Harris' *Chocolat* . . . The ultimate foodie version of *Perfume*, this is an addictive page-turner filled with lavish literary gastro-porn'   *Red*

'*Appetite* by Philip Kazan has had me salivating. Yes Kazan writes good food . . . [Florence] is wonderfully evoked . . . Delicious stuff'   *Big Issue*

'Ambitious and engrossing . . . a novel of exceptional energy and colour'   *BBC History Magazine*

'Kazan brings medieval Italy to life with an astonishing degree of historical detail. *Appetite* has the vivid colours of Tracy Chevalier's *Girl With a Pearl Earring* and the sharp odours of Patrick Süskind's *Perfume* . . . Readers will certainly come away with an appetite for more'   *We Love This Book*

'intense, sprawling and most convincing'
Sydney Morning Herald

'A delicious and mouth-watering read, this is a novel which engages all the senses'   *New Books Magazine*

PHILIP KAZAN is an informed historian,
a passionate cook and a keen traveller.
He brings real gusto and humanity
to his writing.

In Memoriam: William E. Spruill

'O Ariel, Ariel,
How I shall miss you. Enjoy your element.
Goodbye.'

(from *The Sea & The Mirror* by W. H. Auden)

Acknowledgements

Great thanks go as ever to Jon Wood and
Genevieve Pegg at Orion Publishing, for sticking
with me; to Christopher Little and Emma Schlesinger
for their steady hands and warm hearts; to Tara, for
her patience and for her advice which, as I have
learned, I ignore at my peril; and to my parents,
for their wisdom and their love.

The heavens set your appetites in motion – / not all your appetites, but even if / that were the case, you have received both light / on good and evil, and free will, which though / it struggle in its first wars with the heavens, / then conquers all, if it has been well nurtured.

Dante, Purgatorio, XVI

The wheel of Fortune turns; / I go down, demeaned; / another is carried to the height; / far too high up / sits the king at the summit – / let him beware ruin!

Anon, Carmina Burana

↭ I ↫

NIGHT IS FALLING VERY GENTLY, shaking the light from the dusty air. After the clamour of the day, the city is settling its affairs, settling down, grudging, grumbling, a caged lion submitting to its pallet of musky straw. Behind, in the house, footsteps tell me someone is doing this or that. Whatever it is, there's nothing urgent. In the eaves of the loggia a fat brown gecko has woken up too early and is fussing among the beams. The cathedral dome is turning from red to orange, hanging over our rooftops like our own setting sun. The whole city is lion-coloured, and out beyond Careggi the mountains are already fading.

There is a bowl of peaches on the balustrade, ripe enough to have lured a single hopeful wasp. I'm trying to remember something, but remembering can be so hard in a place like this, where every stone has some meaning or other. Florence is always remembering itself, and at the same time creating new things to remember. Confusing . . . Perhaps that's why we have the dome, sitting on us like a giant's paperweight: to keep all the memories in order. Anyway, I have enough to keep in my head. Menus, orders, a man coming up from Pisa with shrimps and cuttlefish. I ferret idly through my thoughts, but it's all distracting. Even the air is complicated. The smells of cooking are weaving through other scents: pine trees, rotten fruit, rubbish piled up behind the houses. So I let myself surrender to Florence, like I always do. I do not have a choice – I've never had a choice. I am up here on my balcony looking down, but I am not separate. I'm just another ingredient.

The peaches are beautiful. They are blushing to the same shades as the dome: the red of the tiles, the gold that's winking off the orb on top of the lantern. A friend of mine helped put that up there. I don't know where he is these days. The world seems to have got bigger lately. But that's the world beyond the walls. Something about the light, the way the city appears cupped by the mountains, makes Florence seem like the centre of everything – it thinks it is, of course. But I don't care about that. I just want to remember something. So I reach out for the ripest peach, pick up the soft ball, feel the nap of its skin. It smells a little like the bowl, and a little of camphor, the way very ripe peaches sometimes do. I don't really like the feel of peach skin against my tongue so I just bite, and let the gobbet of melting fruit burst inside my mouth.

The flavours settle across my tongue in shapes and colours. Sweetness pools, smug and tarry, like pitch seeping from a sun-warmed beam. Quicksilver balls of sourness skitter for a moment, then freeze into shards and fall like icicles brushed from a window sill. Tiny pricks of vinegar mark out the footprints of the wasp. I let it all dissolve into golden light.

A hand settles on my shoulder. I lean my cheek against it, hold up the peach. An everyday gift. It is accepted. I close my eyes, feel the dying sunlight brush against the lids. The city breathes, and its breath is fifty thousand voices, fifty thousand souls waxing and waning, rising and falling. This evening it is hardly a whisper, but I have heard it roar. Many times: when so many beautiful things were burned; when they burned the priest who hated beauty. When our rulers fled; when the French marched in. When the great bell of the Signoria tolled for a boy who was butchered under the great dome, and the dead were dug up and dragged through the streets. When dead men hung like black pears from the palace walls, and the wasps went mad from gorging on spoiled meat.

These things have happened: I saw it all. And still the peaches taste of amber, and of drowsy wasps. So much is lost, but should we miss it? The dome still holds us all in place. The fires are lit and food begins to fry, to boil. Smoke rises up in threads like the warps of a loom. I breathe it all in, all this perfume, all this life. My life, threaded across this great loom.

The hand at my shoulder is gone. Then it returns, brushes my cheek. I turn and catch a finger between my lips. The taste of peach is there, and something else. Another thread of the loom, the thing that takes the complication out of the air, that makes sense of our great beast, our city; of our lives. I've found it, hidden in plain sight. Because it was never lost. It was there all along.

So. Now I remember. Now I can tell you.

Fortuna Turns Her Wheel Once:
'Regnabo' – 'I Shall Reign'

Florence, 1466

MY MOTHER DIED THE DAY before I turned fourteen. I watched her take her last breath, a long, shuddering gasp. It didn't make much difference, really. The figure lying in Mamma's bed – a waxy creature with the translucent skin of a slaughtered hog after it has been bled empty – had stopped being my mother days and days ago. The room smelled of sweat, of lavender and sage and chamber pots: and when the priest gave me a little shove in the direction of the corpse, and I knelt at the bedside, took her already cold fingers, raised them reluctantly to my lips, her skin smelled of the same things. I rested my lips against the veins ridging the back of her hand and did what I had always done: flicked my tongue against her skin and tasted it.

Some people call a talent like mine a gift, and some call it a curse. It is both. I doubt that most people would like to know what death tastes like – we might not like to share the dinner table with those who do. But I, not quite fourteen, discovered it for myself. You will perhaps be disappointed when I tell you that death has no taste. I'm talking about death itself, the moment that removes us. Dead things have flavour. We like some of them, or we would not hang our meat. Really, we wouldn't eat at all, or perhaps only oysters. But death itself is flavourless. It is a void on the tongue. My mother's skin had the saltiness of sweat and the rankness of consumption. I didn't expect to find those tastes I loved: garlic and onions, water from the well in our courtyard, sometimes ink, always the flower water she bought from the apothecary near the Palazzo della Signoria. I was expecting sickness and soap, and there they were, but the tastes were hollow. I staggered to my feet and ran upstairs to a corner of the loggia, and rocked on my heels, trying to shut it all out. It was not that Mamma was dead. I had been expecting that, and people died all the time. I had just realized she had had her very own flavour, and I had discovered it only by its absence. It had gone with her, and I would never quite know what it had been.

She had wanted her brother to be at her bedside, but Filippo wasn't there. He hadn't lived in Florence for years, although the whole city knew what he'd been up to in Prato: how he had made a nun pregnant, run off with her, and then managed to persuade the Pope, no less, to let them marry. He was always a charmer, my uncle Filippo Lippi, but in Florence they still remembered how he'd been caught embezzling, tried to blame someone else, and been racked for it until his guts had popped out – only a few guts, mind, because he'd been sewn up again and sent off to do more mischief. They all remembered that. The fact that he was the greatest painter of our age was less appreciated, though his glorious work was everywhere. Which just proved that flapping tongues are mightier than keen eyes.

But Filippo would have been there if he'd known. If my father had bothered to tell him that Mamma was dying, he would have ridden the shoes off his horse to get to her bedside. He was only her adopted brother – a cousin, from the Lappacchia side of the family – but they had loved each other as if they'd slipped out of the same womb. He couldn't have saved her. I think it would have made it easier for me, though, if I could have seen his stubby, tonsured form at her side. And he would have drawn her, alive and dead. It seemed to me, in the days that followed, as my mother's corpse lay among candles, and then was slipped, without much fuss, beneath its plain marble slab in San Remigio, that if I could have seen it all through Filippo's eyes, through the lines he made with charcoal on paper, trying to capture what it was his eyes saw — really *saw* — it would have made more sense. Filippo might have showed me something I had missed. Because I understood, even then, that Filippo's eyes did something to him, in the same way that my tongue, my palate, did something to me. A real artist has hungry eyes. Filippo, with his appetite for everything, certainly did. He saw things other people missed. I tasted them.

I was still slumped against the wall of the loggia. My father was calling me; pigeons were scraping around on the beams above me; and footsteps were clattering, down in the street. I wanted to scream at them all to shut up, to give me peace, but this was Florence where there is never peace. I got to my feet, slowly, painfully. Papá called again. I looked out over the balustrade, half hoping to see a friend there: Arrigo, Tessina, the Lenzi boys. But I saw only heads, balding or greasy or capped, and no faces turned up to where I stood. So I pulled myself together and went back downstairs to kneel by Mamma's bed. The priest and the surgeon were gossiping about a magistrate. Papá went out to arrange the funeral. Then the others left, and I was alone. Mamma's mouth was open, her lips almost white. I tried not to look at her, but I could not bear the dark oval of her mouth, and so I tried to shut it. The looseness of her jaw terrified me, and as I bunched up the damp sheets to prop it closed I winced with the horror of what I was doing. Mamma was gone, but her corpse was still here, an empty thing with a mouth that could not breathe, or speak, or taste. Empty: a crypt. I finally got it closed, and buried my face in my hands.

But as I shivered, my forehead pressed into Mamma's

hand, a slight breeze rustled the curtains. I remembered the priest opening the window after it was over, and now the air brought me the most ordinary scent. Someone was making a *battuta:* frying an onion, parsley, beet leaves. The sugar of the onions, the metallic edge of the beet, the smoky, barnyard sweetness of the lard plucked at my misery: *This is life,* they said. *This is what we do every day: give ourselves up for your food, for the sake of your Florentine bellies.* And all of a sudden I felt the city all around me like a vast, dirty flower, and there I was at its centre like one of the lugubrious black bees that lumber through our gardens in summer. There was the house, the walls that held us. We were the Latinis, and we lived here, on Borgo Santa Croce. Around the house, the neighbourhood curled, our *gonfalone* of the Black Lion, where people were frying *battuta* as if nothing had happened, and where they would go on frying it if the whole world was coming to an end. Further out, the quarter of Santa Croce with its great basilica, whose bells would be tolling soon, as soon as Papá paid the priests. And all around me, Florence itself, a cobweb of clattering streets, countless alleys, towers, workshops, tanneries, cloisters, churches and burial grounds, where the sky is a thin strip of blue above, and the earth is a great belly of brick-lined guts held in by the walls of the city, with its towers and gates. Out there, thinking of their dinner, sixty thousand citizens: paupers, tarts, guild members, monks, nuns, painters, apothecaries, bankers, cripples; their stomachs all rumbling now that the *battuta* was cooking. I wasn't alone at all. No one is alone in Florence, not even the dead. Mamma would vanish into soil that was black with the dust of other Florentines from other times. And still the onions would be chopped, and the beet greens, and the parsley. The sizzling fat would heat patiently in pans that no one would ever count. And people would eat.

⤞ 3 ⤝

My birthday came and went. I spent it working for my father in his shop on the Ponte Vecchio. Papá was a butcher – the Latinis had been butchers for a hundred years or more, building up the business slowly and cannily. Papá was as patient as the beasts whose flesh he cut up and sold. He had been in the shop the day before his wife died, and he was there the next day. I hated him for it, back then, because it would never have occurred to me that Papá might have feelings the way I had them. But when he asked me to help him with some sheep that needed preparing I said yes – not that I ever had a choice in those things, though perhaps it had been my birthday present, this pretence of free will – and found the hard, meticulous work to be a great gift after all. We stood side by side, sharing a whetstone for our knives, both knowing what to do, because I had already received the teachings he had received from his own father, and I was just the latest link in a chain that stretched back to the Latinis' past as slaughterers in the slaughterhouses of San Frediano, and before that, as farmers in the Mugello. There was comfort in that, or at least the absence of pain. I had been getting used to absence, that summer, but this pain was something new. It was as if Mamma had been my skin, and her death had left me flayed and raw.

It was difficult to look for comfort in Papá. Mamma had been soft and quiet, as neat as a turtle dove, and Papá was a big, untidy buzzard. Everything about him was solid and practical. His shaved head sat on a neck as thick and corded as a Chianina bull's. His nose, a ridged beak, had been broken, his lips were forever gathered into a belligerent pout. Below, the hard prow of his chin jutted like the spur of a galley. That year, he could still put one hand under my armpit and lift me high above his head – I was a big lad, but smaller than a side of Chianina steer. He was always caught up in his work, always happier when he was somewhere other than our house. The house, and Mamma. How could I have known they'd loved each other?

I am ashamed, now, to remember how surprised I was that Mamma's death had upset him so much. I was the one who had loved her, because I had understood her. She had been quiet, where Papá was loud. She had read books and could talk about painting and music, and had grumbled about her husband all the time: he messed up her kitchen, his clothes smelled of the slaughterhouse, he spent too much time at the palace of the Butchers' Guild. She read Boccaccio while Papá crashed about, bellowing about the price of steers. She had been close to her brother Filippo, who my father cordially disliked. So why did he miss her so much? He'd barely seemed to notice her when she'd been alive. She'd been a sort of neglected possession – even her epitaph said as much:

ISABETTA DI NICCOLAIO LATINI

Niccolaio Latini's Isabetta. And now he hadn't spoken to anybody for days, and was more or less living in his shop.

I am laying out cuts of meat with my father. We have made stacks of chops, shanks, glistening frogspawn piles of kidneys, silken heaps of liver. Now I'm struggling to hang up dressed sides of mutton in the front of the shop. I'm not quite tall enough to reach the iron hooks, though I will be, next year. I can't remember if I leaned against Papá then, after we'd done what needed doing, just rested against him for a moment. I'd like to think that I did. I would like to think he pulled me to him, so that we stood, father and son in bloodstained whites, for all the passers-by on the bridge to see. Perhaps he did. I hope he did.

The last carcass was hung when I saw, framed between gently swaying meat, the tidy black-clad shape of my friend Arrigo Corbinelli. He held up a hand, shyly, grinning an uncomfortable little grin. Papá saw him too. He patted me on the shoulder.

'You can go with Arrigo,' he said. 'We've got a lot done here.'

'Are you sure?' I asked, dubiously. I felt safe in the shop with Papá. It was as if, out there in the streets, all the horrors that had come with Mamma's death would find me and pick me to pieces. 'Aren't we going to cut steaks next?'

'I've got to give him something to do,' muttered Papá, jerking his chin at Giovanni, his assistant, who was lurking in the back of the shop.

'But, Papá . . .'

'I can't make you work here all day,' he said. He put down the knife with which he had been trimming flaps of skin away from the carcasses. 'Do you want to go back to the *palazzo*?'

I bit my lip, feeling the horrifying sadness coming up in me again. Mamma was laid out in the main room, candles at her head and feet, lilies all around her. The whole house stank of cloying lilies and guttering candles, but not of my mother, who seemed to have vanished as though she'd never existed at all. Everything needed dusting and sweeping, though Mamma would never have left the dirt from the mourners' boots lie unswept. And yet there was this thing, this effigy, lying on a table in our grand room . . .

'I'll go with Arrigo,' I said. 'But I'll meet you back here, yes? At sunset?' Papá nodded. I went into the back and changed into my ordinary clothes. Arrigo was still standing in front of the shop, scuffing the toes of his shoes against the flagstones. When I came out into the noise and light of the bridge he took a step back, as if the death of mothers was something you could catch, but I understood. We were at the age when our bodies seemed too awkward for our brains. Children hugged, grown-ups hugged, but not fourteen-year-old boys. I folded my arms, just as awkwardly.

'Sorry, Nino,' he muttered. 'About your mother. My parents say . . .' He kicked at the stones again. 'Look, do you want to play dice? There's a game going on behind the church.'

'All right,' I said. I glanced back at my father, who was standing with his back to me, broad shoulders soft and sagging. He'd picked up the knife again, and a whetstone, but just seemed to be staring at them. I wanted to run inside and stand there with him, but somehow I knew I couldn't. So I turned and took Arrigo's arm, and we set off through the shoppers, heading north.

'So what did your parents say?' I asked him, when we were away from the main street.

'Just that your mamma's with God,' he said.

'I know she is.'

'That's what I told them.'

Years ago, I'd often wondered why I was friends with Arrigo. I mean, I'd known *why* we were friends: because our fathers were confraternity brothers. Messer Simone Corbinelli was a middling-well-to-do lawyer who lived in Corso dei Tintori, and he and Papá dressed up once a year and carried a wooden saint around the streets of the Black Lion. Arrigo was skinny, tall for his age, and big-nosed. When we were small he always seemed to have a cold sore in the winter, and in summer the grass seed made him sneeze. Some of us called him 'Priest', because his mamma dressed him in black and cut his hair with a pudding bowl. He was bookish as well – not surprising, for the son of a lawyer. He had an older brother who was studying law at Bologna, and that was what his father had planned for Arrigo as well. I had been five or so when we had first clapped eyes on each other, suspiciously, in the basilica. Our parents had shoved us together and expected us to get along.

To the surprise of us both, we did. It turned out that we shared a love for the streets, for *calcio* – our Florentine game of a ball, thirty men and much blood, played by young nobles on feast days in our great piazzas and imitated by lesser mortals in the back streets and on the wastelands inside the city walls left over from the Black Plague – and for wars and intrigues. Arrigo was a reader, and Mamma had taught me to read as well, though I was never as diligent as my friend. And he believed, quietly but with huge conviction, in Our Lord. *Who doesn't?* you ask. Exactly so – but perhaps I should say instead that Arrigo saw the world as the saints must see it, whereas I have always approached God as the layman that I am. He wasn't a preacher, though, and he wasn't pious – you can't be pious and play *calcio*, and Arrigo was the best *calcio* player in the Black Lion.

'Who's at the church?' I asked.

'The Buonaccorsis, and the signorina.' The signorina meant Tessina Albizzi. 'It was the signorina who told me to get you, not my parents. *They* just sent me to pay my respects to your mamma.'

'Did you?'

'Yes.' He paused, and lowered his head. I wished he hadn't seen her; I didn't want anybody else to see the thing that everyone was telling me was still my mamma. 'I'm so sad for you, Nino. I really liked your mother.' He closed his eyes. 'You know, "it is in dying that we are born to eternal life" – Saint Francis said that.'

'But . . . Arrigo, she's just dead!' I burst out. 'How can she be so dead here, and alive somewhere else? I don't understand . . .' Oh, Christ. I couldn't cry, not in front of someone else. So I turned and kicked out, savagely, at a large pot at the side of the street that held a half-dead sage plant. It exploded in a burst of shards and dusty soil. Arrigo paid no attention.

'You have to have faith that it's so,' he said carefully. 'You have to believe.'

'Just like that? So easy?' I said bitterly.

'It's not meant to be *easy*. What's easy is me talking about your ma being dead, and how you should believe she's in heaven. But only you can do the believing. Saint Francis was really talking about letting your doubts die, so that you can be reborn on earth.'

'Have you done it, then?' I snapped.

Arrigo gave a little snort and shrugged his shoulders. ''Course not,' he said. Then he twisted his mouth into a half grin, as he did when he was trying to show he understood you. 'Come on, then! Someone's going to be angry about their pot.'

We found our friends in a passageway behind San Pier Scheraggio. Tessina Albizzi was playing dice with the Buonaccorsi twins, Mario and Marino. Tessina liked to gamble, though she was bad at it. But it didn't matter, because it wasn't her money. Recently she'd found a stash of almost worthless old coins that she thought her uncle had hidden and forgotten about, and she'd go down behind the church and throw dice against the wall, swearing like a mercenary when she lost. Tessina's mother was dead, and her father as well. She lived with her aunt and uncle, who were horribly respectable, and if they'd ever paid her any attention they would have beaten her for the company she liked to keep.

I knew Tessina had heard about Mamma yesterday because

the whole neighbourhood had known: *Niccolaio Latini's wife won't last out the week.* Tessina didn't say anything when I squatted down beside her. She took my hand and dropped the dice into the palm. Then she lobbed a clunky old coin onto the small pile that lay in front of Mario's bare feet. Mario was always the banker. Though he and Marino were dyers' children and had probably never touched a book or an abacus, Mario could do anything with numbers. Tessina nodded gravely, and I gave the dice a shake and tossed them at the pitted bricks of the church.

I lost, of course. But Tessina dropped her coins on the pile, one by one, and I threw the dice, and lost, until Tessina's purse was empty. Then we stood up.

'You've ruined me,' she said to the twins, and bowed. 'Coming, Arrigo?'

'I have to get home,' he said, dusting off his black tunic.

'Cowards, the lot of you,' said Marino, gathering up the dirty coins. He stood, and dusted off his knees. 'Sorry about your mother, Nino.'

'Very sorry,' said Mario, and the twins crossed themselves solemnly, in perfect unison.

Tessina took my hand and we wandered off down to the river. I don't remember what we said, or if we said anything at all. It was enough just to sit and watch the water, and listen to the noise of the crowds on the bridge. A man was catching eels, and another man was hawking grilled ones. Tessina bought a skewer of them with one of the proper coins hidden in her dress, and made me eat. They were good: the firm meat, rich with fat and faintly muddy, was hidden inside a crust of salt, cinnamon and breadcrumbs. It was the first thing I'd eaten since Mamma had gone, and Tessina fed me, breaking the fish apart and holding it out so that I had to take it from the palm of her hand. Beneath the salty fish and cinnamon, I could taste Tessina, and the coins she'd held, and the dirt of the alley. When the eel was finished, she licked her palm, threw the skewer into the Arno, and led me back to the shop, and my father.

⁂ 4 ⁂

WHEN I WAS A CHILD I put everything into my mouth, and what didn't fit, I licked. As a result of this habit, grown-ups were forever slapping me, yelling at me, and even now there are some tastes that immediately bring back a ringing between my ears, because our cook, whose name was Carenza, caught me and cuffed the top of my head: *For God's sake, child! That's copper polish!* Or perhaps it had been the stuff for bleaching our bed linens: I'd tried everything. It wasn't because I wanted to fill my mouth – I'd never sucked my thumb, so Mamma told me – but the reason was too hard for a small child to explain. I suppose at first I assumed that everyone tasted things the way I did; that a dab of something on the tip of the tongue caused things to appear in their mind's eye: colours, shapes and patterns, or pictures of things, even of people. The copper polish, which Carenza made with sal ammoniac, must have been disgusting. I remember it burned my tongue, sent an intense flash of sky blue through my skull and, for no reason at all, the image of cobblestones. I'd ducked away from Carenza, gone out to the courtyard and spat . . . *Eat some proper food!* They were always yelling that, and I ignored them. There was plenty of time for proper food. Because I wasn't hungry: I was exploring my city, so vibrant and alive. Always searching, I'd tried the moss that grew around the old marble well-head. Moss was just moss to eyes, nose, fingers. On the tongue, a piece the size of my thumbnail became a field of grass rippling in the wind. I licked the marble, which seemed like the flavour of the world itself.

Mamma would have been watching from the doorway. She had shouted at me for trying the polish, but mostly she let me do what I wanted, as long as it wasn't too mad, or too dangerous. Mamma understood, I think, what I needed to do. She had grown up with Filippo, so she was used to people with unnatural senses. She knew her brother was seeing things in a different way from most people. *Drunk on paint* – that's what Mamma called Filippo. But it was the colours that made him drunk, not the paint. Paintings are simple, really. Think of an Annunciation: it's just two people in a room. One of them happens to be an angel, of course. But really, a man with wings is talking to a rather alarmed young woman. Ignore the wings and you could be looking through a window anywhere in Florence. The story – the real story – is told by the colours.

It is Filippo's colours that let us watch as a creature from Heaven – not a man at all, and those wings: they're for flying across oceans of light – performs his miracle and steps through the veil into our world. As that concerned young maid realizes she is carrying the child of God, we feel her terror, and her wonder. A room, a man (ignore the wings just a little longer) and a woman, washed in colour and the suggestion of light: colour and light doing something they don't do in our drab world. Filippo's sight showed him things in their true nature, the way they really looked. My mouth showed me what things really tasted like, and every time I touched my tongue to something, I was reaching through the veil into the angel's world.

It faded, in time. The angels banished me, as angels are wont to do. Everything began to settle down. Perhaps I had mapped things out to my satisfaction, or maybe all the strange tastes had damaged my tongue, but by the time I was five years old I'd realized that I wasn't moving through an endless corridor hung with painfully bright, gauzy curtains, each one dazzling. I could put a spoonful of pottage into my mouth without the room disappearing. There was less wonder, I admit, but relief as well: it had been exhausting, that relentless assault of sensation. Now I began to understand something I'd never grasped before: the notion of food. And with that, I began to notice the kitchen.

When our house had been built a hundred and more years ago, kitchens hadn't been as fashionable as they are today, and ours was quite small, an oblong box of unrendered stone with a fireplace at one end and a small stone larder set into the wall at the other. There was a big table, the top of which was almost the colour of ivory from years of scrubbing. Pots hung from the ceiling beams, between the festoons of braided garlic, the hams, the *salsicce*, bunches of mountain herbs for medicine, strings of dried porcini, necklaces of dried apple rings in winter, chains of dried figs. The smell of onions, of hot lard and smouldering oak wood, of cinnamon and pepper, always seemed to hang in the air. The larder was full of meat at all times, needless to say: not small pieces, but huge joints and sides of beef and lamb, which Mamma and Carenza could never hope to use just for our household, and which were quietly passed on to the monks of Santa Croce so that they could feed the poor. Carenza made salami with fennel seeds and garlic, prosciutto, pancetta. Sometimes the air in the larder was so salty that it stung your nostrils, and sometimes it reeked of spoiled blood from the garlands of hares, rabbits, quail, thrushes and countless other creatures that would arrive, bloody and limp, from Papá's personal game dealer.

Next to the larder, a door led out to our courtyard, which Mamma had kept filled with herbs. An ancient rosemary bush took up most of one side, and the air in summer was always full of bees. Sage, thyme, various kinds of mint, oregano, rocket, hyssop, lovage and basil grew in Mamma's collection of old terracotta pots. A fig tree was slowly pulling down the wall, and a tenacious, knotted olive tree had been struggling for years in the sunniest corner. I had spent a lot of time out there when Mamma was dying. I thought she would have been happier out there too, but the grown-ups wouldn't hear of it. Typical of grown-ups: to want to die in the dark, on damp sheets, when you could slip away on warm stone, with bees and lizards to watch over you.

The kitchen would become more important to me than church. Mamma and Carenza loved to cook the things the people of Florence have always cooked: grilled meats, sausages, stews, *torte*, pies, eels, even lampreys. It was watching Mamma that I first witnessed the smelly, fiddly surgery required to turn those sinister creatures into a delicate, succulent feast. Later, the two women would teach me all their secrets, so that by the time the first hairs had appeared on my chin I could cook as well as any housewife of the city. But first I had to learn how to eat. One particular thing I remember. It was Lent, and Mamma had made something she loved: a *menestra* of elderflowers. We were sitting in the kitchen, just Mamma and me. She put the dish in front of me, and the horn spoon. *Eat*, she said, because people had to tell me to eat in those days. I was a thin child, all sharp corners and bulbous joints, because I hardly ate. It made no sense to me, to force things through my mouth and down into the dark mysteries below, where all their light was snuffed out. That was something an animal would do. I would watch in horror as Tessina and my other friends bolted their food. The way my father chewed meat with a feral look in his eyes frightened me. I preferred to sip or to nibble, until someone shouted in my ear, as they always did, or cuffed me on the skull.

Eat. I hunched my shoulders and picked up the spoon, reluctantly, because the smooth cow-horn had a gloomy mildew-green flavour of barns and old toenails, no matter how often it had been washed. Mamma had set out an olive-wood spoon for herself, and on a sudden impulse I grabbed it and, to avoid a telling-off, hastily scooped up some pottage and slurped it into my mouth. All the flavours lined up, an army getting into ranks: peeled, ground almonds; elder-flowers; bread, sugar, the lush heat of ginger. It is hard, looking back, to remember exactly what a mouthful like that would have done to me, but I think it would have told me some kind of small but complicated story, or perhaps I would have seen a piece of carved ivory, for all the white things: almonds, bread, flowers, sugar. Something obvious like flames for the ginger, or less obvious: a sun-warmed brick or a cockerel's comb.

What I do remember about this particular bowl of *menestra*, though, is that nothing like that happened. I tasted . . . almonds. I still saw them as bright green in my mind's eye, but somehow it didn't take over the whole world. Instead I thought to myself: *There are almonds in this. An almond is a nut. It grows on a tree.* A tree with sweet white flowers, of course, and there's the nut itself, nestled inside its speckled, woody shell. I found myself savouring the milky bitterness of almond meat, noticing how the sugar seemed to flow over the bitter, not destroying it but creating a separate taste. The ginger and the elderflowers fell into each other's arms, and all four things sank into the comforting blandness of the soaked bread. To my amazement I discovered that I could keep each clamour-ing taste, with its colour, in its place; and pick out other flavours too, each with its own colour and image. I dipped my spoon in again, tasted, swallowed. Another spoonful, then another. The flavours weren't disappearing into nothingness, they were becoming part of me.

'Do you like it, *caro*?' said Mamma, astonished.

'They go into you,' I said in wonder.

'What do?'

'All the tastes. They don't just go down and get lost inside you. It's like I'm a birdcage, and they're the birds.'

'Hmm. That doesn't sound very nice.'

'No, it is!' I took another spoonful. 'They're pretty birds, and this way they don't fly away.'

But whether or not I had become a birdcage, or a crystal goblet, or any of the other things that occurred to me over the next few days, I began to eat properly, and soon I looked like the other children and not like some little waif who'd barely survived a siege. I began to notice that different foods made me feel different in my body, something that had never dawned on me before: I thought it only did things inside my head. I began to crave some things: sugary, milky sweets; charred meat; lemon rinds. Then I started to watch Mamma and Carenza as they cooked, the two women working together, arguing quietly over the food, laughing. Mamma was short and fine-boned. Her face was rather long and her eyes were green and very big. She hid her brown hair modestly under a coif of fine linen, and to look at her you might think she was a simple, plain person, but like her brother she saw the world with heightened senses. Carenza stood more than a head higher than Mamma. She was a tanner's daughter from the slums of San Frediano, with a tanner's tongue which she didn't always keep in check. Where Mamma was fine, Carenza was heavy: heavy, wavy black hair that was going early to grey, black eyebrows, earlobes stretched by heavy gold rings. Her arms were as strong as her accent and when she moved around the kitchen you made sure not to get in her way. But her sculpted, square-jawed face might once have been beautiful, and her heart was as kind as Mamma's. If you saw them together you might, for a moment, think that they were sisters, leaning together in the steam from a cooking pot, bickering over the seasoning.

One day they let me knead the ingredients for sausage meat, and the raw foods themselves seized me: lean pork and soft, white fat – *The one talks to the other*, said Carenza. *Without the fat, the lean is too dry, and without the lean . . .* she stuck out her tongue, *too much.* I grated some cheese: dry pecorino that had been in our larder for months, and some fresh *marzolino*, tasting both. Mace went in, and cinnamon, and black pepper. *How much salt?* Mamma showed me in the palm of her hand, *Let me sweep it into the bowl.* Then she broke some eggs onto the mixture.

This is my *secret*, she said, and grated the rind of an orange so that the crumbs covered everything in a thin layer of gold. *Do you want to mix it, Nino?*

Almost laughing with excitement, I plunged my fingers through the cold silkiness of the eggs, feeling the yolks pop, then made fists deep inside the meat. I could smell the orange, the pork, the cheese, the spices, and then they started to melt together into something else. When it was all mixed together I licked my fingers, though Carenza slapped my hand away from my mouth, and after we'd stuffed them into the slimy pink intestines and cooked up a few for ourselves, I discovered how the fire had changed the flavours yet again. The clear, fresh taste of the pork had deepened and intensified, while the cool blandness of the fat had changed into something rich and buttery that held the spices and the orange zest. And the salt seemed to have performed this magic, because it was everywhere, but at the same time hardly noticeable. I licked my fingers over and over again, and if I had seen Mamma hugging Carenza, her face flushed with relief and happiness, I probably thought it was because the sausages were so good. From that day on, I was allowed to do whatever I wanted in the kitchen.

It puzzled my friends, all this fuss about food. Arrigo, who was often at our house while our fathers were doing neighbourhood business, used to sit with me in the kitchen and share the meals I cooked with Carenza and my mother. I remember one particular dish, a *peposo*, that we ate together. *Peposo* came to Florence with the men who made the tiles for the great dome of our cathedral. It's simple: cheap beef, garlic, red wine, bay leaves, salt, and black pepper, lots of black pepper. Simple, yes, but if you get the pepper wrong it becomes uneatable; if the salt is wrong it's revoltingly bland; too much wine, too little garlic . . . That day, Carenza and I both agreed we had got the balance right. I savoured mine, making sure I understood what had happened between the ingredients, how the proportions had created the exact taste we wanted. Beside me, Arrigo was ladling stew into his mouth like a metalworker stoking a furnace. As I watched, he reached absently for the salt, scooped up a fistful and dropped it into his bowl.

'What did you do that for?' I said in horror.

'Not salty enough . . .'

'It's perfect!'

He turned to me, eyebrows high. 'Keep your hair on,' he said.

'No! I mean . . .' I pulled his bowl away from him. 'Can't you *taste* it?'

'Not really,' he said easily, taking back his bowl. Then I noticed. His nose was streaming, as it always was. He sniffed and wiped it on his sleeve. 'But it's delicious.'

'*Delicious* . . . You ruined it! What do you mean, *delicious*?'

'That's what grown-ups say, isn't it?' he said cheerfully. ' "Mmm. Tasty. Lovely." ' He shovelled some more into his mouth. 'Finish up and let's go and play.'

I worked out, that afternoon, that Arrigo could hardly taste a thing because his nose was always stuffed up. But what

26

I couldn't really comprehend was that he didn't seem to care. I almost stopped being his friend, because he must be some sort of monster, but the next day we took on the gang from the Via dei Malcontenti on a patch of waste ground behind San Noferi and while we were busy lobbing stones at the encmy I decided to forgive him.

↘ 5 ↙

AFTER MY BIRTHDAY, PAPÁ VANISHED from my life for a while. He had been at the funeral, of course, but then he'd withdrawn to the shop. It was Filippo who rescued me. He arrived three days later, hammering on the door, bringing the dust down from the beams as he shouldered his way past the serving girl and bellowed for someone, anyone, to tell him what in the name of Christ was going on. I heard his voice and rushed downstairs.

'Nino?' he said. 'It's true, then?'

I had not spoken to a soul since we'd buried Mamma. I'd hidden myself away in my room, drinking well-water, eating stale bread that I took from the kitchen when Carenza had gone to bed, afraid to taste anything in case it reminded me of something I'd cooked with Mamma, because then her loss would flay me all over again. The funeral had been unbearable: long and boring, and I'd been surrounded by old people I didn't recognize, and butchers who'd probably never even met Mamma. Carenza was somewhere at the back of the church. Tessina hadn't come, though I hadn't expected her to: her aunt and uncle would have felt themselves much too fine to attend the funeral of a butcher's wife. But Arrigo had been there, thank God, though he'd had to stand further back, next to his parents. I spent the whole service trying not to cry. I almost chewed through my bottom lip as Mamma was lowered beneath the floor, though in a way I was glad that her corpse was finally leaving me, because its presence in the house seemed to have stifled my ability to feel anything but a soft, prickling horror. That in turn made me feel guilty,

28

and so did my boredom, because the priest droned on and on. I couldn't help being bored, just like I couldn't help feeling as if the world had ended. Only once did I turn my head, and there was Arrigo staring right back at me. He gave me a crisp nod, and I felt a little better. But when I got back to the house I went straight to my room and stayed there. All I wanted was to remember the taste of my mother's skin, and I couldn't. All I could taste was the raw place in my mouth where I had bitten deep into the flesh. It tasted like my own death, but I didn't want anything else. Carenza brought bowls of soup and bread and fruit, but I left them untouched. Arrigo came to visit, but I couldn't bear to see him. Tessina came by, but I was asleep and Carenza hadn't wanted to wake me.

And now here was Uncle Lippo, holding out his dusty arms to me. I ran into him and hit his squat, solid form with all my weight. He gathered me into his road-stained robe and held me tight. Without meaning to, I began to cry. There wasn't anything to say, anyway. Filippo's hand settled around the back of my head and stroked my hair. I breathed in, and the road from Prato to Florence unwound on my tongue as the dust dissolved: sour mountain stones, lowland mud, horse sweat.

'I'm so sorry, Nino. I've come too late.'

'She didn't know that, Uncle,' I said into his robe. 'She didn't know anything for a long time.'

'She's with God, my son.' He let out a great sigh. 'If anybody deserves to be with God, it is my sister. You know those white lilies that Gabriel holds when we paint the Annunciation? I believe she's in a field of those, Nino. I can smell them. I've smelled them all the way from Prato . . .' He stopped. I looked up, to see tears pouring down his cheeks.

He sniffed mightily, wiped his face with a dusty sleeve. 'But now, look at you! You're all bones, dear one. How did a butcher's son get so skinny, eh? And your mother wouldn't want you to starve yourself to death. I think we should have something to eat, don't you?'

He led me into the kitchen. When Carenza saw Filippo, she bowed her head respectfully and asked him for a blessing. Normally I would have found that amusing, because I had never really believed that Uncle Lippo was a proper friar. It seemed so unlikely. True enough, he almost always wore the white cloak of the Carmelites, but he didn't look like one. He didn't look like an artist, either. My uncle was wide, solid, and a bit bow-legged, with a generous belly and big, thick-fingered hands – labourer's hands. His face was framed by ears that stuck out from his close-cropped hair but seemed too small for his head. His jowls were starting to sag and were usually covered with three or four days' worth of stubble. His nose was delicate and starting to redden from years of wine, and his cheeks, too, were filigreed with broken veins. It was a plasterer's face, or a bricklayer's. Or perhaps a butcher's. Maybe that was why my father didn't like his brother-in-law: because Filippo's father had actually been a butcher, and so had my mother's father, who had adopted Filippo when he was small. The meat business was in my uncle from head to toe. Slop some blood onto his monk's whites and he could have walked into the Butchers' Guild without anyone blinking.

And his reputation . . . If you'd heard of Filippo Lippi, you had heard all about the girls, and the drinking, and getting caught for forging a contract. You would certainly have heard how he'd seduced a nun over in Prato and given her a baby, and then married her, even though he was in Holy Orders. You'd heard he had done some painting, and that old Cosimo de' Medici had taken a shine to him, but just look: do you ask him for some veal cutlets, or to build you a wall? And for Christ's sake, don't leave him alone with your wife.

But then you noticed his eyes, a deep slate grey, and set wide apart under arched, questioning brows. By their shape, they didn't seem to belong in Filippo's face at all. They gave the lie to everything you might have assumed about my uncle, but you had to look closely. And if you did, you would discover that he was looking back at you. But if you felt uncomfortable, or perhaps even naked under his level gaze, you really had nothing to fear. Because Filippo was searching out what it was that made you beautiful. You might not think that you possessed any beauty at all – the whole world might find you repulsive, even, but Filippo Lippi would find something. Then you'd find yourself shaking his hand, laughing at something he'd said in his raspy voice, still heavy with the tones of Oltrarno across the river. You'd be charmed. You might even find you'd lent him a little bit of money. And though you'd never know it, your nose, or your hair, or a shoulder – whatever morsel of beauty Filippo had seen in you – might end up in someone's altarpiece.

Carenza was chopping onions at the great rough oak table. Carrots and celery were already chopped; beet leaves and parsley for the evening's *battuta*. She was from Oltrarno like Filippo, and she liked him because of that. She said horrible things about him sometimes, about his women and all those debts, but he was a man of God, and more important, he was from her side of the Arno.

'More comely than ever,' my uncle bellowed, in an accent so thick I could barely understand him. Carenza blushed redder than the onions and the steam had already made her. I could see that Filippo was right: she had been almost beautiful once upon a time. When she saw me lurking behind Filippo's broad back she beckoned me over with her knife.

'Nino, come here! Where have you been, *caro*?'

She knew where I'd been. She had been leaving food outside my door since the funeral: everything plain, white, *in bianco*, as befitted a family suffering bereavement. I had brought it inside, sniffed at it, but I didn't want anything. I was trying to remember the taste of my mother's skin, as it had been when she had been healthy, and I didn't want to be distracted by food.

'You look like a skeleton, little one! Have some sole – fresh from Pisa this morning. White as a virgin's slip.' I shook my head. 'Some rice and peas? Some bread and milk?'

'I'm not hungry, Carenza.'

'How about some . . .' She winced, as she did when she was wrestling with her conscience. 'Your father left us some *Cinta* Senese. You love that, Nino! I'll cook it in milk, the way you like it.'

'Is it loin?' I asked, despite myself. My stomach had come to life. There is nothing quite like *Cinta* Senese.

'A lovely piece. Your uncle will have some, of course?'

'You are a temptress, Donna Carenza,' said Filippo, somewhat thickly.

'All right,' I said. 'But . . .'

'But what?' Carenza was wringing her hands. I couldn't bear it.

'Only if I can cook it myself.'

'Anything! You little bastard, anything! Your mother didn't leave you with me so that you could starve yourself! Don't torture me any more! Cook, if that's what you want! Cook!'

Filippo settled himself in the kitchen's one decent chair. Carenza tried to keep her place in front of the fire but eventually she gave up and retreated, muttering complaints in dialect. I went and had a look in the cold room. Papá had been wandering in and out of the house, dropping off bloody, greasy parcels of meat and then leaving, word-lessly. There was some ordinary pork, a heap of pigs' livers and some caul fat. Carenza had been to the market that morning and bought fronds of bronze fennel with their pollen-heavy flowers still on them; sorrel; bitter lettuce. I chose the fennel, went out to the courtyard and picked marjoram, thyme, parsley and mint.

I decided to make some *tomacelli*, because I liked them and it was the kind of fiddly, absorbing dish I could lose myself in. So I put the livers on to boil, and then cut up some veal haunch. Carenza liked *mortadelli* and so I'd make her some with the veal. I chopped the veal up finely with a bit of its fat and some *lardo*, mixed in some parsley and some marjoram. The livers were done, so I drained them and put them in a bowl. Into the *mortadella* mixture went a handful of grated *parmigiano* cheese, some cloves, cinnamon and a few threads of saffron. An egg yolk went in too, and then I sank my hands into the cool, slippery mound and mixed it with my fingers. When it was smooth I shaped it into egg-sized balls, wrapped them in pieces of caul and threaded them onto a spit.

While the *mortadelli* sizzled over the flame, I took the livers and crumbled them up, added some minced pancetta, some grated pecorino, marjoram, parsley, raisins, some ginger and nutmeg and pepper. I bound it all together with a couple of eggs and made the stuff into balls, smaller than the *mortadelli*, wrapped them in more caul and set to frying them in melted *lardo*.

I put them on two plates: one for Carenza, one for Filippo. My uncle fell on them, licking his fingers and mumbling delightedly. Carenza nibbled one and frowned. 'What's wrong with it?' I demanded.

'Nothing's wrong with the food. It's delicious. But you're behaving like a *pazzo*, a madman. I'm scared for your brains.

First you starve yourself, then you start doing St Vitus's dance all over my kitchen.'

I shrugged – I wasn't finished.

'*Porca miseria* , , , What the *fica* are you up to now?' demanded Carenza, when I started flouring the table top.

'Ravioli,' I said.

Carenza sighed bitterly and crossed herself.

I kneaded for as long as I could bear it, soothed by the rocking back and forth over the table, letting my muscles ache and start to tire. Then I borrowed Carenza's rolling pin and began to roll out the creamy, elastic sheet. Carenza was watching me, growing more and more indignant. Finally she stood up, gave her gown a shake and stamped over to the table.

'Now what, *pazzo*? Stop it! *Madonna strega* . . . Here.'

She snatched the pin from me, bumped me out of the way with her well-padded hip, and started, delicately and methodically, to roll out the dough. Carenza's hands were one of my earliest memories. They had always been there, to hold, to feed, to scold and comfort. Big hands, almost as big as mine, they were red and puffy and chapped from steam and water. The ball of her left thumb was a great pad, hardened from years of chopping vegetables against it. Her fingers were getting rheumaticky and the knuckles were swollen, and yet she ran her palms over the dough as if she were smoothing a bridal bed.

'Gently. No madness.'

'Madness? You can talk,' I said.

'*Pazzo*.' She went on rolling: pushing away, drawing back. All the heaviness, all the bad temper and love that was Carenza, seemed to hover over the table with the lightness of a sparrow's wings. I stood close, and listened to her sigh gently with the effort. 'There. Done. What are you going to fill the ravioli with, *pazzo*? Your brains?'

'I thought some cheese, some breast of capon, a bit of calf's udder . . .'

'Raisins?'

'No.'

'Good. Didn't like them in the *tomacelli*.' She rested her red fists on her hips and examined me. Depending on her mood, Carenza could make you feel like the baby Jesus or something hanging in a cold room when she looked at you like that. But right now her eyes were warm. 'Your mother, God rest her soul, did this as well,' she said at last.

'What, made ravioli? Of course she did,' I said.

'No, no. Cook like a madwoman when something was wrong. She would come down here and, oh! she'd get in the way. And she wouldn't eat anything. Just serve it up to you – and your father, the ungrateful beast.' Carenza sniffed pointedly. She was devoted to my father, because loyalty was more important to her than her own skin, but she had honestly loved my mother. 'All he ever wants is half-raw meat, and plenty of it. And there was your poor mamma, serving up aspics and fried *zucca*, *torte*, the most beautiful sauces . . .'

'*I* ate them,' Filippo pointed out.

'Yes, but then you went away east, didn't you?' Prato was less than fifteen miles away, but Carenza had never been out of sight of the city walls.

'I didn't know that about Mamma,' I said. 'Was she unhappy very often?'

'Some people think that life is a field strewn with peach blossom,' said Carenza. 'While some see things as they really are – that we live through every trial the Lord sends us, just to get to the next one.' She crossed herself.

'And your mother saw that better than most,' said Filippo sadly.

'Anyway, she came down here because the food did what

35

she wanted it to do, and I paid attention to her, which none of you lot ever did.'

'That's not true,' I muttered. 'I did. I do. I miss her.' I started looking nervously around for ingredients, but sud denly Carenza grabbed me and hugged me, hard. I was engulfed in her scent: sweat, onions, and the bergamot oil she bought, once a year, from the apothecary around the corner from Ognissanti.

'You really are like your mother. She couldn't take care of herself, only other people. Foolish way to live. But I loved her, yes? Now do something useful.'

Later on I went out with Filippo, because Carenza said I should stop moping. We'd made the ravioli, arguing happily about ginger and sage, then boiled them, saying the *pater noster* together twice, because that was the time it took to cook the little walnut-sized balls perfectly. Then the three of us had sat in front of the hearth and eaten a bowlful each, and talked about Mamma, not as she'd been since the beginning of the year, but when she'd had her health. I'd wanted to tell them what I'd discovered about death and its taste, but I didn't. If Carenza thought I was *pazzo* now, she'd be calling the surgeon to drill a hole in my head if she got wind of the thoughts that were filling it up to the brim.

We crossed the Ponte Vecchio when the sun was halfway down the slope to evening and the swallows were swooping through the arches, calling to one another as they chased flies across the river that shone like burnished copper in the sultry light. Papá wasn't in the shop on the bridge, or perhaps he was in the back. Anyway, he wouldn't have been happy to see Filippo, and I didn't know what I would say to him, so we walked on into Oltrarno. The threatening bulk of Luca Pitti's new palace, still unfinished, reared up in front of us, and Filippo, who hadn't seen it for a few years, made us walk around it while he muttered about Pitti's vanity and cursed him for levelling the streets he had played in as a boy. Then we headed west, threading our way along Via Sguazza, past the basilica of Santo Spirito, down Via Sant'Agostino and into the Piazza del Carmine.

The big old church hunkered down at the far end of the square was almost empty except for a priest reprimanding some choristers, a few black-draped crones and a younger priest who was pacing around absently, as if he was slowly going out of his mind with boredom. Filippo led me around the corner to the chapel of the Brancacci family, where we lit candles for my mother's soul and knelt for a little while in front of the altar. But I knew we were here for something else.

On the walls around us, the frescoes glowed in the fading light. Filippo leaned back against the wall and I settled down next to him. My eyes flicked over sad old Saint Peter chatting to Paul through the bars of his cell, and across the crowd watching Christ wake the son of Theophilus from the dead, but they didn't rest there. The real drama, my own drama, was being played out above Saint Peter's head, where the gates of Paradise had just closed behind Adam and Eve.

Filippo was mad about these paintings. He'd start twitching, almost: more excitement than I'd ever seen in a grown-up. I would have been four when he first brought me here, and I'd have been trying to tear the place apart, I'm sure; but I wouldn't have been as excited as my uncle.

Just look at that, he'd said, hand clamped on my shoulder, turning me to face Adam and Eve as they staggered, wailing, from the Garden.

That's Tommaso Simone's work, that is, he'd said the first time. *Masaccio. The father of us all. My master – and he was only five years older than me, God rest him. Well, what do you think, eh?*

I had loved all of it. The way Eve lurches, her head back

and her face blurred and ugly with despair and terror. The way Adam's prick is right there on show, hair and all, just like some man at the bathhouse. The angel hovering overhead, orange, if you please – but looking at him, you think, well of course, angels *are* orange. And the blue sky. I'd wanted to dive into that blue, fly into it like a pigeon.

And look there: Saint Peter curing the sick with his shadow.

It's . . . I hadn't finished, too busy gaping at the people who seemed to float there, unearthly, ghostly even, but then again more real than me and Uncle Filippo. It was the clothes I liked best, I'd decided: all those gorgeous apricots and blues and pinks, the folds so real they might have been sticking out of the plaster. There was a long painting of a naked man kneeling in the middle of a crowd of rich Florentines, bankers and guildsmen by the looks of them, and I thought, *It's more real than life.* And there was Jesus, young and stern and draped in blue, all the apostles or whoever they were looking cross about something. And behind them, a rocky mountainside with a little village hanging from its slopes. I wondered what it would be like to go there.

Where's the rest? I'd said at last.

He died, Filippo had said. *Didn't finish it.*

What's died?

Died means stopped working, for ever, he'd said. And then he'd ruffled my hair.

After that I had come here many times, sometimes with my uncle, sometimes on my own. I'd always loved the way the cherub glides over the two naked people on a tidy square of his own coral-coloured robe, his finger pointing to some unseen wasteland, his sword heavy and black as death. I'd never really seen the humans themselves, though. I mean I'd looked at them. I'd even studied them, because Filippo had told me to, but I don't think I'd ever really seen them until today. Because, like them, I'd just been thrown out of

Paradise. I stared at Eve. That mouth, black and dug out of her face like a grave, was howling the way I wanted to howl. Her eyes were screwed up and crying for all the millions of her children yet to be born, and I was one of those too.

'It hurts, doesn't it? My master knew,' said Filippo, putting his arm around me. 'I don't know how, but he could touch pain. And he was such a kind man . . .'

'I can't help wondering about the apple. She *had* to taste it. Adam didn't care, but she did. I would have done the same thing. I'd have to have known.'

'The flesh is weak,' said Filippo. 'We're compelled to do what is forbidden.'

'No, Uncle. I wouldn't have cared about it being forbidden. If God had said "Don't steal my gold" or "Don't swim in the river", I would have obeyed him. But what did the apple taste like?'

'I don't know,' he sighed.

I wanted to know: had the fruit been sweet or sharp? Had its flesh been crisp? Had the juice spurted into her mouth, or had it been bland, woody, tasting of wasp? I still felt sorry for Adam, but not for Eve. I stared at her mouth, and felt nothing but envy.

6

FILIPPO WOKE ME UP THE next day, sitting on the edge of
my bed and saying matins in the rumbling voice he used for
church.

'Get dressed,' he said. 'I'm going to Verrocchio's studio.
You're coming too.'

'I'm not,' I snapped, pulling the bolster over my head.

'You are. When was the last time you drew anything? Eh?
You've a good eye, a very good eye. And a good firm line.
I'm not letting the butchers have your soul, Nino.'

'I just want to sleep, Uncle. Leave me alone.'

'Verrocchio is working on a new commission. Have you
seen it?'

'The Doubting Thomas?' I mumbled, despite myself.
'There isn't much of it yet. Some sketches for Christ's face,'
I conceded, sitting up and rubbing my eyes. 'They're quite
good. Sandro's been helping.'

'Well, that's what I want to see.'

'But I don't want to . . .'

'Stop whining.'

'I'm not!'

'You are, my dear boy.'

'I'm in mourning.'

'Well, so am I. So's your father. He's mourning with his
cleaver and his knife, and very sensible too.'

'It's . . . it's unchristian.'

'I absolve you. Now get up.'

'I don't feel like drawing, Filippo! I'm no good, anyway.'

'Don't, then. Don't draw. Sandro will be there, though,

and you know what he's like. His stomach will be going off like siege artillery come noon. Verrocchio's too. You can make them something for their lunch.'

'Go away. I'm not an artist – I draw like a two-year-old. And I'm not a cook. I don't care about any of it, Uncle! Get Carenza to make something. Buy something in the market. Some tripe from Ugolino . . .'

'Ugolino be buggered. Get up, you idle little sod, or I'll have you excommunicated.' Filippo's hand shot out and got me under the armpit. I convulsed in reluctant laughter and before I knew it, my uncle was throwing clothes at me and I was pulling them on, cursing him.

'There's no time to make anything,' I said. The clock in the Signoria had just struck eleven – Filippo had let me sleep late, after all – and I knew that Carenza wouldn't ever give me the run of her kitchen at this hour. 'We'd have to go out and buy the ingredients, come back here and prepare them.'

'We'll buy things on the way and cook them there,' said Filippo, clapping his hands together and rubbing them, as if to seal matters.

The *bottega* of Andrea del Verrocchio ran the full length of a two-storey house a little more than halfway between the Bargello and the Porta alla Croce. You entered through a wide brick archway into a world of noise and seething disarray. The space was vast. It stretched away under receding brick vaults like a nightmare exercise in perspective. The vaults were festooned with winches, ropes and pulleys that dangled among a mismatched forest of stepladders, half-finished armatures, wooden scaffolding and easels. That day, the kiln at the back was lit. Verrocchio got his wood from the cooper down the street, and the *bottega* was filled with the sour incense of burning oak and pine. Near the front entrance, a tangle of metal rods was on its way to forming the outline of a human figure, like the drawing of a man scratched out by a child. A slab of marble bore a complicated frieze of bodies in frenzied motion. Near the centre of the room, a large model of the dome of our cathedral stood on a table like some outlandish dessert for titans with a taste for architecture.

Two boys were arguing loudly in shrill, unbroken voices. A heavy woman was trying to make herself heard over the racket, pointing to a large basket of fruit and holding up her fingers, bargaining with a man whose back was towards me. Someone was sawing a piece of wood, and a girl was trying to open one of the windows. Further off in the outer regions, a hammer was striking something hollow, and a chisel was tapping against stone. The cool, mineral tang of marble dust fought with the acrid fumes of hot metal and the tang of vinegar from the fresh tempera. Verrocchio himself was banging away with a pestle, surrounded by a slight haze of greenish pigment. The pestle had been carved out of porphyry, I guessed from a scrap of the stone for Old Cosimo's tomb. One of the boys pushed the other one, who shrieked with rage. I couldn't understand what they were saying, because they were speaking in a heavy street dialect as thick and rich as pig's blood. Just when I thought they would come to blows, the market woman turned and unleashed an appalling torrent of oaths on their blond, curly heads, and they both shut up.

Andrea di Cione – I called him Andrea because I knew him, though he liked his customers to call him Verrocchio, which I suppose sounded more impressive – was thirty-one, but just then he looked a lot older. The pigment had settled on his face and every time he had wiped the sweat away he had rubbed colour into every line and pore. His handsome, rather heavyset features looked like a glazed terracotta bust that had been fired wrong, webbed by cracks and fissures. Only his bright blue eyes had escaped.

'Why are you doing that, Andrea?' demanded Filippo. 'Can't you put someone else to work? One of those little horrors, for instance,' he added, nodding to the boys.

'Them? All I need those little sods to do is stand still and look pretty, but even that's too much to ask. Christ knows what would happen if I let them near the paints.' He held up a finger and then sneezed thunderously into his cupped hands. They came away trailing a string of vivid green snot.

I went over and found a more or less clean kerchief for him. He took it and blew more *verderame* out of his nostrils. There was a fair bit on his face, smeared in with some lemony streaks of orpiment and some expensive-looking red that had got into one of his eyebrows. It looked bright enough to be lac. Of all the painters in Florence, only Verrocchio was rich enough to throw lac around like that. But there again, he wasn't really a painter. This was a hobby for him — or so Filippo had told me once, a bit ruefully. Sculpture was what brought in the money. When you'd made a tomb for Cosimo de' Medici, and been paid for it, you could afford to dabble a bit.

'Is Sandro about?' I asked.

'Hmm?' Verrocchio muttered, distractedly. He gave another bright green sneeze and his face cleared. 'In the back,' he said. 'Botticelli!'

He bellowed again, and a fair-haired boy joined in, trilling hoarsely like an eel seller in the market, then high and airily like a courtly girl summoning her maid. I hadn't seen him before: he was about my age with a pretty face, but his arms were strong and muscled, as if he'd already worked hard in his life. He was drawing on an unprepared board with a stick of charcoal. I peered over his shoulder. He had already half covered the wood in tiny sketches: faces, a bird with a straw

43

in its beak, stars, and an outstretched arm with a latticework of exposed muscles. It looked like his own arm, only peeled. I winced.

'Could you all please shut up?' A deep voice boomed from behind a loaded easel at the back of the studio, set up to catch the light from the back doors, which were open, letting in the sound of chickens scratching and clucking around the well-head in the courtyard beyond. Then Sandro Filipepi himself appeared: Botticelli, the Little Barrel, though he was anything but little. Heavy-jawed, big-nosed, his lips curling like a cherub who'd just drawn a bad hand at cards. His grey eyes were fixed on something not necessarily present in Verrocchio's *bottega*, but when he saw me he stepped out, looked for somewhere to set down his brush, chose an almost empty glass cup of wine and dropped it in handle first, and held up both hands in greeting. I went over and kissed him on both cheeks.

'Nino!' he said, raking his thick fingers through the tangled curls of his butter-yellow hair. As always he had the look of an overfed angel who had been sleeping in a ditch somewhere on the very borders of Purgatory. 'I'm so sorry about your mamma . . .' He crossed himself and glanced back at his painting quickly, almost as if something had moved or muttered out of the pain. He frowned, then his face cleared. 'What brings you here?'

'My uncle Lippo thinks you artists need feeding up. I'm to be your cook today.'

'Hmm,' he said. 'And what will you make us?'

'A *cibreo*,' I told him, dangling the bulging, onion-scented bag I had brought with me. Which is a Florentine way of saying: *something really good*.

'From you, I would expect nothing less.' He sat down, bent his head and scratched it vigorously with both hands. '*Dio*, I am so hungry! I've been standing here since . . . since

44

last night.' He looked around, found the wine glass, noted with surprise that there was a brush sticking out of it, took out the brush and tipped the inch or so of wine down his throat. 'Damn . . .' He examined the bottom of the glass, and held out a huge hand, finger pointing as imperiously as a Roman consul selecting a town to be razed. 'Just there, Nino.' I looked, found a pitcher of wine, poured him some and, not finding a cup for myself, took a sip from the pitcher.

'What are you working on?' asked Filippo, who had wandered across.

'Another Madonna,' Sandro said.

'Can we see?'

Sandro wagged his finger in the direction of the easel.

'Almost done,' he mumbled. 'I don't think it's bad. Hmm?'

'No, not bad, Sandro. Not bad.' Still looking at the picture, Filippo reached out and took Sandro's hand. He squeezed it, silently. Then he went back to Verrocchio's table and left me in front of the easel.

'I have to finish just this piece,' Sandro was mumbling into his cup. 'Jesus, my eyes are crossing by themselves, I've been looking at it for so long. And I'm starving,' he added, as if I'd forgotten.

Towards the back door was the area set aside for making clay models and casting small bronze pieces. Today it wasn't being used: the one calm spot in the studio. Everything was covered in black, powdery dust from the kiln. There was a bucket of dirty water on the floor and a rag, so I wiped off a table and dumped out the contents of my bag.

I'd done something bad, but Filippo had been the instigator. The loin of *Cinta* Senese had been sitting in the cold room, begging to be cooked. I'd shown it to Filippo – *This is our supper*, I'd said, and he'd replied that supper was too far away, and didn't the painters deserve the best, serving God as they did? So I'd grabbed it, along with some garlic, thyme, rosemary, peppercorns and a nutmeg. Surely they'd have salt at the studio . . . Filippo had bought some onions, a flask of milk and a hunk of prosciutto on the way. I hunted around in the small, chaotic niche where the artists kept their food and discovered a dusty flask of olive oil. Sniffing it dubiously, I found it was quite fresh: the dark green oil from the hills behind Arezzo. In Florence we almost always cooked in lard, but oil would do in a pinch.

The kiln was lit but not being used for anything, and the fire was dying down. I threw some pieces of oak onto it, chopped the onions and the ham with a borrowed knife, cut the loin away from the ribs. The artists had a trivet and some old pans which they used to cook with every now and again, though mostly they lived on pies from the cook-shop up the street. There was an earthenware pot with a cracked lid, which seemed clean enough. I put it on the trivet, poured in a good stream of the green oil, browned the meat in its wrapping of fatty rind. Sandro gave up a cup of white wine, unwillingly, which I threw over the pork. When it had cooked off, I crushed two big cloves of garlic and added them along with the rosemary I had brought, and a handful of thyme. The milk had just foamed, and I poured it over the meat. The air filled with a rich, creamy, meaty waft. I added salt and a good amount of pepper, covered the pot and pushed it just far enough away from the flames. I had saved a finger of Sandro's wine for myself, and with it I went off into a corner to wait. But I had only just sat down when Verrocchio's voice came barking down the length of the studio.

'Nino! I need you, please!'

Downing the wine, I went to see what he wanted.

'I've run out of green. If I give you the money, your uncle says you can be trusted to buy some more.' I bristled:

Verrocchio had had me running errands like this for years. Seeing my expression, though, the painter's pigment-caked face split into a wide grin. 'I'm sorry! I meant *your uncle can't be trusted*, so would you please go and buy me some malachite from Bonetti's?'

'And take young Leonardo with you,' added Filippo, waving to the pretty boy who had stopped drawing and was mixing a pot of gesso.

'Why?' I said rudely. I didn't want to go out and leave my pork, and I certainly didn't want company.

'Because he's new to the city, and he's your age,' said Filippo. 'It won't kill you.'

I sighed. 'Only if you watch my pot on the fire over there,' I said. 'Don't let it burn.'

'Trust me.'

I looked at his reddening nose, and at the just-refilled goblet of wine in his hand. 'I won't be long. Just check on it, please?'

So, with misgivings, I went out with Leonardo to Bonetti the apothecary, whose shop is on the other side of the Bargello, near Santa Margherita. We were silent most of the way there – I admit I was sulking, because I resented having to entertain this stranger, so I paced along, tight-lipped. But Leonardo didn't seem to mind. He seemed to be quivering with energy. He followed the flight of pigeons, paused to peer into a doorway, reached up to pluck leaves from trees that reached out over walls. As we passed the Bargello and went further up the Via Ghibellina, the street became noisier, rougher, a neighbourhood of artisans. We passed forges, a brickworks, carpenters' shops from whose doors wood shavings drifted out like huge snowflakes. Leonardo sniffed the air like a dog. He scooped up a curl of wood and held it up against the sunlight.

'Where are you from?' I finally asked, when we were almost at Bonetti's.

'From Vinci,' said the boy. 'Near Empoli.'

'And what are you doing here in Florence?'

'I am Maestro Andrea's apprentice,' he said. And he said it, not quite proudly, but as if he knew what it meant. I liked him for that.

'You're very lucky,' I told him. 'How on earth did you get in?'

'My father is a good friend of Maestro Andrea. He arranged it.'

'From . . . where did you say? Empoli?'

'No, Vinci. And my father lives here, in the city. He's a notary. His house is in Chiasso di San Biagio.'

Chiasso di San Biagio – his father must have money. 'What do you make of it?' I asked. 'The city?'

'Wonderful,' said the boy seriously, and held up his hand so that the sunlight outlined the flesh in a vague red translucency.

A man with a basket of food came out of the entrance to a courtyard. Something he carried smelled good, and so I stopped him.

'What do you have?' I asked, and he showed me: nothing special, just some sausage and olives and cheese. I took an olive and bit off the end. It wasn't fancy, but it was how it should be: the sensations of salt, meat and grass danced across my tongue and merged. I bought some and the man wrapped them in a cone of vine leaves.

'Try the cheese,' said Leonardo. He was standing to one side, watching me.

I shrugged and nodded at the man, who shaved off a sliver of the ivory-coloured stuff and gave it to me. Again, nothing special: a pecorino, aged, but a good one. I could taste the sheep's teats, buttery caramel, earth . . .

'Are you from up past Pistoia?' I asked. The man beamed. 'Yes! From San Marcello,' he said.

'Thought so. This is *pecorino di Cutigliano*, yes?'

'Of course! The best cheese in Italy!'

When I heard the price, I grumbled and asked him who did he think I was, Filippo Strozzi, and offered him half. He was so happy that I'd guessed his birthplace that he accepted without a grimace. We left him, and I broke off a piece of cheese and gave it to Leonardo.

'Thanks,' he said. 'How did you guess where it was from? The man had an accent: was that it?'

'I didn't notice his accent,' I said, and shrugged. 'It's just cheese from the Pistoiese Mountains. It has that taste.'

'Tell me.'

'The sheep eat the grass, and their milk tastes like what they eat,' I explained patiently. 'There are certain kinds of wild flower that grow on the hills around Cutigliano, I suppose, and they flavour the cheese. There's something a little bitter – someone told me there are a lot of gentians up there. Then they age the cheeses on spruce boards, and you can taste that.'

'Can you?'

'Yes. It's strong.' I took a bite and smacked my lips. 'Like pitch.'

'I can taste cheese,' said Leonardo, biting off a corner of his piece. 'My mother's is better.'

'Your mamma makes cheese?' I laughed. 'What, in Chiasso di San Biagio?'

'No.' Leonardo narrowed his eyes a fraction and he changed. It was like a sea anemone – I had been to the sea once, at Livorno – which, when you poke it, pulls all its questing fingers in at once and disappears inside itself. 'My mother lives in Vinci,' he said.

'Ah. Well, my mother's dead,' I said. He nodded gravely,

then brightened, and I got the impression of curious golden tendrils spreading out again to probe, to investigate.

'You're right. The cheese is good,' he said, and, popping an olive into his mouth, looked up with complete attention to where a sparrow was cramming a long piece of straw under the eaves of a house. 'So my mother's cheese tastes of Vinci,' he said.

'Yes. Of course it does. Everything tastes of where it's from, among other things. It has to.'

'How do you mean? There are gentians all over the mountains. How do you know that cheese didn't come from the Casentino? Or the Lunigiana? Monte Amiata?'

'Because it didn't. These are Pistoiese gentians. And you can taste the mould.' Leonardo wrinkled his nose. 'There's mould in the caves where they age the cheese. And the stone of the cave. It all tastes like itself, nothing else.'

'And you can tell the difference? How?'

'Look. Do what I do.' I licked my finger and dabbed it onto the brick wall next to us. I licked it, and then touched the stone lintel of a door, licked that. 'So. Can you taste the brick? And the stone? Are they the same?'

'No.' Leonardo frowned. Then he threw back his head and let out a delighted laugh. 'Can you tell the difference between bricks, then? Do streets taste different?' He wasn't mocking me, though. If I had said yes, I believe he would have licked every brick in the parish of Sant'Ambrogio.

'I expect so.'

'Nothing is the same, is it? It's all so . . .' He licked his lips, his face almost transfigured. '*Complicated.* I love that, don't you? Look at those two birds up there.' Leonardo pointed to a pair of swallows perched on a washing line. 'Are *they* the same?'

I squinted. 'Yes. I mean, they look alike.'

'No,' he said, as if to a very small child. 'One's male and one's female.'

'Oh. Well, there you are. They look exactly the same to me.'

'They aren't.' Leonardo reached into his tunic and pulled out a battered drawing tablet and a stylus. He glanced up at the birds and then seemed to let the stylus tip loose on the white surface of the tablet. The birds appeared before my eyes, shaded as the light was striking the living creatures above us, exquisite, almost bursting out of their two dimensions. 'That's the boy, and that's the girl. They're probably two summers old.'

'How did you do that?' I asked.

'With my eyes.' He paused, and licked the tip of the stylus. 'I'd like to know how eyes work. Aristotle says that the eye contains some kind of hidden fire. The light enters from outside and the fire inside reacts and duplicates the image within us, like the stylus on the tablet. But . . .' He blinked. 'Where would the hidden fire *hide*? Anyway, you taste like I see. I think I see things the same way that everybody else does, but apparently I do not, though I think it's just them: they aren't paying attention. You think everyone tastes things like you do. But I can't. I'd like to, though! I wonder if you can teach me?'

'I can try.'

He looked at me, pleased. 'I wonder if the eyes are like the tongue,' he said, perhaps to himself. 'The tongue picks up sour, salty, sweet, and tells the intellect, which is the soul, so . . . Does the eye taste light?' He seemed delighted with the idea, and began to stare at his fingertips with fascinated concentration. I was worried he might bump into a passer-by, so I tapped his arm.

'We should hurry,' I said. 'I'm making *arista* with an

incredible bit of pork. I don't want it to burn. When you taste it, you'll fall over.'

'I don't eat the flesh of animals,' he said simply.

'Really? Why not?'

He regarded me with wide eyes and blew his cheeks out as if to say, *Where could one possibly start?*

We bought the malachite, a satisfyingly heavy, knobbly green lump, and hurried back to the studio. To my relief, Filippo had been as good as his word and my pork was still unburned. In a few minutes it was ready. I dumped the contents of the pot unceremoniously onto a clay charger, borrowed a stiletto and carved the meat into thick slices, laying them out on a dish and ladling the thick, curdled gravy over everything.

The artists and assistants, all except for Leonardo, gathered around, carrying hunks of bread that Sandro was sawing from a huge loaf. I took the dish and offered it first to Verrocchio, making sure he took the best piece, near the end where the gristle had melted to a divine softness, and then to Filippo. They ate carefully, critically, watching me the whole time while I watched them. At last they licked their fingers and nodded. The other artists dived, and in seconds the dish was empty. I'd kept a little for myself, though, from the fatty end, already in a little dish which I'd had to rinse clean of yellow paint. I took the dish off to my corner and set to.

Cinta Senese does not taste like pork, exactly. It is gamey, almost ripe, like well-hung pheasant or bustard, but with an almost muttony texture and juiciness and an aftertaste of briny sweetness. I could taste the woods where this pig had rooted: the wild garlic it had found, the lily bulbs, last year's acorns. I sipped the gravy. The milk had been curdled by the wine and the curds had soaked up the juice from the meat, along with the herbs. It was rich, and almost caramel-sweet, shot through with the resinous bite of the rosemary and the woody, slightly overripe tang of the pork. I was still eating long after the others had finished and gone back to their work. Filippo was busy again with Verrocchio, so I went and found a drawing tablet, the kind smeared with the ash of chicken bones made into a paste with spittle, that takes a line well but is easily cleared with the brush of a wet finger. I settled down near the back door and began to draw.

I sketched one of the assistants, who was sorting out wires for an armature. Then I did my bowl, my shoe, a chicken that was fussing around in the courtyard. Rubbing out the chicken, I started on a face I knew well. Curly hair – I always started with the hair. Then the nose, small and upturned. The eyes, delicate but heavy-lidded like the mouths of seashells. A Cupid's bow for the mouth . . . Not quite right. I changed it a little, made it pout. Then made it smile.

'She's pretty.' I jumped. Sandro was standing behind me, hands on hips. 'You're not bad, you know,' he said. 'I can see your uncle's style all over it, can't I?'

'Of course,' I said proudly. 'But it's no good. I couldn't . . . you know . . .' I jabbed my stylus in the direction of his easel.

'With a bit of practice.' He shrugged. 'I'd prefer it if you practised with the food, though. Any fool can draw. But that *arista al latte* . . . Dear God.' He gave back the tablet. 'Who is she, anyway?'

'No one. Just a friend. Her name's Tessina. Tessina Albizzi.'

7

AFTER FILIPPO HAD COAXED ME out that first day, I spent less and less time at home. The streets were where I felt happiest now. I played a lot of *calcio* in those days with my friends. It was our obsession – that, and *beffe*, the elaborate practical jokes that Florentines are so fond of. We would sit in our hideouts and discuss the famous ones again and again: when Maestro Brunelleschi, with Maestro Donatello and Giovanni Rucellai, tricked Grasso the woodcarver into believing – actually believing, mind you – that he was the famous wastrel Matteo and not himself, breaking into his house and even throwing him in jail for debts he didn't owe . . . Then there were men tricked into collecting supposedly magical stones, or persuaded that they were dead, or women, or rich, or poor – in short, whatever they were not, and whatever would best punish their lack of *virtù* – and *virtù* was everything. It was the way real men behaved. It was what made a beggar remain a beggar, and Messer Lorenzo de' Medici into what he was: Il Magnifico. If you overstepped your bounds, got airs, thought you were better than your equals or, God forbid, better than your betters, you risked becoming a *beffato*. No one was funnier than a *beffato*. If you fell victim to a *beffa*, you'd have to leave Florence or be laughed into an early grave.

Arrigo was our captain, the *condottiere* who led our gang of boys from the part of the Black Lion that lies between Piazza Santa Croce and the river. Arrigo, the Buonaccorsis, the Lenzis, an Albizzi, Marco di Bosco, and all the other dusty, smiling faces whose names are lost to me now. *Calcio* was our life. We called our team *I Denti del Leone*, the Lion's Teeth, and we regularly gnawed up the boys from the streets around the old Roman amphitheatre, where the Peruzzis have their palace, though we usually came off less well when we played the thugs from the dyers' quarter to the east. When we weren't playing we gathered behind San Pier Scheraggio and chewed over games we'd played, or the more serious business of the grown-up tournaments: how the team of the Dragon neighbourhood across the river had brought in farm boys from outside the wall to give them more muscle up front; how one rich man was too fat to play; how another went down if the other side so much as farted at him. I was supposed to be in mourning now, though, and it would have shamed Papá if his son was seen roistering in the streets. So instead I watched from the shade if there was a game, or roamed the market with Tessina or Arrigo.

Meanwhile, Filippo was getting ready to go back to Prato. Spending too much time in Florence made him nervous. He said it was because he missed his Lucrezia, but I think he was worried about bumping into one of his many creditors.

'I *have* to go, *caro*,' he insisted. 'Little Filippino will have forgotten what I look like.'

'Filippino is nine years old,' I reminded him. 'If he doesn't remember you after a fortnight, there might be something wrong with him.'

'*Dio* . . .' Filippo crossed himself.

'I'm joking, Uncle!'

'I do love my little boy. And of course my dear wife. But I've also got a piece of work to finish – Herod's feast, you know. The diocese is being extremely irritating about payment.'

It wouldn't have occurred to me to remind my uncle that, as he had absconded with one of the nuns to whom he'd been chaplain, and under their employ, the diocese of Prato was being very forgiving indeed, and insisting that he finish the work they'd commissioned him to do was fair enough, under the circumstances.

'I'll have to come and visit you,' I said.

'Do. Lucrezia loves you, Nino. And the little one too.' I hardly knew Filippino, who had been a small, petulant creature with a mop of black curls and a very nasty rash on his face the last time I had seen him. Aunt Lucrezia, though, I could conjure up in my mind with no trouble at all. You really couldn't blame Filippo for what he'd done – well, Papá could, of course, and probably a good-sized portion of Tuscany's gossips could, too – because Lucrezia Buti was certainly one of the most lovely women I'd ever seen, as beautiful as an almond orchard in full flower. Filippo had painted Lucrezia often: she was the Virgin in one heart-stoppingly tender fresco in her own convent's chapel.

'Come to the market with me,' I begged him, but he shook his head.

'I have to pack my bags,' he said. 'But I shall see you later. I'm off tomorrow morning – I couldn't leave without one more of Donna Carenza's stupendous lunches.' So I went by myself.

That day was as hot as July can be in Florence. Crossing the Piazza Santa Croce was like venturing out into a small piece of the African desert – there was even sand underfoot, left over from a joust the week before – but one dotted with small crowds of black-clad merchants from England and Flanders, gawping at the wonders of our city, watched by feral children who lurked, sensibly, in the shade of the colonnades. I squeezed past barrows full of bricks heaved by sweating men, past farmers on their way back from the market leading donkeys with empty panniers across their backs. Sometimes I felt as though I was pushing through heavy curtains of stench from the piles of rubbish and shit that spilled from alleyways or the doors of empty houses. The air was so thick with reek that I could taste it in my mouth: rank, with a metallic edge. I pushed on, through a sudden gust of perfume from a rose seller, out into the Piazza della Signoria.

Someone was yelling about the Medicis in front of the Signoria itself. That had been going on a lot recently, because Luca Pitti didn't like Piero de' Medici any more. Opinion in the Black Lion, which was a Medici stronghold, held that Messer Luca's problem was the size of his *uccello*, because a man with a prick of dignified length and girth wouldn't always be trying to do things bigger and better than everyone else (this usually accompanied by a gesture that showed the prick and stones of the Medicis and their friends to be of serious heft). The Medicis' symbol itself was a set of golden balls, eight *palle*, which were meant to be coins or pills, though it didn't seem to matter; and those who loved the family took them as their talisman and cried '*Palle! Palle!*' whenever there was a *calcio* game, or a festival, or a riot. So I ignored the sweating man's babble about the endangered republic, crossed the road in front of Orsanmichele and entered the *mercato*.

Coming this way, you first pass by the tables where the bankers do business. Ever since I could remember I had been annoying these rich men, playing with my friends around the exquisite hosiery of their legs until they kicked or threatened. I was too big for such sport now, though – big enough to be arrested or taken around the corner and whipped by the liveried men who guarded the bankers and their customers. But they didn't interest me any more. I didn't like the way they bit their gold coins with such relish – gold doesn't taste as nice as it looks. Long ago I had thought that it must be warm and rich, like an egg yolk or saffron, but when I had sneaked my father's signet ring into my mouth I found it tingled against my tongue with a slightly threatening insistence, and that the taste itself was bland and a bit sour, like snow – a greyish-blue taste, not yellow at all. Much more exciting were the crumbs of red sealing wax hidden in the intaglio. tiny bursts of honeyed pine resin laced with dangerous, acrid pinpricks of poisonous vermilion. So at fourteen I understood that gold was useful, but I couldn't fathom why the world had made it the symbol of wealth. One nail-scraping of fat from a good ham held more richness than all the gold in the Medici bank. But still I yelled '*Palle!*' with the best of them.

For me, the real world began further along the street, where it plunged into the ancient warren of the market itself. This was where Florence had always been. It was our heart, set to beating by Julius Caesar himself, and if you doubted that you only had to dig a vegetable patch or a cesspit, because when you scratched the skin of the *mercato*, out jumped ancient tiles and bricks and coins, and sometimes even a marble head or hand, still staring, still reaching out for you.

Papá had first brought me here early in the morning, when the real business is done. He'd dragged me around by the wrist – I would have been an unwilling five-year-old – and showed me off to his suppliers and favourite dealers. The sort of thing a little boy finds dull beyond belief: much more fun to sit underneath a piss-stained pillar and play with rubbish. But I don't think I was unwilling. The *mercato* was my world from the moment I breathed its air. Half awake at such an hour, I'd been amazed to find that the market was alive already, though the sun had barely heaved itself above the rooftops and everything in the square had that strange, washed-out look, as if the shadows had feasted on colour all night long. We had gone straight to the stall of Ugolino the tripe seller, and Papá had bought me my own bowl of tripe, which I had slurped and chewed until my jaw ached, feeling like a man alongside Papá, although I had stood no higher than his purse where it hung from his belt.

There was Ugolino now, eternally poised over his pots, tall, angular and scowling. He always reminded me of the grey herons that would stalk along the shallows of the river in the early morning, spearing frogs with their beaks. I waved, as I always did, and he ignored me, as was his custom.

At the centre of the *mercato* is a Roman column, on top of which stands the golden figure of Dovizia as made by Maestro Donatello. Dovizia — Abundance — is coy but purposeful, a country girl in the city, and she balances a basket of fruit on her head, a handy roost for the market's pigeons. Chains trail from the foot of the column, where pilferers and short-changers are secured, to be kicked and jeered at, and pelted with old fruit and spoiled offal. There were no prisoners today, but among the rusty coils of chain sat a small figure with hair more golden than Dovizia. The column's plinth was a waist-high block of marble, but even when the figure jumped up and began to wave at me, I could barely see her over the heads of the market-goers. I stood on tiptoe and waved back.

'Tessina!' I yelled. Tessina Albizzi waved again, then grabbed a length of chain and wrapped it around her wrist. She held her other hand out to me imploringly. I barged through the crowd and vaulted up beside her.

'What have you done this time?' I asked, pretending to struggle with the chain. 'Turned the milk sour? Put paupers' bones in the bread?'

'Worse. I stuck my tongue out at the chief justice.'

'Of course you did.' Tessina was always making up crimes to shock me: stealing the shoes off a corpse on the gibbet, drinking consecrated wine . . .

'No, really. I really did.' She was scowling at me. 'I'm serious.'

'Christ!' I was quite impressed. 'Really?'

'Yes, really.' Tessina unwrapped the chain, looped it around her neck and goggled her eyes. 'Of course, he didn't notice. Nobody noticed.'

'That was lucky, then. And how did he earn such a foul attack on his dignity?'

'Trod on my foot, the bastard. He didn't notice that, either.'

He wouldn't have. Tessina Albizzi had always been small. Her mother had been so ill after she was born that she couldn't nurse her, and the neighbourhood gossips said that the wet nurse was getting the *uccello* so hard from Tessina's father, Girolamo il Grande, that her milk had gone thin. It wasn't hard to believe that of Girolamo, and Tessina ate as much as any other child, seeming to grow at half the speed of the other children in the Black Lion. But she was as wiry as any boy, and it had caused quite an uproar when Tessina first flexed her arm and a little muscle popped up, hard as a walnut, while us boys could hardly produce anything.

But she never looked like a boy. A mass of curls, the colour of August straw, made a halo around her head, tight and springy, as if a goldsmith had put them there. Her skin was pale like the flesh of hazelnuts, dusted with little freckles, except when she stayed too long in the summer sun and it burned. Like a peach, her arms were covered in fine golden down, which also clung, fainter than faint, to her upper lip. By our tenth birthdays, she only came up to my chest, and in our fourteenth year I could still nestle my chin on top of her head as we stood together.

We had known each other all our lives, and that was really true, because we were born on the same day, at the same hour, and our fathers had bragged about us up and down the streets of the *gonfalone*, and had us christened together in the great church of Santa Croce, around which all our lives turned like the spokes of a wheel. Girolamo Albizzi had been a wool merchant, rich, with powerful friends in the government, but he approved of Papá, who wasn't rich, but who shared his passion for Black Lion politics, and for the Medicis.

Even when we were younger we had played together every day, running with the others through the streets and joining in the complicated games of territory and pride that raged back and forth across the Piazza Santa Croce, invisible to the grown-ups, but just as desperate and bloody as the fights which, once upon a time, had split Florence in half before the Medicis healed all the old wounds. We'd been prince and princess, leading magnificent, invisible processions through the alleys. We would peer out from our boltholes at the farmers trundling their carts to market, and she would dare me to jump out and steal fruit for her. I would do it just to see the juice run down her chin. And then I'd ask her how it tasted.

'Have some!' she'd say, holding out a half-mauled nectarine.

'No, just tell me,' I'd say, and so she would. Even then I liked to know how things tasted to other people, and in those days, other people usually meant Tessina.

I chained myself up next to her on the plinth. People were giving us funny looks, but most of the stallholders knew us, so no one threw anything. Tessina kicked her legs, and I settled back against the warm stone of the pillar.

'How did the chief justice tread on your toes, anyway?' I asked.

'He came to see my uncle. Something about his land claim over by the Porta Ghibellina, I expect.'

Tessina's uncle was a running joke between us. A bitter

joke, though, because he was nothing like her dead father, who had been loud and kind-hearted, with a big belly and a bigger laugh. Uncle Diamante was wiry, pallid and old-fashioned. His face was drawn and beaky, and he dressed like old Cosimo de' Medici had probably dressed when he'd been young: careful, plain and fifty years out of date. The only thing that wasn't outdated about Diamante Albizzi was his ambition, and he had his nose in everything that went on in the Black Lion, sniffing out a deal or a way to get his foot up on someone else's neck. His wife, Maddalena, was almost as bad. Tessina said she had lemon juice in her veins. The air in the Albizzi palace was cloying with piety. Tessina complained that it got into her clothes like the stink of soured milk.

We were almost equal now. Tessina was an orphan, and I only had my papa, who had become so withdrawn since Mamma had left us that I might as well have been an orphan too. Words weren't always important between Tessina and me. They weren't always needed. I leaned against her gently, feeling grateful that she was there. Mamma was dead, Papá was sleepwalking through his days and Filippo was going back to Prato. But Tessina was with me. Tessina had always been next to me. One of her springy curls tickled my ear. Her head sank onto my shoulder.

'D'you fancy some tripe?' I asked, feeling all warm and contented.

'Mmm, tripe,' she said. And elbowed me hard under the ribs.

'Ouch! What?'

'Couldn't you think of something else?'

'But you can't get it at home!' I protested. Which was true: Maddalena Albizzi thought tripe was common, and wouldn't allow it or any number of other good honest Florentine dishes to be served under her roof. 'And you love it.'

'Are you *always* hungry?'

'No. But what could be better? A bowl of Ugolino's tripe . . .'

'God almighty.' Tessina got up and stretched. 'You have one then, you glutton. I might have a taste. A small one.' She jumped down from the plinth and looked up at me, squinting into the light. I noticed some new freckles on the bridge of her nose, faint and rather adorable. A peasant strolled by with a cockerel under his arm, and gave her an admiring look. That surprised me. But what surprised me more was the splinter of anger I felt in my chest. Who did he think he was?

'You know, you should be enormously fat,' she said, ignoring the man. 'All you think about is food.'

'I don't eat that much,' I protested. Surprised again: I seemed to be feeling hurt, but we tore into each other all the time, and this was mild stuff. I jumped down beside her. 'Anyway, look where we are! It's all food! People eat. You eat . . . you know, I could say you're *always* eating as well.'

'If you say I'm getting fat, I'll kick you,' she warned.

'I think maybe a bit plump . . .' Tessina's foot collided with my shin.

'Animal.'

'I'm not going to share my tripe with you.'

We burst out laughing, although she'd actually kicked me quite hard and my leg was throbbing. She set off through the maze of stalls and I followed, limping slightly. As we passed a fruit seller, Tessina's hand darted out, quick as a praying mantis, into a pile of scarlet cherries. No one else noticed, and after we'd gone a few more steps she turned and opened her fingers to reveal a glowing cluster of fruit.

'Here,' she said, holding one out.

'But I'm *always* eating . . .'

'Shut up. You really are a baby sometimes. Here.'

I leaned forward and she popped the little orb into my mouth. 'Well?' she asked.

'*You* tell me.' I took another cherry and put it between her lips. She puckered, bit down. Her eyes narrowed, and then she smiled. A bead of wine-red juice appeared on her lower lip and she sucked it back in.

'Cherry-like, I'd say.'

This was a game we played all the time. 'And?'

'Mmm . . . Sour. Not like a lemon. More like a pomegranate. Then sweet. Like jam. And a bit of almond,' she added, spitting out the stone.

'Really? Pomegranate?'

'Yes. Now you.'

I had been rolling the cherry around in my mouth, letting it slip across my tongue. There was the flicker of salt from Tessina's fingers, and her own flavour: saffron, violets, the liquor of oysters. There was another taste as well: perhaps from the one who had picked the cherry from its tree.

'If you go back and ask that grocer, "That cherry I stole – where was it from?" I bet he says Celleno,' I said. 'Good choice – very expensive.'

'And why?'

'A bit crunchy, a bit undersized. Also not as fresh as it looked – it's come from the other side of Monte Amiata, been on the Via Salaria for days . . .'

'But the taste!'

'Blue,' I said. Tessina nodded, seriously. It was true, in a way: cherries have never been red in my mouth, but a bright, rippling azure. 'It's a good cherry: blue like the Madonna's robe in San Marco. Around the stone it's white, and the stone . . .' I spat it out. 'Bitter! Like dandelion milk.'

'You're so strange, Nino,' said Tessina admiringly. 'What about the pomegranate? Was I right?'

'Except that pomegranates aren't blue, are they? No,

you're nearly right. It's a difficult sourness, though . . .' I smacked my lips, trying to puzzle it out.

'*Dio Mio!* Difficult! Only you could think such a thing. Do you want another one?' She took a cherry and stuffed it between my lips. Then her hand paused for a moment, caressed my cheek gently.

'How did you get this way, Nino?' Tessina had asked me this many times, and I'd always shrugged and said *don't know* or *like what?* She was usually teasing, or exasperated, but today she didn't seem to be either. And anyway, I didn't really understand it myself.

'Do you really want to know?'

'Of course. Why, are you going to tell me?' The little smile said she didn't believe it.

'Yes.'

'Really? Why – because I said you only think about food?'

'Probably. It's true, though. I'm . . . I'm not quite right.'

'Oh, Nino.' Tessina took my arm and pulled me against her side. 'You're still getting over your mother. I didn't mean it. You aren't getting fat.'

'No, no. It isn't that! But I've been spending a lot of time with my uncle, and thinking about Mamma all the time. There's so much, and it's already going away. I just remembered something from a long time ago, that's all.'

'So tell me, and we'll both remember.'

I shut my eyes. *The arched board was up on an easel in a pool of sunshine, and the light was glowing on the faces of Mary and her angel. I marched up to the easel – this I do remember, but maybe only because Mamma never let me forget it – and stared at the Madonna. Then I spun round and located Uncle Filippo, standing in the dusty shadows.*

'Uncle!' I demanded. 'Where's Mary's dress? Is the angel telling her to put some clothes on?'

'You didn't say that, did you?' Tessina blushed and crossed herself, though the look on her face wasn't pious at all.

'I did.'

There must have been a deep, stunned, grown-up silence in the studio. And then Filippo's laugh, warm and rich like spiced wine.

'Yes, little one. You're quite right. Would you like to help me get her dressed?'

'But where are her clothes, Uncle?'

'I have them over here. Come and look.'

He led me over to a stained trestle table. I didn't see any clothes, just a lot of pots and bottles and lumps of rock, and two mortars with their pestles, one big and one small. I probably frowned and scratched my arse in puzzlement.

'It was always total chaos in there,' I told Tessina. 'And then he bends down and fumbles among all that stuff – real treasures: lumps of malachite and lapis lazuli, bones . . . And what does he come up with?'

'That's an egg,' I'd told him, with the kind of world-weary, condescending patience that only five-year-olds can manage.

'Well done – complimenti! Take it.' I did, giving him a funny look. 'Now watch.' Another egg had appeared magically in his hand. He cracked it against the lip of a clay pot. With great care, he broke the shell in half and let the white fall into the pot. Then he held out one half of the shell to me. In it the yolk nestled, softly wrinkled, perfect, golden. With another conjuror's flourish he produced a white kerchief, laid it on an uncluttered corner of the table and gently tipped the yolk out onto it. It rolled for an instant and settled, quivering. He lifted a corner of the kerchief until the golden ball began to roll, slowly, down the little hill of white cloth, leaving a glistening slug-trail as it went. The last bits of white came away in threads.

To my astonishment, Uncle Filippo leaned forward, the end of his tongue caught between his teeth, and picked up the yolk with the very tips of his fingers.

'Pass me that,' he said, pointing to a square dish of plain white glass. 'And that' – the smaller mortar. I obeyed. 'Good lad. Now the stylus.' I gawped. 'The pointy thing just there,' he explained. I handed it to him. Very gently he pushed the metal point of the stylus against the bag of egg yolk. It yielded and gave. A bead of golden fluid oozed out and dropped onto the glass dish. Then another and another, until the bag emptied and the dish was filled with yellow.

'Ecco. Now you do it.'

And I did. I don't recall exactly what I did, whether or not the egg divided gracefully into white and yolk, whether the yolk survived the kerchief, whether or not I made a complete pasticcio of the stylus. What has always stuck in my memory is a pool of yellow in a dish – perhaps mine, more likely Filippo's – and my uncle's hand holding a spatula, tapping from it a dull greyish powder into a heap next to the yolk. He gave me the spatula.

'Pigment. Mix it up, Nino.'

Clumsily, I pushed some powder into the egg and swirled it around. I'm not ready for what happened next: not ready for the colour. Pure blue, pure, dark blue, stronger than the sky in August at midday, when it seems to hang like a polished iron helmet over the city; clearer than my friend Tessina's blue eyes, that the old women in our street are saying will be the loveliest in all Florence.

'Oltremare,' breathed Filippo. Ultramarine. 'That's the most precious thing you've ever touched, little Nino. The most expensive, anyway. It will make a pretty dress for Our Lady, won't it?'

He took the dish from me, nodding approval. He added a little more pigment, working it deftly with the spatula. The little blade reminded me of a cockerel wiping its beak: side to side, peck, peck. 'You can't waste a speck of this,' he'd said, 'though for once I've got a lot. Messer Piero has shelled out for the very best this time.

'Now Nino will help me dress the Madonna,' he said. And that is how I came to take up a brush, drag the glossy hairs through the paint and make, under Uncle Filippo's calm but watchful gaze, a blue mark somewhere in the region of the Virgin's left thigh.

'Steady. Feel the brush. You're clothing the Mamma of God. We are doing this for Messer Piero, but when we paint holy things, God watches us.'

'When we got home, there was a bit of ultramarine on the nail of my right thumb. It glowed – I thought it was like a scale from an angel's wing. And I was hungry. Eggs . . . I built a great pile of eggs on the table in our kitchen and started doing what Filippo had shown me: separating the yolks and whites. When Mamma found me I'd done over a dozen.'

'Gesù! My mother would have killed me,' said Tessina.

'Lucky for me she was a good and patient woman. Do you know what she did? Instead of yelling at me for wasting good eggs, she helped me make a frittata – I mean, she made the frittata, but I beat the eggs and poured them into the hot butter. I put in the herbs: borage and grape shoots, I think. She even let me fuss around the edges with a wooden spoon, and I pretended I was mixing a huge dish of golden paint, enough to paint haloes on a legion of angels, or to feed them. Then we ate it all, the two of us, and I fell asleep with my cheek on the table. When I woke up in the morning – someone had put me to bed – I pulled my thumb out of my mouth and discovered the bit of ultramarine was gone from my thumbnail. I wandered downstairs to find Mamma, and showed her: Look! I've got paint in my tummy. My father wasn't pleased, at all. I think he'd always known that Filippo Lippi would make one of us crazy, and it seems to have been me.'

'Do you think it was the lapis lazuli?' asked Tessina seriously.

'No. I think it's because I'm just pazzo.'

'You aren't. You're fine, my old Nino. If the rest of the world think cherries are red, that's their hard luck.'

We were standing in front of Ugolino's stall, and he was

looking at us with undisguised suspicion. Ugolino was a peasant from somewhere near Lucca; a little heavy, a bit wall-eyed, rather slow-tongued, he cooked tripe and only tripe, every day of the year when the city allowed it, from dawn until dusk, and it was a masterpiece. Two great pots steamed on their braziers. One held a pottage of tripe, the other was *lampredotto*, the fourth stomach of the cow, which he served up on bread. His recipe never varied, but it didn't need to. Ugolino's food could have been served to the Pope himself – he was the cardinal of tripe. But it was hard to imagine Ugolino outside the *mercato*, let alone in Rome. He was one of the constants of the place, and as he stood there, rain and shine, stirring his pot with a long, gnarled spoon of olive wood, he seemed as permanent as Dovizia's column.

I handed over my coin and took a big bowl of the stew and a hunk of rough, saltless bread. My spoon was ready in my pocket, but to begin with I just sipped carefully at the piping-hot broth. There it was: Ugolino's genius. As the broth cooled on my tongue I wondered, as I had wondered since I was a little boy, what he did to make this stuff so perfect. It isn't difficult to cook tripe. You just have to clean it properly, boil it and add some spices and herbs . . . Well, perhaps not quite that easy. You should boil the tripes – after you've scrubbed them as diligently as if they were the Duke of Milan's bed sheets – with a bit of white-wine vinegar and the bone from a *prosciutto crudo*. Perhaps you are of the better sort and buy your tripe already washed: even so, give it another rinse. Laziness never rewards the tongue. High or low, people like their tripe to be white, and if you don't add salt, it does not colour. While the tripe is bubbling, take some fine lard – the *lardo* made in the marble quarries of Colonnata is best, but if you can't afford that, don't think that something cheap and rancid will serve just as well – cut it up into little dice and add it to some good broth made from a capon, white wine, some leaves of the bay laurel and a handful of fresh sage leaves that you have torn into pieces by hand. When your tripe is tender, take it out of the water it has cooked in, throw the bone to your dog or the kitchen boy, cut the tripe into strips and add it to the broth, with some mint and some pepper. And now you may add all the salt you desire, because your tripe will stay as white as a Madonna lily. Serve it hot and sprinkle on as much of the sweet spices – cloves and cinnamon – as you fancy, and of course some good hard cheese.

I'll admit that my way is a little fancy, but I'm a good Florentine and I would be nothing better than a traitor to my city if I messed around with *trippa* too much. Ugolino probably did much the same thing. He added calves' feet, certainly not heretical. There was saffron, pepper – it was long pepper: you could tell by the bite on your tongue – sage. But there was something that puzzled me. Something intangible. I had decided, through a process of elimination, that it must be the mint he used, but it was some variety I couldn't place, and of course Ugolino himself would have offered up his own *uccello* on a spit, roasted with onions and figs, rather than give away his secret. It was mint, but it had the force of *nipitella* and the lemony tang of *melissa*, with a sweet, smoky depth that invited you to chase it around your mouth. I'd come to believe it was something that only grew somewhere like the dungheap in Ugolino's home village, because try as I might – and more than once, after the house had gone to bed, I had gone down to our kitchen and blended every mint-like herb for sale in the market – I could never make a good copy of the taste. I had come quite close, but my tripe was just tripe. Carenza liked it well enough. 'Does it taste like Ugolino's?' I would ask her, and she'd always shrug. 'Better,' she'd say, more often than not, but if I pressed her she'd shrug again. 'What do you want from me, *pazzo*? Tripe is tripe.'

'More cheese?' I asked now, and Ugolino grudgingly dropped another pinch into my bowl. He saw me almost every day, and I was still an annoying stranger.

'Signorina Tessina!' The voice was coming from the north-east corner of the square. Tessina shrugged and dipped her finger into the tripe.

'Who's that?' I asked. She shrugged again.

'More than one Tessina in Florence,' she said. 'Lend us your spoon.'

But she had only just fished out the first frilly strip of *trippa* and sucked it into her mouth when there was a burst of obscenity behind us. Turning, we saw a squat man barging his way between two narrow stalls. He was paying no attention to the people he was elbowing out of his way, and his face was puckered into a furious scowl.

'Signorina Tessina!' The man stopped, red-faced, right in front of us. He wasn't scowling on purpose. His face was gathered and ridged like a piece of leather left out in the rain and dried by the sun into a permanent mask of rage. Brown hair, cut to the very letter of fashion but so coarse it might as well have been hacked at with a billhook, stuck out from beneath an expensive cap of Persian red. He was stocky and slightly bow-legged and not much taller than me, and a short-sword hung from his belt.

'Marco Baroni! What on earth d'you mean by this?' Tessina was holding out my spoon as if to keep him at bay. I sometimes forgot – in truth I hardly ever remembered – that Tessina came from one of the city's better families, but she could certainly put on airs, and she was doing it now. She didn't seem worried, but my stomach suddenly felt as if it were full of frogs.

Marco Baroni had been lurking on the edge of my life more or less for ever. He was four years older than me, but had already started to strut around town as if he had a dozen more years' worth of life and experience. And he could get away with it. His father, Bartolo, was as rich as the Grand Turk. In fact, Bartolo Baroni was probably the richest man in the Black Lion, a broker of Flemish wool who controlled the Arte della Lana — the Guild of Wool Merchants — and who was just about to start a two-month stint as Gonfaloniere di Giustizia, the highest political office in the republic. Nobody crossed Marco, and if they did they suffered for it. At eighteen he had already killed a man, and blinded another over a gambling debt. The fact that he looked like a dog-breeding experiment gone dreadfully wrong, that he was often to be seen around the sodomite brothels, only made things worse, because people who didn't know better, or thought they could handle themselves, soon found out that Marco would do anything to avenge even the smallest affront to his vanity, because his ugliness was outdone only by his pride. He usually went around in the company of four or five close friends, all of them his equal in belligerence. Corso Marucelli was his particular favourite; a lout who stood to inherit a large part of the western suburbs. Marco had killed, and so had Corso. No one crossed them. In all these years I had never so much as stepped in Marco's shadow. I'd never even seen him up close. With good reason: I'd known a boy my age who, at ten, had thought it would be a laugh to throw a toad at him. Marco had snapped his arm like a twig and he'd never thrown straight again.

And yet here he was, panting a bit and all but simpering in front of Tessina. 'What do you want, Marco Baroni?' she asked again. I admired her nerve: my tongue had gone as dry as a fillet of salt cod.

'I came to tell you that you are required at your uncle's house,' said Marco.

'*Required*? Is something the matter?'

'No, no. Nothing at all.'

'Then what are you doing? Have you turned messenger boy? Did my uncle give you a penny to find me?'

I was really alarmed now. Tessina of all people must know that you didn't talk to Marco Baroni like this. He wasn't known to be especially fond of women; in fact, there was a rumour going around that his father had had to pay the owner of the Chiassolino, a popular brothel, quite a few florins after Marco had beaten up one of the girls.

'Tessina . . .' I hissed. It was a mistake, because Marco noticed me for the first time.

'I know you,' he said. *No you don't*, I wanted to say, but I couldn't have made a sound right then.

'I'll go when I'm ready,' said Tessina. 'Do you need to tell my uncle? If you do, perhaps you should be getting back to him . . .'

'No, no.' He bowed, fashionably but not elegantly. 'I just happened to see you, after talking to your uncle Diamante, who was wondering where you might be. I'm on my way . . .' He nodded past Ugolino, which happened to be the direction in which the Chiassolino and other far less respectable fleshpots lay. I might have smiled. My lips might have given a small twitch. I'd done something, though, because all of a sudden Marco was standing right in front of me, the toes of his boots almost touching mine. I couldn't help noting that he was only half a head taller than me.

'I do know you. The butcher's son. Latini.' I nodded painfully. 'Are you bothering Signorina Tessina? Are you troubling her with your filthy, meaty butcher's stink? Eh? Because I can smell you, and you're certainly troubling me.'

'I don't think so,' I said, forcing the words out.

'You don't think you stink of the rotten meat your father sells?' I shook my head, hoping that he'd appreciate an honest answer. 'Well, something stinks, and it's coming from you.'

It was all going to happen now: I knew it. My hands were

73

clamped around the hot bowl but I knew I couldn't drop it and raise my fists, because if I did, he'd kill me. I was going to get hurt, and there was nothing I could do about that. If Marco would just get it over with . . .

But instead he leaned in close and whispered in my ear. 'You know, butcher's boy, I've worked it out. You've been cuddling your dead mamma, haven't you? And she's been dead for . . . ooh, three weeks now. That's where the stink comes from.' He stepped back. 'Go home, *signorina*. You're expected,' he said, very sweetly, to Tessina. And then, rolling slightly on his bandy legs, he stalked off and was swallowed up by the crowd.

Tessina was prising my fingers away from the bowl of tripe. My knees started to shake.

'He's a devil. He's a demon,' I whispered. 'I haven't wet myself, have I?'

Tessina glanced down. 'No. Well done.'

'Thanks.'

'Um . . .' I didn't fancy the tripe any more. It looked like a glutinous mass of worms, and after the thing that Marco had said . . . I took the bowl from Tessina and set it down on the stall. 'How do you know him?' I asked.

'Marco? I don't *know* him. My uncle knows his father. Worships him, more like. Every time Bartolo comes to the house, Uncle fawns all over him. It's disgusting.'

'Christ. I'd have thought Baroni would be too common for your aunt and uncle. I mean, they don't allow tripe, but they suck up to that old wineskin? Wasn't he a mercenary, before he got rich?'

'I think so. And his father made barrels.'

'I heard he had his rivals drowned in his cellar.'

'Really? I heard he sold them to the Turks as galley slaves. Anyway, it's because he's going to be *gonfaloniere*. Uncle thinks it's going to rub off on him, I suppose. He'd give one

of his eyeballs if he could get into office. And should the
Medicis take notice of the Albizzi family again – he'd probably give both eyeballs.'

'My father . . .' I was going to say something mean just to
be companionable, but Tessina cut me off.

'Your father isn't a snob,' she said. 'He works hard and
everyone respects him. And he isn't trying to crawl up
someone's backside because he thinks there's a pot of gold
up there.'

I thought of the house without Mamma, and Papá's pale
face when I happened to see him. And I thought of us
together in the shop, working in silence. 'Thanks, Tessina,'
I said.

'I suppose we'd better go and see what Uncle Diamante
wants,' she said.

'All right.' I turned, to say sorry to Ugolino about the
wasted tripe, but he was busy chopping ham. The bowl was
already gone. And in its place, my coin. Ugolino looked up,
glanced down at it and gave me a barely perceptible nod. I
picked up the coin. My cheeks were burning, and I was
about to stammer something when he gave a grunt and went
back to his chopping. Tessina was already walking away, and
I hurried after her. When I caught up, Tessina snaked her
arm through mine and we slipped, gratefully, into the shade
of the alleyways.

The Palazzo Albizzi was just around the corner from the
church of San Remigio. In fact, Tessina's father was buried
on the other side of the aisle from Mamma. Not so long ago
– within my own lifetime, in fact – the Albizzis had been a
big family in the Black Lion. A hundred years ago they had
been linked in business with the Peruzzis themselves and had
managed to survive when Bonifazio Peruzzi, so the story
went, had loaned too much money to an English king who
had never intended to pay it back. After that disaster the

Albizzis had shifted their allegiance like clever fleas from one rich host to the next, but they'd never quite managed to get their teeth into the Medicis, and since Cosimo and now Piero had extended their power over Florence, so the Albizzis had begun to wither, and with the death of Tessina's father, the rot seemed to have set in for good.

I was a familiar face at the Palazzo Albizzi. The family treated me as a sort of honorary cousin because Diamante and his wife had no particular liking for children – they had none of their own – and I was a convenient playmate for their niece. I kept Tessina out of their hair, and in return they were willing to tolerate my father's inferior guild. So I wandered in through the front door without giving it a second thought.

Diamante Albizzi was a nondescript man who always looked as if the surgeon had given him a week to live, and his wife had the air of someone about to be bereaved. Long ago, I had decided that this must be why they had got married. They rarely spoke to me, and I took no notice of them, an arrangement that seemed to suit us all perfectly. Sure enough, they paid no attention to me now, although they seemed to be more than usually pleased to see Tessina. In fact, I couldn't remember them ever smiling at her, but here they were, grinning like a pair of Barbary apes.

'My dear niece!' exclaimed Uncle Diamante.

'The *podestà* came to see us this morning, child,' said Maddalena, breathlessly.

'I know. He stepped on my foot,' said Tessina tartly. As ever, though, her aunt wasn't listening.

'And do you know why he came? Of course you don't.' Maddalena frowned, then decided to pass over this short-coming. 'He came to bring a suit—'

'A law suit? That's not good, though, is it?' Tessina put in.

'Not that kind of suit, girl. He came on behalf of a friend –

a very *important* friend — to ask a question of your uncle and myself.'

'Get on with it, Donna Maddalena!' After years of marriage, Diamante still addressed his wife as if she were wed to someone else. 'The point is, niece, that the next *gonfaloniere* of our city is a great friend and guild brother of the *podestà*,' he went on, plainly deciding that his wife wasn't to be trusted with the telling of this tale. 'And because of that, the *podestà* agreed to put forward his suit.'

'But what suit?' said Tessina.

'A proposal of marriage,' they both said, more or less together. Perhaps that was why it took Tessina a moment to react.

'It's true! Bartolo Baroni has asked for your hand in marriage,' cried Maddalena. 'Don't fear — we said yes, of course we said yes!'

The room seemed to swell and then contract around me, the black shapes of the heavy, ugly furniture dancing crow-like through the musty air. I opened my mouth to say something but all that came out was a fit of coughing. Diamante Albizzi glanced at me as if I were a cupboard that needed dusting.

'There is only one thing to cloud your joy,' Maddalena added, her face falling. 'Messer Bartolo could not, of course, be expected to wed during the two months he will be in office. And directly afterwards he is journeying to Burgundy on business. And besides . . .' She grinned, even more horribly than before. 'Messer Bartolo has stated he would prefer his wife with some endowment in the . . . in the . . .' Maddalena's hand fluttered in the region of her heart.

'He prefers a girl with breasts,' stated Uncle Diamante, bluntly. 'And has deigned to wait until such time as you grow some. I have assured him that breasts will be forthcoming,' he added, looking at her sternly.

'Bartolo Baroni?' whispered Tessina. 'Why? I don't understand.'

'Of course you don't,' said her uncle, more kindly. 'But rest assured it is an excellent match. Messer Bartolo—'

'Please don't!' said Tessina. I could tell from her voice that she was fighting tears, but I knew her so much better than her guardians ever would.

'No, don't be modest,' said her uncle, not comprehending. 'The Baroni family is what one might call *young* in terms of years, whereas the Albizzis have their roots in Julius Caesar's time. It's a most attractive match to Messer Bartolo. Your dowry is to be the castle in Greve which Baroni wants to rebuild. And your children will be Baroni-Albizzi – we pushed him for Albizzi-Baroni, but—'

'You mean, you've been plotting this for . . .'

'Well, for several weeks,' said Maddalena brightly. 'Your uncle has been working *so* hard on your behalf. Now you must thank him for finding you such a match.'

If I had been a bit older, or more confident . . . If I'd come from a family with its roots in Julius Caesar's privy, perhaps I would have stepped forward and tried to save Tessina. But instead I stood there like a piece of wood, and finally Diamante noticed me, so I never found out whether or not Tessina thanked him for condemning her to marry Bartolo Baroni.

'Now then, you, sir!' he said. 'Latini's son, is it?'

'Yes, sir,' I mumbled.

'You'll leave now.'

'Wait, Uncle! Nino and I were going—'

'Have you been listening, Tessina?' Maddalena's voice was back to its usual vinegar. 'You are betrothed. To all intents and purposes you are a woman now. Running about the streets with this *butcher's* son? No, no. You will remain in this house until it is time for your husband to take you away.'

'But she's . . .' I was about to say, *she's just a girl*. But I would have been too late anyway. Tessina was a woman now, but I was still a boy. A butcher's boy. 'Can we just finish what we were doing?'

'Can we at least say goodbye?' said Tessina.

'Why?' said Diamante Albizzi simply. A hand dropped onto my shoulder, and the *palazzo*'s steward, silently and with perfect efficiency, turned me around and threw me out into the street. I just had time to hear Tessina's voice, no more than a shriek of desolation. Then the door rasped shut and I was on all fours in Via delle Brache. I sat down and wrapped my arms around my knees. Two monks walked by and one of them cursed me under his breath. Further away, somebody was frying up a *battuta*.

8

FILIPPO WAS ALONE IN THE kitchen, the remains of a roast duck in front of him. He looked up when I came in and gave me a broad, greasy grin. When he noticed my expression, and the beaten slope of my shoulders, his eyebrows shot up.

'Something troubling you, dear one?'

'No.' I went straight to the pantry and came back with a basket of onions. Silently, I began to strip off the papery outer skins. With Carenza's sharpest knife, the one she never let me use, I sliced one, then another, piling them into a green, translucent mountain. The tears ran down my face, down my neck and soaked the collar of my tunic so that the rough wool started to chafe. Still I chopped.

'Do we need quite so many onions?' said Filippo softly. He had come quietly to my side, and now he laid his hand on mine where it gripped the knife.

I nodded. 'You always need onions,' I sniffed, and wiped my sleeve angrily across my face.

'What's happened, Nino? Did you get into a fight?' I shook my head. 'Are you in trouble?'

'No, of course not.'

'Then . . . Hmm. How old are you?' he said, as if to himself. 'Fourteen. Nephew, are you by any chance in love?'

'What? Go away, Uncle!' I put down the knife and shook him off. 'I want to be by myself, can't you see that?'

'Oh, no. I fear I'm right. You are in love, and it has gone badly. Tell me.'

'Filippo . . .'

'Girl or boy?'

'What? Girl!' I burst out, shocked.

'Aha!' Filippo clapped his hands.

'She's just a friend.'

'Of course she is. That's a good start. Not the best, perhaps, but you're young.' He stood up and, hooking his arm through mine, led me out into the little garden. 'So you've been thrown over.'

'Thrown over?'

'Given the boot. Rejected.'

'No! She's done nothing. And there's nothing anyone can do.'

'Is she dying? Ill? Gone to a convent? Betrothed?' Filippo was studying me keenly. 'That's it. Betrothed – not to you, obviously.' He nodded to himself, satisfied with his deduction, and regarded me, his eyes twinkling.

'Who cares about her?' I said angrily. 'Go away, Uncle. Because I don't bloody care . . .'

I ended up telling him everything. Filippo listened, like a priest, like the kind of friend I didn't have any more, now that Mamma was dead, and Tessina might as well be.

'I'm so sorry, Nino,' he said when I was done. 'I can't offer you anything but a blessing and a prayer, I'm afraid, and something which will seem cruel, which is to say that this will happen again, and again, and will get a bit less hard every time.'

'How long? How many times?'

'Until it stops happening, or you stop caring,' said Filippo, with a wry smile.

'Is that what happened with you and Aunt Lucrezia?'

'Yes – well, a bit of both. Since we're talking as two men who've had their hearts broken, I have to say that you shouldn't follow my example, dear one – God forbid you should do that, and your poor mother would say the same, ten times over. My advice as a man who has loved many

81

women, many *many* women . . .' He paused, and crossed himself. 'We are in your mother's house, and she would want me to be honest, for once! My advice is, well, perhaps not the most righteous you'll ever receive. But it's honest and I can assure you I can back it up with experience.'

'So all the stories that Mamma never let me listen to were true, then?'

'To my shame. But not to my regret.' He chuckled, then stopped himself with a priestly finger to the lips. 'My advice. I ask only that you listen to it, not that you take it. We've known each other for a long time, *caro*. And I can see that you are very much like me – you don't *look* like me, thank God, but in your eyes, your senses.' He touched a finger softly to his eyes, and again to his lips. 'The world reveals itself most truly through our senses,' he went on. 'And the senses are rooted here.' He laid his hand against his heart. 'You are very much like me, Nino, and unless you stifle all your gifts, which will be hard but not impossible, your life will be like mine as well.'

'You mean . . . I will become a priest?' I frowned.

'No! I don't think you should do that!' He laughed, and rubbed his tonsured scalp. 'I mean you will find that what pushes you onwards through life is not the same force that drives others. If you fight against it, you will destroy yourself. If you accept it, you may be destroyed, but at least you will have come to know yourself, as Our Lord commanded us to do. Follow your heart, Nino, and not your head. Always remember that.'

'Is that what you've done, then?'

'Alas, I've often followed neither.' He glanced down at his lap and rolled his eyes. 'Follow your heart, Nino. If it tells you to be a butcher, be a butcher. If it tells you to paint, come and see me and I'll be happy to teach you what I know. If you want to paint pictures with other things . . .' He pointed to my pile of onions. 'You of all people could teach this world how to do it. And your Tessina . . . you weren't wrong to fall in love with your friend, *caro*, and it isn't wrong to be hurt. Remember it. She will always be your first teacher, you know.'

'I don't understand.'

'You will soon enough. Forget the head, Nino. The heart: always the heart.'

He left the next day. I walked beside his rented horse all the way to the Porta al Prato and watched as he trotted away and was swallowed up by the road dust.

Fortuna Turns Her Wheel A Second Time:
'Regno' – 'I Reign'

9

Florence, 1471

SOME PEOPLE LOVE KITCHENS WHEN they're going full tilt, roaring with voices and heat. When there's a sort of anger in the air, and a mist of hot oil and steam, and the walls seem to sweat onion juice. But for me, the kitchen is beautiful when it's empty. When all is silent except for the crackling of the fire, and I can move around without banging shoulders with a dozen sweating men. When there's silence, and time, because time is more precious than saffron to the cook.

I had come to the Taverna Porco a couple of hours after midnight. A noise in the street had woken me and then I'd started worrying about the *contadino* who was meant to be delivering my game for the day's service, and realized I wasn't going to get back to sleep. I'd let myself in, brought the kitchen fire back to life and sat for a while, watching the flames. Then I had gone to work. Cutting onions, mincing garlic, sorting the good herbs from the ones that had gone rotten. It wasn't much, but it was something. It would prove to my uncle Terino, yet again, that his nephew put cooking before everything else. For five years I had been trying to prove it to him, and for five years he had ignored me.

Other things had happened, to be sure, in our lives, in our city. Florence is like a pan set over a flame that is just too high for what is inside it. Men rise and fall. The great triumph, and then they pass away. There is always something terrible just over the horizon. Things are stirred, and fried, and discarded. Piero de' Medici defeated his great rival Luca

Pitti, and that strutting cockerel, dressed in red silk and always crowing from his pile of gold, was almost forgotten. Piero's son ruled us now, young Lorenzo, the wonder of the age. Life was good if you were a friend of the Medicis. Florence felt new, as if it was something just slipped from a goldsmith's mould. Lorenzo made us all shine, it seemed – unless, that is, you missed the old Florence, where breeding counted above money and skill. If, for instance, you were a family like the Pazzis, nobles who complained that Piero, and now Lorenzo, had done away with the republic and ruled Florence like princes. If you made '*Popolo e Libertà*' – 'People and Liberty' – your war cry and set yourselves up against the mighty *Palle*. Everyone understood, though, that when Francesco Pazzi talked about liberty he meant liberty at the behest of the Pazzis. The old families were finished anyway. They weren't needed. We had golden Lorenzo, and we were the golden centre of the whole wide world. And *Palle* drowned out *Libertà* every time.

If Terino had known I'd been there most of the night, would he have paid me more for all the time I'd given him? The devil he would. My father's brother held onto his purse with something approaching rigor mortis, and I'd begun to think that the Last Trumpet would have to sound before he'd give me a rise. Because he was family, he saw no limit to how much he could exploit me. If pressed, Terino would bark that he was doing me a vast favour, letting me loose in this kitchen. And if I complained, he went straight to Papá and made it clear that he was doing his brother an even bigger one. The problem, for me anyway, was that Terino was right. He'd given me a chance, he paid me enough to keep my clothes in fashion and gave me just enough time off for me to help Verrocchio and Sandro – who had his own studio now – mix paints and size boards. And once Terino had understood I knew what I was doing, he'd given me a free hand.

At first I had served under the man who had led the kitchen for fifteen years: Roberto, a former soldier, who had ended up teaching me how to run a kitchen. Now I was nineteen, and in charge of the food at the Taverna Porco, which was no small thing. Roberto had finally had enough of Terino and had walked out one day. In the chaos that followed I had told my uncle that I could take Roberto's place, and seeing an opportunity to save himself some coin he had grudgingly agreed to give me a chance. It had taken a few months of blindingly hard work to convince the other cooks that I was their master, but in the end I managed it. I hope that my confidence impressed them, but I think they were scared of me. The way I could taste was plainly a gift, but kitchen folk are a superstitious lot. I'm sure they wondered if my gift came from above, or below. As long as I made sure they were paid, and that the food they put out was called the best in the *mercato*, they gave me their loyalty. And if they gave me the horns behind my back, well, I was always too tired to care.

The Porco is right on the market square. My uncle had given it a reputation for decent food at a fair price, a place where you could go to eat and drink without being bothered by whores and whoremongers, because the Porco was one of the few inns in the *mercato* that didn't double up as a brothel. I never found out why my uncle had resisted putting a few girls – or boys – upstairs. Lust brings in more coin than food, and I doubted that Uncle Terino would have minded being a pimp. But whatever the reason, the Porco was an honest tavern, and because of that, our customers tended to be of a better sort. We had scholars, the more successful artists, even bankers. All of them seemed to like my food, so Terino put the prices up, and to our surprise the place became even more popular. That meant more work for me, while Terino's grip on his purse strings only grew tighter.

But what was a boy of almost twenty – in Florence you are not a man, in the eyes of convention and the law, until you are approaching thirty; unless you are poor, in which case you're called a man and put to work as soon as you can stand upright – doing with such responsibilities? Papá was not particularly rich, but he was wealthy enough to let his son piss away his life for the traditional period, and I know he would have preferred it, because an idle son reflected well on the father. I think the future he'd planned out for me was one of late nights, gambling debts – hopefully small – and mistresses, until I turned thirty, married an heiress and got down to the real work of hauling the Latinis into the first rank of Florentine society. But I didn't want to be a butcher, and I didn't fancy being a wastrel, either.

I hadn't wanted to do anything at all after the Albizzis had cut Tessina out of my life. The market seemed empty and colourless. At first, after Filippo left, I spent my time in our kitchen, cooking everything I could lay my hands on in a sort of frenzy while Carenza looked on, getting more and more worried. Some things came out well, some were inedible to anyone but me. After she had thrown away one too many dishes, Carenza lost her patience and banished me. After that I lost my appetite for food, and spent my time tasting things that usually go untasted: the iron latch on my window, the furniture polish on my bedstead, spiderwebs. I lay in the middle of the floor, drawing these things, the way they looked and what the tastes looked like. First Mamma and now Tessina had left me, and I had no one to talk to about the pictures and colours that formed on my tongue. I would write long letters to Tessina full of strange images and sensations. After the first two were sent back unread, I still wrote them, but they went into the fire. Eventually I gave up writing the letters altogether and just sat for hours, sucking the ink from my quill, letting black words beat around my mouth like bats. Papá began to worry that, having just lost his wife, he was about to lose his son as well. I'd never talked to him about Tessina, and it wouldn't have occurred to me to confide in him now. He wouldn't have understood. I didn't understand myself. But Papá, faced with a problem, needed to sort it out. Another man would probably have gone to a priest. It might have been the common sense of a butcher that made my father talk to Carenza, or perhaps it was just luck, but in any case they both cornered me one evening down in the kitchen.

'Do you think your mother would approve of you moping, eh?' said Carenza. 'No, I can tell you that she wouldn't. And you had fourteen good years with her, so give thanks for that. I lost my mamma when I was two. And besides, it's not as if you're alone in the world.'

I wanted to tell her that I was never alone, that every smell that came in through my window came to life like a painting in front of me that didn't go away if I closed my eyes. That I knew what everyone in the street had for breakfast, lunch and supper. That cherries were blue, and a piece of grilled beef was a citadel with battlements of salt and towers of burned sugar.

'I'd give a gold coin to see inside your head, my boy,' Carenza was saying. 'At least when you were doing all that cooking you had a smile on your face.'

'Things are all right when I cook,' I muttered. 'If you'd just let me do what I want down here . . .'

'What do you mean, "all right"?' said Papá. I looked at him. His face was pale, and I noticed that his left hand was different. The little finger was swaddled with a dirty bandage, and it was no more than a stump.

'Did you cut your finger off?' I asked. He nodded. I

reached for his hand, cradled it awkwardly for a moment. It was heavy, and feverishly hot. I knew there was something I ought to do for him, but I didn't know what it was. 'Then why didn't you let Giovanni do the work, and come home?'

'Because I have to do it myself,' he said, as if it was the most obvious thing in the world.

'Not the donkey work!'

'But none of it's donkey work, Nino! I learned it all from my father, and he got it from his father. If it's in here . . .' He banged his chest with his wounded hand, and winced. 'If it's here, all of it is a joy. It's what I do. It's what I am.'

'That's why I have to cook,' I said. Carenza sighed loudly and shook her head. But my father just furrowed his brow at me. 'Papá, why do you have to keep working at the shop, even though you've cut off your own finger? Giovanni's there. Piero is there.'

'Giovanni can sell, but he can't cut. Piero can barely tell a sheep from a . . . from a camel. Neither of them can see it, Nino. They can't *feel* it. Weren't you listening? It's not just meat, it's a whole world.'

'That's what I'm trying to tell you: the kitchen is a world too!' My voice was louder than I'd intended. 'It's where I live – it's the only place I want to live!' And then, overcome with confusion and shame, I ran out.

Papá came to my room later. It was coming on for evening, and I was sitting in the middle of the floor on my threadbare Turkish rug, trying not to think about the smells wafting in through the window: the piece of mutton cooking down at the Berardis', which had been in the larder two days too long, or the stockfish stewing across the street, which needed more garlic and less rosemary.

'Carenza tells me that you cook quite well,' he said, going over to the window. I knew he couldn't smell the things I could, that he was just looking at the pigeons on the roof opposite. 'Apparently you can cook every dish she can – I had no idea. Actually, she says that she's never tasted food like yours.'

'Tell her I'm sorry,' I said. 'I won't bother her any more.'

'No, no. Carenza thinks you have a real talent. Your mother used to think so too.'

'Really?'

'Don't be surprised. We used to talk, your mother and I. Every so often.' He gave a weak smile and it was then that I realized, for the first time: *He loved her.* 'Do you want to come and work with me at the shop?'

'What, now?'

'No, I mean every day. I'm carrying Piero like a sack of turnips. You'd be a help.'

'I don't think I ought to.'

'You mean, "I don't want to."'

I kicked at a fold in the ragged old carpet. 'No, Papá. I would be worse than Piero. If I tell you something, do you promise not to be angry?'

'All right.'

'I like the shop. I like the work . . .'

'And you're good at it, Nino. Honestly. You know I don't say things if they aren't true.'

'Thank you, Papá. But I would be a really bad butcher.'

'I don't think so! Why?'

'Because I only care about what happens to the meat when it's cooked!' I blurted. 'Being a butcher, it's all about . . . it's just *ingredients!*'

'Of course it is, Nino! Nothing wrong with that.'

'Yes, but when you sell someone a piece of meat – a veal breast, say – aren't you thinking *what a good piece of meat I'm selling you, you lucky fellow. And you'll be back for more, of course.*'

'Well, I suppose I'm thinking something like that. Why not? I've chosen the calf. I've taken it to the shambles. I've hung it, and I've butchered it. I should know it's going to be tasty, shouldn't I?'

'Yes, but how is he going to have it cooked?'

'That's none of my business,' said Papá.

'I know. But that's all I would be thinking about,' I said breathlessly. 'Nothing else. I would *need* to know! Is it going to be cooked and cut and fried up with onions and verjuice? Made into *mortadella*? Sausages? A *sopado*?'

'What in Christ's name is *sopado*?' exclaimed Papá, exasperated.

'Exactly! It's a stew with nutmeg, and honey, and red wine . . . cinnamon, cloves.' The tastes enveloped me for a moment and I swallowed. Recently I'd discovered the Jewish quarter to the west of the *mercato*, and had spent hours sampling new tastes and strange ingredients – strange to me, that is. The owners of the little cook-shops put up with my questioning, perhaps because I was so fascinated by their wares that the question of their religion never crossed my mind. 'Do you see, Papá? I'd always want to be on the other side of the counter.'

'So you want to be a cook?' Papá sighed.

'I *have* to cook! If I'm not in the kitchen I miss it. I can't bear it. I know it doesn't make sense.'

'It does,' he said quietly.

'Carenza's right about me being *pazzo*.'

'No she isn't! But she doesn't mean it anyway. Don't think badly of Carenza. She gave me a bit of a telling-off, after you stormed out.'

'I'm sorry.'

'Don't be sorry on my account. She told me an idea she's had – well, that's Carenza. But for once it's a good one.'

'Really? Can I go and use the kitchen, then?'

'No. She said I should talk to your uncle Terino. And I said I would.'

'About what?'

'He's got a kitchen, hasn't he?'

'Of course he has. But the Porco's a real place. I mean, people pay money to eat there.'

'So what? My shop's a real place too. If you're good enough to work there, and I say you are, you're good enough for the Porco. You need to work, Nino. Either that, or calm down and do what other boys your age do. Go out and run around with your friends.'

'My best friend has gone,' I said bitterly.

'Arrigo?'

'No! Someone else.'

'Left the city?'

'No. Gone.'

'Ah.' Papá crossed himself, and I didn't have the energy to put him right. 'Then perhaps work is the best thing. Just for a while, maybe. Terino has a good business. You'll learn a lot. Or maybe he'll put you off the whole thing,' he added hopefully.

'I'll . . . I'll see.'

'So we'll go and talk to your uncle?'

I sucked my teeth for a moment, then nodded. 'I'll be a pot-scrubber, though,' I said.

'No you won't. I'll make sure of it. He's my younger brother, isn't he? And my customer. If he doesn't do what I say, I'll make sure that his meat is all gristle.'

'All right.' I nodded.

'Good!' Papá came over and ruffled my hair, carefully, as if he was afraid he might be scrambling my brains. Then he tugged gently at my earlobe.

'I'm sorry about your friend,' he said.

'I suppose . . . it's God, isn't it? We can't question Him.'

'No,' he said softly. 'No, we can't.'

10

IT WAS STILL HARDLY LIGHT outside in the *mercato*. Coppo, my second in command, arrived just ahead of the curfew. Because I was young, and the boss's nephew, I'd had to throw my weight around to get the other cooks to respect me, and anyway, kitchens need a bloody-minded ogre to make them function properly. But I wasn't in the mood that morning and so I put him to work grinding pepper, which I knew he didn't mind doing. When the rest of the crew arrived, we were set up for *pranzo*.

Now we had to make the dishes we always served: *zanzarelli* soup with almond dumplings; pottages of tripe, broad beans, veal, fennel; spit-roasted squabs, chickens, hares, rabbits, quail, thrushes, lampreys, eels; macaroni in the Roman manner, cooked in a dainty, lard-spiked broth; a fish *torta*; chickpeas, greens, rice fritters. There would be a fruit *torta* and a custard pie for after. I'd just given everyone his orders when Uncle Terino reappeared in the doorway.

'For tonight,' he said, ignoring what should have delighted his miserly, time-hoarding eyes: the sight of a kitchen in full swing at sun-up, the preparation all done, things already bubbling over the fire. 'For tonight, there's special orders. Four roasted kids. Two suckling pigs. A veal head . . .'

I added it all up in my head. The kids would need to be seethed and larded, then stuffed . . . The suckling pig . . .

'Who's this for?' I asked, wiping my forehead. Jesus, I'd have to have a couple of hours' sleep if I was to get that amount of food cooked.

'Never mind who it's for!' Terino's eyes, not large at the

best of times, seemed to recede into his skull as his face puffed and reddened with anger. This was a ritual between us, but he was a fool and I'd long since learned to ignore him. This morning, though, it felt as if he'd slapped me. I gritted my teeth.

'This calf's head. Does it need to be done any special way?'

'Special way? *Special* way? By no means, young master! Let's just give the fine gentlemen a plate of tepid shit for their dinner! Let us serve them a raw head! If you are thinking of putting out something other than a *special* veal head, I'll have you scrubbing—'

'Sorry, Uncle,' I said, feeling as if my jaw muscles were about to snap, so tightly was I clenching them. 'In what way do the gentlemen wish their calf's head cooked?'

'Are you giving me lip, *nephew*?' He knew I hated him to call me that in front of the staff.

'No, not at all. But I need to start—'

'You need to start all right. Why don't you pull your thumb out of your arsehole and do some proper work, eh? Standing around idle, with all these grown men around you . . .'

'*Vaffanculo*, Uncle,' I muttered. Terino jerked his head like a fighting cock.

'What did you say?'

'I said . . .' The lie I needed to tell floated up into my mouth. *I said, whatever you like, Uncle.* But I'd spent four years biting back what I really wanted to say – words that, for God's sake, the money-grubbing, swollen-headed *stronzo* needed to hear – and suddenly they came out, and with them a great relief, as if I'd pulled out a rotting tooth. 'I said, go and fuck yourself.'

The kitchen went as silent as it had been in the dead hours of last night. Even the boiling stock and the frying onions seemed to pipe down in expectation. If so, they weren't going to be disappointed.

'Madonna.' Terino was coming to the boil himself. 'Ma. Don. Na. *Madonna maiala! Dio boia!* Out! Get out, you little *cazzo*! Nobody fucks me up the arse like this! Nobody!'

'Oh yes?' Coppo and the others were staring at me, rigid with anticipation. A lifetime of this stretched before me, a lifetime of pecking up crumbs of praise from among the turds, while this wattled tyrant pranced and crowed . . . 'You must be deaf, then,' I said distinctly, not really believing what I was doing. 'Because the whole city calls you a *buggerone* behind your back.'

'I'll kill you!'

'Oh, don't lift a finger, you fat pig. I'm going. Stuff your own veal head. In fact, stuff it up your *culo*.'

I left. I strutted, in fact; and every eye in the kitchen burned itself into my back as I went. I stared my uncle right in the face as I passed him. His eyes were bulging, fish-like, from his splenetic features, and his lips were moving. Finally, when I was almost at the back door, something came out of them.

'Stop, Nino!'

I turned around. A few seconds ago I'd been terrified, but now I was past caring. '*Vaffanculo*.'

'Don't talk to your uncle like that.' Terino's veins were standing out. The sinews in his neck were practically twanging with the effort to keep his temper under control. 'Now stop this nonsense and come back.'

'You must be joking!'

'I'm not! Come back.'

I gave him the sign of the horns and turned to the door.

'Wait! I'm . . .' He grabbed his own hair and pulled it, hard. 'I'm sorry, Nino. I need you in the kitchen tonight.'

'Why?' I snapped, my hand on the door latch.

'Because I'll be in the shit without you, all right? The rich ones will be out there waiting for food, and what am I going to do, eh? Without you in the kitchen, what in Christ's name is going to happen tonight? Nino . . . Please!'

'I want more money.'

'We can talk about that later.'

'You must be joking.'

'All right, all right! More money! Whatever you want! Just get back here!'

I went back. Where else was I going to go?

As soon as lunch was over I went out into the market square and stuck my head under the pump. It was overcast and humid: there would be a storm later. I waved to Ugolino, standing in his corner stirring his pots as he did every day except Sunday without fail. He ignored me, as ever. Pigeons were fighting for the best spot on Dovizia's column. Out of pure habit I looked for the soft halo of Tessina's hair in the crowd at the column's foot, but of course she wasn't there. I hadn't seen her again since that day, not even in church. She wasn't dead, because I'd have heard – or married, because the whole of Florence would have known. I'd seen Bartolo Baroni once or twice, when he wasn't away in Flanders. He rolled through the Black Lion like a side of beef perched on skinny legs, dispensing favours and settling disputes. Some said he was in the Medicis' pocket, and some said the Medicis were in his. I gave Bartolo a wide berth, and his son an even wider one, and when Papá praised Baroni for his good works in the neighbourhood I kept quiet.

When I had cooled off I went back to prepare Terino's special dinner orders. I stuffed the suckling pigs with their own chopped innards, some boiled eggs, lard, pecorino cheese, seasoned well with pepper, saffron, garlic, parsley and sage. They went onto the spit to cook slowly, the spit-boy told to baste them with a brine of vinegar, pepper, saffron and bay laurel. Coppo was set to scraping the calf's head, which I was going to boil and serve with a green sauce. I decided that kids seethed in milk would be too rich, so I quartered them, stuffed them with whole cloves of garlic, prunes and thyme flowers, and put them in the oven while I made their sauce.

Terino would want something traditional, but I wasn't going to give him an inch. The kids were small and tender, the first of the spring, and I could picture the hills they'd come from, yellow with broom. So I decided to make a yellow sauce using saffron – which was expensive and would distress Terino – almonds, and egg yolks. It all went into the pestle with some verjuice and a good pinch of ginger, then through a sieve. The colour wasn't quite right so I added more saffron, though an egg yolk would have done just as well.

It was much later in the evening. Everything had gone out to my satisfaction, though I had yelled myself hoarse at the turnspit, who had almost singed one of my piglets. The pieces of kid, basted with saffron and verjuice and bright as sunshine in their robes of broom-flower sauce and decorated with real sprigs of broom from the market, the game stew . . . After the last piglet had been arranged on its dish and carried into the dining room I had sat down on the turnspit's stool and realized that I was completely drained. I was staring at the ceiling, gasping like a landed carp, when Terino put his head around the door and beckoned to me, his puffy face more than usually livid with excitement.

'Come out, Nino! Some friends want to meet you.'

'Please, Uncle. I'm done.'

'When you've come back, we'll discuss your pay . . .'

'Christ!' I levered myself upright and staggered past him. My slops were plastered to me with my own sweat, spattered with green and bright yellow. The cloth around my head must be even worse, so I took it off, and my wet hair fell down onto my shoulders. I wandered down the passageway that connected the kitchen to the dining room, Terino breathing heavily behind me, chivvying me along. I hated going out to the dining room in my work clothes. In the kitchen I was in charge. But out here I looked like a pot-boy, and as soon as I stepped into the noisy room, I felt like one too. The customers would be condescending bankers with grease stains on their doublets, and those doublets would be worth more than Papá's shop. When they saw I was just a boy, they'd laugh at me. It had happened before. Terino had better be prepared for what this was going to cost him.

The dining room was long and low-ceilinged, lit by banks of candles. A fire smouldered in the fireplace although it was warm outside, because Terino liked the way it smelled, and the heat kept the walls from sweating. The eating crowd was beginning to drift away, leaving the drinkers. I ran my eyes over the tables, looking for rejected food, but the earthen-ware trenchers were mostly empty. Good. I wondered where my bankers were, but then I saw someone waving to me from the corner beyond the fireplace. Terino would have put them there, of course: in the most private part of the room. I sighed, wiped my hands on my front and set off between the tables. As I got closer, though, I saw that the man waving to me was Sandro Botticelli. That was a relief. I waved back and hurried over. The five people with Sandro were unfamiliar – one of them looked like a lawyer and the others, from their clothes, weren't short of a florin. Bankers, after all? Maybe Sandro was discussing a commission. One of them seemed to be a boy. Another – the one in the best clothes – had his back to me. The others were laughing at something. Then the man with his back to me turned and smiled.

I had seen Lorenzo de' Medici many times from a distance, but here he was, a few steps away, and though I'm somewhat ashamed to admit it, I almost fell to my knees. There was no more famous person in all of Florence, perhaps in the whole of Italy, and he was staring at me.

He had an odd face, full of awkward planes and protuberances. From one angle he looked like a handsome toad, and from another like a Roman senator. The Medici beak, on Lorenzo, looked as if it pecked out the livers of Titans at breakfast time. His mouth was wide but almost lipless, and his eyebrows were heavy and densely black, as was his hair. It was a beautiful face, in fact, because it lacked all compromise. I would have sketched it there and then onto my filthy apron if I had had a bit of charcoal.

'You must be Latini,' said Lorenzo, his voice high and raspy, as if someone had recently punched him in the throat. 'Come and sit with us. Here, next to Angelo.' The boy dragged his chair to one side and I pulled up an empty one and sat down. The boy nodded at me shyly.

'Angelo Poliziano,' he said. He was probably three years younger than me, and I suddenly felt grateful to him: he'd made me look older by comparison.

'I hear that you are Filippo Lippi's nephew?' said Lorenzo. I nodded. 'And Sandro here tells me that you can paint with some of your uncle's gift?'

'I will not boast,' I said carefully. 'Not from modesty, but from honesty, sirs. I'd like to be a painter, it's true, but I will always be running behind my betters, trying to catch up. With a basket of lampreys and some nutmeg, though . . .'

'Well said. We've all enjoyed a feast tonight. Have we not, friends?' Glasses were raised around the table. 'Let me introduce you. This is Braccio Martelli, Giovanfrancesco Ventura . . .' The two men in pricey silk nodded, still grinning at whatever joke I had interrupted, and didn't seem that interested in me. 'Poliziano you've met, and Sandro, of course. And this is Marsilio Ficino.' The man I'd taken for a lawyer nodded courteously. 'I'd like to say he enjoyed his dinner, but alas, our modern-day Orpheus shuns meat.'

'And nothing cooked – fortunately he knows his wine,' Sandro put in. He'd had a fair amount of wine himself, because his face was flushed.

'Welcome to our table!' said Ficino. He was short and a little bit stooped, though he wasn't an old man, and had a mild, rather long face. His blue eyes shone with a gentle calm. I took his hand, feeling much more at ease. I knew who he was, of course, and I was very flattered.

'Sandro here has told me a little about your work, sir,' I said. 'Plato . . .' I rummaged among the litter in my mind for something I had learned from Arrigo. 'I believe Plato says that gluttony makes us incapable of philosophy and music, and deaf to that within us which is divine? I can only imagine what you must think of my own profession!'

'Hear that, Ficino? In our Florence, even the cooks quote Plato!' Lorenzo de' Medici slapped the table, laughing.

'Is it gluttony that you encourage, then?' asked Ficino. It ought to have been a stinging question, but I understood that he wasn't trying to goad me. I let my eyes run across the table, with its empty dishes and piles of bones.

'If so, I don't seem to have done too badly,' I said. 'But my answer is that I enjoy cooking for gluttons in the same way that our Botticelli likes painting for short-sighted patrons.'

'Aha. Interesting. But you must do so, all the time. Isn't that the purpose of a place like this? And I hasten to add that the Porco keeps an excellent cellar, so I cast no aspersions.'

'No, no, of course,' I said hurriedly. I could feel, rather than see, Terino wringing his hands from the kitchen door-way. 'It's true – my kitchen serves men whose main concern is that their bellies be filled, not with that which fills them. For my own part, I would like my food tasted, not bolted. Food can make you think, sir, just like music or words on a page. I believe we don't understand that, because we've chosen not to. If a man is deaf or blind, we pity him. If he cannot taste, then we say he must be lucky, and make some joke about his wife's cooking.'

'Very true!' exclaimed Ventura. The whole table was listening now, and I ought to have been nervous, but Ficino had put me at my ease.

'Now painters like Sandro, or my uncle Filippo – they use their pigments to create light, and movement . . . and even sound! I mean, you can hear the crowd muttering at Peter in Masaccio's painting – the one in the Carmine.'

'It's true,' said Sandro. 'I've heard them.'

'After enough wine, I can hear the wall complaining that I'm pissing against it,' said Martelli. The others laughed, except for Ficino, who had his finger beneath his chin, paying me polite attention.

'Well, taste can do that too,' I went on doggedly. 'We think we use one sense at a time – our ears to hear music, our eyes to see a painting, but that's not true at all. Why do we see, in our heads, a pretty face when we hear a love song? Why do you hear Masaccio's crowd? Food, sirs, is no different. We don't taste with our tongues alone. I mean, what did you think of your kid?' I nudged a dish, and the bones rattled.

'I thought of goats playing on the hills in this lovely springtime, and I felt somewhat melancholy,' said Lorenzo. 'But only for a moment. I suppose it was the broom flowers. But the meat tasted so good that I forgot all about it. In fact, I imagined the goats eating all those fresh herbs, and how good it must be to wander about on the hills with nothing to worry about.' He sighed. 'A devilish trick, Messer Nino, to play on someone trapped by his work.'

'I'm sorry, sire! But I must confess, that's exactly what I intended.'

'Then you must come and cook a meal for me.'

'I . . .' My mouth fell open, as if the muscles of my jaw had turned to aspic.

'I'm sure he'll say yes, Lorenzo.' Sandro filled a cup with dark red wine and pushed it over to me. 'I wouldn't let him think about it too much, though. He does tend to do that, and it isn't good for him.'

'Then it's agreed.'

I don't remember the rest of the evening except as a rising and falling of words and laughter. When I had grown too exhausted to speak any more, I had bowed clumsily to the company and gone off to sleep under the kitchen table. And it might have seemed like a dream had not a boy in the red, green and white livery of the Medicis brought me a message, later that week: a simple piece of folded paper, on which was written:

Marsilio tells me that Socrates said 'Worthless people live only to eat and drink; people of worth eat and drink only to live.' I have always believed that he has it the wrong way around. Thank you for transforming me, for too short a time, into a mountain goat.

And below the words, the spiky signature of Lorenzo il Magnifico himself.

ANOTHER WEEK HAD GONE BY. I was scraping a pig's head in the kitchen one morning when someone came in through the back door.

'Put it down by that big jar,' I called, thinking it was a delivery. But there was silence, so I looked up and saw a short, dark man with lavish eyebrows, his face deeply lined. I saw that one of his legs was slightly crooked.

'Are you Nino Latini?' he asked rudely. His accent was foreign.

'Who wants to know?'

'Zohan di Ferrara.'

I dropped my scraping knife. 'You're not him,' I said.

'Believe what you want. Don't you have someone else to do that sort of rubbish?'

'We . . . we're a couple of men short today.'

'Humph.' He grunted vehemently. 'Tomorrow night. You working?'

'It's my day off.'

'Pity. Looks like you'll be able to make it, then.'

'Make what?'

'The Palazzo de' Medici. A banquet for fifty guests. Just one night, so don't get any ideas. If you're only fit for scraping heads, don't bother turning up. But if you've got any balls, I'll see you in the kitchen one hour before sunrise.'

And with that, he left. I sat down with a bump. Zohan di Ferrara was the most famous cook in Florence. He worked for the Medicis, of course – no one else could afford him. Cooks talked about him as if he were Merlin.

I didn't tell Terino. He'd given me a rise but it was his idea of one, not mine. It was starting to dawn on me that my time at the Porco might be coming to an end. I shouldn't be scraping pigs' heads, should I? On the other hand, Terino was family, and Papá still thought he might leave the tavern to me one day. But then again, Terino wasn't that old, and he might have another twenty years left in him. Twenty years of him pissing in my pocket and acting as if he'd bought me in the slave market . . . I didn't know what Maestro Zohan wanted me to do at this feast, but I decided I'd pluck rotten pheasants all day and all night if it meant I could learn something from him.

So I woke up very early the next day, though I'd hardly slept, and let myself out of the sleeping house. The streets were quite empty. I skirted the Piazza della Signoria, turned northwards through the neighbourhood of the Dragon. The Medici palace is in the Golden Lion neighbourhood, not far from San Marco. I didn't come up here very often: the last time had been a year ago when Piero de' Medici had died, and Papá had taken me to stand outside the palace with him, with all the crowds who'd come to pay their respects, and to show young Lorenzo that they were behind him.

I followed some men who looked like servants and they led me to the back entrance. The palace was just beginning to wake up, sleepy men and women tottering around the corridors, starting on their first chores of the day. I followed my nose to the kitchen, where the fires had been burning all night, and the boy in charge was staring at the coals, glassy-eyed, rocking on his stone seat. Oil lamps were burning on stands, and there were expensive candles made of proper wax. Maestro Zohan wasn't there, and the kitchen was almost mine. It was vast. There was marble everywhere, as white and gleaming as if it had just been sliced from the rocks of Colonnata. Copper pots and pans dangled in profusion.

Shuddering at the thought of all that scouring and polishing, I chose a corner near the fire and changed into my white slops, then set to laying out my tools.

Not long after that, Maestro Zohan rolled in, trailing a retinue of other cooks and helpers. The Medicis' own servants had begun to stream in too, and in no time the kitchens were full of noise. The great personages of the household were gathering: the *credenziero*, whose domain was the palace's second kitchen, where the sweet courses and especially the great sugar sculptures that graced every banquet were made; the *spenditore*, in charge of buying the food and keeping the accounts; the *bottigliero*, who chose and served the wine; the *dispensiero*, who held the keys to all the storerooms, the cellars and the cages and cupboards; the baker and the *panatiero*, who bought the grain, supervised the quality of the bread and rationed it out to everyone in the household who was entitled to a share; the *trinciante*, who carved the meats at table and amazed the master's guests with his skill and artistry; the *canovaro*, who held the keys to the wine cellars. All these men answered to Messer Lorenzo's *scalco*, a very grand person indeed, who looked after every aspect of his employer's entertainments, was an expert cook, a master of etiquette, a dance-master, a stage manager. I don't remember the Medici *scalco* now, except that he was old and fierce, a proper noble-man from one of the city's ancient families – a Peruzzi or a Brancacci, perhaps – and that I did everything I could to avoid his glance. As head cook, Maestro Zohan answered only to the *scalco*, and they were deep in quiet but intense con-sultation. When I had finally managed to get the maestro's attention, it took him an uncomfortably long pause before he could place me.

'Ah, the boy from the *mercato*,' he said. 'I heard you told your uncle to fuck himself. Try that with me, and there won't be a kitchen between Scotland and China that will hire you. All right?' I nodded glumly. Did the whole world know what I'd said to my uncle? Was it so obvious I wanted a different job? 'Good,' the maestro went on, his eyebrows bristling. 'What can you do?' He picked up a long wooden spoon that was lying on the table next to us, and began to tap me with it, absently but quite hard, on the breastbone.

'I can do anything, Maestro,' I said quickly.

'Anything? That's good. Gut those lampreys.' And he waved his spoon at three baskets of plaited, tangled eels.

There are few jobs more vile in a kitchen than preparing lampreys, but it was to this slimy, smelly purgatory that my tongue had brought me. I had broken two immutable rules: I'd been disloyal to my family and I had got above my station. News travels fast through the world of cooks, a shadow world of small-hours gossip and hard drinking, and I'd got myself noticed in the worst possible way. The only thing I could do was get stuck in, and so I did, in the most literal way imaginable. For the way you prepare a lamprey is to remove its monstrous ring of teeth, poke a wooden skewer up its arse and draw out its guts whole without breaking them – if you do, the whole fish is tainted with evil-tasting juices – but you must collect the blood that comes out, because that goes into the sauce. All this after you have, with the greatest care, scraped off every ribbon of thick eel-slime. I was an idiot, but at least I knew that Maestro Zohan was waiting for me to call him a *testa di cazzo* and flounce out. So I rolled up my sleeves and got to work.

Time slithered along, dissolving into a reeking daze, but at last I had three empty baskets and most of the lampreys emptied and slimeless. The front of my tunic was foul, and my hands would stink for days, but I went and told the maestro, as humbly as I could, that the job was done, knowing that he was bound to give me some other nasty chore. But instead he looked me up and down with slitted eyes, seemed to find my revolting appearance to his liking, and tapped me on the arm with his spoon, which he had been carrying around like a commander's baton.

'Now cook them.' And he turned on his heel and strode off towards where the bakers were rolling out dough for *torte*.

This was too good to be true, but I knew it was another test, all the more dangerous because it seemed like a reward. Luckily for me, I knew how to cook lampreys. I ran around the kitchen, finding ingredients, begging for them if I had to. This was a rich dish, in flavour and cost, and if I messed it up I might as well be throwing silver into the river. Each fish got a piece of nutmeg, about the size of an orange seed, in its mouth, and a clove pushed into each of the holes on either side of its head – there are fourteen, as I came to know very well that morning. Then I rolled each one, tail to head, into a compact whorl and nestled it into a pan. When one pan was full, and the fish were packed tight enough that they wouldn't unravel, I put in olive oil, verjuice and some of the good, rich white wine from Liguria, sprinkled on a little salt and put it in a cool place. The delicate flesh would need to be cooked at the last minute, but meanwhile I prepared the sauce: hazelnuts – I considered almonds, but the hazels looked plump and tasty – went next to the fire to brown, then into a mortar with raisins, bread, verjuice and more Ligurian wine, to be pulped. When the lampreys were cooking, I'd add their blood and some of the pan juices, a pinch of ginger, lots of cinnamon and a few more cloves and boil it all down. Maestro Zohan suddenly appeared at my side, sniffed at the sauce and at the pans of lampreys, and nodded briskly.

'Right. Now stop buggering around and get to work.'

I hadn't had time to chat with anyone else – I'd hardly raised my head, in fact, since the maestro had arrived, and that had been hours before dawn. Now I found myself working with a pair of Zohan's own assistants on a mound of at least fifty sheep's feet that needed to be cleaned, boned and soaked for aspic. Like Zohan, they were from Ferrara originally, but had lived in Florence for years, and had lost the outlandish accent of their master. This was to be quite a banquet, they told me. The Neapolitan ambassador would be coming with his wife, and the ambassador from Milan as well.

After that we fell to talking about less civilized matters, and by the time the feet were ready we had more or less decided what everyone else in the kitchen liked to do in the bed-chamber, and with which sex. We made the aspic, and sometime after luncheon, which passed me by, though I was working too ferociously hard to be hungry, the man in charge of the meat had a pan of boiling water spilled down his leg by a clumsy boy and had to be carried out, gasping in pain. Like the mercenary I was, I abandoned my new friends, scooped up my knives and scurried to where the maestro was raging in front of a small company of suckling pigs.

'I'm a butcher – what do you need?' I demanded.

'I thought you were a cook,' snapped Zohan.

'Born a butcher, Maestro,' I assured him. 'It's in the blood.' And I gave him the edge of one of my knives to feel. He seemed convinced.

'But can you do this?' he asked dubiously. 'These need to be turned inside out and stuffed.'

So this was my penance: the dish I had tried to refuse my uncle, returned to me eight times over. 'Of course I can,' I told him.

I have never worked so hard. The fires inside, and the close, still day outside had made the kitchen into a Vesuvius of heat so intense you could feel it every time you moved, and every step felt as if I was pushing through heavy velvet curtains. The air was dense with smells. My nose was full of pepper dust and my eyes were watering. I got the pigs done, but only just. And that huge quantity of food was just one part of the feast. All around me, other dishes were taking shape: for the first service, a group of young girls were gilding candied plums, figs, oranges and apricots with fine gold leaf, and more gold was being smoothed onto sweet biscuits of fried dough cut into witty shapes and drenched in spiced syrup and rose water. There were *torte* of every kind: filled with pork belly and *zucca*; *torte* in the style of Bologna, filled with cheeses and pepper, and *torte* filled with capons and squabs. There were sausages, whole hams from all over the north of Italy. My suckling pigs were for the second service, alongside the lampreys, candied lemons wrapped in the finest sheet silver, an enormous sturgeon in ginger sauce, a whole roast roebuck with gilded horns, cuttlefish cooked in their own ink. Blancmanges of all colours were being turned out, shivering, onto silver platters. It was too much for the eye, let alone the stomach.

I was touching up the edge on my knife when Zohan's spoon rapped me on the crown. 'Over there,' he said. 'Your lampreys are going on. I've got Cino to finish the sauce. But this needs doing now.'

I followed the spoon, and my heart sank. A group of exhausted bakers, their hair, eyebrows, eyelashes and clothes matted with flour, were assembling a pie crust as wide as my outstretched arms, baked in sections and big enough to cover the copper dish, almost a bath tub, that stood next to them on the floor. And next to the tub, six osier cages had just been set down. Each cage was filled with grey, black-headed birds, all screeching their heads off – but the kitchen was so loud that I hadn't noticed them come in.

'You need to help with the flying pie,' said Zohan, and rolled off to inspect a collapsed blancmange.

No great banquet is complete without flying pie, but I

hated the ridiculous things. A lid of pastry hiding a dish full of living songbirds. It must have surprised somebody once, a very long time ago, but there wasn't a reveller in the whole of Christendom who would let out anything more than a sigh of utter boredom as the crust was cut and the birds, the ones that were still alive, flew out to batter themselves to death against the windows, or take to the roof beams from where they could pelt the guests with droppings. The only worthwhile part of the dish was the edible heart, usually a pie a great deal smaller than the dish, and that was usually crusted with bird shit and feathers. All in all, a complete waste of time, but nonetheless I spent the next half-hour dragging terrified blackcaps from their cages and cramming them in under the lid of the pie. When I was done my hands were covered in scratches from their beaks and claws, and I felt like a torturer. I've always had a soft spot for Saint Francis, who my mother loved passionately. Eating birds is one thing, but tormenting them for the pleasure of rich folk is another.

The birds were calling out in terror beneath their pastry roof, the beasts were on their platters, the gold leaf was burnished and Zohan was scuttling to and fro, scattering spices and powdered sugar left and right like some pagan priest. He stuck his finger into every dish, tasted it, and wiped it on his tunic, leaving a wet, dark rainbow of grease that looped from his breastbone to his right hip. Just one dip, then a nod – and once or twice, a curse, and the dish would go back, to be seasoned again or thrown away. Serving men and women were running in and out, sweating, swearing and being sworn at as they collected dishes. A small, liverish man who turned out to be the major–domo appeared and began to scream at Zohan, but scurried out again as Zohan and all his assistants poured out a torrent of Ferrarese blasphemies.

My lampreys – I'd run over, making sure Zohan noticed, and finished the sauce myself as soon as I'd crammed the last bird into the flying pie – were going past, and Zohan stopped the women carrying the great two-handled dish in which they nestled. He stuck in a finger, licked it, nodded. And instead of wiping it, he smiled, dipped again, licked, and waved the dish on. I went looking for the dish they'd been cooked in. There were still some flakes of white meat, and one fish had crumbled and been left behind. I scooped up some of it and popped it into my mouth. The flesh was sweet, not fishy at all, and the texture was a little like young rabbit. The tartness of verjuice fitted into the earthy richness of cinnamon like a sword into a scabbard. A dish to make the maestro smile. I sagged against the table with relief.

The kitchen was even more crazed now, if that were possible, but the first and second service cooks were done. All the reheating and assembling could be left to the servants and assistants, all of us hungry but too sickened by the endless processions of foods that had passed through our hands to eat anything.

I stripped off my soaked and clinging slops in the middle of the kitchen and stood there naked, my skin giving off wisps of steam. All around me, men were doing the same. Serving girls were watching us from the door, their faces a garland of roses. My body was shaking, and it felt as if my muscles were just giving up, one by one. But there was a buzzing in my head, and the blood in my veins was pumping, hot and eager. I'd stayed the course. I'd conquered. Standing there, all those women watching me, I felt, not like a man, but like a big, prancing satyr, with matted, gravy-soaked fur on its haunches. And then I looked down at myself. Twisted into a damp, hot loincloth for hours on end, my tackle had shrunk into what looked like a handful of peeled quails' eggs. I hurriedly turned away from the door as I yanked up my underthings.

A dish rag, more or less clean, was all I could find to wipe myself dry, and then I dragged on my hose, unbearably scratchy against my hot skin, and my shirt and doublet. Then I picked up my slops and wrung them out, and they gave up a trickle of dark brown juice. Now that the fires had died down, the whole kitchen was quickly going stale. The juice I had wrung from my clothes lingered on my hands: sweat, slime and spoiled things. That rankness was rising from the floor, from the tables and the unwashed pots, and from the men and boys who stood about, stretching, blinking and yawning.

It was as if the kitchen workers had become one great, stinking, lurching animal, and now, at last, the beast was hungry. We swarmed over the work tables and ate whatever was lying around. And what we could not eat we wrapped up and stuffed in our bags. I saw one cook shovelling nutmegs from a chest into his purse, and another was stuffing the sleeves of his *farsetto* with sticks of cinnamon. There was a bag of saffron on one of the tables, half hidden by an abandoned piece of flying-pie crust, and I quickly shoved it down my *mutande*, because people don't like to search your underwear as a rule. All this thievery was going on under the indulgent gaze of Zohan, who was holding court at the far end of the room. Every now and then he would beckon to one of the cooks, who would kneel on the flagstones while the maestro leaned over and muttered into their ear. Sometimes it was praise, because the man would smile, and sometimes reproach or dismissal, and in that case the man would stand abruptly and walk off, not meeting anyone's eye. Then it was my turn. I went and crouched down next to the maestro's chair, and he touched me lightly on the shoulder.

'You did well, and I'm pleased. But never say such naughty words to your betters again, eh? If you ever decide to leave your uncle — and of course you'd never do such a wicked thing — you come and talk to me, yes?'

'Yes, Maestro,' I said, feeling dizzy with relief. 'And who pays me for today?'

'You've got at least a florin's worth of saffron tucked behind your balls, lad. Let's say we're even, shall we?' He patted me on the head and sent me on my way. I took a slab of pancetta and a fist-sized rock of sugar, said goodbye to the men I'd been working with, and left.

It was almost midnight, and I'd been awake for half a lifetime. The Piazza del Duomo was deserted save for a man chatting furtively in the darkness to a couple of younger boys. The Fico would be open, and some friends were bound to be there. Perhaps I'd find someone to buy my saffron. I walked slowly, imagining I had left Florence and was up in the night sky, drifting through strange constellations.

❧ 12 ❧

I MIGHT NOT HAVE AGREED to play *calcio* for the Santa Croce team that day if I'd known what was going to happen. And then again, I probably would have said yes anyway. But as I waited for the game to begin, the only future I could predict was that I was going to lose some blood at the very least, because the boar-faced bastard standing across from me had shoulders too wide to fit down half the streets of our city, and because he was giving me the evil eye with everything he had.

It had rained in the night, and the wet sand was cold and clinging beneath our bare feet. But it was sunny now, that delicate April sunshine, warm in the open, cold in the shadows. We stood, fifteen against fifteen, scuffing the sand like angry bull calves, washed by the din of voices that filled the piazza, calling to us, calling across us to rivals. 'The Black Lion pimps their sisters!' 'The Dragon are little bitches!' 'Boys of the Wheel . . .' And then one lone voice, shouted into a moment of near quiet: '*Popolo e Libertà!*'

I glanced behind me, a reflex, the part of my blood that was Florence and nothing else jumping to attention, along with everyone else in that great crowd who had heard those three words. Not many people dared to challenge the Medicis with that cry, not since Luca Pitti had tried to topple Piero the Gouty in the year my mother had died. It was '*Palle*' now for everyone, *Palle* for the eight golden balls on the Medici shield. Not many denied the *Palle*, just a few diehards from Oltrarno, and a few of the old families, like the Pazzis, still saying that they wanted the old republic back, when every-one knew they were just jealous of the *Palle*.

And anyway, nobody was paying any attention. The man we were all looking towards, over to the right of the dignitaries' stand set up on the steps of Santa Croce, didn't move a muscle. Now 'People and Liberty' had been drowned out by '*Palle! Palle!*' and the crowd were cheering and point-ing to the men on the dais. The Medicis. They were all there, the great men of our city. There was Messer Lorenzo, il Magnifico, straight-backed and haughty in a magnificent robe. Next to him stood his younger brother, golden Giuli-ano; and the head of the Medici bank, Messer Francesco Sassetti, with his hand on Giuliano's shoulder. And there were the Medici allies: Soderinis, Tornabuonis; the Milanese ambassador, Nicodemo Tranchedini. There were the big men of the Black Lion, drinking in the admiration of their home crowd.

So there I was, staring at a line of big, riled-up lads, and particularly at the one who was built like an ox and had the outraged face of a wild boar's head sitting on a platter. You could tell the sons of rich men – *calcio* is for the rich, or supposed to be – by their smug mouths and perfect hair, but this boy looked like he'd just been dragged away from a busy morning at the slaughterhouse. No doubt he could tell that I was an impostor as well. I glared at him and spat. *You're right, my friend*, I thought.

The ball went in but we were already charging at Santo Spirito. My feet felt slow and clumsy on the spongy sand and, sure enough, the huge slaughterer's apprentice was coming straight for me, with all the grace of a storm cloud. There are no rules in *calcio*. You get the ball into the other team's net, and how you get it there doesn't matter at all as long as you stop short of murder. One tactic – if you have the nerve to call it that – is to hurt the other team so badly early in the game that they can't stop you scoring later on. That was what the brute ahead of me had in his little mind, so instead of letting him rip my arms off, I dived sideways and sliced my legs under his feet. He went down like a dead oak, and I scrambled up and dived into the thrashing scrum that was already heaving backwards and forwards over the ball. After that, there was no time to think. I got the ball a few times, set off up the field, only to be pulled down and savaged by the enemy – that's what they were, pure and simple – but mostly I just attacked any Santo Spirito player who wasn't fighting with someone else.

In our city it often feels as if there are no coincidences, that a sneeze outside the Palazzo Vecchio will get a girl knocked up in San Frediano. So when Paolo Soderini brought his elbow back sharply into my face and the bridge of my nose popped with the sound of a boiled egg dropped onto a flagstone, the first thing I thought was, *Of course, his brother owes me six soldi from that* tarocco *game at the Taverna Bertucce*. I let myself lie on the sand for a minute, because it was cool, and because I couldn't see a thing. Blood was pouring between my fingers. I pinched my nose between thumb and forefinger to keep it straight and looked up, blinking tears, blood and sand out of my eyes. *Get up, you bardassuola*, I told myself. A broken nose in the *calcio* is nothing. If you can't shake off such a thing, you have no business playing the game. One of my teammates pulled me to my feet and I tore what remained of my shirt off my back and clamped it to my face. Soderini had already disappeared into the ruck of yelling, sweating bodies further upfield. And, as soon as my head cleared, I dived in after him, which was how I tripped over the ball, and that, in turn, was how I scored the last of Santa Croce's eight goals after a mad, stumbling dash towards the net, choking on my own blood. After that there was chaos. I grabbed the ball and held it up, yelling like a soul in hell, blood flying. Above me on the dais, Lorenzo and his friends were applauding. I yelled again, caring only that the power at the very heart of our city saw what I had done. Lorenzo turned and whispered to someone behind him, and perhaps he learned my name, in any case, he gave me a dignified wave. One of the other team grabbed at the ball and I punched him hard in the face as the crowd screamed and I was pulled under a roiling scrum of bodies.

As we eventually beat Santo Spirito by eight goals to seven, I was a popular boy in the quarter of Santa Croce, and the pride of my neighbourhood. When the heralds sounded the end of the game, it was men from the Black Lion who hoisted me onto their shoulders and ran me round and round the piazza. I basked in it all, as I flew past the blurred faces I could barely see, the screaming girls and the roaring men.

There was a great flagon of wine, and I was just about to fill a clay bowl when a hand gripped my shoulder. I turned, expecting to find another admirer, but instead found Carenza, frowning at me.

'What are you doing, you idiot?' she snapped.

'Sorry, Carenza?' I began, but she had already taken the cup from my hand and given it to a surprised bystander.

'Look at you. Coated in blood – you look like Saint Bartholomew.' She crossed herself with a sturdy, water-chapped hand.

'I know! I scored, Carenza – did you see?'

'Come back to the house. Now. There'll be time enough for this buffoonery when your nose is sorted out. Can you breathe, you donkey? Eh?'

I went with Carenza. My energy was gone, and besides, Carenza brooked no nonsense from anybody, let alone me. She sluiced me down with freezing well-water, smeared my cuts with salve, and ordered me to the kitchen table, where a steaming bowl of soup was waiting. It was *ribollita* – I could tell only by looking at it, because I couldn't smell a thing. Carenza was staring at me, arms folded, so I dutifully plunged my spoon in, scooped up a helping of cabbage, broth and bread. I inhaled the steam but there was no aroma, and my nose started to throb nastily. I sipped, expecting the straightforward, solid tastes of Carenza's soup, but it might as well have been hot water. I took another hasty gulp, letting the liquid dribble down my chin. Carenza beamed at last, but I was in a panic. I couldn't taste a thing. No smell, no taste. My tongue was dead. I glanced up, thinking the world must be changed, but nothing was different. I tried to blow my nose, but the only reward was a great gout of blood that began to spatter the table, and made Carenza dive at me with another towel. I grabbed the cloth and hid my face behind it, because I did not, at that moment, know what I was going to do. No taste . . . So this was what I got for giving in to pride when the rich boys had asked me to play *calcio* with them. Without my tongue, without my nose, I had nothing, nothing at all.

It might seem a minor inconvenience to some. I had my eyes, my ears, my limbs, my wedding tackle – what more could a man in the full bloom of his youth possibly require from life? So I couldn't taste a bowl of *ribollita*. Didn't I know what it should taste like? Could I not remember? The answer to that was yes, I could remember, because I could remember almost everything I had ever tasted. Not as fleeting impressions or half-recalled likes or dislikes, but as detailed and bright as a newly painted fresco. A fresh loaf of bread, hot from the oven, I had eaten at a fair fifteen years ago. My first oyster. The difference between squab and pigeon meat, a revelation which had come to me like the voice of the Lord speaking to Moses. It was gone, all gone. I laid my head in my hands and sobbed, as my blood began to stain the table and Carenza's lovely *ribollita* cooled, its simple pleasures locked away behind a door to which I had just lost the only key.

13

THEY HAD HANGED SOMEONE FROM the Palazzo della
Signoria, dropped him out of an upper window so that he
dangled, back flat against the wall. He'd soiled himself, like
they always did, and far below his feet urchins were trying to
push each other into the pathetic little puddle.

I had felt something in the air as soon as I'd left the house,
as the city had closed in around me. Just a strip of blue sky
overhead. Two red kites soaring, weaving gently in and out
of sight. I'd walked through what should have been curtains
of scent and stink: new bread, a basket full of lilies heading
for church, the reek of a baby's soiled linens; trampled bulbs
of garlic, smouldering charcoal, armpits, the manure of men,
women, dogs, cats, pigeons, rats, bats and flies; the slippery
tang of fresh fish; a man on his way home from the brothels,
ripe with the toil of flesh upon flesh. I could smell nothing,
though, so it was like walking through the background of a
painting.

A couple of lads dressed in the over-laundered, much-
mended finery of two years past were throwing dice against
the steps of the oratory of San Fiorenzo. In the distance something was building, a roar like the Arno when it came down
wild and brown in spring and flung itself against the bridges
and the banks. Men were running down the Via de' Gondi
and women were craning their necks from the windows
above me, all looking towards the great square at the centre
of our world. It was obvious from the look on every face – a
leer: part shame, part savagery – what was going on. I had
decided to go the long way around the piazza, but there were

too many people in the narrow street and I didn't fancy fighting my way upstream. I had to rest for a moment, feeling bruised and liverish, keeping my eyes out for pickpockets. People swarm to see thieves hanged, which makes it easy for other thieves to rob them. Every cutpurse in Florence would be here today, and I wanted to be sure that it was the country bumpkins and the paunchy moralizers who got fleeced, not me. People were already drifting away, because one dead man can only amuse you for so long.

I was going to the Porco, because I had to tell Uncle Terino what had happened, and that I wouldn't be able to work until my senses righted themselves, if they ever did. As it turned out, he was in a good mood – perhaps he'd been to the hanging – and he let me off with a few muttered threats, because I was a hero of the *calcio* and people were coming into the tavern just because I was his nephew.

I was free. Nothing to do, no responsibilities. I dreamed of times like this when I was up to my elbows in onions or hog intestines, Terino cracking the whip, customers begging or complaining like greedy fledglings. But without my nose and my tongue, I found myself drifting. I had never realized that my whole life was built around three senses: taste, smell and sight. Without the first two, the market was hollow and eerie. I was hungry, but the goods laid out on the stalls were just shapes. It was purgatory.

Across the Porta Santa Trinità and a short stroll towards the south lies the church of Santo Spirito. It is a vast, lovely place, built by Maestro Brunelleschi and therefore the merest hair's breadth from perfection – and perfection, as the Turks say, is the preserve of God alone. I stepped into the long, column-lined nave and immediately the heat and noise of Florence became a fast-fading memory. I felt better. Everything was beginning to settle: all my remaining senses, which had been working madly to make up for my ruined nose, started to relax. I listened to the sound of my shoes tapping across the tiles. In the chapel of San Frediano, someone had lit a few candles. I lit another – for Carenza, because Frediano was her patron saint – and said a prayer to Frediano himself, who was up on the altarpiece, kneeling in a red robe before the Virgin and Child.

Filippo had done these panels ten years or more before I was born, and I still remembered Mamma bringing me to look at them when I was a tiny boy – although I don't suppose she had brought me for that, but to seek Frediano's blessing for something or other.

I sat down and let my eyes wander over the scene. It was a crowded one: Filippo had imagined, or seen – the best art is a record of things seen, firm and solid, in some place between dreams and the everyday – a room packed to bursting with furniture and figures: the two saints; Mary and her Son; and at least six angels, their thick, soft wings trying not to be in anybody's way. There are stalls of carved wood on either side, behind which an assortment of frustrated children are straining to catch a glimpse of the miracle. And there, in the shadows on the left, is a face: young, round-cheeked and dark, with a couple of days' stubble on the chin, which rests carelessly on the wooden rail; a clipped halo of curly black hair; and wide-set, almond eyes that, alone of all the eyes in this busy painting, are looking out at you.

At me. 'Hello, Uncle,' I whispered. The eyes twinkled: whatever Filippo had used to bind the pigments had kept an almost liquid freshness. I didn't quite recognize the face Filippo had painted: the man I knew had already settled into middle age. But I knew those eyes. I had last seen them when Filippo had leaned down out of his saddle just beyond the Porta al Prato, cupped his big, broad hand around the back of my head and kissed me on the brow. Then he'd ridden away and I never saw him again. He went down to Spoleto that winter, and within two years he was dead. I always meant to go and visit him, but I never did, and then it was too late.

At least he had left a bit of himself here, and in one other place: in Sant'Ambrogio, in the *Coronation of the Virgin* he made for the church, he kneels on the left, head propped on a hand, exhausted by the proceedings, or by the painting, or more likely by the night he had just spent with the golden-haired girl he is staring at, a girl whose face seems to glow and dissolve in such a way that it forces us to see her with Filippo's own eyes, to see what he sees: love, of course, but desire as well, and devotion. I would go there next, wander up to Sant'Ambrogio and be with my uncle as he gazed at beauty.

I had come to Santo Spirito first because, as Carenza would have told me with no hesitation whatsoever, I was *pazzo*. I knew I was mad. I had to be, because I had the vague idea that I'd be able to taste the Virgin's robe as I'd tasted it so long ago. But now, as I stared at it, I tasted nothing. I still felt myself dropping into the depths of all that blue, felt my heart lift, felt the air of the church shift and gather, as if it was about to announce something. But I could not smell the incense I knew must be there, or taste the dust motes – church dust, the leavings and sloughings of all those worshippers, all those golden robes, all that coffin-wood and candlewax and hope. I couldn't taste anything at all. And there was Filippo, watching me as I tried to find my world in his paint. He understood: *follow the heart, not the head*. If he'd been there in flesh and blood I'd have asked him if I could lick the board, and he'd probably have said yes, but he was pigment and oil and egg yolk, and the face he'd left behind said: *Life goes on. Virgins have babies, saints kneel, angels crowd in and make everyone sneeze with their dusty wings. Fingers cramp on the brush, eyes blur. But even so, it's all a miracle.*

Filippo's son Filippino told me, years later, that his father had painted me in one of his frescoes in the Duomo of Spoleto. From memory, of course – he must have been remembering my face as it had looked when he'd last seen it. Masaccio had taught Filippo, given him all that colour and light. But for some reason he hadn't passed on his knack for showing pain. Filippo had just soaked up his master's beauty. He found it hard to paint brutes, or coarse faces – somehow they all became angels under his brush. He did it to me: Filippino showed me his drawings, and there I am, tucked away in the *Coronation of the Virgin*, a curly blond angel, although my hair is black and barely wavy. But then I suppose all hair is golden in Heaven, and besides, I like to think that Filippo painted what he wished for his nephew, not the boy he remembered, struggling painfully into manhood.

Down below, Filippino showed me where his father had painted himself solid and earthbound in his Carmelite robes, trying not to watch as the Virgin dies. She looks a little bit like my mother. I'd closed my eyes then and tried to imagine myself in the faraway place where he'd died, standing by his tomb. I wanted to tell him something, but the only thing I could find to say was you were right: I did end up like you, down on the ground, not quite comfortable with holiness, knowing that the angels don't approve of us as we follow our hearts and our senses, because the one thing that angels will never understand is appetite.

14

I CAME OUT OF THE church like an owl woken into sun-light: almost blind, dizzy with brightness, groping through a dazzling world. How long had I been staring at the badly lit painting? Blinking frantically, I made my way uncertainly out into the square and almost collided with a plump, grey-haired man in servant's clothes and a decent pair of boots, one of the heels of which I had trodden on. He turned and cursed me peevishly though with restraint, and his hand stayed away from the hilt of the cheap short-sword at his belt. As I blinked some more, apologizing, trying to get the throbbing, whirling blots of inky colour out of my eyes, I saw his restraint was due to his being the escort for a young lady. She was obviously rich, because the hem of a beautifully embroidered gown fluttered below the drape of a modest shawl of undyed linen that she had drawn up over her head into a loose hood that shadowed her face.

'Sorry,' I said for the eighth time. I tried to make my way around the man but he, in his efforts to get clear of me, kept stepping into my path and for a spiky few moments we were caught up in an embarrassing little dance. 'I beg your pardon . . .'

'Come, Salvino! We . . . Nino?'

I looked around for the person – a woman – who had said my name.

'Nino! Nino Latini? It is you, isn't it?' To my surprise it was the lady in the linen shawl who was speaking. I stepped away from the servant, who was beginning to redden in the face, and bowed, wondering: an old friend of my mother?

One of my Oltrarno cousins, who I hadn't seen for years? 'You don't recognize me . . .'

I was confused. The light, my jangled senses . . . I stooped to peer beneath the heavy frill of the lady's shawl, only to find the servant's outstretched hand shoved into my face. But not to keep me at bay: he was reaching for my own hand.

'Latini?' He yanked my arm up and down until the joints rattled. 'A pleasure! Christ, a real pleasure! I saw that goal – a masterpiece, my lad! *Porca Madonna*, you really gave Santo Spirito a good . . .' He released my hand and began to pump his fist back and forth between us.

'Thank you,' I said, taking an expeditious step backwards.

'Like I said, you gave those bastards a good—'

'Yes, Salvino!' The woman laid a gentle hand – it was a small hand, very fine-boned, with a faint scatter of freckles – on the man's thrusting arm and he stopped abruptly, looking sheepish. I stared at the hand, at the fine robin's-egg blue of the vein that snaked across the delicate bones beneath. Not a woman's hand: a girl's. In the place behind my eyes I saw it turn palm up, fingers cupped loosely, a living goblet holding stolen cherries. In the real world it rose and brushed back the hem of the veil.

Five years had passed since I'd last seen Tessina. Five years: a whole lifetime, more or less. I hardly knew my fourteen-year-old self when I stumbled across him in the half-light of memory, but at least I had watched him grow up, observed *him* change into *me*. Tessina survived as nothing more than bad sketches in my mind's eye, paintings by an overeager but sloppy apprentice. Like my mother, in a way, who had left my world at the same time, and whose memory I had gilded and burnished, draped with the finest blue robes, anything to block out those last sights, the waxen woman on her bier, jaw bound with fraying linen. And Tessina, too: I hated to remember her tear-stained face as the Albizzi servants had dragged me from her house. She might as well have died. In a way, I *had* let her die: it was easier to think she was gone out of the world than to know she was just around the corner but unreachable.

'Nino? It is you, isn't it?'

I seemed to have turned to wood. So we stared at each other, a little desperately, until the slender fingers moved from Salvino's arm to mine. I let my eyes fall and studied them dumbly, until suddenly they pinched me.

'Did the *calcio* scramble your brains, Nino? What are you doing, sleepwalking in broad daylight? Are you all right?'

'I'm . . .' I turned my head. There she was.

The same, and yet a different person entirely. A woman – of course, a woman: in the same way I called myself a man. So Tessina had become a woman, with cornflower-blue eyes, brighter than Filippo's best paint; and thick, wavy hair that had darkened a little to the colour of old amber or perhaps chestnut honey, shaved back in the fashionable way from her smooth forehead. She still had freckles, the tiny upward curve to the end of her nose, but her face had changed. It had become itself.

I did a ridiculous thing. I bowed, because that was what one did when one met a lady, especially a lady whose silver and pearl coif, whose milk-white kidskin slippers and Venetian silk dress told one that she was of the highest rank. I bowed, felt my hair flop down across my face, felt the blood throb into the bruises around my eyes, into the disturbed innards of my nose. Something caught hold of my left ear and pulled, gently but firmly. I straightened up. Tessina let go, adjusted her shawl, pulled it down over her brow, which was creased with amusement.

'I saw you play,' she said.

'Did you? I didn't see you. I looked, but—'

'You looked? For me?'

'Of course. I do. I always . . . You were there with Messer Bartolo, I suppose.'

'I was at the *calcio* with my aunt and uncle. Messer Bartolo has been in Flanders for the past two years, and not expected back for another year.'

'I never congratulated you on your marriage.'

'But I'm not married yet!' she exclaimed, then dropped her voice. 'Still betrothed. Bartolo has been away so much.'

Her eyes seemed to have become an even brighter blue. 'Salvino?' Tessina turned to the servant, pointed to a woman selling peaches from a basket in the shade of the church. 'I'd like one of those. Could you buy me one, please?'

The servant gave her a surprised look, but trotted off obediently.

'He worships the *calcio*,' said Tessina, staring after him. 'So I'm sure he'd never dream that you might be a danger to my virtue.'

'What? Never!' I laughed, disconcerted. 'So . . . so . . . Tessina. You . . . You've . . .'

'So have you.'

'And you're out in the city. I didn't think . . .'

'Twice a week I go to the Convento di Santa Bibiana in Oltrarno. My aunt Maddalena has a cousin, a nun. She's old, the nun, and dying, and I sit with her.'

'I'm sorry.' I shuffled my feet, caught myself, stopped. 'So twice a week you've been walking down here from the Black Lion? And I never saw you!'

'But you were looking?' She glanced quickly towards the church, where Salvino had paid for the peach and was ambling back across the square. 'If you go around behind the convent, there's a tiny alley that leads to the garden wall. You can climb it. The garden is all overgrown: the nuns never go there and the gardener died last year. On Tuesdays and Thursdays . . . I'm going away tomorrow for three weeks, to

131

our place in Greve. But after that, if you climb over the wall when the bells chime two in the afternoon, on a Tuesday or a Thursday, I'll be there.' She raised a hand, waved to Salvino. I stood, hands clasped behind my back, stiff as a wooden image, Tessina's words clattering around my head loud as pebbles thrown down a dry well. 'Nino. Do you understand?'

'Yes.' I nodded. Took a step back, bowed again. Raised my head and looked into her face. Our eyes met and my body flared with heat, like a dull hearth blown back to flame. 'I—'

Tessina shook her head quickly, turned away from me and walked briskly towards her servant. Who raised his arm to me, pumped it again in brutal celebration as if he was trying to deliver a reluctant calf. I saluted with as much bravado as I could manage, spun on my heel and all but ran out of the square, north towards the bridge, towards the river, feeling as if I would have to jump into its sluggish, smelly waters before the fire inside my heart burned me to a crisp. My face was blazing. My hair felt like burning wires, like something pulled out of a goldsmith's oven. My heart was thumping, a big, red-hot coal smacking against my ribs. And my arm, where Tessina had touched me . . . I raised it to my mouth, kissed the cloth of my sleeve. And there, jumping from the weave to my lips, a taste.

Saffron — of course: what else would she be? A flavour that takes the lives of ten thousand lovely flowers. As it had done all those years ago, the taste rose again on my tongue as a ravishing, barbarian palace of domes and spires. Tessina. There she was, all of her: salt, the crystals that grow on oyster shells that have dried out in the sun; violets; lemon leaves; nutmeg; myrrh.

And with that, Florence burst in on me: all the smells, the stinks, the miasmas, the perfumes. I staggered, had to catch hold of a stone hitching post, because it felt like wings were beating around my face. I could smell everything, and I could taste: and lingering in nose and on tongue, the golden shimmer of saffron.

15

I WENT BACK TO WORK the next day. Terino had sent
Coppo round to the house in the evening to check on me,
who found that I'd recovered my senses, or at least the ones
that mattered to my uncle. He came back again first thing
in the morning, bearing gifts and threats from my uncle: a
businesslike letter outlining a laughable pay rise, which I
scanned while Coppo watched, and then some veiled threats,
voiced reluctantly by Coppo in Terino's unmistakably bilious
words. The carrot and the stick – always both with Terino,
and the stick always bigger than the carrot. So I took myself off
to the Porco, to boredom, the beady eyes of my uncle all over
me and my kitchen, looking for an excuse to complain; the
same dishes to prepare, the stink of Coppo's armpits, the ache
in the small of my back and in my legs as the hours passed.

But for all the tedium and numbing familiarity, nothing
was the same. I went through my tasks like a sleepwalker,
grunting orders, moving like a marionette in the hands of a
puppeteer who has put on his show a thousand times before.
Tessina Albizzi was inside me like lemon juice dropped into
oil; and like oil does when something sharp and arousing is
dropped into it, I was starting to change, to take on unfamiliar forms and tastes.

I rubbed my hair dry with a barely clean rag that reeked of
onions and went into the privy set into the corner of the
yard, because it was the only door in the Porco with a lock.
The courtyard was where we washed. It was where we piled
up the baskets of live fowl before we killed them, and where
we threw their guts and feathers, together with all the other

leavings of the kitchen: guts, peelings, and the scrapings from the guests' plates. Terino paid a man to clean it every so often, but because he was a tight bastard it wasn't that often, and the pot-boys had to shovel a path, every morning, from the kitchen door to the pump and to the privy. The stench was bludgeoning, but I needed peace and quiet, at least for a few minutes, so I sat on the smooth old plank and stared at the peeling whitewash that hung from the wall, and at the dusty cobwebs full of insect husks.

What did flies taste like to the spider? I wondered. The ones I had swallowed by accident – and once, on purpose – had been bitter like ash. But when the spider sucked them dry, were they succulent, like oysters? Was it like biting into an orange, or sucking on a marrowbone? These were the things I'd talked about with Tessina, I realized. The old Tessina, the wild-haired robber of market stalls, not the lovely stranger I had met yesterday. The Tessina of my childhood would have caught a fly for me to eat and describe, and I would have done it too, but only because I'd loved to please her. The woman in Piazza Santo Spirito . . . had she been the sort of young lady to wonder about the taste of flies, or whether cherries tasted blue or red? She had seemed far too . . .

I scratched my cheek – my face had been so bruised from the *calcio* that I hadn't shaved for days. Here was I, hiding in a jakes, feeling surprised that Tessina Albizzi had grown up, but what had she thought when she'd seen me? Who or what had she seen? A stubbly brute with a newly broken nose, pale from a life spent working indoors, his eyes knowing, a little cynical – in other words, a man. We had changed – it had only been five years, but God, how we'd changed. But I would see her again. She'd held that out to me, out of nowhere, a golden promise, as if she'd reached up, scratched off a curl of the sun's bright rind and given it to me. I leaned forward and began to sketch a face on the rough wood of the door with my thumbnail. At that moment someone kicked roughly at the door.

'*Cazzo!*' I shouted.

'Wipe your arse, and hurry up about it,' said a familiar voice. 'I want a word with you.'

Zohan di Ferrara was standing in the little courtyard, prodding a calf's skull with his toe. He looked up when I emerged, and wrinkled his nose. I went and washed my hands at the pump – I am slightly fastidious in this regard, but I resent tasting other people's dung in food (a cook's dirty fingers can make the journey of the most expensive spice from India a wasted one), let alone my own – and wiped them on my apron. Zohan spat, turned and made for the gate, crooking his finger for me to follow.

'Do you like working in that shit-hole?' he asked, when we were both standing in the street.

'There are worse places,' I said, trying to sound casual. 'Try taking a shit at the Fico.'

'I heard you've become some sort of hero,' he said, regarding me through narrowed eyes. 'Kicking a ball around. I don't understand your city at all. Buggery and ball games . . .' He cleared his throat and spat again.

'I was lucky,' I said. My heart was beginning to thump: surely he hadn't brought me out here to insult me?

'Were you lucky the other night at the palace?' he said.

'Anybody can play *calcio*,' I said. 'But cooking . . . That's different, isn't it, sir? Luck has nothing to do with it.'

'Messer Lorenzo seems to agree with you. Whether it was your lampreys or your *ball-kicking* . . .' One of his eyebrows twitched upwards. 'Can you still smell?' he asked, pointing to my swollen nose. I nodded hurriedly. 'That's fortunate. If you'd damaged yourself with your bloody games, you wouldn't be able to cook tonight for the master's banquet.'

'At the banquet?' I said stupidly.

'Yes, the banquet, the damned Arnolfini banquet,' he said impatiently.

'I'm working tonight,' I said. 'Here.'

'Not any more. I've given your uncle one of my own men. Not one of my best, mind. A dislikeable man, your uncle. A *buggerone*, is he?'

'What? He is not!' I said, trying to be affronted, trying to sound as if this big-nosed Ferrarese needed to think twice about insulting Florence, and now my flesh and blood. But all the time I was trying not to laugh.

'He wanted money – too much for what you're worth, boy.' Zohan shrugged. 'It's not my money, anyway,' he said. 'You'll work tonight. If Messer Lorenzo isn't poisoned, and still finds you *amusing* . . . If, by some miracle, you win through, you'll work for me. Thirty florins a year. Get yourself some clean slops.' And with that he marched off in the direction of the market.

I leaned back against the wall of the Porco, feeling lichen crackle against my clothing. Loose mortar trickled down my neck. They would be cursing me in the kitchen, but instead I followed my memories out into the marketplace, bought a punnet of cherries and sat down on the pedestal of Dovizia. Ugolino, over in the far corner of the square, was packing away his things. He moved with great dignity, doing just what needed to be done and nothing more. Once he looked in my direction and I waved, but he gave no sign that he had seen me. I sucked on a cherry. Thirty florins a year! That was an insane amount of money. Was I being taken on as a cook, or as a banker? My father would be proud, wouldn't he? I watched Ugolino, wondering what he made in a year – next to nothing, probably, though he was the finest cook in Florence. It didn't seem fair. But then my elders were always telling me that life had nothing to do with fairness, that a man took what he wanted, that respect was earned by setting your foot on the faces of your enemies.

Perhaps Ugolino didn't care about respect, though. I did. I was going to kick my way up the midden until I was eye to eye with the best of them. Now I could buy some decent clothes. Something beautiful to wear when I climbed the convent wall. Because I was going to do that, as soon as I possibly could. I popped in another cherry, bit down. The fruit burst in my mouth. *Blue*, I said to myself. *Blue*.

I went back to the Porco to collect my knives, and the kitchen staff stared at me like a gaggle of owls. The new man was already bossing them about: I could tell by the tense hunch of their shoulders, and the way they were trying to avoid his eye. I strutted over to Coppo and stuck out my hand for him to shake, and he glared before giving me a curt nod. Then Terino came in. I waited for him to say something unpleasant, which would make it easier to leave his employment, but instead he came over and squeezed my shoulder.

'So, Messer Lorenzo de' Medici will be eating our food every night, eh? You've brought honour to the Porco, nephew. And to the name of Latini. I know talent when I see it,' he went on, loudly, and the new man smirked, condescendingly. *Just you wait*, I thought. *You'll be hiding in the privy soon enough.*

16

Zohan di Ferrara ran the Medici kitchens like a *condottiere*, which some said he had actually been once upon a time, serving the Duke of Milan as a mercenary captain. It wasn't difficult to imagine. He had the nature of a warlord. The kitchen staff functioned as one creature bent entirely to his will – we were the bees and he was our queen, though if he'd suspected that I had even once dreamed such an image into being, he would have spatchcocked me – and yet he also seemed to know every last thing about each of us: our vanities, our strengths and most especially our failings.

I hardly remember these bees, my companions in toil: they are strained, sweating faces, snarling with effort or scrubbed blank by fatigue. Names like Pippo and Beppi, dogs' names, more or less: easily commanded, easily whistled to heel . . . There, I have made Zohan a soldier, a queen bee and a shepherd, all at once. I am a cook, though, not Ovid, and I am struggling to explain, with my poor store of words, the power that resided in this beak-nosed, swarthy, round-shouldered Ferrarese.

It was not confidence: Zohan knew he was a foreigner, and he was always ill at ease in Florence. Besides, a cook knows he is only as good as the last mouthful of food eaten by his customers at each and every sitting. I knew very well that he lived in dread of some piffling mistake made by one of his Beppis or Ginos, which was why, every night, he strained to drive his very soul into each one of us. Zohan trusted no one, took nothing for granted, expected disaster. This would have hollowed out a lesser man, but the Ferrarese seemed to draw his strength from it. The more embattled he was and the bigger the demands made of him, the more stolid and implacable he became.

I was a stranger in the maestro's kitchen. Every man there had been hand-picked by Zohan, had worked a long and painful apprenticeship, from turnspit to fish-scraper to onion-chopper. They had all scrubbed the pots and the floors. They had been bruised by the maestro's heavy spoon and cringed before the carronade of his tongue. They did what they were told, and they did it perfectly and without question. I was a boy from a tavern, ten years younger than the youngest man who Zohan trusted with any responsibility. I should have been carrying firewood and pots of boiling water.

But that wasn't to be my lot. Zohan cornered me the first morning and placed his spoon hard against my breastbone.

'Do you know why you're here?' he demanded.

'Messer Lorenzo liked my food,' I'd replied. I wasn't there for any other reason, was I?

'Messer Lorenzo can't boil an egg by himself,' said Zohan loudly. The din of a great kitchen starting up for a hard day's work dimmed magically and all those faces turned to where I stood, backed up against the storeroom door. 'As a consequence, he believes that those who have mastered the art of egg-boiling' – he shoved the spoon into my sternum – 'have *demonstrated* some small flair in the boiling of eggs, are useful and worthy creatures. And because Messer Lorenzo believes that egg-boiling, let alone more complicated operations, are mysteries akin to Our Lady's impregnation' – the spoon dug deeper – 'should the man who boils Messer Lorenzo's eggs deign to add, shall we say, something truly miraculous, such as salt and pepper, Messer Lorenzo might well take that man to be a genius. A Petrarch of the culinary arts, perhaps? But I'm a mere cook – what could I possibly know about such things? Messer Lorenzo, however, is a great and unfathomably clever man, and as such is disposed to admire genius wherever it might be found. You, boy, have caught his fancy. Your egg-boiling skills have ensnared him. Therefore you are required to display your rare genius not just for Messer Lorenzo, but for all his friends, relations, enemies and rivals. Honoured? I should say so, eh?' The spoon came up and tapped me gently under the chin. 'But don't for one moment think that you are a cook, boy,' he said, smiling tightly. 'You are entertainment. You are the new toy. You are the master's new dancing girl. So you'd better dance, eh? You'd better dance.' The last words were punctuated by the spoon clacking against my ear, my shoulder and finally my arse as he sent me on my way with a blow that stung my backside for an hour afterwards.

The kitchen throbbed with purpose. And we danced, all right: a tight, careful masque, stepping in time to Zohan's orders, or to the sweep and stab of his spoon. Everyone knew his place, of course, though not me, not at first. I was in the way. I was under every foot, at every elbow, over every shoulder. I should have been slapped and kicked and cursed, but they held their tongues: they didn't dare do otherwise. Because I was the pet, the experiment of the great man who presided, more or less invisibly, over every life in the city, let alone the palace and its kitchen workers. I was just another refinement in the conditioned torture of their days: they had to figure me out, accommodate me and, on top of everything else, keep their thoughts to themselves. Zohan bellowed at me – 'Dancing *Girrrl!*' – cursed me enough for all of them, so in a way that was all right. And as terrifying as he was, I loved him as much as he must have detested me, those first few weeks. I watched him like a young wolf watches its parent: learning, learning. But I still felt like an ape dressed up like a gentleman and sat at the high table for an evening's sport. For two weeks I suffered, knowing I was upsetting the mechanism. I went home to toss and turn in my bed, skimming over seas of fretful dreams.

The third week began. I crept in and dragged on my whites, feeling the nervous dread pooling in my belly. It was going to be another day of *Dancing Girl, shake your arse.* And sure enough, Zohan greeted me with a disdainful rattle of phlegm and stabbed his spoon in the direction of a huge rush basket that was leaking grey fluid onto the stone floor.

'Where have you been?' he snapped. I opened my mouth to tell him that I was the first man there, but the spoon caught me a stinging blow on my shoulder. 'Those bastards have been waiting for hours,' he went on, pointing to the basket. 'Get them done, and quick. The whole city is sagging beneath your idleness.'

Stinging with the affront but keeping my face a mask of unconcern, I dragged the heavy basket over to my work station. Pulling off the lid, I found a glistening corrugation of tentacles and bulging, unfocused eyes. It was cuttlefish, arrived just that morning on a barge from the coast. Though they were no more than a day out of the sea, they had already started to turn – very slightly, and perhaps a less acute nose than mine would not have noticed. I grabbed a cuttlefish, slapped the limp, slimy tube onto the table. With a twist I pulled off the head, dug my thumbs in behind the eyes and pushed. The beak, about the size and shape of a rosebud made out of fingernails, popped out between the flaccid bloom of tentacles. I threw it to one side, took each hard eyeball and severed it at its root. Then I picked up the body and pulled the membrane from the milky mitre of flesh, turned the tube inside out, ripped out the guts, taking care not to burst the ink sac, pulled off the yellowish inner membrane and reached for the next animal.

By the time I was done, there was a mound of pallid flesh

and a towering nest of tentacles; a huge, sullen peacock's tail of eyes fanning out across the table, and a spiky pile of beaks. The guts, a wet skein of greys, browns, greens, sucked at my fingers as I slipped them, fistful by fistful, into a bucket. The beaks snagged my skin; the eyes tried to escape, like beads from a broken necklace. The lonely, semen tang of cuttlefish was all over me: hair, arms, clothes. I thought that at least I would be told to cook the things – stuffed with pine nuts, raisins and herbs, perhaps – but when I came back from slinging the bucket of reeking dross onto the midden, Zohan put me to cutting the ribs from a huge sheaf of black kale. I sliced mindlessly, drawing the knife's edge again and again across the crinkled, curling leaves, and when I was done there were herbs to chop for a *battuta*.

Meanwhile, the kitchen was clanging and clattering at full stretch. I was dying to get in front of a sizzling pan, to make something, but as usual I might as well have been the pot-boy. I was halfway through a basket of beet greens, knife working automatically while I watched the other men at their tasks, when my eyes settled on a pan set too close to the fire. It was filled with seething white liquid – a precious blancmange. Zohan had gone out to the privy, otherwise he would have jumped on the cook. Without thinking I pointed at the man, heavyset, who was standing next to the fire, scratching his nose. He was called Nenè, a fellow who moved around the kitchen slowly and deliberately, full of confidence but never actually seeming to do anything except get in the way.

'You! What the hell are you doing? Take it off the flame, and stir it! Who told you to stop stirring?'

The man did as he was told, and then glared at me, betrayed by his reflexes.

'And you!' I went on, my eyes coming to rest on a young man – older than me, though – who was chopping onions.

'Is that how you slice an onion? Why not serve Messer Lorenzo a whole onion on a plate? *Cazzo* . . . like an apple? Are you trying to kill Messer Lorenzo, eh? How is he supposed to digest those great chunks?'

Nene was stirring his blancmange now, but sullenly, wagging his spoon to and fro in the thick white stuff as if the whole thing was beneath him. I snatched the spoon from his hand and shouldered him out of the way. 'Watch me, yes?' A blancmange is a delicate thing, hard to make, harder to perfect, and ruined in the flutter of an eyelid. Goat's milk, rice flour, pulverized capon breast, sugar and rose water. It should be as white as a virgin's inner thigh, and its purity is the benchmark of a kitchen's ability. 'You have to be gentle, as if you were holding a baby.'

The crew stopped what they were doing and looked at me with all the disgust and hatred that had been marinating inside them. Everything went quiet. I realized what I'd done, and then the thought that came into my head was *They're going to murder me*, because knuckles were going white around knife handles, pot handles, pestles. I looked from one face to another. Perhaps I was trying to judge who was going to come for me first. At that moment, though, Zohan walked back into the kitchen.

No one said a word, but he knew. He *knew*. Without so much as the twitch of an eyebrow, he walked slowly, calmly, over to where I stood next to the pan of blancmange. He looked from Nenè to me, then his glare took in the table, the fire, every soul in the kitchen, all standing stock-still, waiting. The maestro raised his finger, dipped it into the blancmange, stuck it thoughtfully between his pursed lips. His eyes closed, then opened again, and when they did they were drilling straight into mine.

'Scalded,' he said.

'Maestro! It's fine!' protested Nenè.

'I told you!' I said to Nenè. 'He was stirring it like a sleeping man playing with his *cazzo*, Maestro.'

'That wasn't very professional, was it, Nenè?' said the maestro.

'But—'

'You're idle, Nenè. We're all carrying you. Me, all your friends here. The sweet little Dancing Girl, trying to do you a favour. Get out of my kitchen, and don't come back. I'll send someone round with your pay.' With that, he turned to me, leaning into the table so that the back of his head was mere inches from Nenè's face. I saw the poor man's mouth working, the colour ebbing from his usually florid cheeks. He hesitated for a moment, waiting for someone to come to his rescue, perhaps; but the kitchen was completely silent except for the whispering of the fires and the susurrus of hot water and oil. Squaring his shoulders, he spun round and walked, unsteadily and too quickly, out of the kitchen.

'And you, Dancing Girl. What sharp eyes God has given you. Such a keen nose for the shortcomings of your fellows. What should we do with this blancmange, would you say?'

'Throw it out and start again,' I said, brightly, searching the maestro's face for any emotion at all.

'Quite right. Quite right. Take it out to the jakes, then, would you? And do you think you could make us another one in time for service?'

'Of course, Maestro!' I said, joy swelling my ribs.

'I don't doubt you could. But instead, you will take shovel and broom and clean out the jakes and the midden yard until Messer Lorenzo could eat his dinner off the cobbles.'

Silence. But I could feel them, all the eyes fixed on me, and every look hot with loathing, anger, and joy at my downfall. And there in front of me, the maestro, solid and unmoving as a way-marker standing at the crossroads where I had suddenly arrived, not lost a minute ago but now faced with . . . with what? The front door or the back door. Escape or humiliation. Life, more or less, or the death of everything I had imagined for myself. Then I thought of Tessina, how I'd wanted to tell her that I was working for the Medicis, that I was going to be someone. And with that, I chose. With a nod to the maestro I reached past him for the pot of blancmange, picked it up and walked with it down the long tables, the laughter starting now, the relief and the scorn bubbling out into the open with a sound like the low hum of flies – worse, though; much worse than the flies that waited for me in swarms as thick as wet bed sheets, out in the midden yard.

All day I toiled in the privy and the yard, gagging at first, sweating and growing stained and saturated with the filth I was shovelling, until I was more repulsive than any of the reeking labourers I had spent my life mocking. The other cooks came and went, pissing and shitting, throwing pails of rubbish, hooting with laughter at my sorry state. But not a word did they speak to me. The maestro did not appear.

I didn't dare go home that night, too ashamed and disgusted with the state I was in and what stupidity I had brought upon myself; and instead crept into the stables and huddled up in an empty corner. In the morning I was stiff and starving, but I set to and worked until noon, when, unable to bear my hunger any longer, I slipped out and made my way, through back streets and alleys, to the man I had been thinking about ceaselessly for hours.

Ugolino was stirring his pots, the great gnarled spoon carving gentle arcs in the seething stews. When he saw me, and the filthy hand that was holding out a coin, he showed no sign of disgust or even surprise. I took my bowl of tripe and began to shovel it into my mouth like an animal.

'Messer Ugolino,' I gasped, when the sharpest thrusts of hunger had been cauterized. 'You have saved me.' He looked at me for a moment from beneath his grey eyebrows, then went back to his stirring. 'I mean it,' I went on. 'There is no food like this in all the republic. I cook in the Medici kitchens . . .' At this, his eyes flickered for the briefest instant over my repulsive, shit-smeared clothes, my black hands, my streaked face, and then returned to the inspection of tripe and *lampredotto*. 'And Messer Lorenzo never – mark me! – never eats a finer meal than this. At his noble table, off golden plate . . . Nothing like this.' I slurped again, and again, until the brown earthenware of the bowl was revealed, speckled like a thrush's wings. I found another coin, held out the bowl.

'Can you give me the recipe, so I can cook your tripe for Messer Lorenzo? I'll call it *trippa alla Ugolino*. I'll pay . . .' And then the stench of my clothing, the horrible, creeping itch of all the filth against my skin, descended upon me. I looked around. People were starting to stare. No one I recognized, no friends or acquaintances or – *grazie a Dio* – enemies, but in a minute they would appear. The bowl wavered in my hand, my other hand found another coin. But it was no good. I set the bowl down.

'Thank you, Maestro Ugolino,' I said.

I went back to the yard, to more stench and misery, and another night spent with the mice and the heavy breath of horses. It was almost the end of the third day when the heavens grudgingly let down a little rain and helped me sweep the last few feet of cobbles until they were more or less clean. Even then I stayed outside, letting the rain soak me, until I knew the evening's service had ended. No one had come to move their bowels for an hour or more, and the last bucket of chicken skin and carrot peelings had been flung. When I was good and wet, and did not seem to reek quite so horribly of ordure and offal, I went back into the kitchen.

Zohan was sitting in his chair, waiting for me. Or perhaps he had no idea I was even a part of his world any more. In any case, when he looked up from the ledger he was reading, there was nothing to show that he hadn't been expecting me to come crawling back, or that he cared either way. As I slunk towards him he stuck his hand between his legs and retrieved his purse, from which he took a coin. He flicked it towards me; I caught it.

'Fine work. That is what you've earned for it. Go to the bathhouse. And be back here tomorrow morning.'

The coin was a *soldo*, about half a day's wage for me.

'Tomorrow morning, then?'

But Zohan had already gone back to his ledger.

The next morning I got in early, and helped the turnspit light the fires. I was sharpening knives when the others started arriving. Each man greeted me with narrowed eyes and a curt nod. But a greeting nonetheless. Zohan arrived, looked me up and down – for signs of shit or fish guts, no doubt – and called me to his chair.

'So you did come back,' he said. 'Fair enough, Dancing Girl. Not just a pretty plaything after all. Get to work.'

'Right away, Maestro,' I said, and turned, thinking to find a basket of onions to prepare, or some herbs to pick: some mindless task suited to one who yesterday had been scrubbing a privy floor.

'Wait a minute.' Zohan's spoon jabbed me in the kidneys. 'You were right about the blancmange, of course. And right about Nenè. I've made sure that the boys know it too. I was going to give Nenè's job to Tino. But seeing as you're still here, I'm giving it to you. Yes? Are your fingernails clean?' I held them out for inspection. 'Good. Make me a blancmange. If it isn't perfect, you're out for good. Understand me?'

'I do, Maestro. Thank you!'

'You *should* thank me. And every other bastard in this kitchen. They could have drowned you in their filth, but instead I saw men going out into the alley to move their bowels, just so you weren't inconvenienced.' He sniffed. 'I can't think why they bothered. Perhaps they pitied you.'

'Perhaps, Maestro.'

'Yes . . .' The wooden spoon hovered, then settled at his side. 'Get to work, then, boy.'

Time moved like a drunkard across the next few days. Messer Lorenzo had gone to his villa at Careggi for the rest of that month and so the tension in the kitchen had lessened, a little. Which was a good thing, because I had to ask the maestro to be excused Tuesday's day shift. I'd spent hours trying to dream up some plausible reason for this, and daydreaming about how things might be when I met Tessina in the convent garden; but in the end I just traded Tuesday mornings for my biweekly day off, and Zohan agreed quite readily. What did I need a day off for, anyway?

Because the master wasn't at home, Zohan let me cook a few dishes. These he would criticize loudly, finding fault where I was certain none ought to be. Most of the time I was doing the mundane tasks that Nenè had done before me. It was tedious, but I was far too busy thinking of Tessina and not my status or my self-regard. I didn't complain, glad, for once, of the distraction and the mindlessness. I was doing the things I had done for years and I might as well have been a sleepwalker.

17

IT WAS GETTING FEROCIOUSLY HOT. Summer always turned Florence into an oven, and that May it was already as if we were being licked by the tongues of invisible flames. I went from stifling kitchen through streets rippling with heat to my airless bed, and back again in a horrible, sweltering gyre. Summer was binding clothes, stinking gutters, the Arno thick and sluggish with offal and tannery muck. It meant nothing to me, though. I had two things on my mind: the kitchen, and Tessina Albizzi. It could have been snowing for all the notice I paid to the weather.

The first time I went over the wall and into the garden of the Convento di Santa Bibiana, I had no idea what to expect. The garden wall – or a small square of it – lay at the end of a dark and narrow passageway presided over by an old, half-blind woman who squatted on the steps of a disintegrating house, swathed in the dusty black of a widow. She paid me scant attention as I made my way cautiously past her, through the fallen doorway of a deserted pigsty that had been built against the wall. A huge fig tree was twisting up behind it. There were plenty of handholds in the wall – plenty of scorpions too, no doubt, I thought to myself – and it was easy to scramble up and over. On the other side the trunk of the fig was knotted and curved like the body of a huge serpent. I swung myself across the wall and stepped down into its coils. The scent of the leaves – burned sugar, nettles, old Marsala wine and wasps – enveloped me. I paused, and peered through them at the garden beyond.

I saw an ancient raised pool surrounded by a lip of marble

on which the carvings had long since been rubbed smooth by time and the rain. Behind the pool was a tiny hut – a shed, really – built of rough stone blocks, with a roof of cracked tiles through which ivy was growing. A stone statue of Christ three centuries old was being smothered by a dog rose. All of it – the pool, the statue, the hut – was hidden behind a dense thicket of unpruned fruit trees, bay laurel and figs, woven through with great ropes of vine and ivy. Behind that was the convent itself, but only its bell tower showed above the wilderness. It did not feel like a place of God at all. It was abandoned to the workings of nature: it did not belong to mankind any longer. There were paths, slowly being choked by weeds; the wide eyes of the stone Christ awaited, year by year, the slow creep of ivy tendrils. A leaf stirred – I jumped, thinking of unseen feet, of nuns long dead, but the tail of a large bronze-coloured lizard whisked another leaf and vanished beneath the statue.

'Nino?' Tessina was standing in the doorway of the hut. My heart lurched: she was dressed from head to foot in white. In that deserted place, my fancy already working as it was, I almost took her for something unearthly.

'It's me!' I said. But my voice was swallowed by the leaves and the buzzing of insects. I jumped down from the tree; dry leaves and twigs crunched beneath my feet. Pushing my way through cobwebs and wiry strands of columbine, I skirted the pool. Tessina followed me with her eyes, silent, her hands grasping the edges of her hood. It was as if I had jumped down from the wall and landed in the middle of some vast and deserted forest. Then my leggings snagged on a bramble and I fidgeted with the stem, trying not to rip the wool. And Tessina giggled.

'Are they good ones?' she enquired, her face almost hidden in a crescent of deep shadow, all except for her eyes, which shone speedwell blue.

'My best,' I said. The bramble seemed to have stopped me in my tracks. The scent of the dog roses was heavy, cloying. Neither of us moved. A huge bumblebee lurched through the air and landed on a flower, bending the stalk almost double under its weight. Then a single bell rang out noon from the convent, sweet but lonely, as though it chimed only for itself. As the last chime sounded, all the bells of the city began to ring.

'You were early,' whispered Tessina. I could barely hear her, and stepped over the last few paving stones to where she stood. 'We were both early,' she said, as I stopped in front of her. She slipped the hood back from her head. It settled heavily across her shoulders and suddenly I was looking at the perfect amber cascade of her hair.

'I thought it was going to rain, but . . .' I began, much too loudly. It didn't even sound like my voice, and why had I said it anyway? I wasn't completely sure that Tessina was actually here. Perhaps none of this was real. It didn't feel like real life, the way I lived it on the other side of the wall.

Tessina frowned, put her finger to her lips. Her hands went up to the folds of her cloak, and I thought she was about to pull up her hood again, but she paused, and I felt her searching me with her gaze. Her face was a little tight, I realized, and there was something else: almost desolation. I opened my mouth to say . . . what? I raised my hands instead, without thinking, and put them together in an unconscious prayer. Prayers do not work, in my experience, save for that one. It broke the drowsy spell of the garden. Tessina smiled. Her face, which had been ghostly white, came to life. Freckles appeared, and little lines, bracketing her lips. 'Come with me,' she said, in her ordinary voice. She turned and slipped through the door of the hut.

I had to duck slightly under the lintel. Inside, the hermit's retreat was larger than it had seemed from the outside, but only a little. The walls had once been plastered and painted, but only the rough outlines were left, all their colour bled out long ago. The roof was sagging, and ivy had forced its way in and was hanging in a great proud swag from one corner. The rafters were festooned with spiders' houses, and bat droppings had piled up in the little fireplace. But the floor of plain trodden earth had been swept clean. There was no furniture except for a milking stool riddled with wormholes, and along the far wall, an old bed of wooden planks, with a grey blanket draped neatly across it.

We looked at each other, reached out our hands. I could feel the air growing thick again, or perhaps it was just my blood. *Should I kiss her now?* I was thinking, when Tessina untied the cord of her cloak and let it fall to the floor. She stepped away from it, reached up and put her cheek against mine, very softly. She pressed harder and I closed my eyes and let my head loll, alive to nothing but her scent, the smooth touch of her skin against my newly shaved cheek, hot, almost feverish. Then our lips touched. We kissed, very softly, and then harder, as we forgot ourselves, and re-membered . . . Because it was our destiny, after all. The same stars had made us, the same experiences, smells, tastes had shaped our lives – and our blood, we discovered, beat through our bodies with the same rhythm, the same heat.

'Do you remember, we did this once before,' she whis-pered. 'In the saddlemaker's shed near San Remigio. We dared each other. I closed my eyes. And you ran off.'

'I won't run away this time. I promise.' I reached for her, and she sank against me. We were utterly still for a few long moments, skin pressed hard against skin, and then . . .

. . . it was different. It was all different.

A large white gecko was nosing about in a corner.

'Did a hermit really live here?' I asked.

'The first abbess retired here. She started a fashion: there was a hermit here for generations, but the last one died twenty years ago.'

'But you've been coming here for . . .'

'A couple of years. I slip away from the nuns and play the hermit. It's bliss. Do you think it's very dreadful, us doing this in here?'

'No.' I leaned back against the wall, feeling the cold of the stone, the warmth of Tessina's body along my side. 'How could I think this is dreadful? But are you sure no one ever comes out here?'

'No one ever has. They only go out to the paved yard right next to the house, and never at this time of day. The nuns are all in their cells, and Salvino is full of food and snoring in the refectory.'

'So you just slip away?'

'I said I was coming out here to meditate on Our Lord's mercy.'

A bell sounded somewhere nearby. 'Do I need to go now?' I asked her.

'In a minute. Salvino will be waking up soon. We don't want him blundering out here. Although as you are his new hero, perhaps he would forgive us.'

'Better not to risk it.' I suddenly felt a chill, though the hut was stifling. Perhaps Tessina felt it too, because she pressed herself against me and her lips searched for mine again. Then she pulled away.

'You're right.' She paused. 'Perhaps you should go now.' There was a moment of awkwardness, but then we were kissing again. 'Were you always so sensible, Nino Latini? Will you come on Tuesday?'

'Of course.'

'Good. Then go.'

'I don't want to.'

'But you have to.'

'I'll miss you.'

'Then you won't be late next time, will you?'

'I wasn't—' But she hushed me with a finger pressed to my lips and before I had even realized it I was alone in the little hut.

18

AFTER I'D SCRAMBLED BACK OVER the wall, I made my way to the Ponte Vecchio. I had to be at work soon, had to go home and change out of these fine clothes, and so I walked carefully, trying to seem carefree.

I arrived at the *palazzo* just in time, and walked into air thick with tension. Messer Lorenzo was back from Careggi, two days early and with no notice given; and there was an intimate meal to be prepared. Tino had the day off and Tino's understudy Andrea was down with a fever, and so to my amazement Zohan put me in charge.

'Am I cutting my throat, Dancing Girl?' he demanded.

'No, Maestro! I'll make you proud!'

'Proud? I haven't felt proud in years.'

I had to scramble about, concocting a menu from what was to hand, making sure the other men would obey me. Zohan sat on his throne, twirling his spoon, watching me but doing and saying nothing.

Fortunately there was no shortage of things to cook in the vast larders and storerooms. Looking around, my eye was instantly held by a rope of quails, hanging like strange upholstery from a hook in the cold room. The quail would do for the main dish. There were fish: carp, pike and tench. Fish was good, but I needed something else, something salty. I sent one of the Ginos out to the market to buy me a basket of mullet and a big bunch of watercress.

The boy I assigned to pluck the quails tried to give me some lip so I laid into him: a short, acidic diatribe loud enough for the whole kitchen to hear. After that they all calmed down and fell into their proper places. First I made a tart with some tender young leeks, sweet butter, some fresh pecorino, galangal and sugar. When the watercress arrived I had a green sauce made, chopping it finely with parsley and mint and garlic, mashing it with vinegar and passing it through a sieve.

The quails were roasted and dressed with a sauce I made with crushed blanched almonds, verjuice, the mashed pluck of the birds, some raisins, pepper and a very good dose of cloves. The mullet, also roasted, were sent to table still sizzling, their bronze skins decked out in the green livery of watercress. When the leek tart was presented to me for inspection I threw a handful of sugar onto the golden crust, and some pine nuts. To round off the meal, there had been a simple tart of sweet grapes.

Over the next hour or so, Zohan drifted in and out of the kitchen but said not a word to any of us. I had to snap at some heels, but we had the place tidied up and scrubbed down in good time, and when each man's task was done I sent him home. That earned me some gratitude: it was Zohan's habit to keep the crew waiting until he himself was done. So when the maestro came back for the last time that night, he found me alone, drawing up tomorrow's market list by the light of a single lamp.

'What in Christ's name did you think you were doing tonight?' he said at last, but though the words seemed angry there was no heat in them.

'Preparing an intimate meal, Maestro,' I said. 'I hope it was to the company's satisfaction?'

'Satisfaction . . . A queer turn of phrase,' said Zohan. He flicked my list away with the spoon and leaned next to me, blocking my light. 'Of course, you knew who was in the company tonight.' I shook my head. 'Don't play the innocent with me, Dancing Girl.'

'Messer Lorenzo and his lady wife, I assume,' I said truthfully. I had been so flustered when I had arrived, that I really hadn't paid much attention to the day's briefing, other than the word *intimate*.

'Ha! The Lady Clarice remains at Caroggi. And she is eight months with child. But if you thought she was here, were you trying to kill her, eh?'

'Maestro, I swear I have no idea what you are talking about.'

'Good Christ! Mullet? Leeks? Quail . . . Madonna. *Quail?* Clove and garlic in everything . . . By the Virgin's sweet milk, I know you used to cook in a brothel, but . . . but what possessed you?'

'Oh.' I understood. The saltiness of the mullet, the dryness of the quail, the warmth of the cloves . . . Without meaning to, I'd selected a menu of foods notorious for their heat, for their quality of arousing the blood.

'You lucky whelp. It wasn't the Lady Clarice at table; it was Lucrezia Donati and a couple of milk-faced poets.' Lucrezia Donati was Lorenzo's beautiful, and married, mistress. 'You knew. You did know. You devious little—'

'Did they like the food?' I cut in.

'Like it? They liked it, all right. Not that they weren't in a hurry to leave the table. If you understand me. I would be surprised if they even made it to the bedchamber.'

'Right. I understand you, Maestro.'

'Of course you do. Messer Lorenzo is very pleased with you. He'll be even more pleased tomorrow morning. You little weasel,' he added, with frank admiration.

19

A WEEK LATER, I JUMPED down into the convent garden, and hearing nothing except a blackbird foraging beneath the rosemary bushes, I made my way over to the hermit's hut, expecting to find Tessina waiting for me. But the hut was empty. I sat down on the rickety bed to wait. The convent bell chimed, to prove I was early, and I grinned: *Who is late this time?* I thought. But the minutes passed, and after they had turned into half an hour I decided that Tessina must not have come to the convent that day. *She could at least have warned me.* But how? She had no means to get word to me, I reflected. Every minute of the past week I had thought about Tessina at least once. Damn. I would have to drag myself back through Florence now, but I would see her next week.

Zohan stamped into the kitchen and found me cleaning up my station.

'Dancing Girl!'

Someone started to giggle. The entire kitchen was watching me, their pink, sweat-streaked faces expectant, hungry, like spectators at a bear-baiting just before the dogs are loosed. Zohan rapped his spoon three times on the edge of the great table. The men nearest to him edged away. The maestro beckoned me with one imperial jerk of the spoon. I cleared my throat and obeyed.

'You're wanted,' said Zohan. The spoon hovered in front of my face. The maestro narrowed his eyes. Then he tucked the spoon beneath an armpit. 'Wanted by Messer Lorenzo.'

'What for?' I asked, trying to sound normal, though my throat felt like a rusty pipe.

'No questions. Follow me. The rest of you can get back to work.' Zohan raked the other cooks with his eyes and they all cringed appropriately. He spun on his heel and left and I bustled after him, trying not to catch anybody's eye.

'What have I done?' I asked, as soon as we were out in the passageway. For the first time in years I felt as if I might start crying.

'Done? What do you think you've done?'

I thought I'd been careful. I'd tried to follow the maestro's orders and put just enough of my own spirit into the dishes, but had I done too much? Not enough? Dreadful pictures were painting themselves: a bishop retching up his guts under the dining table, a Soderini choking on a fish bone.

'I don't know, Maestro!' I blurted, wringing my damp fingers.

'You played the *stronzo* with my capon recipe, didn't you?' Zohan didn't slow his pace, but in the dim lamplight his face looked like a terrible surgeon's instrument: something to crack bone or excise mortification.

'I . . . I did. I'm sorry, Maestro.'

'You took out the sugar.'

'I didn't think it needed sugar. I shouldn't have presumed.'

'And the bitter cherries: where did they come from?'

'I thought the . . .' Lost for words, I smacked my lips, conjuring up the sensation of mouth-furring cherry juice. 'I thought the tartness might be a nice foil to the meat, after I'd rubbed it with lard and cinnamon . . .'

'Lard and cinnamon. Lard and bloody cinnamon. Who told you to do that, eh?'

'No one. I sometimes do it that way. Such a simple dish, Maestro: just a few capons! I didn't think there'd be any harm.'

Zohan began to chuckle. My stomach rolled over. But there was warmth in the sound. Amazingly, the maestro seemed to have shed his anger.

'No harm done, you say? Depends what you mean by harm, Dancing Girl. If Messer Lorenzo smacks his lips and licks his fingers clean after polishing off one of your capons, I should say there's no harm in it.' He laughed, a terse bark. 'Shall I tell you what I had planned for you, pretty dancer?' I nodded, reluctantly. 'Good. Nothing. I planned nothing. I expected you to soil your *mutande* and run away, or to give up. Bury yourself in onions. Meanwhile, Messer Lorenzo forgets about his latest passion, doesn't he? He forgets, and I quietly get rid of you. You go back to your uncle with a few good stories and I get back to business. My kitchen's been juddering along like a cart with a broken spoke since you arrived. My boys are all trying to get one over on you, or stick a knife into your back.'

'That's true,' I admitted.

'Ah, not completely in a daze, eh?'

'I know they hate me.'

'Getting above yourself again. They hate *me*, as is right and proper. You they just fear.'

'Why would anyone fear me?'

'Are you stupid, Dancing Girl? They fear you because you've dropped down on them like the Archangel himself; you go straight to the good jobs, and meanwhile your mother's still wiping your arse.'

'My mother—'

'—is dead. I know. That, as they say, is life. So . . .' Zohan stopped in his tracks and pulled me so that I was facing him. 'Am I to understand that you don't take to being feared? Because if so, we are walking in the wrong direction.' He turned me, firmly, so that I was facing back down the passage, towards the kitchens and the back door. Then he gave me a gentle shake. 'Messer Lorenzo – Lorenzo il Magnifico – licked your capon off his fingers, in front of Signor Tornabuoni, Messer Tommaso Soderini, and the Bishop of Pistoia. Then he asked me if I'd cooked it. Because I'm an honest man, and because there was a bishop staring right at me, I said no, it was that young Nino Latini. And do you know what? He'd forgotten all about you. *From the Taverna Porco*, I said. Then he remembered. Asked for you in person. I should have kept my mouth shut, and sent you back to the Porco, where I found you hiding from your fat uncle. But I didn't. I reminded him who you were.'

'Thank you.' I said it as sincerely as I could, considering my teeth were chattering with nerves.

'Don't thank me, boy. Thank your capons.' He put his face very close to mine, so that his nose was almost touching my own. 'Did you think I'd let you meddle with my food?' he asked. 'Did you really expect to send your food out to the master's table without my noticing? I taste everything that comes out of my kitchen, boy. Everything. I could have had the master's hounds eating your capons quick as that.' And he snapped his fingers next to my ear. 'But that would have been a waste, Dancing Girl, of a nice plate of food. Now you're going to speak to Messer Lorenzo, and when you come back to the kitchen the men are going to fear you – properly, this time. And do you know what? They're going to start to hate you a little bit too. Because I'm going to make you my lieutenant. Messer Lorenzo's going to expect it, and I'm telling you now so you don't wet yourself in front of the fine company.'

'But you have a lieutenant . . .'

'Tino? Too bad for him. You won't find Tino when you get back from the high table.'

'You're just going to kick him out?'

'Why not? He's worked ten years at my side and never so

162

much as added one extra peppercorn to my recipes. He's never caused a disaster, but he's never made anyone clean their plate with their finger, either. If you feel so bad, though, you can trot home now. Out the back door with Tino. Or you can come with me to see Il Magnifico.'

I looked back down the passage, to where light was spilling out of the kitchen. Further off, the great door that opened onto the street closed with an almost palpable *whump* of displaced air. Ahead, in the opposite direction, there was a low murmur and the scent of candles, perfume and food. At that moment a serving boy appeared around a corner and jogged past us bearing a silver charger piled high with bones: the remains of a roasted kid I had sent out earlier.

'All gone,' said Zohan. 'One of yours, I think. Ah, well: lots of stories to tell the little boys at the Porco. Get out, then, since you can't make up your mind.'

'But I've made up my mind,' I said. 'You'll have to teach me, Maestro. And hit me with the spoon – often. So the boys don't resent me too much.'

'I'll thrash you half to death,' Zohan said, nodding. 'We're going on, then?'

'Yes, Maestro. If you teach me everything you know.'

'Conditions, Dancing Girl? Since when did a creature like you have conditions?'

'Since Il Magnifico licked the food I prepared off his fingers. Maestro.'

'You little shit . . .' Zohan scowled, then whipped the spoon out from under his arm and caught me a mighty crack across the temple with it. I reeled backwards, rubbing my scalp. 'And what do you say?'

'Thank you, Maestro!' I almost yelled it.

'You'll curse me before you thank me, boy.'

'Yes, Maestro!'

'But when you thank me, you'll do it with the whole of your immortal soul.'

'I will, Maestro.'

'Then let us get on with it.'

In the days since I had come to the Medici palace, every time the dishes for luncheon and dinner left the kitchens, like a merchant fleet setting out from some Indian port, I would picture them bobbing away – propelled by the sturdy legs of serving boys and girls – towards a vast, airy space like the nave of a cathedral that would surely be crammed with a small army of extremely hungry nobles. As we left the service quarters behind and climbed a staircase of veined marble lined with busts and hung with paintings, my excitement grew. But when Zohan prodded me through the open doorway of the *sala*, as he called it, jabbing his spoon into my kidneys with greater force than was strictly necessary, I realized that the most fevered of my daydreams had been . . . ordinary. The room was long – it must take up half the length of the palace. Five high, arched windows looked out onto the dim lights of Via Larga, two more faced onto the little church of San Giovanni on Via de' Gori. There were people seated around a long table clattering plates and talking with wine-loud voices.

Lorenzo de' Medici was beckoning me from the far end of the table. I glanced sideways at Zohan, who gave me a curt nod. I made my way along the line of chairs, feeling as out of place as I'd ever felt in my own city. But the other diners ignored me. Only Lorenzo watched me, his eyes narrowed. My teeth were starting to chatter again, but then I happened to notice a man, his velvet cap slipping backwards off his grey-stubbled head, devouring a slice of *torta*. I'd made the filling myself: pears roasted in embers, mixed with some boiled pork belly, some eggs, rose water, cinnamon . . . He was licking the stuff off at least eight heavy gold and jewelled rings, and I caught the faint click of them against his teeth. Amazingly, this was my world after all.

'Not so different from your uncle's tavern, is it, really?' Lorenzo appeared to have read my mind. Not a difficult trick, under the circumstances, but it put me suddenly at ease.

'My uncle would like to think so, my lord.'

'Tell me: is Maestro Zohan treating you well?'

I glanced towards the doorway, where the Ferrarese was standing, straight as a sergeant-at-arms, watching us. 'Very well, my lord. It's a great honour to serve under someone like Zohan of Ferrara.'

'You don't approve of his methods, though.'

'My lord?'

'I've been sensing a new hand in the kitchen. The maestro and I have known each other a long time. His work does not require improvement, Nino Latini.'

I hung my head. Here it was, after all: merely a round-about way to the executioner. What would I tell them, back at the Porco? Terino would make me beg, or worse.

'I humbly—'

'What I'm attempting to say, Nino, is that you seem, very sensibly, to have decided not to improve upon Maestro Zohan's methods, but to simply cook what you want.'

'I'm sorry, my lord. I hope I haven't given too much offence.'

'Offence? Doubtless you've offended Zohan, but that's no concern of mine. No, you've given delight, Messer Nino.'

Then it was over. I went back to the kitchen, and Zohan made me his lieutenant. And the only thought in my head was that I couldn't wait to tell my darling, my Tessina. Because I wasn't just a tavern cook any longer. I talked – *conversed* – with Messer Lorenzo. Give me a few more months, and I'd have something to say to Diamante Albizzi about his niece. Fortune had put her hand on me. I was shining. I was a golden florin.

Another week went by. I leaned against the peeling white-wash in the hermitage, watching the spiders in the rafters. Two bells sounded. I gave it another half-hour, then left.

A week later, the sky was bruise-grey and the air was thick with thunder. I crouched, peering down the overgrown path towards the back wall of the convent. Now and again a figure, a shadow in a white head-covering, drifted past one of the windows. The bells rang: two, three, four. I sat there for so long that the birds got used to me. I sat until my legs had gone numb. It would be so easy to walk down that path, knock on the convent door. Perhaps the old nun had died. Or Tessina was lying at home, struck down by marsh fever, which was bad that year, or plague, which was rippling round the fringes of the city. I went through every reason a dozen times. And still she did not come.

A week later, I hauled myself up onto the wall. But there was no one there. I knew the hut was empty. I dropped back into the alley. As I passed her step, the old lady held out a little bunch of flowers to me: wild basil. I bowed and took it, to be polite. And as soon as I had turned the corner into the wider street I crushed it against the wall, watching the constellation of tiny white flowers turn to black against the dirty stone.

20

Florence, July 1472

A YEAR WENT BY, SO quickly I barely marked its passing. I was Maestro Zohan's lieutenant, and I worked all the time. No afternoons off for me any more – what was the point? They had been for Tessina. I didn't need any time for myself. I did the maestro's bidding, sometimes cooking his food, sometimes trying my own ideas. I worked, sometimes I suffered, and always I learned. I barely thought about Tessina any more. It seemed long ago, that strange afternoon in the hermitage. I visited my mother's grave, but I could hardly recall her face. My father I saw at those odd times when our busy paths crossed, which was hardly ever. Carenza fretted, those rare times when we sat together in her kitchen, and told me I was working myself to death. I had no time for my old friends from the streets: if I went out it was late at night, with other cooks, and we talked our own language.

If there was one constant in my life it was perhaps Ugolino the *trippaio*, because on most days I would slip out of the kitchen and buy myself a helping of his tripe. It was partly an excuse to keep an eye on the market, to feel that I was a part of things; and partly the tripe – simple, perfect – was the measure against which I judged my own taste buds. Every day I asked him for his recipe, and every day he narrowed his eyes and kept his lips tight shut. I could never tell if he was displeased, or if he even remembered my face from the last time he had served me.

It was after one such meal that I ran into an acquaintance

of mine, Piero di Ghisone, who everybody called La Scimmia, the Monkey, because of his long skinny arms and clever, spider-like fingers. I'd always thought he'd have made a splendid pickpocket, but fate had given him an eye for colour, and the master Alesso Baldovinetti had taken him on as an assistant. He spent his days mixing paints and pouncing out drawings onto prepared boards, and that was probably all he would ever do, because, while he could mix reds that would make a cardinal throw himself into the Tiber with envy, his drawings were harsh and unfeeling.

'Nino!' he said, grabbing me by the sleeve. The Monkey had appeared out of the crowd, all arms and legs and sharp eyes. 'Can you do me a favour?' he said, not letting me get a word in.

'Depends what it is,' I said, my mind on an order which the kitchen would need for an important lunch service at the end of the week.

'Maestro Alesso gave a job to me and Cosimo — Cosimo Rosselli? You know him, don't you?' I nodded. Rosselli was older than me, a good painter already on his way, though he was still Baldovinetti's pupil when it suited him. He'd done some frescoes for the church of Sant'Ambrogio, and the commissions were trickling in, but they wouldn't be enough to keep him afloat. 'Trouble is, Cosimo got offered a bit of work by the Pazzis, and . . .' He rubbed a spindly finger against his thumb. I nodded.

'So?' I asked.

'I daren't tell the maestro. He'll skin me. You know what he's like.' I didn't really. But I nodded again. Baldovinetti was a wonderful painter but he rode his pupils and apprentices hard. 'Cosimo was supposed to draw this girl for a Madonna. Has to be done tomorrow, because the maestro has the plasterers booked for the day after.'

'Where's the fresco going to be, then?'

'Santa Trinità,' said the Monkey. 'But the model's coming to Cosimo's rooms. With a chaperone,' he added, with a simian leer. It wasn't difficult to imagine those bony fingers rummaging through petticoats. 'I know: too bad,' he said. 'Listen, Nino. Can you do the drawing? I've seen your stuff: just as good as Cosimo. The maestro won't notice. She's going to be in the background – probably get one of the others to paint it anyway.'

'How much?' I was blunt, hoping to put the Monkey's back up so that he'd leave me alone, but he didn't notice.

'One lira.'

'Two,' I said, automatically. Cosimo would be getting at least three. The Monkey was looking to pocket a nice little sum and use it, no doubt, to go exploring beneath petticoats.

'One and a half.'

'Two ten,' I snapped.

'*Dio maiale* . . . Two, then.' The Monkey's heavy eyebrows were corrugated with annoyance.

'Better than being skinned by the maestro,' I pointed out. He brightened, slightly.

'No doubt, no doubt,' he said. 'All right, then. Done. Meet me at Cosimo's rooms, ten of the clock tomorrow.'

Why not? I said to myself as the Monkey melted back into the market crowd. Messer Lorenzo was travelling to his villa at Careggi tomorrow and I had been given the next three days off. Besides, a little bit of extra money wouldn't hurt. I could buy some new clothes. Better, though, was the thought that I could make a drawing – a proper one, a cartoon for a fresco, no less – without anyone breathing down my neck. I didn't care if Cosimo Rosselli got the credit, assuming there was any. My friends often paid me a few coins to help them with their own stuff. I'd been spending what spare time I'd had over the past year, at Verrocchio's studio, picking up odd jobs. I was good at hands and feet, so I sometimes did them for a crowd scene while the real artist concentrated on the exciting bits further up the board. Flowers, leaves . . . Clouds were easy and were good for a few pennies. I was happy to do it, because I loved to draw. And now up popped the Monkey, offering me two lire to draw an entire woman.

Cosimo Rosselli lived on the other side of the city, in the Unicorn neighbourhood beyond Santa Maria Novella. I knocked on his door at the appointed time, and the Monkey opened it. He looked decidedly relieved to see me.

'Come in, for God's sake,' he whispered. 'You're late.'

'I am not.' We were standing outside on the landing, and the Monkey was wringing his hands fretfully.

'Ach. In that case they're early. Lovely girl – I mean, really lovely. But her chaperone: Christ's pox, I've been turning myself inside out trying to get the old carp to smile, and I've had enough of it.'

'You won't get anywhere. With the girl, that is – maybe you'll have a bit of luck with the chaperone, though. What is she, a nun?'

'Very funny. No, she's an aunt or something. And don't you try anything, either.'

Cosimo Rosselli lived and worked in one large room on the top floor of an old building that had been some sort of factory in the past. The artist's unmade bed stood in one corner, and the rest of the floor was taken up with the articles of his trade: a table buckling under the weight of a large bronze pestle and mortar, jars of pigment and a jumble of brushes, knives and scrapers; a piece of Roman marble that might have been someone's knee; stacks of wooden boards, an easel, piles of robes and vestments. Two windows, not large, were allowing a couple of sunbeams to explore the chaos. In one of the bands of light, perched on the edge of a rickety-looking chair, her face turned away from me towards the window, was the girl I had come to draw. She was short, which surprised me. The artists generally liked tall, skinny women for their models, women who tended towards the innocence of last century's Madonnas, or the muscular tautness of Roman statuary. But the girl who sat there in the drifting dust motes was . . . my mind searched for a word to capture her, and what rose to the surface was honeycomb.

'Bit small for my liking,' muttered the Monkey beside me. But I barely heard him. I was absorbing the girl's long curls that fell in tendrils across her shoulders, giving me a glimpse of white skin at the nape of her neck. She wore a dress of butter-coloured silk, and a simple strand of garnets at her throat. Her hair had been shaved back from her brow in the fashionable style and two thick braids wound around her head like a crown, held in place by a strand of pearls.

The Monkey, impatient, nudged me hard in the ribs and I made some small, indignant noise. The girl turned, and with a jolt I saw blue eyes, a lightly freckled nose . . .

'Nino Latini?' she said, her voice low and measured.

'Tessina?'

'Is anything the matter, niece?' A greying woman – she was grey all over, from her iron-coloured hair to the hem of her Flemish-cloth dress – stepped into the light. I knew her with no trouble at all: Maddalena Albizzi.

'This is Nino Latini, Zia Maddalena. From our Black Lion. He scored in the *calcio* – don't you remember? In the spring. I pointed him out.'

My credentials – neighbourhood, family, guild – seemed to be satisfactory to the aunt, because she did nothing worse than fix me with a disapproving look. She evidently had no recollection of that terrible day when she and her husband had ordered their servants to throw me into the street.

'A butcher's son is an artist? Sometimes I fear for our city,' she muttered. 'Young man, you look most disreputable, but you *did* uphold the honour of our quarter, so . . . Well, then, we should get it over with. Where do you require us?'

'It's just the Donna Tessina we *require*,' the Monkey said, tactlessly. I took his shoulder.

'Show us what the maestro needs, and then why don't you go and buy some honey pastries from the place on the corner. Signora Albizzi, some chestnut cake for you? It is famously good.' I had suddenly remembered that Tessina had once said her aunt's one weakness was her sweet tooth, and to my relief she permitted herself a minute smile and nodded stiffly. I shoved some coins into the Monkey's bony fist and patted him on the back. He looked aggrieved, but after another nervous glance at Zia Maddalena, he shrugged and pointed to a clearing in the middle of the studio.

'You should stand there, miss,' he said to Tessina. 'Maestro Alesso wants this pose.' And he drew his angular frame up, twisting his shoulder coyly and letting his long hands flutter against his thighs.

'One foot in front of the other?' I asked, demonstrating.

'That's it – you've got it,' said the Monkey, relieved. 'Oh, yes: and she needs to wear this . . .' He picked up a long shift of very sheer white silk.

'Could you ask your niece to slip this on over her clothes?' I asked the aunt. Maddalena nodded, frostily; but I was suddenly aware of Tessina's eyes, studying me with amusement or perhaps annoyance.

'No, no!' said the Monkey, too loudly. 'Not over the clothes. Maestro said *very clearly* that she had to be naked underneath. Said it *very clearly* . . .'

'Young man . . .' snapped Maddalena Albizzi, reaching for her niece's hand.

'I'm sure we could manage,' I began. But Tessina shook her head, sending her curls flying.

'For goodness' sake, Zia!' she said. 'I am representing Our

Lady! I do not think any impropriety will be attempted by these men, who are doing the Lord's work . . . Are you not doing the Lord's work, Nino Latini, by representing His mother for a holy painting?'

I swallowed. 'Technically, yes, of course that's true,' I said hurriedly, crossing myself – perhaps that was overdoing it, I thought, but Zia Maddalena's hand withdrew minutely from Tessina's. 'Piero and I will wait outside. We will go and buy you cakes and sweetmeats together,' I babbled, backing away and grabbing hold of the Monkey's shirt as I went. I pulled him through the door and together we clattered down the stairs.

'*Jesus* . . .' The Monkey ran his fingers through his hair and we walked down the street towards the bakery. 'But you know them? How?'

'Neighbours from the Black Lion,' I said. 'You heard – family friends. Her parents died and we didn't see each other any more. We'd have been so big.' I held my hand in front of my breastbone.

'She's *still* that big,' the Monkey pointed out. 'Anyway, what a nice childhood for you, eh?'

'She didn't look like that back then,' I mumbled. 'How does she come to be modelling for Maestro Alesso?'

'How do you think? The girl is betrothed to Bartolo Baroni – lucky bastard. Fat, old, ugly, lucky bastard.'

'Luck has nothing to do with it,' I muttered.

'Oh?'

'I mean that Bartolo Baroni doesn't need luck,' I pointed out. 'He's got money and he's got power. He didn't woo her, did he? He bought her.'

'You sound bitter,' said the Monkey, cocking his black eyebrows at me.

'No, no,' I said hastily. 'I wish him joy. What would the Black Lion be without old Baroni, eh? As you say, he's a

lucky bastard. And he'll have a pretty painting. Pretty painting, pretty wife. She'll make a nice Virgin.'

'I was thinking the exact opposite,' rasped the Monkey,
licking his lips. I shoved him into the bakery with orders to
buy the sweetest thing they had.

When we got back to the studio, Tessina was almost
hidden behind Zia Maddalena, who stood, solid and grey,
arms folded tightly, in the middle of the floor. I could see
Tessina's bare foot and above it, a fold of gauzy cloth. As the
Monkey bowed his way across the floor to lay out the
dainties on a somewhat clean pewter plate, I started assembling the things I'd need for the drawing. Meanwhile I
was stealing glances at that foot. There was a glint of the
finest golden hair, almost invisible. Where the sole arched up
from the floor, though, the skin was stained, dirty, and all at
once I was back in the passageways with Tessina, both of us
nine years old, barefoot, waiting like two nervous cats to
pounce on a couple of older children and steal the apricots
they were eating, on *our* territory. And at that moment,
Tessina stepped out into the light.

The robe hid nothing. In a way, Tessina was more naked
wearing it than she would have been without any covering at
all, because the fine silk tissue clung, highlighting and making
dark shadows. The effect was ethereal and painfully of the
flesh, all at the same time. I began to fumble with charcoal
sticks, but I couldn't stand it, and raised my eyes to Tessina's
face.

'It really is you,' I said in amazement.

'I might say the same,' she replied evenly and, tilting her
head to where the aunt was sampling some honey-soaked
chestnut cake, lifted a finger to her lips.

'And now you work for *him*?' Tessina enquired, nodding
at the Monkey with undisguised distaste.

'Piero? Christ, no! He's Alesso Baldovinetti's dogsbody.

One of Maestro Alesso's pupils was supposed to be here, but he had better things to do. So . . . *I didn't know,*' I hissed, glancing over at the aunt.

Tessina winced and took a deep breath. 'We should start, Signor Latini!' she said, rather too brightly. And she shifted her stance to the timeless pose of the Madonna, one foot extended demurely in front of the other, a hand raised in tremulous blessing. The gauze shifted and tightened against her breasts, revealing the dark circles of her nipples. I swallowed and made a great show of setting the paper against the board of the easel.

'I promise I'll make a good portrait of you,' I mumbled.

She settled easily. I have seen artists rage at models and abuse them horribly, because they could not be still. And I've tried to draw girls who writhed and twitched so relentlessly that they could have been suffering from Saint Anthony's fire. But not Tessina. She took a deep breath, shivered almost imperceptibly so that the tremors fluttered down her arms and out through the tips of her fingers. Then she was still. Nothing moved except for her eyes, which should have been fixed on a point far past my left shoulder, though every now and again she shot a glance at me. I forced myself to ignore her. The first part of a drawing was always hardest for me. I had to push my mind out of the way, otherwise I found myself criticizing each line as soon as it was drawn. My body, I've since decided, is the artist; my mind is like a tiresome and badly informed patron, forever finding fault, slowing things down or filling them with complications that shouldn't be there. Which is, I suppose, what Filippo always taught me: pay attention to the heart, not the head. Today, though, it wasn't hard to get rid of my mind. I simply let it wander over the extraordinary fact of Tessina Albizzi's presence while my hands got to work with the charcoal.

I would have liked to take two or three days to distil Tessina onto the paper, but that was a luxury I didn't possess.

So I made the outline quickly, with long, swooping lines –
Don't hesitate, Nino. Don't let the line stutter, Filippo would
have said. I caught the drop of the robe, where it hung free in
soft pleats, where it clung to the jut of a hip or smoothed
itself over the roundness of a breast, a knee. Then her legs,
feet, then arms, sketching rough shapes for the hands. Only
then did I put in a neck, rough oval where a face would be.

The face . . . I wasn't ready for that, not quite yet. There
were some adjustments to the drape of the robe I did quickly
– the maestro would know what to do here. A little more
attention wouldn't hurt – he'd be grateful for it, wouldn't
he? So I made sure he would be in no doubt where the girl's
breasts were in relation to the little fold at the bottom of her
stomach, from which the whiteness of the robe fell, just
skimming the springy hair below it.

'It must be a very detailed sketch,' murmured Tessina. I
felt myself blushing, and I coughed to cover my embarrassment. It turned into a paroxysm, and when the fit had passed
I looked up to see that Tessina was still perfectly arranged.
Only her eyes glittered.

'That's what the maestro needs,' I said placatingly. Then I
glanced at what I'd drawn. Dear God. I quickly smudged
some lines and added more, blurring the almost naked figure
I seemed to have drawn, a figure with alarmingly lovely
breasts, legs quivering with taut energy, and all faceless.
Crossing myself feverishly in my mind, I clothed the Virgin
and went to work, concentrating furiously, on Her feet. I
drew them conscientiously, proficiently.

The hands were easy – I can draw hands, because Filippo
had made me work on them over and over again, forcing me
to draw his, mine, my mother's, until they came to life.
Tessina's were easy because they were slender and smooth. I
didn't have to worry about calluses or arthritis, or age. I'd
finished the first thumb and three fingers when Tessina cleared

her throat. I looked up, reluctantly, because I'd been hiding behind the paper, trying to keep myself calm, businesslike.

'I need to pee,' she whispered.

'Go, go!' I said, much too loudly, waving her away. I watched her sway gently away across to the tiny room where, I'd already discovered, a hole opened above a small, reeking space between houses, choked with nettles, rotting food and flesh, animal bones and glistening, tarry heaps of shit. A pig's corpse had been heaved over the wall and lay, blue-yellow and bloated to twice its natural size. That was where the all-pervading reek was coming from. Sniffing at the memory of it, I added some dirt under Tessina's toenails.

'Can I look?' She was back.

'No! I mean, not yet,' I said. 'Superstition. Anyway, you're faceless.'

'You're so *thorough*, Nino Latini. And you've almost run out of charcoal.'

'Not quite.' But there were a fair number of stubs scattered around my feet. 'Keep still, please,' I added, like a real professional.

'You've got charcoal all over your face,' she noted.

'Then it's lucky that I'm drawing you and not the other way round, isn't it?' I snapped.

'Is everything all right?' called Aunt Maddelena. She was sitting at the cluttered table with a kerchief – soaked in Hungary water – pressed to her nose, reading a psalter; but I knew she'd had one gimlet eye on her niece the entire time.

'Yes, yes! Just broke a charcoal stick.' I caught Tessina's eye by accident, and felt myself blush. Wondering how the devil my uncle had ever got any work done, I started again on Tessina's right hand.

We stopped for lunch soon afterwards. Feet were finished, hands almost done – I'd finish them when the face was ready, to give the drawing some unity. The Monkey and I went off to find a cook-shop, leaving Tessina with her aunt, who had brought a small basket of food with her. It would take a long afternoon to capture Tessina's face and I didn't know how I was going to manage it.

But in the end it wasn't difficult. In fact the time went much too fast. When I came to set my new stick of charcoal to the paper, I found that I had memorized Tessina, or at least a distilled image of her, and the charcoal seemed to pick out all the light and dark, all the shading, the perfection of her lips, the fine down, almost invisible except in the light, that shimmered on her forehead . . . I'd found the taste, I realized. Tessina's flavour, not in my mouth, but on the paper. It was a revelation I understood from the kitchen, where an ugly tangle of greenery, flesh, powders and oil or water meets the alchemy of fire, and comes together to present you, the cook, with a gift very different from the sum of its parts. So it was with my drawing. When it was done, the shadows were very long on the floor, and my eyes were watering.

'That's it,' I said. 'That's enough.'

Tessina stretched – I didn't look, couldn't bear to see what the silk was doing against her skin – and padded over. I heard a sharp intake of breath from Aunt Maddalena, but Tessina ignored her. She came to my side and I stepped out of the way, carefully, deferentially. She said nothing, but stared at the drawing for a long time. She breathed. I did not. My eyes flicked over the drawing, finding everything I wished I hadn't done. The aunt was scraping back her chair, letting out a meaningful cough. Tessina turned to me. All the ease had left her, all the merriment. She looked from me to the drawing and then back again. She opened her mouth as if to say something, and I remembered the little gap between her front teeth. It all vanished: the painting, the room, the boards beneath my feet, as if a great bolt of lightning had struck Cosimo Rosselli's studio. It was just the two of us, Tessina

178

and me, hanging in golden space, in a cloud of golden dust motes.

At that moment the aunt took her, not that gently, by the arm. I stepped back and bowed, keeping my eyes on the blackened ends of my fingers. When I looked up, the aunt was already leading Tessina over to the far corner. Finally I took a breath, and up through my nose crept a thread of something. Salt, lemon, rose water, vinegar, cinnamon . . . It was the ghost of Tessina, swirling in the space where she had just stood. I wiped my hands across my face, knowing they must be streaking me with black, but not caring. The Monkey was sidling towards the easel. I craned my neck to look past him, but Tessina had her back to me, nothing more than a white shape in the shadows.

'It's good,' said the Monkey.

'Is it?' I said, barely knowing what he meant.

'Mmm. Wish you'd given it a bit more . . .' And he flexed his fingers so that his hands became two upside-down crabs plucking at the air.

'It's the Virgin Mary,' I snapped.

Meanwhile, Aunt Maddalena, who had been throwing ever more anxious glances towards the door of the privy, was helping Tessina with the last of her clothing. When her niece's modesty was arraigned to her satisfaction, she whispered something in her ear and made for the privy. The door shut and for a moment there was silence. Then from down below came a muffled detonation. Immediately, an indescribably hideous smell came pouring through the window, and a moment after that a desperate cry sounded from behind the door of the privy. I wrenched open the door and found Aunt Maddalena, half collapsed against the wall. The buzz of flies was almost a roar and I stole a glance through the hole. The pig had exploded in the heat, and its bloated corpse had split. The Monkey arrived at my shoulder, and between the two of us we hauled the aunt out into the studio, where she fainted dead away, almost felling the Monkey as she did so.

'Let's get her out into the hallway,' I said. 'The smell isn't so bad out there.'

We half carried, half dragged Aunt Maddalena out onto the stone-flagged landing. 'Wait here with her,' I said to the Monkey. 'I'll get her kerchief.'

'Why me?' he complained, looking at the stricken woman with distaste. Ignoring him, I slipped back into the studio.

Tessina was standing next to the easel, Maddalena's vial of Hungary water in her hand. I found myself staring at the perfect heart of her face, as if I were still drawing it: her eyes, cornflower blue and almond shaped, heavy with tears, but I didn't want to remember that. My fingers brushed the tears from her face and I tasted them, closing my eyes as the salt grew strange crystals on my tongue.

Tessina caught my hands, pressed them tightly between hers. Then she was kissing me. Her back arched as my palm slid down the furrow of her spine, gliding over the heat of her skin. There was saffron in my mouth. The gold motes drifted.

'Oh, God,' I moaned as she pulled gently away from me. 'Tessina . . . I tried to forget you. But how can I?'

'I tried to forget about you too. I made myself. I couldn't go back to the garden because . . . because . . .' We were both talking in ragged whispers, half turned towards the door. 'I wish I'd never even been born. Because now I'll never love anyone else. I'll never love Bartolo Baroni.' She sobbed, a dry, ugly heave of despair. '*Dio mio* . . . I can't bear this.'

'I've always loved you, Tessina.' I could feel tears on my face. 'I should have told you before.'

'You don't understand. Bartolo's coming back.'

'He'll leave again. He always goes back to Flanders.'

'Not this time, Nino. My uncle . . .' She let go of me, and her hands flew up to her mouth.

'What about your uncle?'

'He told Bartolo,' she whispered through her fingers.

'I don't understand, Tessina.'

'Uncle wrote to Bartolo in Flanders and told him . . .' She grabbed one of my hands and clamped it roughly to her breast. There was no tenderness in her touch at all. 'There! That these have come! That I'm fit to be his bride! Bartolo's already in Genoa – he'll be here in . . . not even a week, and he's sent word to prepare for the wedding. He even ordered this painting.' She let go of my hand and buried her face in my neck.

'But what about you and me?' I blurted. 'I'll do whatever you want me to do. I'll join a monastery. I'll leave Florence. But don't marry Baroni!'

'I have no choice. It's Fortuna's doing . . . or perhaps the world is a prison. This isn't real. It cannot be real – it never was. I'm sorry.' I kissed her hands, but she pulled them away. 'I must go. And we can't see each other again. You know that, don't you?'

I pulled her against me, not caring if we were seen, and kissed her lips. I knew I'd never remember her taste: it was too complex, too precious. But still I tried to catch it: saffron, salt, cherries . . . no, that was the past. The present: where was that? Where was the joy? Where was all our delight? It was going; it had vanished, and Tessina was slipping out of my arms.

She ducked her head and brushed past me, the scented kerchief pressed to her face to hide her tears, and I heard her cooing to her aunt out on the landing, and the aunt's flat, peevish voice scolding her, the Monkey, me, the privy, everything. All the things I still wanted to say were withering in my throat: *I'll become a famous cook – the Pope's cook! The most famous in Italy. And then we can be married. Become a nun, Tessina, join the convent and wait for me in the garden. I'll come and rescue you, like Filippo rescued his Lucrezia.*

The Monkey came and stood next to me, giving my sketch a narrow-eyed appraisal. 'Well, that will do very nicely,' he said.

'Pay me, then.'

'All right, all right.' He fished around reluctantly in his tunic and pulled out some coins. I didn't bother to count them, just rolled them into the top of my hose.

'I'm going now,' I said.

I went out into light the dirty pink of fish gills, wearing the stink of the privy like a cloak. I walked fast, head down, and when I bumped shoulders with strangers, I felt nothing at all.

21

August 1472

IT WAS TWO DAYS AFTER the Feast of the Assumption when I came home for a quick sleep between the luncheon and supper shifts, and found a very pale man waiting for me in my father's hall. Prematurely grey hair, pale skin shadowed with dark stubble; pale eyes; all of it made even more pallid by his dark maroon doublet and hose.

'I take it you are Nino di Niccolaio Latini?' he asked, rather perfunctorily. I nodded. 'Then I have the right house.' Did I imagine the sniff, the flick of the eyes? 'My name is Raffaello Ditieri.' He paused for effect. His name did indeed have an effect on me: not a pleasant one.

'Messer Bartolo's steward,' I said, on guard straight away, bristling like a cat and trying not to show it. 'I . . . Welcome to the Palazzo Latini.'

'Your father has a *shop*, does he not?'

'Latini *e figlio*,' I said. 'The finest butchers in Florence. And of course my father is a consul of his guild.'

'Hmm. The Arte dei Beccai,' said the steward. He knew all of this, of course. Besides, he was here to see me, apparently, and not the old man. I couldn't see how that could be anything but dangerous. Which made his next words more of a surprise.

'Messer Bartolo Baroni is holding a banquet to celebrate his betrothal to Donna Tessina Albizzi. He has asked me to enquire whether you would do him the honour of preparing the food.'

'Me?' It was all I could manage. I cleared my throat, noisily, and tried again. 'Me?' The steward's eyebrows told me he was dealing with an idiot: an idiot, and a child to boot.

'Yes, you, *Master* Nino. You are a cook? Or is my master under some misapprehension?'

An insult. That brought me round. 'I am employed by Messer Lorenzo de' Medici as a cook, so no: your master is quite correct.'

Messer Raffaello sighed, and composed his features into something resembling a smile. 'Messer Nino, that is of course why Messer Bartolo wishes to make you this offer. You have quite a reputation for one so . . . so young.' He could have said *so lower class* or *insignificant* so, on balance, he hadn't insulted me again. I bowed politely and hopefully showed a bit of modesty.

'You are very kind,' I lisped, as I was expected to do. 'Unfortunately, as I am already required by Messer Lorenzo . . .'

'Messer Bartolo is of course very good friends with your employer,' said the steward dismissively. 'It's already agreed as far as he is concerned. I take it you accept? Excellent, excellent.' I'd said nothing, but apparently there was nothing to say. 'Now then, Messer Bartolo is expecting you.'

'Is he?' I said, alarmed.

'To go over what is required,' said Ditieri, with the kind of patience reserved for those who were dropped on their heads as babies. And so, instead of a nap, I had a stroll over to the Palazzo Baroni. I shook my head and spat to ward off the evil eye as we passed Via del Corno – street of horns.

When we arrived and were shown into the main room of the palace, Baroni greeted us warmly. Ditieri bowed and introduced me, and I bowed and smiled rigidly behind him, feeling as if I had been holding my breath for too long. Ditieri's bit of ceremony over, I looked up to discover that Baroni was staring at me. He was even larger than I had expected: a good head taller than me, his arse as broad as his wide shoulders. He had thick, muscled arms and big, blunt hands. His hair had gone grey years ago. In that puffy, spreading face was a nose that at one time must have been heroic, but had been broken and had long since turned into a bulbous, wine-filled raspberry. Everything was red, so red it seemed you would certainly burn yourself if you happened to touch his cheek or his blazing, almost raw ears. I thought of Tessina being required to kiss that face, and had to grind my teeth together to stop from groaning.

'Don't I know you, young man?' he asked.

'Son of Niccolaio . . .' I said, smiling carefully, vacantly, teeth still clenched.

'The *calcio* in April. It might be said that you saved Santa Croce, eh? Spirits flagging in the second half, and then that goal? Magnificent.'

'Messer Bartolo is too generous,' I muttered.

'Seem to remember your nose was smashed. Does it trouble you?'

'No, not at all, sir. Fortunately. I need it for my work.'

'Of course, of course – we have much to discuss. I've often wondered, though: does Niccolaio Latini *need* to send his son out to work?'

Who are you, barrelmaker's son, to talk about my father that way? I thought to myself. 'My father would be happy to see me waste the days of my youth. But I am ambitious, sir,' I said instead, because that was the kind of thing that *men* said to one another. 'One day I should like to cook a banquet for His Holiness in Rome.'

'Well done, well done.' The vulture eyes studied me carefully. 'Wasted, though, in the kitchen, I'd say. I might offer you a job myself. Make better use of what I saw on the *calcio* ground. Tell me: are you for the *Palle*?' He leaned forward and fixed me with one rheumy, vulture's eye. Curling my toes in distress, I nodded. 'Of course you are: working for Il Magnifico himself. Well, then. If you really are ambitious, we might help each other.

'Come and work for me, for the *Palle*. Forget all that kitchen nonsense – after, *after* you have made me the finest betrothal feast ever served in Florence, of course. I can make something better of you. Do some good for the Black Lion, some good for the Latinis.'

'I'm very flattered,' I said, but inside I was imagining Baroni roasting on a spit like a badly stuffed *porchetta*. *I'd rather go to work in a boy-brothel than run errands for you*, I wanted to say. Instead I bowed again. 'Such an honour. But perhaps we should discuss the banquet before anything else?'

The thought of food was making me sick, because all I could imagine was Tessina in the clutches of this sclerotic beast. The man's ideas were all very conventional, though, as I'd guessed they would be: a big, flashy roast – I suggested a boar, but Baroni wanted a quarter of beef; an expensive sturgeon, the biggest that could be found; *torte*; a fine blancmange. The dessert he pictured was a sugar sculpture of a ram – a black ram's fleece hanging on a gold background being the self-made wool merchant's coat of arms; I suggested, politely, that for a betrothal, a stag might be more appropriate, as the beast symbolized fidelity. And I hinted, as tactfully as I could manage, that his cultured guests – *all* his guests were cultured, of course – would be impressed by the conceit. He growled at that, but it turned out to be approval.

So it was settled. A price was named: enough to tempt me away from the Medicis for good, which was how I was intended to view it. And all the time I was thinking, *Does he know I love his bride to be? He must know. This is my torture.* He didn't, though. It was plain enough. I was something to be acquired. It would never have occurred to him that I had any sort of existence beyond his regard. *If you knew what I desire*, I thought, *horns would be bursting out of your temples*. And then I was dismissed, waved out, already forgotten. I bowed, with florid courtliness, and left his presence.

The Palazzo Baroni is big – I suppose, because I am a Florentine, what I mean to say is *bigger than* our *palace*, though compared to a true palace of one of the great families, like the Tornabuonis, the Pazzis, or the Peruzzis, just around the corner, it was quite modest – and as I walked across the tiles in the long and darkly imposing hallway, I shuddered to think of Tessina trapped in here. There was even a bust, in the ancient Roman style, of Bartolo. Like a suspicious, bibulous minor senator, it kept watch over the front door. I was just about to bite my thumb in its direction when I caught sight of Marco Baroni standing in the entrance to another corridor.

Maturity – relatively speaking – hadn't done Marco any favours. He still looked like an inbred mastiff, but if anything the choler inside him had grown, as if rage was bubbling from his orifices like the dirty water from an overboiled pot of black kale. We'd rubbed shoulders every now and again in the night-time world of the market, and I'd always been excruciatingly polite to him. Not that he'd ever taken much notice of me, because he was always surrounded by his tight little knot of friends – cronies and arse-lickers – and he was usually on his way to somewhere else.

Someone with Marco's natural gifts probably learns that they have to pay to lie with willing playmates, and whenever I encountered Marco in the Fico, he was on his way upstairs, to where the landlord kept his working girls hard at it. Though perhaps he didn't like paying for it, because he had pursued terrified women – boys as well – and cut up their more successful suitors all over Florence. If Marco had found out what I had been doing with Tessina Albizzi, I'd end up looking like an apprentice butcher's first carcass.

That evening, as we were winding down after the main courses, I told Zohan about my afternoon – as much as I could. The maestro hadn't heard, which made me uncomfortable. I hated the idea of Bartolo discussing me with Messer Lorenzo, as though I were another of his slaves. Zohan merely asked what I was going to cook and, when that met with his approval, he congratulated me.

'You don't seem particularly thrilled, Dancing Girl,' he said. 'Already taking it all for granted, eh?'

I couldn't tell him about what might be described, politely, as my conflict of interest. Nor could I tell him that every time I thought of Tessina in that ogre's cave, I wanted to take my meat knife and slip it into my heart.

'It's going to be boring,' I said instead.

'*Life* is boring, you little *cazzo*,' said the maestro. 'Besides, I expect you'll push things a little bit.'

'Is that what one does?'

'I don't know what *one* does, but I know what you're like.' He stopped, looked around, eyes narrowed. 'Come with me,' he said. I followed him out to the cold room. He shut the door.

'Nino,' he said. 'I'm leaving.'

'For the day?' I said, my eyes on the hanging game, calculating if we needed to order more.

'Leaving Messer Lorenzo. Leaving Florence.'

'You can't do that,' I said.

'I've been offered a position in Rome. *Scalco* to His Eminence Cardinal Federico Gonzaga. The pay is good, but the position . . . It's about time I was *scalco*. I'm getting old, and I want to save some money.'

'What do you need money for, Maestro?' I could barely speak, I was so shocked.

'For a little farm outside Ferrara. Vines, some wheat, bees.

What does anybody need money for, Nino? The point is, will you come with me?'

'Me?'

'Who else, Dancing Girl?'

'I can't leave Florence! And I can't leave this place! You don't understand: I'm a Florentine . . .'

'And I'm a Ferrarese. People wander. Sometimes they come home, sometimes they don't. Meanwhile, you're still the best cook, apart from me, that I've ever seen. Come and work for me, and I'll make you a maestro as soon as your balls have dropped. Which they haven't yet, not by a long chalk. And the money will be excellent, that I can promise as well.'

'I can't! I mean, when are you leaving?'

'I want to be gone by the end of the week. They're finding a replacement for me, but until that happens you'll be head cook.'

'Jesus.'

'If you change your mind, I'll be at the Palazzo Gonzaga, San Lorenzo in Damaso – that's in Rome, near Piazza Navona. And that's all I will say on this.'

After that, I barely saw him. My master was busy interviewing prospective head cooks, or out settling his Florentine affairs. And I was busy running the kitchens – too busy to even think about Bartolo Baroni's feast, and, mercifully, about Tessina. When Zohan stamped into the kitchens on Thursday, dressed in tatty riding clothes, I had almost forgotten he was leaving – or perhaps, that he was still with us. True to form, he growled at us, threatened us, told us he'd know, even in Rome, if we were making a *cazzata* of things. Then he went around the kitchen, shook every hand, and into one he pressed a florin. I was last of all, waiting for him by the door.

'Nothing for you, Dancing Girl,' he said gruffly. 'I've

already given you everything I have.' And he reached up and clamped my head between his two rough hands. 'I put it in here,' he said. 'Don't let it run out of your ears.' Then he dragged my head down, planted a kiss on my cheek and left. I went back to work.

That afternoon the new maestro appeared, a gigantically fat, blond man from Brescia whose name I couldn't pronounce. He took me aside and yelled at me in a dialect that was almost unintelligible, though whether he was happy or angry was a mystery. But at least I was able to curse Zohan and wish him ill on his travels, which made me feel less heartsick at his going.

The reality of Zohan's departure did not fully strike home until a couple of days had passed. I was the last of the crew, because I'd stayed behind to prove to the Brescian that I was harder than they were, than he was; and because I'd needed to prepare something for tomorrow, because Messer Lorenzo had already said yes to it. There was an old man in the Jewish quarter who sold little grilled mutton sausages which I had loved for years, and I was going to make them for the master's table. The old man, who had tended his grill in an alley near San Leo for as long as I could remember, was from Oran on the Barbary Coast. I had made friends with him, slowly, over the years, and he had warmed to my persistence and the fact that I, a Christian, could look him in the eye and question him so voraciously about his food. Sometimes he spiced his sausages – mutton and rice mixed with chopped parsley and mint, coriander leaves and celery leaves, finely minced onions and garlic, all stuffed into sheep's intestines – with a powder of dried rosebuds, cinnamon and pepper, and sometimes with ground coriander and caraway seeds. I preferred the latter, but it was the rosebud recipe I was going to prepare for the master, along with both shoulders of a gigantic ram which had come in that morning, horned head and all, and was now filling the meat store with its oily, woolly reek. Then there would be a dozen hares, some partridge, and a basket of pike. A small dinner, then, for Messer Lorenzo, his wife and Signor Sassetti, head of the Banco Medici.

You can't get the stink of mutton off your skin just like that. It takes soap and a scrubbing brush – and time. There was plenty of it still clinging to me like a rancid woollen tunic, along with everything else that had seeped into me during the day's work. All at once it was too much to bear. My fatigue, the strange void that Zohan had left behind him in the kitchen. His leaving suddenly appeared like some kind of dreadful omen, like a comet or a two-headed lion. Fortuna had turned on me. She had taken my life in her hands and ripped out its innards as a hunter does to a rabbit. I had lost Tessina for ever. My maestro had deserted me . . . Though I was dog-tired and footsore, I needed, more than anything else in the world, a lot of wine.

So I limped to the *mercato*. I wanted to be alone, but sometimes it's better to be alone in company. I chose the Taverna Fico.

The Fico was the place where all the artists were gathering that summer, from the paint mixers to the ones who landed the big commissions. Tonight it was full and more people were squeezing in. It was hot outside, and that had fired up everyone's blood. There would be fights later, and the women in the knocking shops all around here would be welcoming the dawn. The Fico itself was a brothel, but you had to know Galeotto Braccesi, the owner, to make it upstairs. The girls – and the boys, so I'd heard – were clean and inventive, but I'd never taken advantage. Anything that happened at the Fico was all over Florence within hours. And besides, the only company I wanted tonight was some- one to keep my cup full. And sure enough, I hadn't been sitting for long when Arrigo walked past with a jug of wine in his hand.

'Dear Christ, Nino!' he said. 'You look like a hanged man. And shouldn't you be preparing morsels for Il Magnifico?'

'Night off,' I mumbled.

Arrigo sat down. He'd only recently come back from Arezzo, where he'd gone on a business errand for his father, so I'd barely seen him the whole summer. I hadn't told him about Tessina – I'd told no one, but if anyone ought to know, it should be Arrigo.

'A night off?' Arrigo cut through my thoughts – luckily, as I'd been about to blurt it all out. 'Cause for celebration, surely! I'm with them.'

He nodded over to where a noisy group of young men, some already quite drunk, were playing a game with coins and wine. Arrigo persuaded me to join them and I hadn't needed much persuasion. The conversation descended into the usual idle gossip and lechery. Food was ordered and we stopped paying much attention to the others. We ate, and I gave my friend city gossip, all the things he had missed. In return he was spinning out a few of his own tales. My attention had begun to drift a little, wafted on the cheap wine that was starting to rise to my head, when two words brought me back with a jolt.

'Santa Trinità . . .'

'Hmm?'

'Were you listening? I said I happened to be in Santa Trinità the other day. There's a new fresco – really beautiful, the paint's still fresh. The Madonna. Well, I went over to take a closer look, and do you know what?'

'What?' I croaked, knowing exactly what was coming.

'I said to myself: *cazzo*!' breathed Arrigo. 'That's the signorina! It's little Tessina Albizzi!'

'I know,' I said quietly.

'What a likeness!' he went on. 'At least, I suppose it must be. Haven't seen her for years. And now, what a beauty! *Madonna!* It's a long time ago, isn't it? When we all used to play dice together?'

'A long time ago,' I muttered. 'Sandro Botticelli took me to see the painting. I didn't even recognize her.' Arrigo didn't deserve the lie, but I had no choice. 'Sandro told me who it was. My father told me she was getting married, finally. Good for her, eh?'

'I suppose so. He's a fat . . .' Arrigo stopped himself, looked around cautiously. Baroni was a name you didn't speak aloud unless you were fawning over it. 'He's a big man. They say he'll be Gonfaloniere di Giustizia again next year. And then . . .' He stabbed his finger at the ceiling.

'Well, lucky little Tessina.' I raised my cup and we drank a silent toast. But something had happened. The Fico didn't seem familiar any more. The rise and fall of Florentine voices all around me, the smells of food and unwashed flesh . . . It was enough to make my skin go cold. I stood up, too fast.

'That bastard Braccesi. Can't he afford fresh meat? I think I'm going to puke,' I said to Arrigo. 'And I have to work tomorrow. Come and look for me at the palace. I'll feed you some leftovers.'

'I'm off to Prato tomorrow for two months. My father's business is killing me with boredom. Nino . . .' He stood up and put his hand on my shoulder. 'Are you taking care of yourself? You don't look very well.'

'The meat. I'm glad I saw you, Arrigo. Come to the palace when you come back, yes? I'll cook you something better than this.'

'Fair enough!'

I had to shove my way through to the door, but at least I was out. I'd kept my mouth shut. I hadn't defended Tessina, but if I had done, the disaster would have been complete. I walked home fast, on stiff legs. Everything felt broken: the night, the streets, the city itself. And next week I had to cook Tessina's feast. I stopped at the corner of Via dei Cimatori and Via de' Cerchi, and really was sick. And then, as I was wiping my mouth, I thought. *I'll give him a love feast*. He didn't deserve it. But I'd give him my best. I'd give him a masterpiece.

❧ 22 ❧

Bartolo Baroni must have been a great friend indeed of Messer Lorenzo, because I was given time off from the Medici kitchens to prepare for his banquet. And I needed time. Whenever the Brescian let me go, I set off into the city in search of the things I needed. The first place I went was Andrea Verrocchio's *bottega*, not to see Sandro – I couldn't even bring myself to look over his shoulder in case I saw him working on some version of Tessina – but young Leonardo. I bought him lunch and asked his advice on a number of matters. After that, I spent hours in the market talking to dealers of feathered game until I found a man who could get me what I needed. I went to the fish market, to apothecaries, even visited an alchemist recommended to me by Leonardo. I pestered the other cooks I knew with all manner of odd questions, and even crossed the river to look for something in the noisome tannery quarter of San Frediano. I went back to the Palazzo Baroni to investigate the kitchen, which was big – bigger, that is, than our kitchen at home – and equipped with a more or less new range, just like the one in the Medici kitchen, except with only two fireplaces. Messer Raffaello introduced me to the *scalco*, an old man called Jacopo, who must have been a gimlet-eyed slave-driver in his day but now was beginning to stoop and had the unmistakable smell of someone who drinks. The servants were all bored: they almost never saw their master, as he had spent most of the last few years in the north, and they didn't seem to feel a great deal of loyalty to him. It all suited me very well.

There was a lot to prepare, but most of it had to be done by me alone. So I took over Carenza's kitchen, which didn't please her.

'What are you up to now, *scimmia*? *Pazzolino?*' And I didn't blame her for asking. Things were being skinned, cured, dyed, wires were being twisted, scribbled notes were all over the table.

Three days before the banquet, Scalco Jacopo sent me the guest list. I had been pushing ahead, fuelled by a stinging concoction of rage, jealousy, and pure broken-hearted misery. But after I had scanned the list of names I had to go and sit outside in the little garden. Because Messer Lorenzo was on the list, and his wife; Agnolo della Stufa the *gonfaloniere*; two priors of the Wool Merchants' Guild and the head of the Arte di Calimala, the Cloth Merchants' Guild; a manager of the Medici bank; the current *gonfaloniere* of the Black Lion. Diamante Albizzi, of course, and Maddalena. A dozen other names I knew well, names that seemed to be in everybody's conversations that year. I was doing this for the men of the hour. *Don't fuck it up*, Zohan had said. And so, in similar but perhaps less florid words, would everyone else: Father, Carenza, Arrigo, Sandro; Mamma, no doubt, if she were here. Filippo? I knew what he'd say. Why was it I always listened to Filippo, even though he was a dead man? And Tessina? The old Tessina of the *mercato* . . . Oh, yes. But what of the Tessina who would be at table on Friday night? What would she say? I thought, and realized I didn't know. But that didn't seem to be a reason to change my course. No: it seemed like as good a reason as any to cleave to it.

In Bartolo Baroni's kitchen the fires had been burning all day, and I had been on my feet since before sunrise. The servants were lined up for service. Scalco Jacopo was drunk on the three flasks of strong Greek wine I had presented him with that morning as a token of my esteem, and the serving men and women had all been bribed with my entire month's wages to do what I said. Dishes had been coming in all afternoon, brought over from our kitchen by paid runners. I had kept Baroni's cooks at arm's length by the sheer force of my energy, and in any case I had concocted each dish so that the various parts made no sense on their own. Only in the assembly would the banquet reveal itself, and by then . . . The guests were seated. Bowls of rose-scented water to perfume their hands had been carried out. The first cups of wine had been poured. I crossed myself.

'Let's get on with it,' I said.

The first dishes, carried out on Baroni's exquisite silver platters, were a selection of marzipan fancies, shaped into hearts and silvered; a *mostarda* of black figs in spiced syrup; skewers of prosciutto marinated in red wine that I had reduced until it was thick and almost black; little *frittate* with herbs, each covered with finely sliced black truffles; whole baby *melanzane*, simmered in olive oil, a recipe I had got from a Turkish merchant I had met in the bathhouse.

I set about putting the second course together. I heated two kinds of *biroldi*, blood sausages: one variety I had made with pig's blood, pine nuts and raisins; the other was made from calf's blood, minced pork and pecorino. Quails, larks, grey partridge and figpeckers were roasting over the fire, painted with a sauce made from grape molasses, boiled wine, orange juice, cinnamon and saffron. They blackened as they turned, the thick sauce becoming a lovely, shiny caramel. There were roasted front-quarters of hare, on which would go a deep crimson, almost black sauce made from their blood, raisins, boiled wine and black pepper. Three roasted heads of young pigs, to which I had added tusks and decorated with pastry dyed black with walnut juice so that they resembled wild boar, then baked.

Meanwhile, there was a whole sheep turning over the fire,

more or less done, but I was holding it so that it would be perfect. The swan – there had to be a swan, Baroni had decided – was ready. I attached it to the armature of wire I had made, so that it stood up regally. The sturgeon, which I had cooked last night at home, and had finally set in aspic at around the fourth hour after midnight, was waiting in a covered salver. There were black cabbage leaves rolled around hazelnuts and cheese; rice porridge cooked in the Venetian style with cuttlefish ink; and of course the roebuck, roasting as well, but already trussed in the position I had designed for it. The sheep, too, had a crude armature, which I had borrowed from my uncle at the Porco, that would allow it to rear from its platter.

'The food . . .' Jacopo tottered in. I guessed he had finished his three flasks, so I pointed with my knife to another in the corner of the room. He brightened and made straight for it. 'Food . . . delightful . . .' he said over his shoulder. 'One or two of the guests have commented, I should tell you, on its overall colouring. It seems a trifle dark . . . or am I wrong? A preponderance, if you will allow me, of black . . .'

'Really? Coincidence,' I said curtly.

'Ah. Exactly,' he breathed, and took a long drink. I went back to work.

I put the sturgeon on its plate while everyone else was out of the kitchen, sent by me on various pointless errands. By the time they had returned, it was time to serve the next course, and no time to talk things over. And whether any of them would have dared to speak to me in any case is doubtful. And they had my silver in their purses. So while they gasped, and shuffled their feet; while I heard a muttered curse, and saw wide-eyed disbelief, they carried out the sturgeon, boiled and set in jet-black squid-ink aspic. They took the swan, neck held majestically erect, a silver crown upon its head, its beak and legs also silvered; clad, as in life, in a regal suit of feathers, though this swan was not white, because I had dressed it in the cured skins of three ravens I had procured from a bewildered game seller and stitched together in my room, the wings set so that they curved across the back, the tail arranged as a swan's tail. The four biggest servants took up the great trencher, which now held the sheep and the deer. Except that the sheep was now a ram, a rearing, prancing beast, upon which I had just secured the luxuriant, silken fleece of a black goat, obtained at great cost from one of Carenza's tanner cousins. Upon its head were curling, silvered horns. At its feet cowered the little deer, curled into a half-moon, its head sinking towards its hooves, and all enveloped in a crust of white sugar. From its head sprouted a single pointed horn, a stub of narwhal, bought from Leonardo's alchemist and only affordable because we both knew it was a fake. The trencher left on its stretcher, borne aloft like a noble corpse, and I followed it into the hall.

I walked into a silence so profound that I could hear the mutton sizzling beneath the black fleece. Faces were set in disbelief, in revulsion, horror, amusement, delight; even fear. Lorenzo de' Medici's heavy features were twisted with some sort of effort. Marco looked like he had charged out of his kennel and reached the end of his chain. Two faces only had no expression at all. Bartolo Baroni sat, his engorged lips slightly apart, his eyes fixed on the swan – or perhaps the ram and unicorn, which were just being set down in front of him. And Tessina might have been one of Sandro's drawings for all she seemed to be really in the room. Ghost-white, whiter than the sugar paste of the unicorn, it was as if she had left herself. Marco gave a snarl and made as if to rise, but his father pushed him back down. I stepped forward and gave a deep bow.

'Honoured guests!' I said. 'May I present: for the honour of the husband and wife to be, a black swan, symbol of the extraordinary union of two great and ancient families: Baroni and Albizzi, good fortune of a kind seen once in a dozen lifetimes. The magnificent black ram, embodying the dignity and majesty of Messer Bartolo Baroni; and the unicorn, who is the pure, virginal and devoted woman who is to be his wife.'

The silence hung for a moment, then to my disbelief, I was hearing applause. Disbelief and disappointment, mixed with anger. Messer Lorenzo was laughing and slapping Baroni on the back. People were on their feet, pointing at the swan, the unicorn. Lorenzo turned to Tessina and she gave him a bright, mechanical smile. Marco was trying to catch his father's eye, muttering something under his breath. Only Bartolo Baroni was silent. He had gone the colour of the blood sausages he had been served earlier. I suppose he was staring at the princely cock and balls I had fashioned from silvered dough, and attached to the undercarriage of the black ram. Alas, the dough had not set, and the magisterial *uccello* pointed not at the heavens but drooped in a soft arc towards the table. Baroni stared, and darkened until his skin was almost ebony. Something had come from all this work. I bowed again, turned on my heel and went back to the kitchen.

Ditieri was waiting for me. Where rage had turned his master the colour of a prune, in him it had merely achieved the rosy blush of, say, a poached sea bream.

'Traitor!' he hissed.

'Traitor? Is Messer Bartolo the republic? And how am I any kind of sinner, I who have toiled night and day for the past two weeks to bring things into being that have never – never! – been seen in Florence before, and only to honour your master! Answer me that, Master Ditieri! What have you done for your master that even comes close? When have you plucked a dream out of the air and made it real? Eh? And fed people with it? And if we're talking *traitor*, I saw Messer Lorenzo de' Medici out there, and he was clapping with delight. Likewise the Gonfaloniere di Giustizia. There's the republic for you. Do you want to finish cooking this supper? No? Shall we let Messer Jacopo do it? Except that he's staggering drunk. In fact, why don't you have a drink, eh? Why don't you find someone else to call a traitor, and let me get on with my work!'

He ranted at me while I put out the next course: a dish of boiled pigeons enveloped in a blancmange, the best I had ever made, with pulverized chicken, rose water, almonds, sugar, capon broth, ginger, verjuice and cinnamon. I had them placed in a deep dish, poured on the blancmange and scattered the snow-white surface with a thick covering of poppy seeds until the silver dish seemed to hold nothing but tiny black grains. Over this I arranged stars cut out of fine silver foil. There was a breast of veal, stuffed with cheese, eggs, saffron, herbs and raisins, upon which I scattered the darkest rose petals I could find at the flower market. There was a soup of black cabbage; boiled calves' feet with a sauce of figs and black pepper; and boiled ducks with more sliced black truffle. It all went out. And Ditieri let it go, because a steady procession of servants had come and announced that Messer So-and-so had told him that he'd just eaten the tastiest dish of his life.

The desserts were arranged, and I was done. They were ordinary sweets, done in their usual colours, because the truth was I hadn't expected to be in the kitchen after the swan went out. Cheese, quinces cooked with honey, marzipans, candied fruits, and for everyone, a *torta*, each adorned with the crest of the person to whom it would be served. They all had the same filling of delicately spiced fruit and custard, all except one.

The night before, while the sturgeon was poaching, after

Carenza had stumped off to bed, I had gone out into the garden with a lamp, a paring knife and a bowl. Though I couldn't remember ever sitting out there at night with my mother, still I felt that she was very near me. Which was sad, because she wouldn't have approved of what I had come out to do. I took the knife and cut a small but deep nick in my arm, just above the wrist, deep enough for the blood to flow out into the bowl. Then I bound up my arm and went back into the kitchen. I stirred the blood into a little pot of aspic, added sugar, nutmeg and a pinch of grated orange zest, mixed it carefully, and when it was ready, filled a little mould I had carved especially for it. The other *torte* were filled, but one case was unfinished. I had lined it with a sweet custard, left that to set, and then pressed pink rose petals into the custard. It was almost dawn by the time the little mould was ready. I turned the aspic out very carefully, laid it in the *torta* case, then poured in another aspic, completely clear and flavoured with sweet wine. Then I closed the lid.

Ditieri watched me icily as I changed out of my disgusting slops and into my best clothes. I set the *torte* on a long trencher and chose two serving men to carry it. Out in the dining hall, I served each guest their *torta*, starting with Messer Lorenzo, who tried to catch my eye. I kept my face a professional mask, though, and went around the table until I had reached Baroni. I gave him his pie, and he turned his face to me and contorted it into a horrible contrivance: a proud, a benevolent, a grateful smile for the benefit of his delighted guests. I ignored him. Tessina was staring into the distance, pretending to listen to Messer Lorenzo, who was talking about alum mining rights. It occurred to me that I would never stand this close to her again. How easy it would be to bend down and put my lips against the white slope of her neck. Instead I gravely rolled up my sleeves, revealing the bloodstained handkerchief that was still wrapped around the wound in my arm. Tessina looked up, gave me the sort of glance that a lady gives a serving man. It was perfect, except for her eyes, which were empty. Perhaps we were simply mirrors of each other's desolation. Her eyes strayed to my arm. She turned back to Messer Lorenzo and his alum mines. I picked up the last *torta* and placed it carefully on her plate.

'A strange fact, my lady,' I said. 'The English, so I have heard it said, call their pie crusts something quite extraordinary. They call them coffins.' Baroni, his smile tacked onto his face like velvet nailed to a broken chair, lifted the lid of his *torta*, blinked with relief. Messer Lorenzo was eating.

Tessina picked up her spoon very slowly. She prised up one side of the pie lid, then the other, and lifted it off. I was sure that only she saw what was inside: a little blood-red heart, suspended in crystal-clear aspic, in a nest of rose petals. She hesitated, glanced again at my bandaged arm and closed her eyes. Then she bent her head and very gently dipped her spoon. All around her, the guests were digging into their *torte* and toasting the forthcoming marriage so clearly blessed by Fortune. Tessina's spoon came up, a scarlet morsel in its bowl, and there was the rest of my heart. I stepped back, bowed to nobody, because nobody was looking at me, and left the Palazzo Baroni

23

THE WHOLE OF FLORENCE KNEW about it the next morning. How some boy had cooked a mourning feast to celebrate
Bartolo Baroni's fast-approaching marriage. How he had
served fat Bartolo a black sheep with a flaccid *membrum virile*,
and a hundred other black dishes, so that the table had looked
as if it were dressed with coal. How Messer Lorenzo de'
Medici had howled with laughter, and how Bartolo had tried
to save face by . . . by what, exactly? What Baroni had actually
said was not reported. There were a number of rumours
abroad: that he had hired an assassin, or several of them, to
kill me; that he had actually died from the humiliation; that
he'd enjoyed the food so much that he'd succumbed to a
terrible attack of gout, or apoplexy, or stroke; that he'd
thrown Tessina out of his house; that he'd married her there
and then. The first rumour concerned me, of course, though I
knew the others were all rubbish. But that evening, after a
strange day in the Medici kitchens, with the staff all whispering about me, I was summoned by Messer Lorenzo.

This was no longer the extraordinary event it had been a
few weeks back. I had been summoned three times since,
always drawn into deep subjects I didn't understand, and
which I tried to steer back to food. Except for once, when
the great man had, rather unexpectedly, talked wistfully
about his grandfather's love of the simple food of Florence. I
had suggested that he visit Ugolino the tripe seller – in jest, of
course: I couldn't imagine Il Magnifico supping tripe out of
a clay bowl in the middle of the market crowds – but he
replied that he knew it well, and that he agreed with me.

We had always talked in the dining hall, at the end of the meal. That evening, though, I was shown into the walled garden that lay at the heart of the palace, a place I had only glimpsed through half-opened doors. Feeling strangely as if I was trespassing, I stepped out onto one of the gravel paths that radiated from the central pool, dividing carefully tended grass with low hedges of bay, box and myrtle.

Messer Lorenzo was alone, sitting on a stone bench. There was a book in his lap. When he heard my feet crunching on the fine stone he closed the book and put it aside, then turned to watch me. I felt quite out of place and I didn't know what etiquette was required of me. So I halted a few steps from the bench. Messer Lorenzo beckoned me closer, though he did not indicate that I should sit.

'You are the man of the moment,' he said, and to my relief he grinned, the same mask of amused mischief I'd seen the night before. And it seemed that this was a mischief he wanted to share.

'Am I, my lord?'

'Believe me, you are. What an evening. I – do you know, I don't think I can remember another like it? The food, of course, I recognized. Exquisite as ever. But I have a suspicion that you perhaps deviated, however slightly, from poor Bartolo Baroni's commission?' He didn't seem angry. In fact he sounded in high spirits.

'I cooked a meal to reflect the event . . . As I saw it,' I said. There wasn't any point in trying to wriggle out of what was coming.

'Ah, yes. You saw Bartolo Baroni's engagement to Donna Tessina Albizzi as a cause for mourning – granted, mourning is a celebration, albeit of things past and not to come. Now, why? Hmm. Painfully easy to work out, of course. You love Donna Tessina.' I opened my mouth to speak, then closed it again. 'Don't tell me you didn't expect the whole of Tuscany to have caught on by sunrise this morning. All I can say is, you must love her very much.'

'I love her, that is all. All the other things I thought I loved – my father, my mother's memory, my friends, our great city – put against my love for her, those are just affection.'

'Really? So her betrothal was the death of what?'

'Of me,' I said without hesitation. 'Bartolo Baroni flatters himself if he imagines I was thinking about him at all, except that in marrying Tessina he has killed our love, and that means my death. I'm dead now.'

'My poor Nino. Tell me: how old are you?'

'Nineteen, my lord.'

'Yes. Well, in some ways – in most ways – last night's display was the act of a child. But executed by a man of, I dare say, quite extraordinary talent. Where did you get those ideas?'

'I don't know, sir. Dreams, I suppose. And paintings. But mostly it was just how I feel.'

'Please don't make my dinners into funerals, Nino. Plainly, we'll have to cheer you up.'

'I expect you'll want me to leave your service right away, sir?'

'Leave? Why on earth would I want that? You are the prodigy of Florence. People are telling the story of Baroni's feast as if it was something they read in Boccaccio. I'm very lucky to have you in my kitchen. In fact, I want to help you.'

'Help me?'

'Certainly. The first thing you need to do, Nino, is put any worries you might have about Bartolo Baroni from your mind. He is an old, old ally of mine. Of my father. Even my grandfather knew Bartolo. He's no fool, though he might look it. I think he knows that he's overreached himself.'

'I don't understand . . .' I didn't. Not one word of it. But it was the sweetest music I'd ever heard.

'With Donna Tessina. A beautiful young woman. And he is three times her age. He looks a trifle ridiculous, doesn't he?'

'Completely ridiculous,' I agreed eagerly.

'And, because I am such a close friend of his, I happen to know that he's a little . . . anxious, shall we say? He knows that he's cutting a *brutta figura*, but it's too late to back out without losing face.'

'Is that really true, my lord?'

'I swear it. I think – this is strictly between you and me, Nino – that he's desperate for a reason to call the whole thing off. Last night merely strengthened that resolve.'

'I thought I'd given him a deadly insult.'

'Bartolo? Lord, *no*! He thought it was quite exquisite! Hilarious! I doubt you'll get paid, mind you, but no, in many ways you played into his hands. And I say again: don't worry. There are no daggers looking for you. You're under my protection.'

'Thank you, my lord!' I was almost melting with relief.

'Not at all, not at all. Now. To business. You can't waste any time. You must press your suit with the lady Tessina as soon as possible. Steal her from Bartolo. He'll thank you for it, strange as that seems.'

'He . . . he told you that?'

'As I said, I've known Bartolo a long, long time.'

'I'll fetch her tonight! We'll slip away and go somewhere north. Milan, where they like Florence and good food!'

'But Nino: wouldn't that be a waste? As you've amply shown, you have a love of spectacle. And this is a great, burning love. You've done a feast of black. Why not bring light to the darkness? A love feast for Donna Tessina. There's not a soul in Florence who wouldn't applaud you.'

'A feast?' I wasn't sure if I'd heard right.

'A feast! My dear Nino, you may have the use of my own banqueting hall.'

'I don't think . . .' But I did. Already my mind was painting pictures. Snow-white lilies – where could I find lilies in August? Never mind. The stag I should have made for Baroni. A swan – obviously, a swan, white this time, and never mind the vile taste. The guests wouldn't care. Guests . . . Father, of course. Carenza – Carenza in a gown! Sandro, Arrigo. Uncle Terino. And the neighbourhood. The butchers . . .

'But before the feast, the invitation,' said Messer Lorenzo, cutting delicately into my reverie. 'You must be fearless. You must be like a hero, like one of King Arthur's knights. On a horse, a white horse – you *can* ride?'

'I can,' I said, utterly bewildered by delight. I hadn't sat on a horse for years, but how difficult could it be?

'We must act fast – Bartolo may change his mind, with so many tongues wagging. At the moment he's right here.' He held out his cupped hand and shook it slowly, as if it held something heavy. I could all but see Baroni crouched in his palm, a little mulberry-skinned homunculus. 'Three days. Give me three days, Nino.'

'My lord,' I said, plucking up as much courage as I had left. 'Forgive me, but I don't understand. Why would you help me like this?'

'A sensible question,' said Messer Lorenzo. He picked up his book, ran his finger carelessly down its tooled, gilded spine. 'I think you are very, very talented, Nino. And you have a remarkable intellect. There are great honours in store for a man like you in my city. To be frank: Bartolo Baroni belongs to yesterday. He'll be *gonfaloniere* in a few months, and then he'll retire. You have your life ahead of you. I see you as head cook – that's obvious – now that Maestro Zohan has left us. The fellow we have now is merely adequate. Or perhaps you would rather be *scalco*? But why waste your talent serving other men? I could use you in the Signoria. Think of it. With Tessina di Nino di Latini at your side, you could be anything. I recognize a fellow poet in you, Nino, and a fellow intellect. So there's my first reason. The second is as I told you: Baroni would like to be free of his obligation. And for a third, the plainest: I wouldn't mind taking Bartolo down a peg or two. So you'd be helping me, Nino. Do you agree?'

'Agree? Of . . . of course!'

'Good. I think you need to leave Florence until the day. I'll prepare everything. Meanwhile, I want you to carry out an important errand for me. I have a letter I need delivered to my villa at Cafaggiolo. If you ride there, stay the night and come straight back here, all will be ready. After that, the feast is in your hands.'

'The head cook?'

'Leave him to me. Leave everything to me. Now, the *maestro di casa* will prepare a horse for you.'

'I need to go home, get dressed . . .'

'Nonsense. You have ordinary clothes? A sword? What more do you need? I'm sure we can find you a cloak. Now go, Nino. Or should I say, Paris. Go, Paris. Think of nothing but your Helen.'

24

CAFAGGIOLO IS A DAY'S RIDE north of Florence, a pleasant ride in summer, up through hills and fields and woods. I set out gingerly on a large though fortunately placid horse, who seemed to know that the creature on his back was an amateur. Cafaggiolo was further than I'd ever been from the city. This was all new to me, riding alone through a strange landscape. But I was on an errand for Lorenzo de' Medici. If he had trusted me, I could do it.

Towards evening, the villa was visible in the distance and the bones and muscles of my arse felt as if they'd been beaten with an iron rod. Despite the pain and the concentration it took to keep the horse doing what I wanted, I followed Messer Lorenzo's command and thought of nothing but Tessina. Fortune, who had gutted me only a few days ago, had reached out again and healed me. I was to have Tessina back. But not as my lover: as my wife. I thought of her sitting next to Baroni at the feast, and it was all so clear. That choleric old buffoon could never have had the perfect girl at his side. He had known it all along. And Tessina: the wife of Messer Lorenzo's trusted companion. She'd sit at table with us, with Ficino and Poliziano and the rest of them, and we'd speak of Plato. Things other than Plato, of course: the government, the Signoria. Tessina at my side. I could, in a way, have stolen that kiss at the feast. But there would be a lifetime of kisses. What had Lorenzo said? *I recognize a fellow intellect.* It was the natural order of things. A worthy man was on the rise.

I delivered the letter, ate a lacklustre meal of cold meats – I would set all of Messer Lorenzo's kitchens in order, I said to myself – and slept in a servant's bed, though I was so tired that I barely noticed any of it, save that the Villa Cafaggiolo was very large and imposing. And when I left the next morning, I didn't trouble to admire it more, because as Messer Lorenzo's friend I would be coming here again soon.

As soon as my arse had gone numb, I found I could more or less ride properly, and so arrived back at the Porta San Gallo before sunset. I went straight to the Palazzo Medici, where I was greeted by the *maestro di casa*. This august man, who usually treated me like a trained ape, told me that everything was prepared. Messer Lorenzo was dining at the house of Francesco Sassetti, so I should retire to the chambers that had been set aside for me, eat a moderate supper that he'd ordered from the kitchens, and – Messer Lorenzo's strict instructions – go early to bed. Tomorrow I was to put on the clothes prepared for me, and meet Messer Lorenzo in the courtyard.

I disobeyed Messer Lorenzo in that I didn't sleep. I couldn't. My room was grand, by far the most richly ap pointed room I'd ever tried to sleep in. It overlooked the Via Larga, and when I'd realized that sleep was impossible I went to the window, knelt on a chair and rested my elbows on the sill, staring down at the dark street lit faintly by other windows, watching cats fight and chase each other back and forth across the cobbles. Then I went back to bed and tried to imagine tomorrow. I was going to ride to the Palazzo Albizzi with Messer Lorenzo. And then what? Invite her to a banquet. And Uncle Diamante? I'd have to invite him too, I supposed. People would notice. It would cause a bit of a stir. But that was the whole idea.

I suppose I did sleep for an hour or two, because it was morning all of a sudden. I had the nerves I got before a big *calcio* match: fear, of course, sensible fear, tempered by the knowledge that I could deal with anything that was to come. Excitement, and a strange sort of calm. I was going to the Black Lion to claim what was mine. Tessina – oh, miracle! – was waiting for me, though she didn't know it yet. Feeling lightheaded and a little shaky in the knees, I found I had slept so soundly that I had not heard a suit of clothes being laid out for me on a settle by the door. As I was admiring them, a manservant entered and said he had come to dress me. And so he did: in hose divided down the centre into red and white; a silvery-white *farsetto* of silk; and a breathtaking cloth-of-gold cloak. There was also an exquisite white hat, festooned with golden feathers which, so the servant told me, came from a pheasant only found in China. I understood, for the first time in my life, what a nobleman must feel like every day, though there was a small voice in the back of my mind whispering, *You look like a gilded blancmange* . . . Feeling I was letting things down a bit, I buckled on my sword, because a gentleman has to have a sword.

Down in the courtyard, Messer Lorenzo was waiting for me on a gleaming chestnut horse. Four others were beside him. All five were, to my complete amazement, rigged out in armour. Not the thick, ugly armour that men take to war, but the light, fluted, chased, engraved, embossed creations made for processions. Messer Lorenzo's armour was silver richly inlaid with gold, or perhaps the other way around. He wore a fluted breastplate over a doublet of flame-coloured velvet. On his legs, thigh plates and greaves forged to look like leaping dolphins were buckled over more red velvet. His helmet had an intricate crest and a visor like the beak of a galley. Over his shoulders was a cloak of cloth-of-gold. His four companions had their visors down but Messer Lorenzo's was up and he was grinning at me under the galley's beak.

'Hail, Paris!' he shouted, and the other four took up the cry, their voices tinny and hollow inside their helmets. A page was leading a pure white horse towards me, beautifully caparisoned with a red leather saddle and gilded harness. I gritted my teeth, made a mess of getting my foot into the stirrup, and gratefully allowed the page to help me up. My backside was not yet ready to return to the saddle, but I barely noticed the pain. Lorenzo walked his horse alongside mine.

He handed me a huge bouquet of flowers, and a roll of parchment. 'I've written this for you. We'll stop in the street outside the Albizzi house. The trumpeters . . .'

'Trumpeters?'

'Waiting for us outside. The trumpeters will blow a fanfare, then – as soon as your Helen appears, you will read that. And then, invite her to your love feast!'

'Should I say anything else?'

'Tell her what's in your heart. It's a day for love, my dear Nino.'

I rode out of the palace gate and into Via de' Gori. Sure enough, there were two trumpeters and a small troop of soldiers, all carrying banners. Lorenzo's companions ushered me to the head of the procession, where we waited for a moment until Messer Lorenzo himself joined us, his visor down. We set off, down Via Larga. I settled into the easy gait of my horse, all of Florence watching us. We were going to call on the loveliest woman in the world, and Messer Lorenzo and I were both young men who knew what it was to feel the senses burning with life's pleasures, and some of her pains.

As we went along, a crowd fell in behind us. By the time we reached Via dei Rustici, it seemed we were heading a carnival parade. The two trumpeters, their instruments hung with white banners, stopped before the dowdy front of the Palazzo Albizzi. The trumpets sounded, and Lorenzo called out in a high, cracked voice:

'Bring the lady forth!'

It had the desired effect. There was a commotion, and an upstairs window was flung open. Diamante Albizzi poked his head out, ready to snarl at whoever was down in the street. But not at Lorenzo de' Medici. He went as white as my cap.

'We have come to pay homage at the feet of the lady Tessina,' trilled Lorenzo.

The crowd behind us had swelled to fill the street, the whole city hungry for a bit of jollity to break the grind of August's heat and stink. I was trying to keep a straight face, as if I did this every day. Lorenzo prodded me and pointed to the roll of paper he'd given me.

'Read,' he whispered.

I looked up, and there was Tessina peering down at us, confused. Swallowing, I unrolled the paper and began to read.

'I saw my lady by a rushing stream . . .'

Tessina saw who was shouting poetry at her and clapped her hands across her blushing face.

'The sun sank early in the western skies . . .'

Every window in the street was open now, scores of people, young and old, leaning as far out as they dared. Tessina's aunt and uncle were standing in their doorway, writhing with confusion.

'How short a while all mortal joys endure,
But not so soon does memory pass away.'

I ran out of words, and sat, staring up at the woman in the window, one face in a blizzard of faces, but the only one born at the same hour as me, under the same Florentine stars.

'Talk!' hissed Lorenzo.

I raised my hand, waved it. Then, still unable to say anything at all, I flung the bouquet as hard as I could towards Tessina. But I threw too hard, and the flowers struck the wall under Tessina's window and exploded onto the party of merrymakers.

'I'm sorry, Tessina! I missed,' I called out, because she had started to laugh, and it was as if we were children again, playing down in this street where I was sitting, on a horse of all things, feeling like a statue made out of marzipan and gilding. 'We were wondering . . .' This wouldn't do. 'Tessina, you are Helen of Troy and I am your Paris. Do me the honour of attending a feast of love, a banquet of delights . . .' None of this was real. The words, the costumes . . . There was only one thing worth saying. I took off my hat and dropped it into the street. 'Do me the honour . . . oh, *porco dio*, Tessina! Will you marry me?'

'What in the name of Christ's bowels?' There was a roar. I turned towards Diamante Albizzi, assuming he had spoken, but he was still staring dumbly at the pageant outside his house. It wasn't Diamante at all, but the looming, crimson-robed figure who had appeared next to him, the man with the broken nose and the spilled-wine skin, who had pushed through the crowd, followed by five men with their hands on their swords. One of them was Corso Marucelli, Marco Baroni's tall, straw-haired lieutenant. Bartolo Baroni pushed Uncle Diamante aside. Aunt Maddalena screamed. Marucelli already had his sword out. More steel whined from scabbards. Someone else screamed.

I turned to Messer Lorenzo for reassurance, but found that he had already ridden back a good few paces. The soldiers had kept a passageway open behind us, and for a moment I thought he was gesturing at me to come over, but instead he raised his visor. The face that leered at me was not Lorenzo de' Medici. It was a man I'd never seen before, eyes too close together, mouth too small, a fair beard that needed scraping off his upper lip. The other visors went up too, and showed four laughing faces, four ordinary market faces.

And now the soldiers were laughing, and the trumpeters were pointing at me and stamping their feet. The laughter flared from mouth to mouth until the street seemed to be trembling with raucous, unstoppered mirth. I watched as the men in armour slipped down the side passage, followed by the trumpeters and then the soldiers. I was left alone, with the eyes of the Black Lion flaying me from all sides, from above and below; with the laughter that comes when we delight in another's shame beating at me. I looked up at Tessina, my mind completely frozen, my body frozen along with it. Tessina was a white flame against the dark square of the window. And then a hand snaked around and clamped itself over her mouth. For a moment a snarling, twisted face appeared next to hers: Marco Baroni, yelling down at me, or at Tessina, or the whole city. Then they were both gone.

Baroni's men were fanning out across the street between me and the Palazzo Albizzi. Corso Marucelli was grinning, his sword raised high above his head. Out of the corner of my eye, a little half-naked boy was dancing in front of the crowd, my white cap on his head. Suddenly the horse gave a frightened neigh and lunged forward. I almost went back over its tail but Fortuna had tangled my hand in the reins and I managed to right myself. A man had grabbed the bridle and was running full tilt at the crowd, who were screaming, in fear or delight, and at the last moment parted for us. The man glanced back.

'Arrigo!' I yelled.

'What the *cazzo* are you doing, you madman?' he yelled back.

We were through the crowd. Arrigo slowed and turned

and suddenly he was in front of me on the horse, pulling the reins from my numb fingers. 'Hold on!' he yelled. The horse lunged again. People threw themselves out of our way. Houses flew past, we turned a corner, galloped across the suddenly familiar void of Piazza Santa Croce. We didn't stop until we were well into the dyers' quarter and the Via dei Malcontenti, along which condemned men are driven on their way to the gallows.

There are a lot of open spaces out there, fields, gardens and patches of waste ground between the mean little houses of the dyers and their workshops. Arrigo reined in the white horse. I slid down to the ground, one red leg and one white leg, planted in a stream of pale blue, piss-scented water that was flowing out from a nearby dye-works. Arrigo tethered the horse to a broken gatepost and left it standing in a patch of blotched mud. It looked utterly dejected. The poor beast had doubtless never been so humiliated in its pampered life.

'What have you done?' said Arrigo. He took me by the shoulders and shook me, not gently.

'It wasn't Messer Lorenzo,' I stammered.

'What? What are you talking about?'

'In the helmet. It wasn't him.'

'Lorenzo de' Medici? Why would it have been? Nino, have you gone mad? Why are you wearing these ridiculous clothes? How could you *afford* them? And the Albizzis . . .'

'I was Paris,' I said, feeling as if someone was holding my head under cold water. 'I was Paris. Tessina was Helen. He said that Baroni wanted to break it off. He said I'd be doing everybody a favour.'

'Who? Who said all this nonsense?'

'Lorenzo de' Medici! After Baroni's feast . . .'

'I heard about that.'

'Wait. Arrigo? Aren't you supposed to be in Prato?'

'I got back last night. I came round to see you, but your

father said you hadn't been home for two or three days. Actually I was just on my way back from your house when I saw the crowd running up Via dei Rustici. I thought, *That's the Albizzi house*. I thought it must be on fire for all the noise people were making. But no, it was you on a white horse, done up like a . . . like a royal *bardassuole*, if I may say so.'

'I've ruined everything, Arrigo.'

'That's plain enough. But tell me what happened.'

So I did, from the betrothal feast . . . no, I had to go back earlier, to Tessina in Rosselli's studio, then what came afterwards. Then the feast, then Messer Lorenzo in the palace garden, Cafaggiolo, the knights in the courtyard, the trumpeters, the soldiers, the banners . . .

'Oh, Christ, my friend.' Arrigo had started to laugh, bitterly. 'Nino, you're a *beffato*. Didn't you see it? Lorenzo has set you up for a grand *beffa*.'

'But why? Why would he do such a thing?'

'Because he's a prince and you're a cook with big, fancy ideas. A cook who thinks he's entitled to the betrothed of the next *gonfaloniere*. I don't know. Because you talked about Plato to the cleverest man in Italy. Mainly, I should think, because he knew you'd walk right into it. *Virtù*, Nino – weren't you thinking at all? You broke every single rule of *virtù*.'

'I can see it now . . . Oh, *Gesù*! I could have been murdered.'

'Oh, you would *definitely* have been murdered. I expect that was just bad luck. *Mala fortuna*. Lorenzo probably set out to humiliate Baroni a little bit, with you as the sacrificial ram.' He kicked a stone into the weeds. The horse flinched, rolled its eyes. 'I'd say his *beffa* has misfired. Someone forgot to tell Bartolo. Or maybe he intended the whole thing. In any event you've got to leave Florence right now. Your life isn't worth a tanner's fart at this moment.'

'Messer Lorenzo will protect me!' I protested, knowing – the instant the words left my lips – what a fool I'd been. What a blind fool. I'd never even heard Fortuna's sword as she swung it at my neck. And all the grand *beffi* we had analysed, over and over again – I'd learned nothing. Instead I had made myself into the perfect *beffato*: arrogant, blind to my own faults, flouting the laws of good conduct, of society, of *virtù*. And I had done it all with my eyes wide open. Committing the worst sins of all: pride and self-regard. 'Oh, God, Arrigo. What will I do?'

'Get as far away as you can. Arezzo, or Perugia? Further, I'd say. Rome.'

'Zohan's in Rome,' I muttered.

'Then go there. But now. This morning.'

'Like this?' I held out my arms.

'No. Better not. Do you have any money?'

'Not on me. There's some in my room at home. Enough, certainly.'

'Good. I'll fetch it for you. And some proper clothes. And a horse. You can have mine. I'll tell my papá that it turned its ankle on the way from Prato. I'll take this one back.'

'To Lorenzo?'

'Yes. You don't want to be a horse-thief into the bargain, do you? I'll say I found it running about in the piazza.'

'Be careful, Arrigo. Don't trust him. And the Baronis will be out.'

'Pfff.' He blew out his cheeks scornfully. 'The Baronis. *Bardasse*. Though I don't think anybody saw my face. Give me that cloak as well – you can't be poncing about like the Queen of the Fairies.'

'Where shall I meet you?'

'Go out of the gate. Past the gibbet. Keep walking. If I remember right, there's a ruined barn about half a mile to the east, quite near the river. Now, your doublet – what's it lined with?'

He helped me turn it inside out. Thankfully it was lined with plain grey fustian, and once it had been buttoned I looked merely eccentric and not like a carnival effigy. And at least I had my sword. Arrigo swung up onto the horse, which seemed to flinch, no doubt expecting further humiliations.

'Wait! Arrigo, I can't leave without saying goodbye to my father, to Carenza!'

'What do you think that scene in Via dei Rustici was, Nino, but the most spectacular farewell in the history of Florence? But I'll do all that's necessary. You just need to get away. Your father will understand.'

'No, he won't.'

'If you think he'd rather bury you tomorrow, by all means stay. I think he'd prefer a live son to a dead one.'

'You're right. Go. And Arrigo: thank you.'

'You'd have done the same.' He waved the cloak at me, tucked it under his leg and cantered away towards the roofs and towers of the city. I turned my face away from them, towards the Porta della Giustizia, the gibbet and the unknown world beyond.

Fortuna Turns Her Wheel A Third Time:
'Sum Signe Regno' – 'I Have No Kingdom'

25

Arrigo was as good as his word. I had waited at the barn he'd described, sitting against the wall on a pile of rotten boards, watching a family of scorpions move up the wall opposite me. It seemed like a dream, which became real again when Arrigo appeared, riding a horse with white ankles, a pair of leather bags slung over the pommel. One held a set of plain, slightly old-fashioned clothes in fusty grey.

'These are my brother's,' said Arrigo. 'He's more or less your size.'

Peeling off the rest of my ridiculous white flummery was what brought me back to the present. 'What's going on in the streets?' I asked, imagining myself burned in effigy.

'The Baronis are running about in the Black Lion, trying to cause a fuss. No one likes them, though, do they? Luckily. The Butchers' Guild have gathered in the Borgo in front of your house in case there's any trouble, so at the moment it looks like the Baronis against the Arte dei Beccai, and I wouldn't bet against the Arte.'

'Did you see my father?' I grabbed his arm and nearly toppled over, as I was trying to pull on the dingy woollen hose at the same time. Arrigo righted me calmly.

'No. The butchers said he'd gone to the Signoria. Carenza was in tears, I'm afraid. But don't worry. It'll blow over. Everyone's talking about what a good *beffa* it was, how clever Messer Lorenzo was for putting it on. They're talking about you too, of course . . .'

'What are they saying?'

'That you're a fool. That you were too clever for your own good, too much in love with yourself.'

'With myself . . .'

'What did you think they'd say? Anyway, that's good. At least they aren't saying you're in love with Tessina. It's all about you and your stupidity, not about her.'

'Thank Christ!'

'Exactly. As I said, it'll fade away soon enough.'

'How soon?'

'Couple of years? Four or five?'

'Five years? *Five years?*'

'Not much longer than that. Five years in Rome – you're a lucky man, if you ask me.' As if to cut off the blasphemous rebuke that was forming on my lips, he held up a leather purse. 'Your money. You have your sword and your dagger: good. Oh – I almost forgot.' He reached into his doublet and took out a folded piece of parchment. 'I met Sandro in the street – he was coming to see if there was anything he could do to help. I said there wasn't, but he made me come to his *bottega*. He gave me this for you.'

I unfolded the paper clumsily, thinking I knew what it had to be: and I was half right. It was a sketch, and for a moment I thought it was one of the drawings he'd made of Tessina. But instead it was a simple study for a Virgin and Child, the child's face no more than a few lines, the young woman staring into the distance past my left shoulder.

'He was trying to find something else,' Arrigo said. 'Really, he was cursing the ceiling down, trying to find his portfolio. But you know what his place is like: bloody chaos. And I was in a hurry, so he sent you this.' He peered over my shoulder. 'Hmm. She's wonderful.'

'Tell Sandro . . .'

'I will. Don't worry. Now get going. There's a ferryman

just a bit further on. Cross the river, head for San Gaggio, and once you've found the Siena road, stay on it.'

'Thank you, Arrigo. Will you be able to tell Tessina . . .'

'Forget Tessina, Nino. Just forget her. It has to be this way. There's no point in pretending otherwise. Forget it all.'

'But I'll see you again . . .'

'Of course. I'm leaving too. I decided in Prato: to hell with Father's business. I'm going to become a soldier. You're going south, and I'm heading north to find a *condottiere* band. I'll see you in Rome. All mercenaries end up in Rome, sooner or later.'

'The world is ending,' I said numbly.

I slept that first night away in a ditch, somewhere in the shadow of the Chianti hills. Not strictly speaking a ditch, perhaps: in fact, it was a small stone-built shed with a serviceable roof of furze and flat stones in the corner of a vineyard. But it might as well have been a ditch, for all the comfort it gave me, and the fact that it looked very much like the hermitage of Santa Bibiana only made things worse.

There didn't seem to be a homestead within sight, and the nearest smoke was rising a good mile and a half distant, so I tied the horse up in a small grove of almond trees behind the shed where he would be hidden from the road, and laid out my blanket on the stamped earth floor. I took out the wine I had bought at Poggibonsi and laid out my dinner on a handkerchief: two sausages, a slice of pecorino, an apple, a quarter-loaf of hard, chestnut-flour bread, a handful of raisins squeezed into a ball. None of it looked good; none of it looked like food at all. I drank the wine and picked at the raisins, watching the valley turn orange and then grey as the sun set behind me. When my head felt heavy enough, I laid myself down by the half-closed door so that I could see out into the tangle of vines, and fell into a sort of sleep. When I did at last fall asleep enough to dream, I found myself hovering, pitching like a boat on rough water, above the streets of Florence, which teemed with man-sized insects, all rustling around busily and sending up a great, verminous stench. I floated higher and saw that what I had thought was my city was really a half-rotted corpse, and the wind on which I rocked was the foul steam of its putrefaction. At that, mercifully, I woke up.

My throat felt like the ditch I had almost slept in. I tottered outside and relieved myself against a vine. The vineyard was a mass of shapes in the faint light of a quarter-moon. I shuddered, suddenly aware of how quiet it was; but there was no human sound at all apart from my own ragged breathing. I had spent almost every night of my life in the company of fifty thousand people, and here I was in the foothills of Chianti, alone except for a horse, some bats and God knew how many insects.

There was no wine left, and no water. My thirst was painful, but I remembered the apple, and devoured it. Luckily it was the tart, juicy kind and did something to relieve my suffering. But I didn't dare go back to sleep and instead wrapped the blanket tightly around me and sat propped up in the doorway. I had nothing to think about except Tessina, and that was like touching freshly burned skin, so instead I let the cold light deaden my wounds and settle like frost around my heart.

I saddled the horse early, before sunrise, and a few miles down the road we came across a farmer heading north towards Florence with a cart full of his produce. He was happy to sell me, at *mercato* prices, some peaches and a decent-looking salami. A bit further down the road was a hamlet with a cold, fresh spring gushing from a marble pedestal next to the locked chapel. By now there were little knots of people on the road. They all looked like pilgrims, and I caught snatches of talk in clacking northern tongues. By lunchtime the way was almost crowded. There were wagons full of nuns, old men in litters, nobles on expensive horses. By the time Monteriggioni came into view it was clear that I wasn't going to find a seat in any decent tavern. The streets were packed with men and women all jabbering to each other in strange languages. I pushed on towards Siena, stopping by the side of the road to eat my dry and salty provisions. The road was leading me through gently rolling, thickly wooded country, quite empty of people. The horse seemed to relish the solitude and the shade of the trees, because he broke into a trot and then a canter, which I discovered I could manage quite well. So it was that we came to Siena a little before sunset.

Because I had seen almost no one on the road, and had left the noisy pilgrims far behind, I had thought I would have an easy time finding a bed in Siena, but I was quite wrong. It seemed as if the whole city was working just to funnel travellers into the waiting hands of overpriced taverns and louse-ridden hostels. I knew the name of an inn – my father had stayed there once, many years ago, so I set out to find it.

As I rode up the main street I was whistled at, jeered from the shadows, importuned by tarts and yelled at by men in the doorways of foul-looking eating places and lodging houses. All the cooking smells were rank or sour: burned oil frying rancid bacon. A lot of cabbage was being boiled, and more was singeing in the bottom of a dry pot. Into this swam a shoal of half-rotten carp, chased by sausages scraped together from the ooze of a week-old offal bucket. I gagged and pressed my sleeve against my nose and mouth. The stench was about to make me sick, but all around, pilgrims were crowding into the steaming doorways of the very taverns that were belching out these stinks, all filled with high anticipation of the fine meal awaiting them. A pimp was hopping backwards in front of me, leering like a monkey and trying to catch my eye.

'Do you know the taverna of the Golden Fish?' I barked at him. Instantly his face hardened and he spat. 'Where can I find a place to eat that won't be like taking my supper in the jakes?' I demanded, urging the horse on, making the man skip out of our way. 'Eh? Is there anywhere in Siena that doesn't stink like *il culo del diavolo*? If so, take me there. If not . . .' I carried on up the hill.

I found the Golden Fish eventually, by asking some men who were repairing the wall of a house. The inn was on the other side of the city, away from the pilgrims, though there were quite enough of those already ensconced in the plain but comfortable public room. I enquired after a bed, and was told I'd have to share one. After my experience in the shed I reluctantly agreed.

There was room at the long dining table for me, and I was starving, so I handed the horse over to a stable boy and poured a pail of well-water over my head. Then I took my place on a bench in front of a pewter charger, its face scratched into a spiderweb by countless knife strokes. There was a portly Frenchman to my right and a tall, grey-haired man in scholar's robes to my left, who came from a place he called Wales. A pretty girl with a pock-marked face went up and down the table, ladling something from a big dish. When it landed on my plate I found it was *ribollita*, our good old Tuscan soup of kale and bread, boiled down into a sort of half-solid sludge. The man from Wales fell on it with his spoon and shovelled it as if it was manna, and the French-man, with a little more hesitation, set to with a grunt of satisfaction. I prodded the stodgy heap with my spoon, leaned forward and sniffed. There was the flatulence again: farts and dishwater. This wasn't *ribollita*. This wasn't food at all. And yet, all around me, men and women were slurping and guzzling like so many hogs.

I pushed the plate away, stood up. None of my fellow diners looked up from their plate. *I could be in Florence right now*, I wanted to shout. *I could be eating tripe from Ugolino's stall, which is finer stuff than any of you have ever tasted. I could be eating a* bistecca *of Latini beef, cooked by Carenza over oak shavings*. The serving girl was frowning at me. I pushed past her and ran to the door.

There was nothing familiar anywhere. I was walking, head down, just to keep myself moving. Siena is hilly, and I went up steps and down steep alleyways until I came to the square in front of the cathedral. It was filled with pilgrims, of course, all squawking and screeching at each other. I kept walking, and did not stop until I had walked clean around the city. Then I went back to the inn and climbed into bed between a cleric from Burgundy and another man from Wales, wherever that might be. The Burgundian snored and the man of Wales had a bony arse that he kept digging into me as he wriggled through his strange Wales-ish dreams. Again, I woke up long before dawn and was through the city gates before the sun was more than a slice of fire above the eastern mountains. I rode south towards the hump of Monte Amiata, stopping only to feed and water the horse and to fill my own water bottle. For myself I bought only bread, and even for that I had little appetite.

In two days I was at Radicofani, and passed the night in the one verminous inn, where bedbugs pricked me all night, and where I awoke to find one of my bedfellows' hands fluttering between my thighs. The man was a Florentine and was quite unabashed when I told him he could fuck himself and not me, and in the end we had a friendly, whispered chat about *calcio* until the rest of the men in our bed told us to shut up in Frisian, Breton and Portuguese. Another day and I had crossed over into the papal states, spending the next night shivering on the threshing floor of a deserted farm somewhere near Monte Cimino. The rain vanished overnight, and the country ahead of me turned brown and dry, shimmering with heat and hissing, like fat frying in a pan, with the cries of cicadas.

And still I had eaten nothing but bread. My tongue had rebelled against any other food, and the smells of cooking in the towns and villages I passed through repelled me. Even the bread, as I had left the lands of Siena for those of the Pope, had turned salty. My body was protesting all the time now, but I couldn't bring myself to feed it.

Hunger was like a strange new country, far stranger than the one I was riding through. Before there had been food for me whenever I'd wanted it. Mamma or Carenza had always been hovering about, waiting to cram something into my mouth. I'd say *I'm starving!* and there would be food, delicious food. Now my insides were screaming for food. They were eating themselves. But I ignored them. Because I had found something familiar in among the pains and the cravings: the same distance I had felt as a little boy, before I'd learned how to eat like everybody else. There was a purity inside me that I hadn't felt for many years. An emptiness: how *full* I'd always been. Crammed with tastes, with textures – with thick, heavy matter. As I rode, my mind showed me all the things I'd ever eaten, and that I'd prepared for the table. Red meat, livid and glistening, its grain rippling, engorged. Fat like ivory. The outline of other people's teeth in things I had cooked, come back half eaten.

Every village I rode through brought the same smells: old oil, old bacon, old cabbage. *But that's just food, boy*, my senses whispered. *That's what food smells like*. Not the food of Florence, I would mutter to myself. *That too. Even your precious*

Ugolino and his tripe. But as I wandered south, I found I'd forgotten even the taste of those magical stews.

I was glad of it. If I could forget Ugolino's food then I could forget other things as well. I let my tongue liberate them: Papá's cheap red wine which he always poured for me; Carenza's vile medicines; my mother's bread. Away they flew, little coloured butterflies melting into thin air. I began to feel lighter and lighter. I was casting it all off. Soon I would melt into the air myself. At last, I summoned up the most terrifying taste of all: the salty, spicy tang of Tessina's skin and the pure saffron of her lips. Out into the air they went. I breathed them into the sky. I was empty at last.

In the end I found myself drifting through an endless landscape of golden wheat and red poppies, ranks of olive trees and strange craggy valleys carved out of rock the colour of old ivory, the constant bumping of my arse against the saddle my only clue that I was actually alive. My mind was usually somewhere else, dabbing like a paintbrush at ghostly memories, bringing them to life and watching them fade back to grey. Tessina was always there. She was following me like a guardian angel, always just out of sight – or perhaps she was Michael, expelling me from paradise.

It had been a day or more since I had really thought about where I was going, or about food. I hadn't even wanted bread for . . . for how long? I couldn't remember. I sipped water from time to time when I came to a spring or a well. At first I would taste it, looking for something in nothing. But I kept finding nothing and gradually I became heedless, cupping my hands into anything that the horse would drink. I knelt in muddy village squares and in farmyards. Once I opened my eyes to find I was sucking down green scum from a stagnant well. After that I hardly touched water either. My guts produced hot, angry fluxes that sent me reeling into the roadside bushes, but there didn't seem to be a time when that hadn't happened, so I climbed back onto the horse.

The road was empty, and its white dust had stripped away my taste and smell, leaving only a searing, chalky void. I found I didn't have enough strength to hold the reins, and after a while the horse began to meander. It kept to the road for a mile or so, and then wandered off to the side, through a gap in a high stand of reeds and out onto a stony hillside dotted with scorched plants. I breathed in, hardly noticing that my throat was rattling like a rusty bridle. The air caught on my dry tongue and colours built behind my eyes: pink and green dust, dark yellow from the dying bracken in the ditch; the black and white of the flies that clustered around the ears of the horse; the rich amber of the horse himself. So beautiful, this invisible world that only I could see. The horse plodded on. The stones grew whiter under his hooves. I needed to piss, so I began to tug at the reins, but the horse paid no attention. I pulled again, marvelling at the soft, greasy feel of the leather in my hands. I bent down, touched them to my lips, tasted salt, my own dirty hands. My face was in the horse's mane, pressed into the damp, wiry thicket, and my backbone seemed to have melted into a nice warm drizzle of syrup. *Everything melts*, I thought, seeing butter sinking into itself, the miracle of solid stuff becoming liquid. *Everything melts*. Now it was me dissolving, running down off the flanks of the horse like fat running from a joint of roasting meat. I was a drop of fat, falling lazily, heading for the welcoming coals. Then I was nothing.

∗ 26 ∗

WOOD KNOCKED AGAINST WOOD, THEN another sound: the dull clank of something being stirred in a clay pot. I opened my eyes, sat up, blinking. My eyelids were crusted together, but even after I had rubbed them clean it was hard to see. Smoke-blackened walls of rough stone . . . I was in a small room with a smoking fire at one end. By the fire, a squat black shape. It rustled. The clanking sound came again. Sitting up had made my ribs cramp together and I bent over, coughing. A hand touched the back of my neck, very gently.

A very old woman was studying me intently, her lined face even more puckered with what I took to be concern. But perhaps she wasn't so old. Sun, rain and smoke from cooking fires had cured her skin, creased it and painted the creases with indelible lines of soot. Her lips were thin and dry, and her eyes were bloodshot, rimmed with smoke-inflamed lids. She was all in black, with a black coif pulled down over thick, wiry grey hair. I jerked back in shock. I seemed to be lying on a bed of dried bracken, but shouldn't I be in an inn? No, I should be on the horse, following the pilgrims.

'Where's the horse?' I blurted. The old woman peered at me through fingers whose knuckles were swollen and crooked with rheumatism.

'The horse?' she repeated, in a heavy, sharp-edged accent.

'My horse. I thought I was riding him. I should be riding him.'

'You fell off,' she said, bluntly, and started to laugh: a thin, creaking trickle at first, then her shoulders began to shake. She took my hand in one of hers: it was very strong and hard.

'You fell off!' she said again, and her mirth doubled her over so that my nose filled with the smoky, animal scent of her hair.

'But how did I get here?'

'We found you in the bottom field. We brought you in. *And* your horse.'

'Thank you.'

'We thought you were dead. But then you pissed yourself, like a baby.' She chuckled. 'So we brought you in. Why were you in our bottom field?'

'I've no idea.' I coughed again, but things seemed to be more or less in order down in my insides, which seemed strange. My last memories were of odd things – pain, mostly, but a lot of ideas and half-dreams and nothing solid. I'd been trying to get to Rome, hadn't I? Following the pilgrims, with their constant squawking about food . . .

'I'm starving,' I said.

'You *were* starving. What were you doing, you stupid boy? Your guts were as empty as a blown egg.'

She reached behind her and produced a big, shallow earthenware bowl, which she rested on her knees. There was an old horn spoon leaning against the rim. She dipped it and raised it to my lips. It was heaped with something very white, running with gold. Without thinking I opened my mouth and licked it. Clear light burst on my tongue. The woman dipped the spoon, offered it again. I ate.

She made the ricotta from the milk of her goats, she told me. The honey came from wild bees in the chestnut forest nearby. She had tried keeping bees once, but . . . And she beat her arms about her head, giggling like a child. This was later, when I had managed to stand and walk a few tottering steps outside and she had helped me sit on a weathered block of ancient masonry jutting from the foundations of the house that served her as a bench.

She had brought me more of the ricotta, which I ate, slurping at the spoon like a child while my companion watched, beaming. My mind showed me the bees working high in the chestnut trees, swarming through the polished, ridged leaves and over the long white brushes of flowers. I saw the dark heart of the nest, dripping gold. Goats clattered over rocks and tore at cushions of herbs. Something was waking up inside me. It was all so familiar, this business of tasting, swallowing . . .

'That's done you some good,' she said. 'You look like a human being again.'

'Thank you.'

'Didn't say it was a compliment, did I?'

'I mean for this . . .' I licked the spoon. 'For finding me. My name is Nino Latini. Who are you, *donna*?'

'Velia,' she said, and nodded, as if to confirm it to herself.

A thought struck me. 'You said, "*We* brought you in." Is your man out in the fields, then?'

'Man?' She frowned.

'I mean your husband, Donna Velia,' I said quickly, thinking I had insulted her.

'My husband died,' she said starkly.

'I'm sorry.'

'Many years ago.'

'And so you live here all alone? But you didn't bring me in, surely?'

'My girls.'

'Girls?'

'My three girls. Good girls, strong and good. *You* won't see them, though.'

'Well . . .'

'They've gone up to the shepherd's hut.' She lifted her chin in the direction of the scarred ridge.

'But I'm not dangerous!'

'Oh, no? Stupid, though. Stupid enough to starve yourself and fall off your horse. I don't want my girls meeting stupid men, do I?'

'A fair point,' I said, and leaned back against the warm, uneven stones of the wall.

I went and lay down again while Velia went off to the spring with two buckets hooked to a wooden yoke across her shoulders. But first I checked through my belongings, which were piled next to the bed. With a stab of guilt I found that everything was in its place, including my purse, still full, because I'd spent next to nothing on the road. I dozed, lulled by the homely sounds of cooking. There was a sense of coming back into myself, the way a family opens up a house they have left empty for a long time. I was half aware of the smells from whatever it was that Velia was making, and they were good and wholesome.

Supper was a pungent, slightly bitter broth of wild chicory leaves, bread and herbs, with the pale, ragged orb of a poached egg suspended in the middle. *Acquacotta* she called it in her strange accent: cooked water. I sipped cautiously, remembering the disgusting *ribollita* from Siena. Had I eaten anything proper since then? Velia must have fed me while I slept, though, or I'd be dead now. The soup was delicious in the way that very simple things can be. There was no seasoning except for salt: a house like this could never afford pepper. But the olive oil in which Velia had fried the onions and garlic, and drizzled over the finished soup, was peppery enough: spiky and throat-catching, it prickled my mouth, balancing the bitter chicory and the bland crusts of bread. And there was dry cheese to grate into it, good salty pecorino with an earthy whiff of the cave where it had been aged. I savoured it for a long time, because I had never tasted it before – I'd never tasted any of these things. The oil was different from our Tuscan oil: thicker, somehow, and more flowery; and the cheese tasted the way the air smelled outside in the valley.

'What is the herb?' I asked, chasing a strange mint taste across my tongue. Strange, and yet familiar . . . It reminded me of something, and that something was Ugolino's tripe. It was almost the flavour that had eluded me for so long. Not exactly, though, not quite.

'*Mentuccia*,' said Velia, shaking her head. 'Never tasted *mentuccia* before?'

'I don't think we have it in Florence,' I said.

'Oho! Florence!' She clapped her hands. 'I've heard of that place! Aren't all the men sodomites? Perhaps I'll call my girls in after all – they'll be safe with a man from Florence!'

'That's not quite fair,' I said. As a Florentine I ought to have been enraged, but wasn't that the trouble? I wasn't a Florentine any more. 'I'm no sodomite.'

'I meant no harm, boy.' She patted my arm.

'Of course not.'

'Tell me about Florence, then. Sing for your supper.' Velia giggled, slyly.

So I did. I told her about the walls, and the *duomo*, and the churches, and the streets, and the market. I told her about the people, so many people, who were never silent, and the bells, and the dogs. About the bridges, the bathhouses, the taverns. I even told her about *calcio*. She listened, shaking her head gently.

'And you,' she said at last. 'What do you do in that place?'

'I'm a cook,' I told her. She threw her head back and laughed so hard at the ceiling I thought she might dislodge a slate.

'A cook! A cook who starves himself half to death!' She started to cough, and spat into the smouldering fire. 'A starving cook . . . This Florence sounds like a wonderful place!

What else do you have there: butchers who faint at the sight of blood, perhaps? Honest innkeepers? Bankers who can't add?'

'Not those, at least.' I told her about the counting tables in the market, by the wall of Orsanmichele, where the bankers did their business, pushing gold and silver and notes of credit across green felt.

'And people trust them?'

'They do. They have to. The House of Medici stands on trust,' I said, and laughed bitterly. 'Is there any wine, Donna Velia?'

'Not for you. The spring is pure. So all this money – what do people do with it?'

'Do with it?'

She nodded seriously.

'I mean they . . . they buy things,' I said, incredulous. 'Food. Clothes. Everything. How do you get your clothes, Donna Velia?'

'I make them.'

'But you buy other things.'

'I've never touched a coin,' she said proudly. 'What good would money do me, eh?'

'When you go to market . . . to sell your incredible cheese,' I said. 'You must sell your cheese, surely?'

'If I sold it, what would we eat, my girls and me? I'd have a hard time chewing silver.' She opened her mouth, revealing gums planted here and there with brown, crooked teeth.

'Buy other food!'

'Sell food to buy food? I can see why the bankers do so well in Florence, if people are that stupid.'

'A new roof, then.'

She roared with laughter. 'Aren't there enough stones in the fields for that? For a new roof all I need to do is plough!' She poured some more soup into my bowl, which I'd already emptied. 'Now tell me. Why were you on the road? Where are you going?'

'To Rome. I'm going to cook for . . . I don't know. Someone important.'

'The Pope?' Velia crossed herself, grinning.

'Yes, the Pope. Can I have this recipe, Donna Velia, for His Holiness?'

'Will he keep me out of hell if I give it to you?'

'This soup would get the Emperor Frederick sprung from hell.'

'Then I will. Now, eat some more. Cooks should be fat. You're a skeleton.'

I stayed with Donna Velia for another three days, and all we did, it seemed, was eat, and talk, and laugh. A dream woke me very early on the fourth day, while the sky was still dark, and I saw Velia sleeping in front of the fire on a rough pallet of bracken. *Dio cane!* How thoughtless I'd been . . . The old woman had given me her bed, and I had just assumed that she had a proper bedchamber somewhere, because in the city, didn't people sleep in their own rooms? I couldn't allow her to sleep on the dirty floor, and besides, I was feeling much stronger. I'd leave that day. So I waited until Velia woke up, lit the fire and went outside. She would often be gone for some time in the mornings, and I wondered if she went up to see her daughters – if indeed they even existed. I washed at the spring and set about saddling the horse. Hefting the saddle, I discovered that I was still quite weak, but in the end I managed to wrestle it onto his back. I tied my baggage to the cantle and sat down on the stone bench to wait for Velia.

'Off to see His Holiness?' she asked when she saw the horse saddled and me in my travelling clothes, which had been washed and now smelled of spring water and the stones of the valley. She didn't seem at all surprised, made no move either to make me stay or to speed me on my way. As I'd sat and watched the birds and the goats wander through the rocky fields I had planned to give Velia some of my money, but as I stood up and hugged her I knew she wouldn't want it. She couldn't eat silver, after all.

'You saved my life, Donna Velia,' I told her. All at once I was trying very hard not to cry.

'I expect so,' she said matter-of-factly.

'I need to thank you, but I don't think I'll ever be able to repay all you've done for me. All your kindness. You've been sleeping on cold stones, and your daughters, up there in the hills . . .'

'Repay kindness?' She snorted. 'Is that some Florentine thing, like selling food to buy food? Listen, boy. I found you and mended you, right enough, but when I find a bird that's been hurt, or a fox cub, I bring it in and save it if it can be saved. It's the proper thing to do.'

'But I'm a man. And you slept on the floor!'

'So what? I've done worse. Listen: if you want to salve your conscience, when you go to Saint Peter's church and light a candle for your dead mother, light one for me as well.'

'How did you know about my mother?'

'You talked in your sleep. And you haven't mentioned her since you woke up. Nor the other one: that Tessina. Will you be lighting a candle for her as well?' She cocked her head, bluntly curious.

'There's no need,' I muttered. 'But of course I'll light a candle for you. And if I get rich and famous I'll come and buy your cheese for the Pope's table. I'll build you a new house – a proper palace. And one for the goats. And your girls.'

'I expect I'll be dead by then,' she said seriously. 'So you'd better give me a kiss now and be off with you.' She presented one cheek and I kissed it, then the other cheek. 'Wait here,'

she said, and went into the house. There was some rummaging, and then she came out holding a bag. 'A cheese – not a
very good one, but it'll keep you fed. There's good red
onions in there, some bread and a bit of last night's chestnut
cake.'

'Thank you!'

'And a bit of honeycomb. Eat that first or it'll get everything sticky.'

'I will. Thank you, Donna Velia.'

'I'm glad you're better. Now go, and let me have a bit of
peace and quiet. Ride down the path – see that big rock, that
looks like a pig's snout? Follow the path to the right, cross
the stream, and keep riding until you get to the road. And
may God keep you safe, boy.'

There was nothing left to say, and so I climbed into the
saddle and turned the horse's head down the valley. I looked
back once, when I came to a tall thicket of reeds that cut
across the valley like a green wall. The tiny black figure was
standing next to her hut. I waved, and she lifted her arm,
turned, and walked away. I gave the horse a kick and soon
we were through the reeds. It was a surprisingly long way to
the road, but there it was at last, swarming with travellers and
farmers going in both directions under the blazing sun. That
night I slept in an olive grove, after dining on cheese and
honey, and before noon the next day I came over a crest in
the road and saw the walls and towers of Rome fluttering
gently in the heat haze.

27

THE ROAD IN FRONT OF the Porta del Popolo was a deafening, stinking riot of people, animals and wagons trying to get in and out of Rome. Pilgrims, some of them almost hysterical with excitement after Christ alone knew how many weeks or months of walking or riding, were yelling at each other, at men who might be Roman, at peasants and shepherds, as if noise alone would transport them into the holy city. Locals, clearly used to this madness, were pushing their way through the foreigners as if they were cattle. And there were real cattle, some with great curving horns, come down the Via Cassia from the Maremma; some fat and white, others smaller and grey, breeds I didn't recognize. There were no Chianina, I noted: Papá would have been disgusted.

Sheep were gathered in great smelly groups over which flies hung in rippling clouds. The sheep were guarded by large, tense dogs, which were the only things that the pilgrims seemed to leave alone. Wagons pulled by oxen and laden with barrels, with baskets full of agitated fowl, with stacks of pots, were jostling their way through the throng. The oxen lumbered along, placid but implacable. It was a wonder nobody was crushed – a company of cripples, come for a blessing or a miracle, were pushed into the path of one large team hauling a cart piled high with butts of wine, but the beasts lurched to one side, into a small knot of sheep, and the cripples, perhaps, had their miracle.

I had hardly set foot on the ancient, glass-smooth roadway of the bridge when a man walking next to me – a tall, ruddy-faced Frenchman – reached into his doublet and whipped out a large, greasy wad of parchment. Handing his staff to his neighbour, who seemed quite used to this behaviour, he began to riffle through the creased pages, and when he had found what he was looking for he held up the book, for so it seemed to be, and waved it at the sky.

'The Milvian Bridge!' he yelled in French, and the others in his party, who up until now had been trudging along in single-minded silence, all began to *ooh* and *aah* at the top of their lungs. 'On this bridge – on this *very bridge* – the Emperor Constantine defeated the armies of darkness – of paganism, I say!' I couldn't help feeling that this bridge, impressive though it was, seemed to be a bit small to host a battle, let alone one between good and evil, but as I was starting to smirk a bit at the pilgrims and their guidebooks and itineraries, it struck me. I was crossing the Tiber.

I hadn't been a brilliant pupil at the school my mother had insisted I attend, but I'd listened enough to know some Tacitus, some Cicero, Seneca, Livy. At one point I could have recited quite decent mouthfuls of Ovid and Virgil. And here I was, looking down at the Tiber. I remembered a bit of the *Aeneid*, some sort of prophecy, where the Tiber foams with blood – I'd held onto that, taken it home to recite to Papá, because I thought he'd approve of the blood, but instead I earned myself a lecture on how much blood it would take to make a river foam, based on the outfall of blood from the San Frediano shambles, and how Virgil was clearly a bit prone to exaggeration, like all poets. *Now, if butchers wrote history . . .*

It was all so long ago, and I'd never thought I would ever come to Rome. So I was no different from the pilgrims after all. Still, it was hard not to notice that this river was narrower, and muddier, than the Arno. We had left it behind by now, and were moving along surrounded by clouds of river flies and dust – and by chatter and laughter, as if crossing the river had lifted some vow of silence. My river was cleaner, wider, more noble. A little spark of Florentine pride began to glow in my chest, but just as it was spreading, the walls of Rome came into view.

Out of the flat flood plain of the river rose a high barrier of fox-brown brick, buttressed with many square towers. From the bridge the road ran straight as a knife, and along it we all poured: pilgrims, farmers, soldiers, lawyers, priests, monks, nuns, sheep, goats, cattle, geese, pigs. For the first time since leaving Florence I had the sensation of sinking into the crowd, just another bee in the hive, and it was a relief.

Beyond the walls I began to see spires, then roofs. I could see the gate now, a distant arch of white between squat, crenulated towers. The river had snaked around on the right and a hill rose beyond it, topped by a huge church. That must be Saint Peter's . . . And sure enough, the pilgrims had all begun pointing at it, waving their staffs around – God save anyone in their way. Like water in an irrigation ditch when the sluice is opened, the whole mass of travellers began to surge forward and I was carried along with them, struggling to keep the horse from trampling all those blundering Frisians and Catalans and Walesmen.

We finally squeezed through the gate, the horse and I. Was I expecting marvels? I was expecting disappointment, actually, having heard a lot of travellers' tales in the Porco, most of them about tarts or cut-throats (and occasionally, memorably, both). But instead I found confusion. Beyond the gate was a wide open space of ancient cobbles and brown dust. There was a fountain of sorts, and a collection of horse troughs all in use, around which spread a great stain of water and manure. Pilgrims, exhausted from struggling through the gate, stood around blinking. It was all too easy to spot the touts and the cutpurses. They were the men with great big smiles plastered across their leathery drinkers' faces, dressed in the fashions of last year, last decade. They wore jaunty, dirty hats and each had a knife, sometimes two, tucked discreetly into a belt or sash. It was painful to watch them single out their victims and cut them out of the larger crowd like dogs working sheep. Seeing a man on horseback, two of them headed for me, as confident and determined as a couple of ticks.

'Welcome to Rome, signore! You'll be wanting the best meal in the city, and the softest bed, and guess what? You're in luck!' The man's voice was cracked and full of the Roman twang. His mate was grinning and hopping from foot to foot, a mindless little jig. I wondered for a moment if he wanted me to throw him a coin, but I saw he was just excited at the prospect of robbing me.

'No thanks, friends,' I said.

'Oh, come now. You're our guest!'

'Am I? I just got here.'

'And that's why you need us to take care of you. Cheap at the price. Best guides in Rome, me and my cousin . . .' They leered in unison. And now they were shuffling forward, and the jigging one was reaching for my bridle. I did what I would have done in Florence: pulled back my coat as if to scratch my thigh, and let the hilt of my sword catch the light.

'I'm sure you'd like to take care of me, comrades, but I'm all right, thanks.' I could grin as broadly as them, so I did, and threw in a wink for good measure. Then I trotted the horse away across the piazza. *Don't look back.*

So I was feeling pleased with myself, my blood good and up. But I was riding towards a shambolic wall of buildings with narrow streets opening between them, and people were seething in and out of those streets: Romans, pilgrims in their groups, and pilgrims single or in pairs, shepherded by diligent, smiling cutpurses. I had felt quite at home for a moment, but now I understood: I was in Rome, and Rome was not

Florence. Those men I had just brushed off: this was their home, and they had sniffed me out straight away. They knew victims like my father knew steers, and they'd found one in me, all right. Cocky, with a full purse and a nice, expensive sword, not to mention a decent horse – sell the beast as transport, or keep him to eat. Flash boys must ride through that gate a hundred times a day, rolling their eyes with excitement like steers going through the gates of the shambles. So this was how those beasts felt as they sniffed the blood being spilled beyond those gates. Where was I going, exactly? Where was I planning to spend the night? And after, that the whole of Rome to search for Maestro Zohan, which would be like looking for a particular chestnut leaf on Monte Amiata. I'd just walked through the gate and already I didn't have a clue what I was doing. I didn't have a bloody clue.

In the end I did something I never thought I'd ever do: I asked a priest. There didn't seem to be a shortage of them in Rome, and every other building was a church, apparently. I rode down the street that happened to open in front of me, keeping a straight back, trying to look right at home. That was difficult, because the sights, the sounds, and most of all the smells of Rome were beating at my senses, all vying for my attention.

The first thing I noticed was something that wasn't there: that flatulent cabbage fug that had hung over every pilgrim trap between Florence and here. The pilgrims reeked of unwashed clothing and crusted sweat, but the Romans smelled of garlic and onions and wine, and although I knew that, as a foreigner I should fear them, every one, from that moment I began to like them as well.

The second thing that I noticed was that Rome was falling apart. A street of tightly packed houses would suddenly give way to a ruin, an open space, a house half fallen in upon itself, or an ancient building that more often than not was in better shape than its more recent neighbours. Washing hung between proud old columns, and pigs foraged among blocks of marble. Every so often there would be a church, or a fortified tower shooting up from some much older structure. The people in the street were mostly dark-skinned, tight-lipped, with steady, untrusting eyes. Eyes had watched this street for two thousand years or more – after so much time, people have good reason to trust no one. These were city eyes, though, and I understood them.

But what interested me more was the food being cooked behind all those walls. There were proper cooks at work. Pancetta frying in oil; garlic; stewing meat. Fish being grilled and boiled. I caught the steely tang of octopus from one doorway. From another, the familiar barnyard smell of tripe. There were more of those barnyard smells: all sorts of animal bits and pieces being prepared with wine, with herbs, rice . . .

A priest strolled out of a small church right in front of me. He had a pleasant, weary face and I decided to risk it.

'Father,' I asked, 'can you help me?'

He mistook me for a pilgrim: it was obvious from the way his face fell when he heard me. 'That way,' he said, auto-matically, pointing to my left. 'Down to that *palazzo* there – see it?' He didn't wait for a reply. 'Turn left just after it. There's a bridge – Ponte Sant'Angelo, yes? You'll see a big round building on the other side of the river? Cross over, and Saint Peter's is on your left. Basilica, yes? *Cathédrale?* And if you need somewhere to stay, go up past the big round building, listen for the sound of your own tongue, and there you'll find lodgings. God save you, my son.' He had his head down and his shoulders set. Instructions delivered, I was already forgotten.

'Father,' I said again. He fixed me with a look of tolerant

exasperation. 'I'm looking for the palace of Cardinal Federico Gonzaga. Do you know where that might be?'

'Cardinal Gonzaga?' The priest looked me up and down, properly this time. 'Ah – pardon me. I mistook you for a foreigner. You're a messenger, aren't you?' This seemed to bore him only slightly less, but at least he was paying attention.

'Not a messenger, Father. I'm a cook.'

'A cook? Nonsense. You are much too thin.'

'Honestly. My maestro is cooking for His Excellency the Cardinal, and he's summoned me from Florence.'

'Florence? Now then, I thought I recognized your accent. A foreigner after all, eh?' He laughed, good-naturedly, and I humoured him with a chuckle of my own. 'And you've never been in Rome before, have you?'

'No, that's . . .' Could you trust even priests in this city? I cleared my throat, and decided that, if I couldn't put my faith in a man of God, I might as well go back and ask those two bandits to put me up for the night. 'That's to say, you are right.'

'Well then. You'd better find your maestro before the thieves of Rome pick you clean – and they will, my son. They will. So – Gonzaga, eh? I know where he lives. San Lorenzo in Damaso.' He gave me directions, which seemed simple enough.

I should have listened more carefully to the priest's directions, because although he'd described a more or less direct route to San Lorenzo in Damaso, I soon found myself tangled up in lanes that curved, twisted back on themselves or stopped dead. Eventually I came to a place where men were burning lime in the doorways of their houses. The street was thick with acrid smoke and the lime burners, with their soot-black faces and red eyes, leering through the fumes like devils in hell, filled me with terror. When I emerged from that cursed realm I found myself in a thriving fish market. I asked my way again – a fishmonger, this time, gave me directions, and only because I bantered with him a little bit about gilt-head bream. I wasn't in a bantering mood by then, though. I was beginning to feel scared and very alone, not to mention hungry. The horse was cross with me. He needed water and hay, and was beginning to trip on the cobbles. I turned his head north, but no San Lorenzo appeared. Instead we came out onto the river bank. There was a bridge, and beyond it a castle of some sort – the big round building which the priest had told me about, no doubt. And beyond, Saint Peter's . . . I remembered Velia's parting words to me.

'Sorry, horse,' I whispered to the sweating beast, and we crossed over the river and rode up the long, straight road towards the basilica. I was back in a river of pilgrims, streaming towards the enormous building that dwarfed everything else around it. *The men who live in the moon must be able to see this*, I thought, and with that I surrendered and became one with the pilgrims.

There were men waiting to look after horses, and I left mine with someone who looked as honest as I could hope for, paying him well for food and water, though I took my pack with me. Then I joined the long, snaking line of men and women waiting to go into the church. I wandered slack-jawed through the atrium, which seemed as big as the Piazza Santa Croce back home; got lost in the glowing mosaic of Saint Peter walking on the Sea of Galilee that rippled and tossed like real water. Even though I was in a crowd of smelly, jostling people I gasped as I came through the entrance to the basilica itself, because it was so improbably vast inside that it seemed to have trapped Heaven itself, and I swear I felt my soul tugging like a sail, desperate to soar up into the distant spaces. But now the pilgrims were rushing off from shrine to shrine and I went with them, to touch every holy stone, shake my head in wonder over saints' tombs, popes' tombs, marvellous relics.

And then I arrived. There was the altar, and I could almost see the bones of the old fisherman lying beneath it, as though the stones had turned to glass just for me. I knelt, touched my forehead to the floor, lit my candles. One for Mamma, one for Donna Velia. And one for Tessina, though I didn't name her, just lit the expensive little finger of wax and set it in the sand, where its light merged into the wall of light lapping around Peter's tomb. And when I finally emerged into the late afternoon, I found that the honest-faced man had stolen my horse.

When at last I got to the palace of Federico Gonzaga, which wasn't far away at all – in fact, I'd ridden right past it – the sun was almost down and the city had turned a warm, generous orange. I was weary and parched with thirst, not having dared to stop anywhere on the way in case I was robbed, or worse. My hand was almost numb from gripping my sword hilt, and my feet were aching, because I had forced myself to strut, head in the air, stamping down on the cobbles of Rome as if I owned them, and all the time feeling as if the slaughterer's axe was hanging just above the head of this stupid, lost Florentine steer.

The cardinal's doorman was about to kick me down the steps but I told him I was the pupil of Maestro Zohan of Ferrara, come to join him from Florence, and I think I may have begged him to let me in. The doorman stared for a long time at my belly, as if my skills as a cook should be advertised there. He looked at my face, then my belly again, like a father confronted by his unwed and pregnant daughter. Then he snorted, shoved me down onto a bench just inside the door, and disappeared into the guts of the palace. When he returned, Zohan was rolling, bandy-legged, behind him, dressed in kitchen whites, and with his spoon tucked under one arm. I was so glad to see him I almost fell to my knees for the second time that day, but before I could make a move he had the spoon lodged against my breastbone.

'For fuck's sake,' he said.

'Maestro . . .' I rasped.

'Dancing Girl. Good. Get your slops on. My number two has died on me. Died, the bastard! The fucking bastard.'

'What, in the kitchen?' I stammered.

'No, not in the fucking kitchen! In the Tiber. They've just fished him out. Shouldn't have been diddling his landlord's precious little girl, should he, eh? Or go ahead: diddle to your heart's content, like I told him, but keep your stupid country mouth shut. So he did one and not the other. Though Christ alone knows how he found the time. I obviously wasn't working him hard enough, the prick.'

'I've got no whites,' I said.

'No whites? You really are an amateur, Dancing Girl. There are whites. You can have his whites, the fucking bastard. Eh? Come along, then.'

'I'm coming. Can I have something to eat?'

'Eat? You're as soft as a baby's bollocks, Dancing Girl! Have you come to work, or haven't you?'

'Of course I have, Maestro. What else is there?'

'What else indeed. Come along, then.'

I followed him along a corridor which looked and smelled like every servants' corridor I'd ever been in. 'It's good to see you, Maestro,' I said to his back. And it was. He was the only thing left of my old life.

'Hmm. Well, it's tolerably good to see you as well. Though you look like a cadaver. Tell me about it later, eh? There's work to do. A lot of work.'

'This city is a shit-hole,' I muttered.

'Isn't it? Isn't it, eh? And yet you didn't stay with His Magnificence, did you? Fucked up in some way, no doubt. It wasn't your food, or I'd have heard. We'll talk about it. But not now. Got your knives?'

'I've got nothing, Maestro,' I said. Christ, I was beyond caring. This corridor was endless, but the smells coming from the far end were good. 'And no, it wasn't my food.'

'That's all I care about,' said Zohan. 'So, Nino.' He paused in a stone archway. Flames were flickering beyond him, and there was a clatter of metal and a many-layered buzz of voices. A hundred scents came threading through the doorway. 'Welcome to the kitchens of Cardinal Gonzaga.'

28

My life became the kitchen of Cardinal Gonzaga and my tiny garret up under the eaves of his palace, barely wider than my outstretched arms. It was furnished with a bed, a stool, a crucifix and Sandro's little drawing of the Virgin, which I had glued to a board and fixed into an old ebony frame I had asked one of the cooks to buy for me. When the Roman sun licked the roof tiles just inches above my head, I roasted like *porchetta*, turning on the rack of my bed, spitted on the heat, trying to find an inch of cool linen. And on winter mornings my breath froze on the cracked pane of glass in the window, no wider than two of my fingers, through which I looked south-eastwards over a sea of roofs to a distant hill. I went downstairs to work, and upstairs to sleep. Zohan made sure I was well paid but the money, which I kept in an old leather spice bag hidden up in the rafters above my bed, just piled up until the bag became almost too fat to stuff into its space behind a loose brick. I never went out — why would I? Here in the palace I had everything I needed. Work and sleep. Everything was simple. You might think I was no better than a prisoner. True enough, though I might have said a monk in some severe order, in that I was free, but bound to those narrow confines by the power of my own will and desire.

Desire . . . Strange to think of a man desiring to be constrained and controlled so that his life is nothing more than a shifting pattern of walls, of endlessly repeated tasks. But that is what I desired more than anything. I wanted to be like a piece of meat laid in a box and buried in salt. I wanted to be drained and dried out, transformed from what I had been into something else. I didn't care who or what that might be, so long as it wasn't Nino Latini from Borgo Santa Croce in Florence.

So I kept to the *palazzo*. Not because I was afraid of the city outside, although that might have had something to do with it; but because cities were what I knew. Streets and people would remind me of who I had been. They would bring the old Nino back to life, and I was much too busy trying to bury him. I had another reason, though, a more practical one. The *palazzo* was not very far from the quarter of the Florentines. It was a small area that was full of Florentine banks, the warehouses of Florentine merchants, the homes of Florentine prelates, ambassadors, traders and even the odd Florentine prostitute.

On one of the few occasions when I had ventured further afield than the square outside the *palazzo*, I had wandered there by accident, drawn by my nose, because it was late in the afternoon and a thin aroma had found me through all the other complications of the Roman air. People were frying *battuta*. Beet greens, hot *lardo*. I followed like a sleepwalker, only to realize, as I caught sight of familiar heraldries on shopfronts and banks, where I was. There was danger here. I had cooked for many guests from Rome at Medici banquets, and they would have seen me on those nights when Messer Lorenzo had summoned me to the dining hall. I knew, too, that Bartolo Baroni would not have forgotten me. There could be people in these streets who had been sent to find me, men who knew that, by killing me, they would gain the favour of one of the most powerful men in Florence.

As an enclosed little world, the Gonzaga palace was better than most, I knew. It wasn't a prison, after all. I could leave. But I had no reason to. So I let Zohan work me as hard as he wanted, which was akin to giving a drunkard the key to a wine cellar. Zohan ordered, I cooked. The kitchen answered to me, like a country answers to its king. A king is answerable only to God, and here there was no god but Zohan. We were always busy. Our cardinal was a man of gluttonous appetite, though not the worst in Rome. Zohan had been hired to bring some of the magnificence of Lorenzo de' Medici's court to the cardinal's entertainments, but for all his reputation and skill, the maestro had found that his new employer did not wish to be amazed or challenged. His tastes were more traditional: he liked the dishes of Mantua, his home, so we cooked a lot of fish and duck, mounds of squash ravioli and rice. We boiled things. A lot of things.

Nino of the Porco, of the Palazzo de' Medici, would have been bored to death by the endless orders of honest Mantuan food, by the never-ending celebration of lake fish and fowl, the strange worship of gourds. But the Nino whose world was the kitchens, the garret room and the maze of corridors and stairs in between, seemed to have gone beyond boredom. The routine was part of the process that was turning me into someone else: the hollow man whose only concern was interpreting the motions of the maestro's wooden spoon. My one interest in the food was that it was perfect, and that it tasted exactly as it should. I ate it too – we did well in the kitchen, the cardinal being a generous employer – and soon I knew the food of Mantua as though I'd spent my life there. I could tell instantly if a pike had come from Lago Paiolo or Lago Superiore, and in what stagnant channel our rice had been grown. I was learning, always learning, and before long the cardinal's guests were congratulating him on finding a proper Mantuan cook.

I might as well have been. I cooked Mantuan ingredients into Mantuan dishes, and ate nothing but the food of Mantua. For all I knew, the cardinal's home town looked like the one I saw from my window: roofs and a distant hill. I didn't care.

The world was now inside. It existed as a stream of tiny revelations and discoveries. The taste of mud in the flesh of eels, and how it could be separated into a dingy rainbow of minerals; the different-shaped *cucuzza* gourds; the ways Mantuan salami was different from the Tuscan kinds I had grown up with. But all the tench, all the *cucuzza* gourds in the world weren't worth one spoonful of Ugolino's tripe stew.

29

Rome, 1473

I HAD BEEN HAVING A small argument with Donnanzo the *bottigliero*, the man in charge of the cardinal's wine. I felt he had been fobbing the kitchen off with inferior stuff, but he insisted the wine he gave us was quality.

'And doesn't it all just boil away to nothing?' he muttered.

'No, it doesn't. I—'

'Someone to see you, Messer Nino,' said a pot-boy, putting his head around the door. Frowning, I left the unrepentant Donnanzo and went back to the kitchen, where I found a tall, dusty man leaning against the table drinking a cup of wine while the cooks looked at him sideways.

'Hello, Nino,' he said.

'Good Christ! Arrigo Corbinelli!'

'None other.'

I gave him a great hug and kissed his rough cheeks. 'You look as if you've been crawling from one shit-heap to another,' I said, brushing his dust off my own clothes.

'Crawling through them, living in them,' said Arrigo.

He seemed to have grown even taller, and his face had lost almost every trace of youth. His cheeks were sunken and heavily shadowed with black stubble, and beneath dust-matted black hair his eyes glowered, huge and dark-ringed. He wore a doublet of Flemish black that must have cost someone a lot of money at some point, though it was coming apart, with stuffing curling from the shoulders. A bright green shirt stuck out from beneath it, hanging down over his bony arse; and a filthy scarf of red Turkish silk was wound around his neck. His hose had also been black at some point, but they had been patched with many different cloths and even some leather. His boots, though, looked as if they meant business, as did his sword, which looked Spanish and well used.

'So you really did become a soldier,' I said, marvelling.

'I did.'

'Madonna . . . And have you been in battles?'

'Little ones.' He held up finger and thumb, as if holding an invisible grain of rice. 'Skirmishes, down south. I took up employment with a *condottiere* in the pay of Ferrante of Naples, fighting the French, and he's been trying to push his French cousins out of his lands. And then there's the Turks, lapping at the east coast. Then my *condottiere* took a bribe and we went up north to join Montefeltro's army.'

'Remarkable. And what are you, a pikeman or something?'

'Pikeman? I'm an officer!'

'Come on.' I looked him up and down. 'Your bum's hanging out of your hose.'

'I'm an unpaid officer.' He laughed wearily. 'Which is why I'm going south again. Soldiering pays better in Naples – such is the rumour, at least. King Ferrante is always at war. There's opportunity. I'm just stopping here for one night, and, honestly, I didn't think I would find you.'

'You need to be fed, man. Come. Sit down.'

I led him over to the alcove where I had set up my tiny office: a pine bureau with drawers and a scribe's stool. Settling him on the stool, I rushed around the kitchen, piling a pewter dish with good things: sausage (which I'd made myself); cheeses; figs, a cold pheasant, some oysters I'd been saving for my own lunch. When I dumped it in front of him he fell on it like a spider enfolding a plump moth.

'When did you last eat?' I asked, amazed at how he was guzzling. I'd never seen Arrigo show any interest in food, and here he was, sucking down oysters as if they were little clots of ambrosia.

'In Florence,' he said between mouthfuls. 'I went to the Porco – of course! Still the same. Your uncle . . .'

'You saw Terino?'

'Fat as a tick, before you ask. I had to ask for credit and he almost shat himself.'

'And my father?'

'I called on him, of course. In the shop. He looks well.' Arrigo twisted his head away and fiddled with a pheasant leg.

'What else? Come on, Arrigo: what did he say?'

'Nino, he thinks you are dead,' he snapped. 'He doesn't look well at all, to be truthful. He hasn't had a word from you, so what is he supposed to think? Couldn't you have written him a letter?'

'It's been difficult,' I mumbled.

'Difficult? Your father looks as if he's got twenty unearned years on his shoulders. Everyone thought you were dead, Nino. But no, here you are, sleek as a cat . . . Could you not have written one bloody letter?'

'I thought . . . I thought it might be better to die,' I said. 'Considering what disgrace I've brought to the family.'

I sank down onto my heels and rested my chin on the desk, like a dog. I felt like a dog. All this time thinking about the food of home, and I'd neglected my own father. But it was true for all that: it didn't seem likely that he'd ever forgive me for the disaster I'd caused, and if he had forgiven me, I didn't want him to worry. You don't worry about the dead. You mourn them, but the misery they cause you only happens once.

'You idiot!' Arrigo burst out laughing, spraying me with fig seeds. 'You're a hero in Florence! You're Adonis, my boy, to everyone in the Black Lion – save for the Baronis, of course, but then again, the neighbourhood's love for you is the measure of how much everyone loathes the Baronis. Marco in particular.'

'I was worried that they'd do something to Papá.'

'No. Your father is quite safe. As I understand it, Il Magnifico himself has made sure of that by way of payment for his little jest, I suppose.'

'So I can go home!'

'Oh, most assuredly not.' Arrigo shook his head gravely. 'No. If you go back to Florence, all the disasters you imagined will come to pass. While Bartolo and Marco are alive, you aren't safe anywhere north of Viterbo. And they are both very much alive.' He paused, licked his fingers, studied me expectantly.

'You haven't said anything about Tessina,' I said, forcing the words out.

'Do you want me to?'

'No! Yes. Of course I do.'

Some nervous impulse jerked me to my feet, and before I could stop myself I had walked right around the kitchen. My head was spinning and my legs felt like stilts. They took me right out into the street and halfway across the little square before I got them under control. Arrigo was waiting for me, polishing off the last of the sausages. Concern for me appeared to be fighting a losing battle against greed. But when he saw me he got up, took me by the arm. The other cooks were watching us as if we had gone mad. Arrigo, ignoring them, led me back outside.

'I have something for you,' he said, reaching into his doublet and extracting a much-creased oblong of parchment. 'Although I thought I might be carrying a letter for a corpse, I reasoned that I could at least lay it on your grave, should you have died somewhere convenient. And seeing as I almost got myself killed fetching it out of Florence, you can at least settle down and read the thing.'

He held it out. I stood there, staring at the filthy parchment, at the loops and slashes of ink. Then I reached out and took it from his hands, feeling as if I had been entrusted with something as fragile as gold leaf. I broke the seal and slowly unfolded it.

Nino,

Dearest Nino. I am writing to you even though I do not know if you are still living. But, if this comes into your hands, I will know you are safe. I will feel happy the moment your hands touch the paper. Know also, my dear one, that I too am safe. I hope that you care. It seems not impossible that you may care very little. I pray that you are not greatly changed by what has happened. I pray that you are living a life as different from mine as it is in God's power to contrive.

I heard that you had gone to Rome from the gossip that comes through Bartolo's dealings with the Palazzo de' Medici. And Arrigo told me what really happened that day. I will not speak of it again, except to say that it was no beffa *to my eyes, and that I would have gladly braved the scorn of every tongue in Florence to come down from my window and ride away with you. My Nino, you are blameless in my eyes, a thousand times over. But not, you should know, in Bartolo's. He has not forgiven and never will, I fear. Forgiveness, along with mercy, is a quality alien to his heart. And Marco is filled with hatred. Do not come back to Florence, Nino. You will not be safe in our republic as long as they are both alive.*

And if you ever had a mind to fear for me, do not. I am quite well. My life has not changed greatly – I still live in a room with a window, and if I look down on a different street, is any street in Florence so different from another? My husband – I am a wife now, strange as it is to write it – does not trouble me. He is old and though in fair health, he can but attempt to perform the duties of a husband – enough for there to be no question of an annulment, but no more. Mercifully, no more. Messer Bartolo is aware of his shortcomings and that, perhaps, is punishment enough for a proud man. His only sin, besides being choleric and entirely engrossed in his own self-regard, is to have desired a toy he could not use. I am that toy and for now I lie, neglected, on a dusty shelf. I pity Bartolo rather too much to hate him, which I am glad of, because my world is too small to hold strong things like hatred. I wish that I had no room for fear, either; but alas, I fear Marco – enough, though, of the Baronis. Ah! I forget, for an instant, that I am one of them, and it is such a sweet forgetfulness.

I have two escapes, so I am blessed. One you will have to ask Arrigo about, because to tell you here would waste ink and time. The other is – have you guessed? – our dear Convent of Santa Bibiana. Poor Sister Beatrice is still alive. We say the Lord must be keeping her for some great purpose, which is perhaps to save me from the Baronis, if only for a few hours every week.

I will stop writing now. Arrigo is waiting in the chapel. He believes that he can find you. I will lie on the cold stone in front of the Virgin every day until I have some word from you. I will pray without cease that my words reach you and that you read them with a little warmth.

If Arrigo finds you, and you read this letter, write back to me at the convent with a little news. Of your doings, and of the place you live. I will not ask for more. I cannot hope for more. I do not dare to hope for very much, these days.

    Tessina di Bartolo Baroni

I folded the letter very carefully, then unfolded it again and let my eyes run across the eccentric loops and slashes of Tessina's hand. Tessina's hand . . . I folded it again and stood there dumbly, holding the thing in front of my chest. I was shaking, as if I'd just run from one end of Rome to the other.

'You saw her, then?' I said, trying to look at Arrigo, except that my eyes kept focusing on a flock of pigeons wheeling and settling on a rooftop opposite.

'I saw her,' said Arrigo gently. 'In the convent – did she say? It was the strangest thing: she'd sent a letter to my father, months ago, telling me to meet her at Santa Bibiana on any Wednesday of the year, if I ever came back to Florence.'

'And nothing's happened to her? She's well? She looks the same?'

'Completely.'

'Did she tell you anything? About Marco Baroni? I think she is trying to say . . .'

'There is nothing wrong, Nino. Calm yourself. Marco is a *testa di cazzo*, of course, but he's terrified of his father. Tessina's quite safe from him. I'm afraid that her lot is the same as ten thousand other married women in Florence. She's been put away in a drawer like a contract. Think about it this way: she is an investment, so she's as safe as one of Bartolo's warehouses of Flemish cloth.'

'And this other thing? She says she has another escape, and that you will tell me about it.'

'Ah! Your friend Sandro Botticelli, who sends his love and a kiss, has decided that Tessina's is the only face he will paint. He saw the painting that Rosselli did of her – a Virgin, I think. Bartolo had it displayed at the wedding. Meanwhile, the Signoria gave him a grand commission, and he managed to get Tessina as his model. Sandro is famous now, and so is Tessina.'

'What does Bartolo Baroni say about that?'

'Oh, by all accounts it has bloated his self-love out of all proportion. He is married to the loveliest woman in Florence, and he makes sure that everyone knows it.'

'Will there be more paintings, though?'

'Sandro is painting her again – probably at this very moment. And of course the other artists are all fighting each other to paint her as well.'

'This is strange news, Arrigo. Wonderful, though. But did she say anything?'

'She hasn't been struck dumb. Is that what you mean?'

'Come on, Arrigo! What did she talk about?'

'The convent roof, the price of chicken livers . . .'

'*Bastardo!* Did she say anything about me?'

'About you? Dear God. What has become of you in this horrible city, Nino? Did you play *calcio* for the Black Lion, or was that some other Nino Latini? Did you fight Baldassarre Venini outside the San Michele Berteldi bathhouse for treading on your shoe? You're a Florentine, man!' He burst out laughing. 'And yes. She didn't lure me to that bloody convent to discuss my various deeds of bravery. She didn't ask about me once, in fact. Satisfied?'

'Satisfied,' I said, joining in the laughter, though not really feeling it. 'And you said you had some trouble with the letter?'

'That was afterwards, and it didn't have anything to do with that thing. I ran into Marco Baroni outside the Chiassolino.'

'The brothel? Were you a customer?'

'Alas, no. I couldn't afford it.' He chuckled. 'Marco could, though. Came out grinning like a cannibal. Then he saw me – went for his sword, but it was tangled in his laces. Hadn't done up his hose, the filthy bastard. So I ran.'

'Wait – you *ran*?'

'Had to. Your uncle took my sword as surety for dinner.

So yes, I ran – I've learned something of the soldier's art! Went back to my father's house, begged a loan from him, crept back to the Porco and paid off your uncle, who is a bastard of a *bardassuole*. Got my sword, got my horse and left the city at sunrise.'

'It's becoming quite the habit,' I said.

We went back inside. I had stopped shaking, thank Christ, because I had to give the kitchen its orders for the evening's meal. Then I took Arrigo around the corner to a hostelry which I had heard some speak of as honest and free of vermin, paid them in advance for his room and board, then told him where to go for his supper, because I had to get back to work. He was to come and wait for me at the palace at midnight, if he was still awake. I ran up to my garret and hid Tessina's letter up in the roof next to my money. Then I went back downstairs and spent the next two hours gutting and preparing a great slimy pyramid of prime Mantuan tench.

I saw Arrigo off the next day, and he promised to return as soon as he could, in triumph, or at least in new clothes, as he put it. But he never did. We wrote to each other often, but three years later the letters stopped. And years after that, I heard that he had died of marsh fever while campaigning against the Turks in Puglia. He never came north again, never tasted *battuta* and tripe and *arista*, never played another game of *calcio*. But I think he was happy nonetheless. He had freed himself from something – I never understood what, but perhaps it was Florence herself. Unlike me, he left of his own free will and, unlike me, he never looked back.

30

Tessina,

From the day we last saw each other, from that hour onwards I have spent my time trying to forget you. I tried for your sake, thinking that your life would be better if I vanished from it completely. But I confess that I also tried for my own sake, because the last glimpse of your face carved itself into my heart and my mind, and it seemed to me that you were looking down from your window and feeling those things which my behaviour deserved: disgust, rage and, most horrible of all, pity. That was the hurt I suffered, far worse than if the Baronis had hacked me with swords. I was cut in the heart and – for this more than anything else I ask you to forgive me – my vanity was sorely wounded. I have tried to become a new man in Rome – not in the way we speak of such things in Florence: I will never care again for social standing or wealth. No, I have sought to unmake Nino Latini and replace him with an entirely different creature. But I have not succeeded. My experiment has failed. I am the same man, as I discovered when I opened your letter.

Your hand held the pen that set ink to paper. My eyes read the words. From Tessina to Nino in only three leaps – suddenly, the wide world seems as narrow as one of our Roman alleys, where you may lean out of an upper window and grasp the hand of your neighbour across the way. I have longed to feel the touch of your hand. Now I have felt it, and I am no longer living on the edge of the world, exiled from everything I know and understand.

*I beg you to forgive me for my silence. I could not have
dared to believe that you wished to hear from me. I have
written to no one, if that is any consolation. I have
neglected my family, my friends. I spend my days wishing
I was somewhere else – you know where, Tessina. And
there is no one else. I have friends, but my heart is back in
Florence. It is a shade that lingers underneath your
window, in the shadows. If you look, you will not see it.
But it is there.*

*I will send this to Santa Bibiana, addressed to Sister
Beatrice. If it reaches your hand, read it with forbearance,
knowing that I am a cook and not a scholar, and do not
have the skill to lay out my soul in words. But I have tried
to put myself here, in the ink. There is a blot: my quill
needs sharpening. I have tasted the ink. It tastes . . . of
what? Tessina, perhaps you will wet your finger, dab and
lick. And tell me, as you used to do?*

No more now. With all my love,
Nino

THE CARDINAL SENT A COURIER to Florence every week,
and I paid the man more than the going rate to deliver my
letter to the Convent of Santa Bibiana. I watched him ride
off early in the morning, wishing fiercely that I could take his
place.

But after that, the city no longer terrified me. It was as if I
had recovered from a long and fevered illness – the delirium
was gone, the fever broken. It seemed impossible that I had
imprisoned myself for half a year. My terrors, I found, had
been nothing but my experiences of that first day in Rome,
when I had lost myself, then lost my horse. Rome was a
foreign place, and I was a stranger here. Florence was many,
many miles away by road, and even further, it seemed, in

space, or in my imagination. I had learned to exist beyond the walls that had held me tightly as a child, and as a boy straining into manhood. I still longed for Florence in every atom of my being, but I could exist here, too. It was possible, just, for a man of Florence to be, if not a man of Rome, at least a man *in* Rome.

It was the maestro who broke the last remaining threads of the spell. A few days after Arrigo's departure, Zohan marched me to the door of the *palazzo*. 'We need *bottarga*,' he said. He shoved some coins into my fist and pushed me out into the square. I looked back at him, blocking the doorway. We both blinked at each other. Then I set off into the unknown. But not so unknown: I had found the fish market all those months ago, and remembered that it was somewhere to the south-east of San Lorenzo in Damaso, near the quarter of the lime burners. There was a great smoke and stink going up eastwards, not very far away. Before long I had found the fish market, bought the best cured mullet roe I could find. And then . . .

I could have gone back to the *palazzo*. But instead I walked in the opposite direction. I had worked with the maestro long enough now to know what was in his mind, and this was what Zohan wanted me to do: the spoon would be waiting to rap my skull if I came back too soon. The fish market was utterly different from the one in Florence. Fish was laid out on the marble steps of ancient buildings and on great blocks of stone that must once have been part of temples or palaces. Everyone was yelling: fishmongers, fish-wives, customers, urchins. It seemed like chaos but then I began to pick out repeated words. The crowd was like a great choir singing strange and angry music, but there was a tune and a beat and I surrendered to it. I wandered along, examining the fish and watching the army of thin and dirty cats who stalked through the market, fought each other for fish guts and heads, or sunned themselves on window sills. The market people were mostly short and swarthy. The women wrapped their black ringlets in scarves of loud silk, while the men looked as if they were dressed for a riot. To a northerner like me it all looked foreign and exotic, and dangerous as well, but as I walked on I reflected that, if all the stories I'd heard were true, I would have been knifed by now. At the very least I would have seen someone else get themselves knifed, but the only blood flowing came from the fishes.

'Are you buying or looking?' the sellers yelled at me. 'If you're buying, buy. If you're looking, *vattela a pijà 'n der culo*!' And as they turned to their next target, I was already forgotten.

Drifting along, I brushed past priests in fine robes, past the whores who were eyeing up the priests and the pimps who were watching their investments. I kept walking until I came to a road of white stones leading up to a sort of rough square. A large and rather shabby church stood on a low crag next to a big forbidding building crowned with battlements and a small tower. All had seen better days, and there was a large number of beggars lolling about or hobbling up and down the uneven steps that led up to the church. But there was also a steady stream of official-looking men going in and out of the fortified building. I strolled over, asked the least decrepit beggar what the buildings might be. He looked at me as if I'd fallen from the skies.

'The Campidoglio,' he croaked. 'That's the senators' palace.' I thanked him and gave him a small coin. He cocked his ear at my accent. 'Are you from Perugia?' he said, grabbing my sleeve.

'No,' I said, shaking him off.

'I'm from Perugia,' he jabbered. 'Or Perugia's from me, if you like. They called me the Proctor! Did you know that? The Proctor!'

'Jolly good,' I told him, and hurried off, seeking shelter behind a gathering of officials. The beggar had already found someone else to talk to, though, and I walked over to where the land fell away in a sort of cliff that was half masonry, half crag, and beyond . . .

I let my breath out, very slowly. Beyond was a great oblong basin contained by a line of buildings to the left and by the slopes of another steep hill on the right. Beyond, I recognized the huge drum of the Colosseum. A haphazard forest of marble ruins all push up towards the light like mushrooms after an autumn shower. A monstrous arch, so low to the ground that a man would have to stoop to get under it.

'Do you even know what a proctor is, you little turd?' The beggar had come up behind me. I bowed politely, cast around for a means of escape, and went over to the great archway. It was larger than I had thought, and the roof, festooned with thin stalactites, soared above my head. I disturbed a large rat, which scuttled up the wall and vanished into a crack. Back outside, I stood in the thin sunlight, studying the figures carved into the façade, the swarming warriors, the angel leaning over the archway. *Sandro would love this*, I thought. *Papá*. And Tessina.

Ghosts . . .

As if I had invited them, they came to me. The ghosts of the living: there they were, just out of sight behind a column, stepping into the shadow of that ruined wall. My father. Carenza. Sandro Botticelli. I left the arch, walked towards an arc of columns that held up a smashed pediment, and a host of invisible Florentines parted for me, whispering in dialect. And Tessina: I could almost smell the spices of her hair, the flowers of her skin. Everything was coming at me: all the things I'd kept at bay outside my attic room. I should have stayed inside, staring at the blank walls, until the ghosts packed up and went home. But they never would, because they lived inside me. I began to run, but I tripped over a half-buried stone and sprawled headlong. I just lay there, muttering Florentine curses into the chalky soil, which didn't smell like home. Nothing smelled like home. I half felt, half imagined that Tessina was leaning over me, kneeling down, hand fluttering just above my hair. I screwed my eyes shut.

'Have you ever been to Perugia?'

'What?'

He sighed, peevishly. 'Have. You. Ever been. To Perugia. Eh? Where they call me . . .'

'The Proctor. I remember. I come from Florence. Do they call you the Proctor there as well?' I asked bitterly, sitting up to find the beggar perched on a fluted marble cylinder a few feet away. 'Because I've never heard of you.'

'Oh. Well, that explains it. You wouldn't have, would you? It's in Perugia that they call me the Proctor.'

I picked myself up, pinched my nose. I had to do something to banish the haunted feeling that had come over me. I was craving something . . . Then I had it. Ugolino's tripe. A bowl of tripe would let me find my way home, at least in my soul. I just wanted that taste, which was Florence, the market . . . The beggar was staring at me, or possibly through me. He had matted brown hair, an ash-coloured beard that had twisted into solid ropes. His face was almost black with filth, but his eyes, though they were surrounded by rings of sore, angry skin, were strangely gentle.

'Listen,' I said. He came to attention, hound-like. 'Where can I get . . . Who makes the best tripe in Rome? Christ, as if you'd know.'

'Know? I do know. Domenico Fiorentino is the man.'

'Fiorentino? Can you take me to him?' A Florentine,

making tripe? That had to be a good omen. 'And if you do, I'll buy you luncheon.'

The Proctor hawked and spat, stuck his hand down into his breeches, so caked in filth that they were glazed and shiny, pulled it out again and studied the palm, as if he'd found a map between the cheeks of his arse. 'Certainly,' he said, and set off, striding with knees bent so that his body bobbed violently and his hair danced like Medusa's snakes. I jogged to keep up.

He led me through old, decrepit but inhabited streets. I followed, not too close, because he stank and his strange locomotion was causing his clothing to heat up and stink even more. At last we emerged into a square in front of a church with an elegant colonnade. Under one of the arches a man had set up a brazier. My heart jumped: the brazier, the big copper pots steaming thickly in the cool air. The cook was stout and bald but he was stirring one of his pots with a long wooden spoon and I found myself squinting, trying to see Ugolino there in his place.

'Fiorentino,' said the Proctor, giving something between a bow and a curtsy.

'Indeed.' I marched up to the tripe seller, put up two fingers. The man grunted and ladled out two bowls, looking on with frank disgust as I handed one to the beggar, who immediately squatted down where he stood and bent over his prize like a ragged hawk protecting its kill. I blew, dipped my spoon, tasted.

Celery. Pepper. Broth made from cow bones, not that fresh. The tripe was good, though: well cleaned, well boiled. Some sort of mint, very strong: I chased the pungent oils with my tongue, searching, searching. The taste came apart. Something myrrh-like, throat-catching; like thyme chewed with a juniper berry. I slurped again, tasting, not wanting to admit to myself what I'd found. But there was no escaping it.

This was a Roman taste. It was the food I had smelled being cooked in these streets. I smelled it on the clothes of the men who worked for me.

'Are you really from Florence?' I asked the tripe seller.

'Florence? Are you calling me a *buggerone*?' He drew himself up, bristling.

'No, no. Because of your name – Fiorentino, yes? I'm from Florence, and I thought . . . Never mind. I'm sorry.' I backed away, slurped up more tripe, though I wasn't very hungry any more. The beggar, meanwhile, had already finished. He stood up, ran his finger around the empty bowl, licked it.

'*Trippaio!*' he barked. 'Have you ever been to Perugia?'

I slipped away as the tripe seller was forcibly informing the beggar that he didn't give a nun's fart what a proctor was or wasn't. The tripe was settling, warm and wholesome, in the alembic of my belly. The Proctor had been right: Fiorentino was a good cook. The best tripe in Rome? I doubted that, but I knew the very best bowl in the city would still have that Roman taste. The taste I wanted must be here somewhere. I would find it. I had the rest of my life to find it.

In the days that followed that first outing, it was as if Rome had made up her mind to welcome yet another outcast. Little by little, I began to catch glimpses of another place. The maestro had put me in temporary charge of buying, because, as he said, I'd never have bought an egg back home in Florence if I hadn't seen the hands of the man who had fed the hens. So I got to know the fishmongers and the herb sellers, the cheese merchants and, of course, the butchers. The fruit and vegetables that came into Rome from the lush fields of the *campagna* were, I was forced to admit, superb. The butchers, to my professional eye, were slovenly and seemed to waste time concocting schemes to pass off rotten meat to their customers. There didn't seem to be the strict laws governing their behaviour that we had back in Florence, and for every man selling the best meat, fit for a cardinal's table, there were five others whose blocks seethed with maggots. I wouldn't have eaten a Roman sausage from a common butcher, not if you'd paid me a golden florin.

My life was changing in other ways. Zohan introduced me to a man called Pomponio Leto, a scholar with a long, straight nose that bisected his face like the gnomon of a sundial. He lived on the Quirinal Hill, in a tumbledown old house, half swallowed by ivy and fig. He seemed to live on little except garlic and onions. From Leto I learned much about the Rome that had once been, because he loved company and knew countless ruins, tunnels, tombs and pits that he delighted in exploring with interested friends. And from Leto I also learned of the strange ways that the ancients had discerned the senses: as the play of atoms of food colliding with organs of taste and imprinting memories upon them. Given that I existed, so I felt, largely as a concatenation of memories and emptiness, this made a good deal of sense to me.

I also met my employer, Cardinal Federico Gonzaga, a tall, ruddy-faced man with black hair, upturned eyebrows and a little rosebud mouth. Having known him only through the limitations of his taste in food, I was surprised to find he was sharply intelligent and decidedly regal. The food he ate came from muddy, sluggish waters and I would have expected it to affect his temperament, but not at all. And as spring came on, and then summer, I seemed to be happy.

But half of my soul was still in Florence. I had known a man, a butcher, who had accidentally hacked off most of his left hand while cutting up a side of beef. All that was left was the thumb and index finger, but he claimed to be able to feel his other, absent fingers, so much so that he often went to twist the ring that had once rested on one of them. In a way I could still feel my other life, or the lack of it. Sometimes I would be walking down a Roman street and be overcome by the sensation that I was in some Florentine place. But these things existed only in my mind. I craved to see or touch the ghosts of home. But more than anything, I longed to taste them.

If my new friend Pomponio Leto had explained it correctly, a taste will remind one of something. But that something is purely a conjuration of our mind-atoms. Sharp atoms give the sensation of bitterness; soft, round atoms are sweet. Bitterness comes from the atoms tearing the surface of the sense organs. But that bitterness – from a wild plum, for example – does not come from the plum at all, but from the sense organs. 'It is all in here, and nowhere else,' Leto had said, placing a finger in the centre of his forehead.

'So the plum isn't bitter?' I had asked. He'd shaken his head.

'The plum has no qualities at all. Everything you – we – experience is entirely subjective. You may taste this wine . . .' He had tapped my cup and I'd sipped, obediently, 'and find it sharp.' He had taken a sip himself. 'I, on the other hand, think it slightly honeyed. Who is right? The wise Democritus would say we both are, because the taste is dictated by our own disposition, do you see? The wine would taste different to you if you had a cold, would it not? And when you were younger, the taste might have been too strong, whereas now you might crave a more robust flavour. And on and on, everything relative, everything dependent on infinitely variable conditions within ourselves.'

'Who, then, can tell me what this wine really tastes like?' I had demanded. On the one hand, this all seemed like the kind of sophist nonsense that had been bandied around at the Palazzo de' Medici. On the other, if it were true . . .

'No one!' cried Leto in triumph. 'Democritus says we know nothing genuine about what exists, except what changes in accordance with the conditions of the body, and what enters it and presses upon it. Everything is unknowable – simply atoms, and emptiness.'

That seemed quite hopeless. My own feeling was that taste worked deeply with memory, and that the act of remembering was more like visiting a place that existed, somehow, inside the skull. The more accurately a taste was recreated, the more vividly the place would be summoned up. So I set about recreating Florence in tastes, and that meant one thing: the stewed tripe of Ugolino.

The first thing I did was revisit the *trippaio* outside San Pietro in Vincoli. He didn't want to give me his recipe so I bribed him – not very much, which only confirmed my suspicions about the probity of Romans as compared to Florentines. I could have bribed Ugolino with a gold ingot and he still wouldn't have given up his secrets, but Domenico the tripe seller caved in for a couple of copper *baiocchi*, and thought he'd got an excellent deal. The tripe was made exactly as I had guessed: bone broth, salt, pepper, onions, garlic, huge amounts of celery, tripe and that herb, which Domenico called *issopo*.

I went to the herb market where, it appeared, everyone had their own version of *issopo*, which wasn't a mint at all, but a kind of savory. Over the course of a few weeks I bought every mint-like herb I could get my hands on and experimented with them in the kitchen after hours. Some were good and others were vile, but none of them was Ugolino's flavour. I began to cook big pots of tripe just to fiddle with the ingredients, and in the end I could knock out a *trippa alla Fiorentina* that, if you were suffering from catarrh, you might mistake for something cooked by Ugolino on a bad day. But Ugolino never had bad days. I even convinced the maestro, who said I'd cracked it, and to stop wasting my time – but then again, coming from Ferrara, he didn't have a clue about tripe.

Though Ugolino's recipe was still a mystery, I consoled myself with the thought that it had taken him a lifetime to perfect it. So I moved on to other recipes, still trying to cook my way back to Florence, but there was always something amiss. The food of a place should be the sum of its parts, and Florentine dishes cooked in Rome tasted wrong, no matter how slavishly I followed my old recipes. I found a couple of cook-shops run by Florentine men, but even their food wasn't right. When I talked to them, they just shrugged and said they'd been away for years, and what did I expect? I got quite angry at one of the men and told him he'd betrayed Florence, but he just laughed in my face. Why, he asked, was I getting so upset about *battuta*? I wasn't about to admit it to a greasy-aproned man in a cook-shop but I was scared that one day I, too, would stop caring about the proper ratio of onion to garlic to carrot, and then what would become of me?

I requested an audience with my employer. The cardinal was at home, and he summoned me immediately, thinking, no doubt, that I needed some information on the following week's banquet. Instead I asked him whether I was doing a good job in recreating the food of his beloved Mantua. He looked surprised and pleased.

'In every way,' he said.

'I am glad. Is there anything you would wish to change?'

'At this moment, not a thing.'

'So the dishes are identical to what you might expect from a Mantuan cook, in a Mantuan kitchen?'

'Again, in every way.'

'Your Eminence, might I ask whether the fact that most of our ingredients come from the lakes and fields of Mantua affects, in your opinion, the taste?'

'Why, of course it does!'

'So if I were to prepare, say, a dish of pike, but using fish from Lake Nemi, it would taste less authentic?'

'But, my dear young man, certainly!' He frowned. 'Has the estimable Maestro Zohan been making noises about kitchen economy? I assure you, I can afford to have my fish sent from Lombardy.'

'No, no, Your Eminence! I would never trouble you with such a thing. I merely want to satisfy myself that Your Eminence finds my dishes to your liking. And if I may beg your indulgence . . .' I fidgeted with my cap. The cardinal was perfectly friendly, but he was also one of the most powerful men in Rome. He was used to the babbling of minions, though, and he inclined his head patiently. 'I am a humble butcher's son and certainly no humanist, but the processes of taste fascinate me from a . . . a professional point of view. Can Your Eminence tell me what it is that signals a food is from Mantua and not from one of the marshes south of here?'

He blinked. 'My dear man,' he said slowly, as if addressing someone remarkably stupid. 'I know it is from Mantua because I have seen receipts from Mantua. Combined with the knowledge that the recipes you use were written by my personal cook, a Mantuan to his fingernails, it tells me the food I have eaten is, as you put it, authentic.'

'Excellent . . . excellent, Your Eminence.' I sighed inwardly. My suspicions had been correct: the cardinal must have a palate as refined as hopsack cloth. 'If you find my preparations satisfactory, I cannot seek any greater happiness.'

I bowed out and went back to the kitchens feeling more depressed than ever. Perhaps if I sat down to a meal perfectly convinced that all the ingredients came from Florence, as did the cook, and ate while I pored over the housekeeping expenses to satisfy myself of every item's provenance, I would be transported . . . It didn't seem likely. I set to preparing a fine basket of woodcock, reflecting that I could give the man upstairs a dish of thrushes netted in the *palazzo*'s garden instead, and he would never know the difference.

31

CARDINAL GONZAGA ENTERTAINED OFTEN IN those days. He was in favour at the Vatican and so there was a never-ending supply of guests for his table. During one banquet, Zohan called me into the dining room.

'I want you to meet an old employer of mine,' he said. A rather long-faced man was speaking with the cardinal, who towered over him, looking down on the soldier through his thick black fringe like a patient horse. Gonzaga was far too well bred to flinch when he saw his cook approaching him through the company, which left me to do all the flinching. But the long-faced man ignored me. Catching sight of Zohan, he let out a roar.

'Zohan of Ferrara! I thought you had died in Palermo!'

'That is Gian Giacomo Trivulzio,' Zohan whispered to me. '*Condottiere*, and weathercock for all prevailing political winds. I was his cook here in Rome, many years ago.

'Sir, might I introduce Nino di Niccolaio Latini of Florence, lately the personal cook and dietary to Lorenzo de' Medici. Nino, this is His Excellency Gian Giacomo Trivulzio of Milan.'

'Delighted,' said Trivulzio.

'Dietary . . . Good heavens,' said the cardinal. 'Is this true? Why was I not told?'

'Ah . . . Your Eminence, that is to say . . .'

'Family matters necessitated that Messer Nino leave Florence,' said Zohan quickly. 'But I can vouch that he left with the . . . the fulsome blessings of Il Magnifico.' For one horrible moment I thought he would wink at me, but he did not.

'How extraordinary. I find myself speechless,' said the cardinal. 'I assumed you were one of Maestro Zohan's protégés, nothing more. How exceedingly fortunate for my kitchens.'

'Do you have a dietary, Gonzaga?' demanded Trivulzio. 'In Milan, no man of consequence is without his own dietary.'

'I do not,' said the cardinal, frowning.

'Then make him yours. I know for a fact your brother in Mantua has one. Your cousins as well.'

'I had not thought—'

'You need not think. He stands before you. Doctor to Lorenzo il Magnifico. Make him your bloody dietary, Gonzaga.'

The cardinal stared at me thoughtfully, his lips pursed. Zohan spoke briefly to the *condottiere* while I shuffled my feet, then we went back to the kitchen.

'Dietary, Maestro?' I hissed, as soon as we were safely cocooned within the noise and steam.

'Of course. You will make an excellent *dottore*. You think too much, Nino, and about the wrong things. A perfect characteristic for a dietary.'

'I've never . . .'

'There's nothing to learn. It's all moonshine.'

'What will I have to do?'

Zohan gave a deep rumble of exasperation. 'You know about the humours.'

'Of course, Maestro. Everyone knows about the humours.'

'Four humours, yes?'

I nodded.

'The dietary uses his skill and knowledge to ensure they

are in balance. That the great and worthy man who is his master is in possession of a balanced system of digestion.'

'But, Maestro, I'm a cook!'

'Have you read Galen?' I shook my head. 'I will lend you my edition of his works. You need only read the lines I have underlined. The rest is sophistry and . . . and . . .' He harrumphed. 'Anyway. You shall read the book of a former colleague of mine from Ferrara, one Giovanni Savonarola – my edition, just the underlined parts. Read it and imitate.'

'This is something for a scholar, Maestro!'

'Listen to me, Dancing Girl. It's the job of a maestro to look after his people. Donna Fortuna presented an opportunity the like of which comes around only once in a lifetime. You, my boy, were too stupid to take it, so I took it for you. Be grateful. You need to strike out on your own. This is a title, Nino. It is a position. Use it. A few years of this and you can be a *scalco*. I'm tired of you hiding in my shadow. And . . .' He paused, pursed his lips, frowned. 'And in any case, you deserve a good position. This is a gift that I can give you. Take it.'

'I am grateful, Maestro. Always. But what will I do? I know nothing – nothing at all!'

'Shut up. You know a great deal. Read my books. But later. You need to get this food out. The company is waiting.'

The next day, Cardinal Gonzaga made me his personal dietary.

From someone who had cared only that his food came from Mantua, Cardinal Gonzaga had fallen head first into the new fashion for diet. When I had first started in his employment he had eaten everything that came to his table without comment, let alone complaint. Now he examined every plate warily, as if each lettuce leaf hid a coiled asp, and would look at me for

282

reassurance. I would be required to trot out some specious justification for why he was eating leeks or *torta* of hop shoots again, and he would nod and tuck in, entirely satisfied. I would have given anything to be back in the kitchen, but I feared offending Zohan. There is no worse flaw in an apprentice than ingratitude. So I became an actor, done up in the stiff, ugly costume of a medical man, even though I had no qualifications whatsoever, and talked in the jargon of the dietary. Joy was banished from the dining hall, and the cardinal had never seemed so happy. I found myself longing for the days of tench and eels, even heron. One night I dreamed that I had made a huge roast swan with all its feathers, and fire shooting from its eyes and beak, and set it on the cardinal like a fighting dog while I pelted him with a battery of the coldest, most phlegmatic foods. I had woken up as his robes caught fire, and decided to look for another job. So I cornered Zohan that morning.

'Where's your gratitude?' he rasped. The wooden spoon, not much in evidence lately, suddenly appeared, quivering, in the space between us.

'But I can't stand it,' I said. 'It's nonsense. All of it.'

'Of course it's nonsense! So what? You're being paid, aren't you? You have a title . . .'

'A title? I'm a cook, not a doctor! I can't bear serving His Eminence food that I wouldn't give to the cats in the fish market. I am so envious of you, Maestro, cooking the banquets – real food.'

'And I envy you.'

'Maestro! You do it, then. You learned things from that *dottor* Savonarola, didn't you? All sorts of unpleasant ways to rob meals of their joy. Take my robes, with my blessing! For pity's sake, Maestro – I'll pluck chickens . . . I'll wash the pots!'

'Ahh . . .' Zohan sighed. 'Don't you think I'd rather be

standing around, doing nothing, except to rearrange an asparagus spear or sprinkle a little spice? I'm old, Nino. My back's giving up on me and I'm finding it hard to piss. I want to go home to Ferrara, drink well–water, eat fresh figs.'

'Why don't you, then?' I said bluntly.

'Because you, Nino Latini, are the best cook I have ever known; and because you followed me to Rome like a stray dog, I am responsible for you. I'm your maestro. I'm *still* your maestro, Nino. Grow up, you little shit, and then you can do what you want.'

'Grow up? Aren't I grown up, then?'

'A man wouldn't be whining to me about his good fortune. Personal dietary to His Eminence Cardinal Gonzaga . . . What do you think His Eminence talks about to his friends? To all those fat old buggers at the Vatican? He talks about his liver, and his spleen, and how you're keeping them as healthy as a newborn baby's. How his digestion is as regular as his father's famous pocket clock. How he's never felt better, and it's all down to you. No matter that he felt fine before. No matter that his mouth's as sensitive as shoe leather. You're farting through silk, my boy, and until you get down on your knees every day and thank God for your blessings, a boy you'll remain.'

Dearest Nino,

You are alive – that alone has made me rejoice. I do not dare say more, not yet, so forgive me if I give you the news instead of what is in my heart.

I found your letter waiting at Santa Bibiana. Sister Beatrice was keeping it safe for me. I do not believe she read it, although dear Beatrice, however much she claims to be dying, seems often to be more alive than most people I see in my little life – excepting Sandro Botticelli,

*that is, of whom more later – and it would not surprise me
one whit if she had prised it open! I should probably tell
you that Beatrice knows all my secrets, by which I mean
our secrets. Don't fear. I do not believe anything I have
told her has caused her to turn one hair. The hidden life of
convents, my dearest, is quite surprising.*

*I am sitting in Beatrice's cell. We are eating lunch, which
is ribollita – it is always ribollita, and not bad. The cook is
an old nun from San Frediano – I expect she would know
your Carenza, at least they look rather alike and Sister
Docchia has been heard to reel out the most horrifying
oaths on occasion. Her soup is like Carenza's as well – do
you remember how she used to roll her eyes when I turned
up in her kitchen with you? – but not as good. Did
Carenza slip a little bacon into her battuta, the heretic?
You would know better than I. Ha! I smile at the memory,
and now have burned my tongue. Sister Beatrice is
laughing at me: tell him something important, she is
saying.*

*So let me tell you this: nothing in my heart has changed
since we last spoke. I have never, and never will, dwell on
the events of the day when you left Florence, but you
should know that I felt nothing but love for you then, as I
do now.*

*I scribble these last words under the benign but
frighteningly acute gaze of Messer Sandro Botticelli, who
is drawing me at this moment. My aunt – always my dear
aunt – is watching over me in the corner, but she has
started to doze, and so out with your letter . . . I will leave
it with Sandro. The dear man patiently wastes his genius
on my wan little face . . . Ah, my aunt stirs.*

In haste, in love . . .

  T

My dearest Tessina,

What joy to receive your letter, complete with a tiny portrait – not of your face, which I would give my life to see once again, but of my own for which I curse Sandro and also embrace him. I will send this to his workshop, so as not to tempt poor Sister Beatrice.

Carenza would rather be hung from a window of the Signoria than put bacon in her ribollita. Her secret, which I will tell you under pain of your banishment from Florence (so please, dear one, tell everyone, so you will be thrown out of the city and forced to join me here), is to use a pot in which she has previously fried lardo, and not washed afterwards. I believe this was a mistake that I made her repeat, because I was a little tyrant in her kitchen. But I loved the ghost of bacon that haunted her soup. How wonderful that you noticed it.

Such matters are on my mind these days. I have been appointed personal dietary to His Eminence Cardinal Federico Gonzaga, though I know next to nothing about such work. I am up to my neck in books, but alas I understand this art hardly at all, for I think it wishes the poor cook to turn physician and I have no skill in that direction. I fear it is all fashion and no substance, a way to gull the credulous rich. And it does not seem right to choose a dish for its properties as medicine and not for its taste! Fortunately, His Eminence is a man of simple tastes and I do not have to torture him by denying him. And it is his good fortune (and therefore mine) not to suffer from any serious maladies. The cardinal's humours are in perfect balance, so far as I can tell, though he has a penchant for melancholic foods, the dishes of his damp and marshy home. To earn my keep I have prescribed choleric dishes of leeks, seasonings of sugar and cinnamon, and when they come into season His Eminence will learn

*to delight in the artichoke, which the Romans cultivate in
vast numbers, and which secretes a bitter milk that opens
the mysterious passageways of the body. I have a butcher's
knowledge of such things and no more, but artichokes are
delicious, so the cardinal shall feast on them and his
anatomy shall breathe easily.*

*Carenza would think I was a madman to be employed
in such a way. How I long for her food. And Ugolino in
the marketplace – you cannot taste his wares, of course. If
you will allow me a prayer on your behalf, it is that your
husband employs a decent cook in his kitchen. He can
afford one.*

*I shall write to Sandro and beg him for a picture of
you. I hardly need one, though, because I see you in every
lovely thing that meets my eye.*

    Nino

That winter, when I was not poring over technical volumes
on dietary science, I wrote letters. To my father, begging his
forgiveness. To Carenza, I sent strange Roman recipes that I
knew would set her clucking. To Sandro, a summary of the
paintings I saw in Rome, and descriptions of how dreadful
they mostly were. To Arrigo, who was always on the move
with King Ferrante's army. I also began a letter to Messer
Lorenzo, which I knew I would never send, in which I
forgave him in condescending tones. This I tore up and
threw into the privy, along with another one in which I
cursed him with every foul word I knew.

In return I heard from Arrigo. I got letters from Sandro, full
of gossip and little morsels of life in the streets of the Black
Lion. A good *beffa* or two, a murder, a taverna gone under,
another coming up. The current tribulations of Messer
Lorenzo, who had picked an argument with His Holiness
and seemed to have lost. The Pope wanted his nephew to be

Lord of Imola, as Sandro told me in a letter, between Florence and the Garfagnano; but Lorenzo had refused to lend His Holiness the money he needed to buy the title. The Pazzis had lent it, though. To the Medicis, that would be like their old rivals spitting on Messer Lorenzo's perfectly tooled shoe.

I even had a letter from Leonardo, a modest square of vellum covered in spidery writing in some script I could not decipher, with the most perfect drawing of a house spider. In late spring a small package came for me from Sandro: two light wooden boards – old drawing tablets from his studio, all scratched and worn, and between them an ink drawing of Tessina.

The ink snared me first with her hair, because ink loves coils and tendrils and Sandro's hand always seemed to catch things as they unravelled. Tessina's curls . . . I could tell that a brush had attacked them, perhaps an hour or less before she had sat for my friend, but they were already themselves again, settling into heavy ropes: half tamed, half savage. And in her face, I found a new tension: a line of cheekbone, a tiny strengthening of her jaw, a minute softening of the curve where nose met upper lip. She was looking at me sideways, a half-smile on her lips. I held the drawing up like a window and stared through it, into it, let it come alive, until she almost spoke to me.

The drawing I took to be framed, and then hung it in my chamber, where it rested to the side – and below, for propriety's sake – of Sandro's little Virgin. So when I worshipped the one, the other was in my sight, and when I stared at Tessina I was also at worship. Her letters I kept on a little box below the pictures, which did look a little too much like an altar. But I told myself that I went to church as diligently as the next man and lit candles for my mother's soul and in front of the Virgin Herself, and so with any luck She would be turning a blind eye to my private arrangements, particularly as I was guarding her servant the cardinal's health with sugar, cinnamon and bitter herbs.

Florence started to come alive for me again in the letters: the brothel fights and the scandals; the cuckolds and betrayers. The latest dishes on sale in the market taverns, the fashions. *Calcio* games, the price of wine and sausage. Tessina wrote about artists I had known and their appetites. Hers was a strange world, going veiled from her locked house to the convent or to Sandro's studio, and I sensed the suffocation she must be fighting. She was in exile too, in a way, though she could at least look out of her window and smell the city air. I searched every word and went over every detail again and again. I was looking for the same thing I was searching for in my food. I did not know quite what that something was: a key, a spell to conjure me back to Florence. But in the end there was nothing but ink and vellum.

In return I tried to describe for Tessina, as best I could, the streets of Rome and the ruins, the churches, Saint Peter's itself, but words have never done what I would like them to do. Tastes I could bring to life, but a record of tastes set down in ink turns out to be dry and definitively tasteless. Because my descriptions seemed so flat and unconvincing to me I began to draw again: sketches of the great arch in the Forum, fish sellers and tripe sellers. Dogs asleep in doorways, cats on old pillars. The Proctor, staring white-eyed from under his helmet of corded hair. I told her what I was cooking, and the goings-on of the Academy. I seemed to be leading a life of happy ease in those letters, and I hoped that Tessina found a small escape in them, but when I read them before dripping on the sealing wax I couldn't really find myself.

My dearest Nino,
   You press me for news of my life, and I know it is because you wish to share it. But I have told you very

little. Doubtless you believe this is because my days are empty compared with yours.

I must tell the truth at last. It is envy that draws it from me – a sin, of course, and self-pity is another, for I feel such pity for myself, sometimes, that I wish the earth would open beneath this city and swallow us all up, like hell's mouth in the old pictures. I have told you that my husband has found himself inadequate in his duties as a husband. This is true, and a mercy. But his ardour, if I can call it such an elegant word, is far from dimmed. When he is at home, which is more and more often, he presses his attentions on me every night and sometimes in the day. No matter that his flesh does not allow him the means to satisfy his desires; he must needs force me to bring him to life with every means his lustful and agitated mind can devise. All to no avail, which only serves to inflame his bile. His bitterness is directed chiefly against himself, I think, but that is only because he regards me as little more than a mannequin of some sort. If he would even see me as a whore, I would have more dignity, I swear it.

When Signor Bartolo is done abusing my honour, his son takes up the game. Nino, you know what Marco is. There is hardly a man in Florence who would not go to the wall or the gutter if Marco walks by. It is not Marco's anger that frightens me, though, but his passion. As the father, so the son: as Signor Bartolo's ardour fails him, so the son's is kindled. The father retreats, humiliated, and here comes Marco, the young cockerel, ready with his spurs and his beak. He has not dared to touch me – and would not, I am certain, while Signor Bartolo lives – but he is always at me, wheedling with his filthy and cruel tongue. There is no reason in him at all, Nino – no sense. He is entirely spleen and mercury.

Ah, my love, sometimes I feel I am in hell already, and

hell-mouth does not need to swallow me up. But at other times I find father and son so worthless, so laughable, that I can put them entirely from my mind. Meantimes I have your words and your drawings. Make me a picture of yourself, Nino. I love your fat cats and old pillars, but draw yourself. I keep your letters safe at Santa Bibiana, but if you send me your likeness I will seal it in my memory and my heart, and use it as a secret talisman against cruel words and deeds.

    Pray for me.
    T

For the first time in many years I had time to myself, but after Tessina's last letter I filled my empty hours with worry. I ought to have been fretting over my employer's imaginary disorders, paid fretting, as it were; but instead I was haunted by a spectral image of Tessina pressed against the heavy panelling of the Palazzo Baroni, recoiling from Marco's face like something vile dredged up from the deeps of the ocean.

    My Heart –
    You are a fool and a careless and heartless boy and even more to be blamed for causing your poor Carenza to pick up a pen for the first time in many years. Your letter was hard to read my eyes are not good did you send instructions on the cooking of bull's pizzle? If this is the kind of savagery you are up to in Rome then God help us all – I cannot believe such nonsense is practised in Rome the home of Our Holy Father.
    But you are alive and I must forgive you for I miss you as if you were my own and not your mother's God rest her gentle soul even though you are committing barbarities – but I forget you cook for a cardinal surely you do not cook His Eminence pizzle and such things??

*Dear boy I love you very much you ask what Ugolino
uses in his* trippa *it is mint what did you think it was you
fool? Here are my instructions for* tomacelli *as you asked
I hope they are good please cook them for His Eminence!
Darling boy to you my love Caronza*

The writing was huge and scratchy, and veered up and to the
right, like untidy birds taking off from a lake. I held it up and
kissed it, read it again, and as I was refolding the paper I
noticed more writing on the back. It was in a small, tight
hand, and I had to squint to make it out.

Dear Nino,

    *Summer finds us all well – I trust you are also in good
health, although the sultry airs of Rome are dangerous
and I advise you to take great care with your food and
drink. I have your letter, and other news of you from
Simone Corbinelli who has it from his son in Naples.
Plainly, God is watching over you, and may He continue
to do so. M. Pisello was caught undercutting the City –
the fine will ruin him. E. Donelli has died and Donelli* e
fratelli *has closed. I plan to buy it from Donelli's daughter
who has married a poulterer. The plague visited us at the
end of the year but chiefly in the west and the Black Lion
was not much affected. I have had to mend the roof
though not extensively. Terino has made improvements to
his establishment. I have been elected to the counsel of the
Guild.*

    Your loving father,
    Niccolaio di Niccolaio Latini

Nino,

    *I am sorry you have not had a letter from me for so
many months. I have hardly been outside this house since I*

*last wrote to you – nothing but short visits to Santa
Bibiana in the company of Aunt Maddalena who, though
growing quite elderly, has sharper wits than ever. Sandro is
between commissions so I have been here in my genteel
prison while my jailers close in upon me.*

*But suddenly there has appeared a great beam of light.
My husband, advancing rapidly towards decrepitude as he
is, has taken a fancy to make a pilgrimage. Not to Rome, I
must quickly say! But to Assisi, to worship at the shrine of
Blessed Francis and attend His holy festival in October of
this year. We shall be leaving Florence in the second week
of September and journeying via Arezzo and Perugia.
What a miracle! Did you know, dearest Nino, that I have
never been beyond the walls of our city? The preparations
are already under way. I feel able to breathe again. What
joy!*

    T

32

PILGRIMAGE. THE WORD ROLLED AROUND my tongue like a fat cherry. I leaned back against the crumbling bricks of a wall near the top of the Palatine Hill. There was no one else around. Now and then, voices came up from below, where I had seen the Proctor lurking under the great arch. I reread Tessina's letter for what must have been the fiftieth time that day. The bricks were warm, sending gritty trickles down the back of my shirt. The air was hot enough to scorch my tongue, and I was leaning into the shade of a scrubby little fig tree, drugged by the appalling Roman sun.

Up here, I could almost believe that the rasping chime of insects was the creak of Fortuna's wheel, turning in my favour. Because when the messenger had given me Tessina's letter, I had just heard that Cardinal Gonzaga was leaving in late September for Mantua and then Milan and would not be returning until the spring of next year. Zohan was going with him, leaving me to do . . . what? It wasn't entirely clear. Apparently I was to be paid a retainer and continue as part of the cardinal's household, but from the maestro I gathered that my employer was expecting me to make myself available to his friends in the College of Cardinals. I was to be a kind of dietary *condottiere*, which seemed the dullest thing imaginable – if, that is, I chose to do it. But what if I did not? There was no one to make me do anything. I didn't care a fig if the cardinals had unbalanced humours.

And then Tessina's letter. Everything became sharp and clear, like broth when whites of egg are stirred into it. Pilgrimage. To leave all this behind me and ride off alone towards a blessing. To be saved – that was why all those tiny shapes were milling around among the fallen marble. To be saved, and to save.

The Proctor was scratching about under a pillar. He looked up and saw me passing, gave me one of his black-toothed grins.

'I met a man who told me there was a door to Perugia somewhere in this field,' he said. 'I am disinclined to believe him, but then again I have time for a brief investigation. Have you ever been to Perugia?'

'No,' I said, sitting down on the pillar. 'But if you find a door to Florence under there, do tell me, won't you?'

'I'll have to think about it,' said the Proctor, scratching himself vigorously.

I had almost four months to kill before Gonzaga left with Zohan for the north. Before I set out on my own journey. It was pure cowardice on my part, but I could not quit the cardinal's household while my maestro was watching over me. It would be like stabbing him in the heart. Waiting until he was gone, though, would be more like putting the knife into his back – or perhaps, so I reasoned, I would merely be doing what he expected. He was setting me up to be my own master, was he not? And when I struck out alone, surely I would have his blessing? Meanwhile there was a stifling Roman summer to endure in my horrible dietary's robes.

'I need a new employer,' I told the Proctor, though I knew he wasn't listening. 'A greedy man who doesn't care about his humours. Someone who will appreciate a dish for its taste and artistry and not for what it's doing to his *pylorus*.'

That was the latest fad at San Lorenzo in Damaso: the stomach and all its whims. The cardinal had been suffering from a slight case of afflatus – the way he went on about it you might imagine that the palace roof was rattling from the strength of his farts, but as I had been forced to listen and indeed smell them, and had heard nothing louder than the snapping of a small twig, my prescription was a *torta* of fennel fronds.

This should have been the end of the matter, but then the cardinal had found an ancient treatise on digestion and from then on it had been the heat of the stomach-flask, the order of foodstuffs to be consumed for the most efficient combustion, and above all – and this was conveyed to me with a sort of wild-eyed desperation, the cardinal's usually rosy cheeks quite pale with agitation – the paramount, the absolute importance of chewing. For without sufficient concoction, or the wrong concoctive process applied to a given ingredient, disaster was inevitable. *Disaster*, he had repeated, as if invoking a tidal wave or some manner of subterranean explosion.

Fortunately for me, I had been reading up on the stomach, on how the food reaches it through the organ's mouth, which must be plugged up at meal's end with some appropriate sealant like cheese, if concoction is to happen and disaster averted; or pulled shut, rather like a leather purse, by the puckering action of something sour. I had examined many stomachs, admittedly those of sheep, pigs and cows, and could find no strings or indeed any place where a lump of cheese might lodge like a cork.

No matter. Cardinal Gonzaga was convinced that his vessel of concoction was malfunctioning. The problem, he feared, lay with his *pylorus*, the stomach's exit hole. This was unlikely, I countered. The fault was most probably with inconsistent chewing, no doubt because His Eminence was distracted by the weighty matters of his office. But to satisfy his need to suffer I had banished carrots utterly from his diet, stepped up the fennel and introduced more umbelliferous seeds, pondering how the roots of umbellifers such as the carrot promote flatulence and the seeds – fennel, coriander, cumin – cure it.

But no cure was forthcoming for my employer's imaginary ills, and nothing seemed likely to raise the siege set around my dignity. Alas, quite the reverse was true. In the days that followed I progressed from analysing the tunefulness and aromatic qualities of my employer's afflatus to examining his urine for signs of humours fallen out of balance. I tried in vain to tease an actual symptom from His Eminence. He was suffering, plainly, from the disease of employing a dietary, but as I peered into the depths of yet another oracular vessel of piss, I found myself wishing I could detect something serious that would get the man off my hands and into those of a proper surgeon. Or perhaps, if there was something actually amiss, I could use my new dietary's skills, such as they were, to cure him.

That was it. I needed to see some result for my pains. I needed a subject: someone to cure. Someone beyond the reach of ordinary physicians. There were plenty of those in Rome, but I needed to find a subject who knew me, who might even be said to trust me. I thought, and thought. But the answer, when it came, was as plain as daylight.

33

'In Perugia . . .'

'Good morning, Proctor,' I said. The man had been wandering from pillar to pillar, drifting slowly towards me across the Campo Vaccino.

'Good morning.' He bowed, and the ropes of his hair bounced, sending a waft of rare complexity towards my nose: fox, badger, goat, porcini mushrooms, *pecorino di fossa*, more badger . . . How different from the fine, perfumed locks of my employer. Here was a man who reeked of suffering, who truly needed the skills of a doctor. Was this how Cardinal Gonzaga saw himself? From his worrying, his fretting, it almost seemed so. The cardinal needed me to heal him, but I couldn't oblige, because there was no illness. Here, though: here was suffering. Diet might not cure my cardinal, but surely it would demonstrate its powers on a wretch like the one crouching in front of me? And I was supposed to be a *dottore*. Everyone told me I was a miracle worker. Well, perhaps I could prove to myself what Cardinal Gonzaga already believed.

'Proctor,' I said, 'when did you last take a bath?'

To my surprise, the beggar seemed delighted with my offer of a visit to the bathhouse. It makes me ashamed, still, to think I had not realized that the horrifying state of the man – his matted hair, the patina of his skin, which made him look as if he had been carved out of deeply stained walnut wood – was not of his choosing. We went to the *stufa* I usually frequented and I paid in advance for as much hot water as it would take to get his skin back to its proper state, and for a barber to be fetched.

I left the Proctor in the unwilling and patently revolted hands of the bath assistants, telling them enthusiastically of his past rank in the city of Perugia, and hurried back to my lodgings, where I dug out a pair of *mutande*, a frayed shirt, an old tunic, some patched hose and the doublet I had worn on my journey from Florence, which had been savaged by weather and by sleeping rough but still looked more or less like a civilized garment. When I got back to the *stufa*, the Proctor was in his second tub, beaming like a saint through the steam, his skin an angry-looking reddish pink. I almost didn't recognize him, because his great mud-fountain of hair was gone, and all that was left was a finger's width of mouse-coloured stubble, roughly cropped. His beard, too, had been razored away, taking a fair amount of skin with it, by the looks of things. The creature who had seemed uncannily without age, like some artist's invention to fill a space in the bottom corner of a second-rate altarpiece, was revealed as a man of about thirty-five, with regular, rather surprised features.

'Disgusting,' muttered one of the attendants, loud enough for me to hear, and the Proctor as well.

'Shut up and give him what he asks for,' I told him. 'Throw in some Hungary water as well.'

'I am cooked!' said the Proctor. 'I am boiled! I am fevered and flayed and braised!' He rose up out of the bath, revealing a cadaverous frame, pocked with welts and cuts and insect bites. The skin across his ribs looked as thin as cheesecloth. He crossed his long hands in front of his sex, and looked for a moment like a Flemish painting of the dead Christ I had once seen, stood on end. I signalled to the attendants, who advanced reluctantly, towels held out in front of them. They pummelled and jostled him as he stood cringing on the wet marble floor, staring up at the ceiling, yellow teeth clenched in shame or pain. When he was dry, and some Hungary water had been rubbed into his scalp and over his chest, I brought him over to the bundle of my old clothes. He stood, knock-kneed, and stared at them, until I picked up the *mutande* and held them out.

'These may not fit,' I said, looking around at his skinny arse, which looked like a pair of hog's chaps set together on a plate.

His eyes flicked from the undergarments to me, and back again. He scowled, then reached out one hand, the other still cupping his manhood, and held them up in front of his face. Something like recognition dawned, and he bent over, scissoring abruptly in the middle so that I heard the bones of his spine crack, and stepped into the *mutande*, pulled them up past his bulging knees and settled them around his waist. I showed him the drawstrings and he pulled them viciously tight. The shirt was vast and again he pulled every drawstring closed as if he was trying to constrain a body that did not belong to him. The hose went on, and finally I helped him into the doublet. Even when he was dressed he did not move but stood, slightly hunched, looking up anxiously at the ceiling.

'Shall we go to the *trippaio*?' I said. His head swivelled and he fixed his white-rimmed eyes on my face, on a spot somewhere on my forehead. 'Proctor,' I repeated. 'Are you hungry?' He stared for longer, then grimaced, as though a spasm of pain or something else had stabbed him. He blinked frantically, then shook himself like a dog. The outsized clothes ballooned, settled.

'I am an official,' he muttered. 'An official. In Perugia, in Perugia . . .'

'In Perugia, they eat lunch, same as in Rome,' I said. 'Come along now.'

We went to the tripe seller in the arcade of San Pietro in Vincoli. This time, though, the Proctor hung back and only trotted across the square when I had bought him his bowl and was holding it out to him, as you might tempt a dog. We went and sat on the steps.

'What is Perugia like?' I asked. He looked at me, shocked, and then his face went blank. 'Is it like Rome?' He blinked. 'Is it flat there? Hilly? Are the women pretty?' He blinked again, and dipped his head so that it was almost in his bowl. He began to shovel and slurp. 'Come on,' I insisted. 'In Perugia . . .'

'I am bathed but not bought,' he snapped.

'I'm sorry,' I said. 'I thought . . .'

'Shaved like a sheep,' he muttered. 'Shaved and anointed. Shaved and anointed.'

He finished his tripe, and sat, round-shouldered, staring narrow-eyed into the empty bowl. From the half-beast he had seemed to be before, the Proctor had been transformed into a confused man, still young, swimming in someone else's clothes. Now he was not just human, but frighteningly vulnerable. It hadn't occurred to me that a simple act of charity might have such a consequence.

'Where do you sleep?' I asked.

'Sleep?' His head snapped around – the white circles in his eyes were wider than ever. 'Shaved and anointed!' he yelped.

'Oh, good Christ, no!' I said, realizing what he was assuming. 'Master Proctor, I'm not suggesting you sleep with me! I was simply wondering what your sleeping arrangements are. A hospice, perhaps? A—'

'A drain, a hole, a tree, a wall, a ditch, a door,' he spat.

'Oh. But there must be a place you prefer to sleep, when you are in funds?'

'Prefer? Funds?' He blinked. 'The White Fathers are kind when there is coin. When, when, when . . . In Perugia they called me the Proctor, you know. Am I still the Proctor, though?' He sniffed at himself, at his arms, under them; ran his clawed fingers across the patchy stubble on his head. 'I am some sort of ape,' he concluded.

'Where are these White Fathers, then?'

'In the Borgo.'

'Then let us go there.'

'No!'

'You can't sleep in a drain.'

'Young man. I can sleep where I wish,' he rasped.

'Young man? *You* are a young man. Do you think God is pleased with you, wandering around in His holy city, looking like some pagan demon?'

'What do you know about God, eh? Do you think God watches apes like you and me in Rome? God talks to his children in Perugia. Here, there are other voices.'

'Well, hear mine. I wish for you to sleep somewhere wholesome.'

'You have chosen me. You have singled me out.'

'*You* singled *me* out! Master Proctor, you have plagued me with your stench and your gibberish for months. Now I am returning the favour. Take me to these White Fathers, and then I swear I will leave you alone.'

The Carmelite friars seemed unmoved by the arrival of the Proctor, but they cheered up when I opened my purse. A month's board was pitifully cheap, so I paid it all with the cardinal's silver, and left the Proctor staring at his new straw mattress.

I went back to my room and wrote a long letter to Tessina, with a sketch in one corner of the Proctor as he had been before his bath, though I didn't mention him. I felt, somehow, that what I had done with the beggar had been meddling, not real charity, and the feeling would not go away. That night, as I bent my head solemnly to observe my employer pissing into a glass beaker, then held up the warm vessel and examined it as though it was an alchemist's alembic holding some miracle of transmutation, I was thinking of the transformation I had inflicted on the Proctor, who was a person, after all, and not a beast.

'Well?' The cardinal's voice was eager. He wanted bad news. I had to disappoint him.

'Much improved, Your Eminence,' I said. 'The phlegmatic crisis has passed. Heat and desiccation prevail. We shall aid their progress with some . . .' I sighed. 'Some roast mutton with a pepper sauce.' Something I might actually enjoy cooking, for once, but I knew it wouldn't be appreciated. I might as well condense the sheep and the pepper into some sort of pill and stick it up his fundament. No, best not to even consider it. I was already custodian of my master's piss – I didn't want to be put in charge of his arse as well.

The cardinal was still gazing at me, rigid with expectation. I sighed again, dipped the tip of my little finger into the warm fluid, touched it to my tongue. A jagged flash of livid maroon lit up my sense organs, followed by a dull, briny and metallic lapping that, mercifully, died away quite quickly. I was left with the faint taste of pigs' kidneys and vinegar.

Who was the madman here? I wondered. Drinking a man's piss, trying to cure him of a disease he did not have, while there was a city full of men like the Proctor, ignored by doctors – both real and invented, like me. We walked past these lesser beings every day on our way to give our masters the attention they so craved. Meanwhile, there was a man who had been a beggar and now felt like a costumed ape: a madman thrust headlong into the world of the sane. And it was my fault. I was supposed to be a doctor, wasn't I? Well, perhaps I could put the threadbare knowledge I had collected in the service of the rich to some good use. I had tried to help a man by changing his outward circumstances, but the trouble lay within. I wasn't going to go sipping the Proctor's urine, but there were other ways.

'Has His Eminence been paying due attention to his concoction?' I enquired, wishing that I could take a sip of the cardinal's wine to drive the taste of his piss from my mouth.

'I have. The act of mastication is infinitely variable, is it not? I am striving to be diligent.'

'I can tell as much,' I said owlishly. 'In case of difficulties with the *pylorus*, the crasser foods are best avoided — His Eminence will have noted the absence of grains and pulses.' Of course, I thought, what did a beggar eat but the crassest foods? A change of diet — any change — might effect a cure in the Proctor. But his affliction was plainly a horrible excess of black bile. You didn't have to be a dietary to make that diagnosis.

'Hellebore,' I muttered.

'Is that necessary? Obtain some!' said the cardinal.

'I . . . Yes, of course,' I said. 'Not necessary in this case, Your Eminence. A plant of frightening powers, best resorted to in extremis.'

'My man, do not delay if you think it necessary.'

I went back to the hospice early the next day, and was relieved to find that the Proctor had spent the night and was still there. One of the friars had given him a broom and he was using it to methodically trace an invisible net across the flagstones of the small inside courtyard.

'Have you broken your fast yet?' I enquired. The Proctor dropped his broom.

'Shaved and anointed!' he cried. The shaving cuts on his face had turned black, and his hair was sticking out at odd angles, but he didn't look too bad. 'Shaved and anointed,' he said again, backing away warily.

'I know. I'm sorry you had to suffer that,' I said. 'Did you spend a pleasant night?'

'Tolerable,' he snapped.

'Good. I've got breakfast for us both.' I unslung the satchel I had brought with me, sat down on the nearest step and unpacked a clutch of fresh early pears, which I began to peel. I held one out, a pale, dewy oval, to the Proctor. Reluctantly, he sidled over, took an experimental bite and, satisfied, sat down some distance away from me.

'Tell me,' I said. 'Do you eat many cloves?'

'Cloves?' he repeated blankly.

'Or nuts – walnuts? Filberts, perhaps?'

'I'll have a walnut, every now and again,' he said cautiously. 'The trees down in the Campo Vaccino . . .'

'Ah. And venison?'

The Proctor frowned.

'The meat of rams? Rabbits? Swans? Pickled foods? Cinnamon? Ginger?'

'Swans and cloves.' The Proctor reached out a bony hand for another pear. He bit into it, and the juice dripped down between his knees. He chewed, frowned thoughtfully. 'In Perugia, of course, we eat cloves by the handful. Like a donkey with oats. Oh, the spices of Perugia! But in Rome I am accustomed to dine on brick-hard bread and onion skins. There are figs . . .'

'Excellent!'

'It would be beneath me to steal from the gardens of honest people,' he went on, paying no attention to me. 'So I gnaw on bread. Thus.' Suddenly he dropped the core of the pear, held up his hands to either side of his face and contorted his mouth into a snarl, thrusting out his lower jaw and working it so that that his teeth, mostly present but coloured in a rainbow of hues that descended from yellow to midnight black, juddered and clacked together. 'Bread, bread, bread, bread. Give me another pear.'

'Did you know that I am a doctor?'

'I know that you are *not* a doctor. Did you know that I am a proctor?'

'I am a dietary. To a cardinal. To His Eminence Cardinal . . . Never mind. My study is the maladies brought on by the maladjustment of the body's humours.'

'You talk as if the words in your mouth have been farted from another man's arse.'

'Oh!' Despite myself, I felt rather hurt. But I tried again. 'Amusingly, part of my work entails the analysis of exactly those fundamental winds . . .'

'Farts. Call a fart a fart. Shaved and anointed by the cardinal's fart-sniffer. Do you have a swan in that bag?' He squirmed, sat on his hands. 'That was a jest.'

'Listen,' I said. 'Have you always been like this?'

'I don't know what you mean.'

'Mad, is what I mean. Have you always been a madman?'

He sighed. 'In parts of Umbria,' he said with infinite patience, 'they call me the Proctor.'

'So, if you really are from Perugia, which I rather doubt, you were a madman there as well. Listen to me. I can help you. Do you want that? Do you want to find relief from your afflictions? Do you wish to have your black bile, which is plainly present in near-fatal quantities, brought back into balance? This, and more, I can accomplish.'

'Ah. But can you cure me?'

'Ah . . .' I gritted my teeth.

'Because you are plainly a somewhat young man, and it seems to me a strange thing that a prince of the Church has entrusted his winds to you.' He lowered his head and watched me through narrowed eyes.

'But he has!'

'Such an honour,' the madman said quietly.

I sighed and started to peel another pear. 'It is the truth: I am a cardinal's dietary,' I said at last. 'Although that doesn't mean as much as it ought to. He's as fit as a prize bull, and his piss tastes like Rhenish wine. But in his service I have learned quite a lot. And food . . . Food I knew already. Did you know, Proctor, that if the cardinal ate the amount of pears you've just put away, he would probably call for extreme unction? Because his disposition is phlegmatic, and pears give rise to phlegm in a most alarming way. You, my friend, are not cold and wet, like His Eminence, but cold and dry. You need phlegm. How are you feeling after five pears?'

The beggar hawked and spat, messily, onto the flagstones. 'Satisfied?'

'Phlegm. Satisfied, to a degree. It's a start. But never mind. Take the last pear.'

'Have it yourself.'

'No, no . . .' I held it out to the beggar, who regarded me sceptically.

'I'm not hungry. Have a pear, *Dottor* Wind. Have some medicine.'

I shrugged and bit. It was good, crisp for a pear and slightly sour. The grains of its flesh spread out inside my mouth: I pictured wind-tossed leaves; green beech leaves.

'It won't do me any harm,' I said. 'I've got a bile problem too, if you must know. But the yellow kind.'

'Ah. Then you're either a murderer or in love,' said the Proctor. Perhaps it was my imagination, but he seemed almost lucid. Then he leaped to his feet in his usual way, like a puppet jerked upright by a child, and stalked away to retrieve his broom, which he began to push around again, muttering about Perugia.

I went and talked to the friar in charge of the hospice, who told me the place was too small and poor to afford an infirmary or a doctor of any kind, and those men who sickened under their care could be offered kindness and nothing else. I asked if he minded me treating the Proctor, and he shrugged his shoulders.

'But aren't you awfully young for a doctor?' he wondered.

I told him I was a dietary, and he plainly had no idea what that meant. So we agreed that I would pay for the Proctor's meals, to be chosen and prepared according to my desires. Later that day, in between services, I made a list, a week's worth of meals:

Pottage of nettles
Pottage of hop shoots
Boiled pigeon
Poached sole
Poached eggs
Infusion of fennel

And so on. I gave instructions on the making of oxymel, the boiling of two parts honey to one part apple vinegar, and insisted that our patient be given nothing but the whitest bread. This I sent around to the hospice.

The next few days were busy – Cardinal Gonzaga was preparing to leave Rome – and so I didn't get back to the hospice until a week had gone by. I had provided my employer with a strict diet to be followed on the road, embraced the maestro.

'What are you going to do?' he asked. His eyes, sharp as ever, probed like the tines of a *trinciante*'s fork.

'While His Eminence is away? I thought I might go on pilgrimage.'

'Very wise.'

'You approve? I thought of Assisi,' I added, deceit coating my tongue like rancid oil.

'Saint Francis . . . A strange saint for a butcher's son.' He laughed. 'Do as you wish. But do not neglect your studies.'

'My doctoring, you mean?'

'You won't be a *dottore* for ever,' he said, his eyes skewering me again. 'But you will always be a cook, Nino. You've done well. And better than I expected. My little wager with Fortuna has not been wasted. You are steady on your feet at last, Dancing Girl. Go on your pilgrimage. Study what you want. When I return you can show me what you've learned.'

I made to embrace him again, but he held up his hand and placed it on the crown of my head. He rested it there for a long moment, and I felt tears welling up. A sudden rush of love overwhelmed me. He let me hug his short, wide, solid frame against me while he stiffly returned my embrace.

'Good, good . . .' he mumbled. Then he nodded briskly, tucked his knife roll under his arm and ambled off, to be lost in the busyness of His Eminence's retinue.

That night I sat down and wrote my letter of resignation. The next day I went to see the Proctor. I took along some cakes made with white flour and lots of honey. The Proctor was sitting in the courtyard, watching ants. To my delight he had obviously put on weight, and the friars had been shaving him, as I had asked them to.

'Are you well?' I asked, sitting down next to him on the step.

'Ah. The Master of the Winds. I am talking to my friends the ants about our home. Is it a pretty prison? The ants say they cannot see any walls, just a vast desert and an endless sky. They persuade me.'

'I'm glad to hear it.' The honey cakes were slightly squashed but the Proctor took his gravely between long finger and thumb and regarded the beaded syrup. He let a drop fall and waited until the ants found it. Then he ate.

'The honey has properties of heat and dryness,' I explained. 'Eat more. How are you finding your diet?'

'Adequate, thank you,' said the Proctor thickly.

'When you've finished that, I've brought some medicine for you.'

'Medicine? Why do I need medicine?'

'We all need medicine,' I said quickly. 'If that wasn't true, there would be no need for dietaries.'

'You haven't come to sniff my fundament, have you?' the Proctor asked suspiciously.

'God forbid! No, it's just a purgative. Very ordinary.'

I took out the vial I had bought from an apothecary recommended by Leto. I had finally told the *dottore* about the Proctor and my desire to cure him, and I was pleased to find that he agreed with my diagnosis of black bile.

The Proctor was licking his fingers and eyeing the vial. It contained a viscous, dark liquid that left a greenish oil on the glass when I shook it. Dangerous stuff. I thought, not for the first time that day, whether I might not just abandon my experiment with the Proctor. Another week or so, and I would be on my way to Assisi. But then I thought of my master, and how he always insisted that a task, once started, must be seen to its conclusion. And perhaps this was what Zohan had meant by *my studies*. Besides, I wanted to see if I could cure the poor fellow's madness. I was a *dottore*, after all. Everybody said so. This would prove it. *And*, I thought with a delicious stab of anticipation, *Tessina will be amazed when I tell her.*

'I don't want medicine,' he said.

'It's fine,' I told him. 'A mild purgative. We have to drive the black, burned and corrupted humours from your body. The foods you've been eating have been a start. Now a little of this . . . it's extremely effective.'

'What is it?'

'A distillation of some wholesome herbs. From the mountains,' I added breezily. 'Here. Just a small sip – a very small sip.' To my amazement, the Proctor allowed me to tip the vial against his lips and let the thick, tarry trickle run across his teeth and into his mouth.

'*Ghaak!*' He coughed, and stuck out his green-stained tongue.

'A little more.' I gave him another small measure. Then, sensing a change in the beggar's mood, I tactfully retreated to the far end of the courtyard and stood in the doorway that led to the chapel. The Proctor got up and began to pace around crossly. I noticed that my old clothes were fitting him better, that his skin looked slightly less raw.

'How are you feeling?' I called.

'Florentine fart-sniffer!' He snapped. 'Purgative. Purgatory.' He coughed. 'A proctor should have a real doctor. A real doctor!'

'I *am* a real doctor,' I said. 'A real dietary. Don't worry, I'm leaving now – I'll be back this evening with your dinner.'

But when I returned, bearing more hot and wet foods – some boiled beef and a pot of preserved medlars – I found the Proctor curled up on his pallet, naked from the waist down, his knees up to his chin, rocking and moaning. I knelt down next to him. He opened an eye, saw me, closed it again.

'He has been in the jakes all day,' said a friar, coming into the tiny room behind me. 'Raving and emptying himself.'

'Ah. I gave him a purgative.'

'You certainly did, my son! What on earth was it?'

'Black hellebore.' I saw the friar's expression change from mild amusement to horror. 'Only a very mild tincture, and the smallest dose. I can't believe it had this effect on him.'

'What did you expect?' said the friar. 'Hellebore makes men mad, and he barely had any reason to start with.'

'Precisely: I am fighting like with like,' I said hastily. That was, of course, the principle, but kneeling here beside the shivering form of the beggar, I felt like an utter fraud, and a murderous one at that. 'Proctor!' I said, and shook his arm. Sweat had soaked through his shirt and his flesh was clammy. 'Proctor? Can you hear me?'

He shook his head weakly. What I had taken for laboured breathing seemed to be words: I bent my head closer. He was reciting something over and over again, but I couldn't hear what he was saying. It might have been the Lord's Prayer, or it might have been the calendar or the gazetteer of Umbria for all I could tell. I felt his brow: no fever. There was no doubt it had been my purge that had done this. When I had bought the tincture I had insisted on the weakest concentration, because what man with even a fingernail paring of knowledge does not know the power of black hellebore?

'Was there . . . was there any blood in his stool?' I asked, dreading the answer. But the friar shook his head. 'Good. Very good. Umm . . . He was raving, you say?'

'Dear Lord, yes, he was. His speech is usually disturbed, as you know, but it was pouring out of him, just pouring. A fountain of words – and of course the convulsions.'

'Oh, no. Convulsions?'

'Horrible twitches, I should say. He soiled himself and the floor . . .' The friar raised his eyebrows meaningfully.

'All to be expected, good brother. Of course, I'll pay for the laundress and for scrubbing the floor,' I assured him. The friar grunted and left. When we were alone, I bent and whispered in the Proctor's ear: 'Can you hear me?'

He moaned and turned his face into the pillow. The muttering started again. I made out a word here and there. It was the Our Father after all, but different:

'Your will be done on earth as it is in Heaven:
That we may love you with our whole heart by always thinking
  of You
with our whole soul by always desiring You
with our whole mind by directing all our
intentions to You and by seeking Your
glory in everything . . .'

He kicked out with his legs and grunted, then folded back in upon himself.

'And with our whole strength by spending all our
energies and affections
of soul and body
in the service of Your love
and of nothing else . . .'

I recognized it: the prayer of Saint Francis. 'Proctor,' I whispered. He moaned again.

'And may we love our neighbours as ourselves!' he said in a half-shout, half-groan, and sat up. 'Oh God, oh God . . .' He looked around wildly, saw me as if for the first time. 'My guts – good Christ, my guts!' He reached for me and without thinking I took him in my arms. He clung to me, sobbing. I began to sob as well. 'I'm so sorry,' I told him.

'Take me to the privy, for the love of God,' he moaned.

I helped him up – he could barely straighten – and we clung to each other as I helped him along the corridor to the tiny, reeking jakes. He shuffled ever more urgently and dropped down onto the wooden bench with a strangled shriek. I stood in front of him, holding both his hands tightly. Spasms were running through him and horrifying sounds were emanating from beneath.

'Hidden or obvious. Sudden or persistent— Christ!' He

yelped and doubled over, gripped my hands tighter. 'Hidden or obvious,' he chanted, over and over again. It was more of the saint's prayer, I realized. *And lead us not into temptation, hidden or obvious, sudden or persistent, but deliver us from evil, past, present and to come.*

I stayed with him until the purging slowed and stopped, and he could stand again. Then I helped him back to his bed. I offered him a slice of medlar but he turned his face away. So I went to the hospice kitchen and boiled up some oxymel – there was honey in the larder, and apple vinegar, so old that the mother had grown into a great mass, like a ball of translucent wool, that stopped up the mouth of the jar as I tried to pour. The Proctor allowed me to feed him with a spoon, sitting with my arm behind his back, muttering and sipping by the light of a cheap, guttering tallow candle that sent up such a smoke that it seemed to be suspended from the rafters by a black string. Compline was rung. We went to the jakes again, and again I fed the Proctor with drip after drip of oxymel, and sat cross-legged on the floor beside his mattress as his muttering subsided and he fell into an exhausted sleep.

I woke to the nipping of lice and the acrid smell of burned tallow. I was on the floor next to the Proctor's pallet. Judging by the vermin that were crawling over my skin and clothes, the friars had not been strictly honest when they had provided a mattress of new straw. I sat up. The Proctor was sitting tailor-fashion on the sheet. There was a slug-trail of spittle running from the corner of his mouth to the open neck of his shirt, and his eyes were rimmed with a yellow crust, but the eyes themselves were clear, and they were fixed on me.

'You're still alive!' I cried. The Proctor blinked, coughed. He regarded me with a look empty of reproach or anger. If there was anything in his eyes it was a sort of bemused curiosity. 'I nearly killed you. I am so sorry, Proctor. I used you as an experiment. It is unpardonable. I am a beast. I am very, very deeply in your debt. If I can ever repay you . . .'

And then a thought struck me. Not a very wise thought, but it had some value, some promise of redemption.

'I'm going to Umbria,' I said. The Proctor blinked again, and his expression became tense with a sort of canine alertness. 'To Assisi. That's in Umbria, yes? I'm going on pilgrimage. Will you come with me?'

ᨒ 34 ᨒ

ON THE THIRD MONDAY IN September, the Proctor and I rode out of the Porta del Popolo and started towards Assisi on the Ravenna road. The skies were pure blue and filled with threads of birds flying south. As above, so below: pilgrims were still pouring down the road towards Rome, mostly from the north to get back home before winter turned the roads to bottomless mire. The birds were drawn on by the promise of warm lands where winter never came, and the pilgrims by the shrines and relics of martyrs, and by the promise of a glimpse, however fleeting, of Christ's earthly representative. I was pulled north by Tessina. I had begun to see her everywhere: in the pale blond of the summer-burned grass, in the occasional high and perfectly white clouds, in the blue of the sky, reflected in the streams we crossed on ancient bridges.

I had given my notice to the cardinal's agent. He had been surprised, then angry, but I didn't care. I'd already moved out of San Lorenzo in Damaso and into a cheap inn. My few possessions were stashed with Leto. The kitchen was in the hands of Luigino, my second in command, who had been running it for months in any case while I frittered away my time with the cardinal's anxieties. The money I had put aside turned out to be quite an impressive sum, so I bought myself a new suit of clothes, a sober but expensive black hat and a heavy travelling cloak. Then I bought two horses, which took a bite out of my savings. After that, I made sure my purse was fat enough to keep us both in decent food and bedding, and the rest of my hoard I deposited with a Florentine bank (not, I should add, the Banco Medici).

I rose early the first day, long before dawn, filled with the excitement that comes before a long journey, which was further distilled into a kind of fever by the thought that Tessina waited for me at the end of my journey. I saddled both horses, which had been enjoying the dubious hospitality of my inn, and led them through the almost empty streets to the hospice of the White Fathers. The Proctor was waiting for me, pacing up and down in the street in front of the door. He had no possessions, except the clothes I had given him and a good cloak of his own which I'd decided he would need. He gave an exaggerated bow to the closed hospice door, treated me to an abrupt nod, and climbed onto his mount.

The Proctor's horse was a nag, sway-backed, torpid and cheap. I didn't expect the man to be able to ride and chose him a mount that would carry him with as much excitement as if he were sitting in a donkey cart, but when I took him round to the stable, thinking I would have to teach him to ride, to my amazement he swung into the battered old saddle and told me, a moment later, that the beast had a wooden mouth. I felt slightly embarrassed by my own horse, a handsome Neapolitan gelding, brownish-black with a lighter stippling across his flanks, which the Proctor eyed approvingly and, if I was not mistaken, enviously. But after he had trotted his nag up and down the street he decided that she was not so leaden after all, claimed that she had Barb blood and that he had admired her sire at the Perugia horse fair.

We made good time that first day, and stayed at an inn which, though the food was repulsive, at least offered us a bed free of lice. I had brought a small leather purse with me, which held a silver vial each of ground pepper, cinnamon, cloves and ginger, together with three nutmegs and a little rasp to grate them with, so after I had gone to work with these the horror of the food was masked somewhat. After a few more easy rides we came to Narni, where the town broods above a deep and sinister valley. Early that morning we had crossed the Tiber at Otricoli, and immediately, as soon as our horses were on the far bank, the Proctor began to sniff the air like a questing hound.

'Smell it, Dr Wind! The air! Oh, Christ, the air!'

'What's the matter?' I asked, concerned. The Proctor had been calm of late, but it had occurred to me that if his madness came back in full force on our journey, I would be ill-equipped to deal with it.

'Umbria! We are in Umbria! Hmm hmm . . . yes, yes! Free from the dismal miasmas of Latium, free at last. Can you not feel it, *dottore*? Can you not feel how pure it is, how clean?'

'I don't believe the atoms on this side of the river can be so different from those on the other,' I said pedantically. 'And besides, I did not feel any barrier midstream, which if the atoms . . .' But the Proctor had already put his heels to the nag's flank and was cantering away from me. Cursing, I set off after him.

From a distance, Narni had given me the shivers, but we found a decent inn which took pride in its food. Narni is famous for its grapes, and the host brought out a jar of them preserved in syrup, beautiful green pearls that I held up one by one before popping them between my teeth.

The Proctor watched me suspiciously whenever I ate. Since the hellebore, he had been much clearer in his mind, or at least more focused, because he rarely mentioned Perugia or his imagined rank, but took an unusual interest in the people and things around him. I had decided that his every moment had been subjected to a faulty concoction in his mind, influenced by his unbalanced humours, so that each experience had been pounded, boiled, chewed, passed through a sieve and moulded until it tasted of nothing but

Perugia. This process seemed to have stopped, which I put down to the purge and to the dishes I had been diligently selecting for him.

I had not dared attempt the hellebore again, but a few more purges, this time of aloes and wormwood, had been much less violent and I'd been able to convince my patient that they were doing him good. He had put on weight, filling out my cast-off clothes until now they more or less fitted him. His skin had healed and he was no longer covered in sores and welts. All in all, he didn't resemble a madman, at least from the outside. His mind was still tender, and I imagined the soft, ridged blancmange inside his skull strengthening, losing its unhealthy blotches and blooms, along with the rest of his body. The black bile was no longer combusting and sending its deadly vapours up into his brain. Under my scrutiny he was chewing his food rigorously, and judging by the quality of his piss and excrement (which I had observed surreptitiously), he was now more choleric than melancholic. In his mood, too, he was markedly hot and dry: his speech was clipped and he had grown somewhat short-tempered. At the same time he had become very attached to me. I sensed that he hadn't quite forgiven me for the horrors my purgative had wreaked on him, but he understood the good it had done. Or so I decided to believe, because after nearly killing the poor creature I now felt responsible for him. You might have mistaken us for master and servant, though our relationship was more like boy and stray dog.

He had proved to be an entertaining companion on the road, though. He knew the names of birds and plants, and barked them out at unpredictable moments, sometimes making the horses flinch. He reeled out long, rambling stories about the road we were on, the country, the towns we passed, which might have been true or not, peopled as they were with a bizarre crew of giants, heroes, fiends, phantasms, emperors and grotesque beasts. But the newly choleric part of his nature came out at every mealtime. Though he ate everything I ordered for him, he regarded each dish with narrow-eyed enmity.

'Can I not just eat,' he asked once, 'without being prescribed and dosed and regulated?'

'It's a beautiful snipe,' I replied. 'What's wrong with it?'

'I wished for the *scottaditi*,' he snapped.

'Lamb will exacerbate your melancholy,' I explained patiently. 'The flesh of waterfowl is dark and therefore hot. It's what you need. Eat it.'

'*You're* having the lamb,' he muttered.

'I can tolerate it. But it is notoriously phlegmatic, and that, coupled with your slapdash concoction . . . No, it would be a disaster.'

'I have seen disaster. Disaster . . .' He squirmed, cleared his throat (I noted the presence of phlegm). 'I say, I have seen disaster, Dr Wind. It does not resemble a plate of lamb chops.'

He was right, of course: the madman was right. It was all nonsense, and if it wasn't nonsense it was insufferable. Food was food: it had the power to give delight and to sustain, but I was a cook, not an engineer, and all I had been doing, these past months, was raising and lowering, balancing and adjusting. I might as well have been winching stones up a wall, or sinking the piles of a bridge, except that then I might have been doing something useful. The cardinal was still healthy, the Proctor was still mad, though I had to admit he had been making an increasing amount of sense lately. I felt a sweet flood of relief: my medical career was finished. Now I could be a cook again.

That night in Narni I offered the Proctor a grape. He shook his head.

'Prescription and purgation,' he muttered.

'No, no. It's delicious.'

'Meddle, meddle . . .'

'It's delightful.' I ate it, selected another, offered it. He reached out reluctantly, snatched it and jammed it petulantly into his mouth.

'A decent grape. An *Umbrian* grape,' he said, appeased. 'Now, what terrible effects will assail my poor frame?'

'None.'

'So a grape is a grape, no more nor less?'

'My friend,' I said, suddenly exhausted by the whole thing. 'Tonight, I will allow that a grape is just a grape. Make sure you chew it properly.'

We ambled along. In two days we were at Massa Martana. It was the last day of September, and the festival of the saint at Assisi was on the fourth of October. The Proctor went out to walk around the town walls, as was his habit. Years – I didn't know how long, in fact – of being utterly alone had driven the habits of solitude very deep, so I let him go. He still had a tendency to mutter, and he might suddenly hunker down in the middle of the street and draw things in the dust with his fingers, but most of the time he was only a little bit stranger than those around him.

I sat in a corner of the dining room, glad to be alone for a while. The closer we came to Assisi, the more my nerves were growing. In five days' time I would see Tessina. It seemed like an eternity and at the same time terrifyingly close. But then, ever since her last letter had arrived, I had felt each day passing with infinite slowness. The hours crawled. Tessina and I were moving towards each other. In five days' time we would come together, two lines drawn on a map, two alchemist's symbols joining together to form something unknowable. What would happen in Assisi was something I hadn't yet dared to imagine. I got up, shuffled around the room aimlessly, then went out to find a church.

There were two, so I chose San Sebastiano as looking less frequented, went in and lit some candles. I knelt, let my forehead rest on the cool stone rail in front of the Virgin's shrine and began to recite the Ave Maria. But my mind would not remain constant. It wandered, then fixed itself on an imagined road, leading straight to an imagined city. Assisi, which I had never laid eyes on: was it large or small? If it was the size of Massa, a tiny place with one main street, how would I be able to meet Tessina without being discovered by Baroni or his men? Would they be staying at an inn? At a monastery? Were there many inns in Assisi? I supposed there would be thousands of people there for the saint's festival, so I adjusted the size of the town accordingly. A huge throng in a small space would be good: I could hide myself. But then what? I'd never dared go this far in my plans. A stolen moment with Tessina? Or would I be able to get her away from her husband for longer? There was another plan, though, which had unfolded in the furthest reaches of my mind. Suddenly, it burst out into the light. Everything was clear, as if the Virgin had leaned down from her altar and laid her hand on my head.

I wasn't going to Assisi to steal a glimpse of Tessina. I was going to steal her. What else could I possibly do? She had to be rescued from her impotent, jealous husband and his revolting son. All my vague and ridiculous plans vanished in a crystalline flood of clarity. There we were, Tessina and I, galloping down the road I had imagined, as Baroni awoke and realized that horns the size of elk antlers were sprouting from his temples. We'd go south, to Naples and then to Spain. Or north, to Milan or perhaps France. It would work. Why wouldn't it? The Virgin was guiding me. Santa Bibiana was at my shoulder.

It was dark by the time the Proctor stalked back into the dining room of the inn, where I had been waiting for him impatiently. I ought to have been worried as well, but I had been completely, shamefully, wrapped in my schemes for Tessina's rescue.

'Where have you been?' I scolded. The Proctor was covered in sweat and dust but appeared unharmed.

'Santa Maria in Pantano,' he said.

'Where?'

He pointed vaguely out of the window. 'I am hungry.'

'I was waiting for you.' He shrugged. 'What is Santa Maria in Pantano?'

'A monastery. Very lovely.'

'Oh. And who told you about it?'

'Told me? Told me? I know it – I have *always* known it.' He turned his back on me and went into the kitchen, from which enticing smells and interesting dishes had been emerging for the past hour. When he re-emerged, he came and sat down opposite me. 'I was hungry, so I have ordered the food.'

'Good Christ! What . . .'

'Plain food. Umbrian food. It won't hurt you, Dr Wind.' There was a new confidence about him. It seems unbelievable to me now, and shameful, but the realization that dawned on me then was quite new and surprising.

'Proctor,' I said. 'So you really are from Umbria?'

'Where, *dottore*, doctor of fundamental winds, snuffler of golden liquids, O shaver and anointer, O prodder and poker and purgator, where did you suppose I came from?'

'I . . . So do you know anything about Assisi?'

The Proctor sucked his exasperation in through clenched teeth. His neck began to twitch, but fortunately the serving girl arrived with a great platter of steaming food.

'What on earth is this?' I demanded.

'Again, I will say it: Umbrian food,' he snapped.

'But these are lentils. Lentils are the grossest of foods. The most indigestible. The sausages . . .' There was a mound of delicious-looking, plump sausages in the middle of the lentil dune. 'The sausages are fine, I grant you.'

But my warning, delivered from sheer force of habit, was too late, thank God: the Proctor had already heaped his plate and was spooning lentils into his mouth like a metalworker feeding his furnace. I speared a sausage with my knife, bit off the end. Juice and fat exploded: the pork melted. I tasted chestnuts, moss, the bulbs of wild lilies, the roots and shoots of an Umbrian forest floor. There was pepper, of course, salt and garlic. Nothing else. I opened my eyes. The Proctor was staring at me, and quickly looked away. I thought I saw a smile cross his lips before he opened them to admit another wagon-load of lentils.

I tried a spoonful myself. They were very small and brown – earthy-tasting, of course. That I had been expecting. But these were subtle: there was a hint of pine, which came partly from the rosemary that was obviously in the dish, but partly from the lentils themselves. I did feel as if I were eating soil, but a special kind: some sort of silky brown clay, perhaps; something that Maestro Donatello would have crossed oceans to sculpt with, or that my uncle Filippo would have used as a pigment to paint the eyes of a beautiful brown-eyed *donna*. Maybe this is what the earth under the finest hazelnut tree in Italy would taste like – but that, perhaps, was a question best put to a pig.

'Make sure you chew properly,' I mumbled, piling my plate high.

The serving girl came back with a trencher of sliced pork meats: cheek, salami dotted with pink fat, ribbons of *lardo*, peppery bacon. The flavours were slippery, lush, like copper leaf or the robe of a cardinal. I coiled a strip of dark, translucent ham onto my tongue: it dissolved into a shock-ingly carnal mist, a swirl of truffles, cinnamon and *bottarga*. I sighed deeply, and sank back against the wall.

'Why are we going to Assisi?' asked the Proctor, after a few more mouthfuls. 'Because you do not seem like the kind of man to go on a pilgrimage.' He belched, pointedly, as if to vex me with the inadequacies of his concoction. 'If you'll forgive me for saying so, eminent *dottore*, high priest of Aeolus, hmm, hmm? Your saint is Bibiana, unless I've misheard your mutterings and mumblings. You chitter away like a dowager's pet monkey. Bibiana – or is it Santa Tessina, eh? Hmm, hmm? I am not cognizant of that saint's holiday.'

'What has got into you?' I said, blushing. The food, and now the Proctor's pointed words, had put me quite off balance.

'You are the doctor, *dottore*. What is the diagnosis when a man eats a slice of prosciutto as if he were snuffling under a woman's skirts? What humour is in the ascendant? Hmm, hmm? Which of us needs a purgative, I ask?'

'I'm not a doctor,' I said, knowing I sounded ridiculous.

'A doctor who is no doctor, but who doctors. A tasty riddle, that one.'

'I am – I was – a dietary. Somewhere between a cook and a doctor.' Without thinking I took another slice of ham, let it overpower me. 'But really I'm a cook,' I said after a while. And so it was that, over lentils and cured pork and the red wine of Montefalco, I told the Proctor my story.

'Assisi will be stuffed like a sausage,' said the Proctor. 'It will be boiling over. It will be . . . I am using the metaphors of the kitchen, Master of Winds, in the hope that you will grasp them, hmm, hmm?'

'I've grasped the main thrust, I think. Can we get on with it?'

'Now you say your lady's husband is a strutting, puff-breasted creature of pride and vanity, for whom appearance is all, hmm?'

'More or less exactly.'

'Then he will be staying at one of the great hostelries.' He reeled off four names. 'But he will have reserved bed and board by the agency of letter. Which you have not done, hmm? So we will stay in Bevagna, which is only a morning's ride.'

It was decided. We would spend the night of the fourth of October in Bevagna, and then I would ride to Assisi early, slip into the crowds of pilgrims, and look for Tessina. Simple enough – it seemed that way, as we rode down the hill towards Bevagna, a walled town sitting at the edge of a broad, flat valley cut off by mountains. I liked the place at once. It was peaceful and the buildings were patchworks of ancient stone and timber. Though it was more than fifteen miles from Assisi, Bevagna was still bustling with pilgrims, and we were lucky to be given the last bed in a clean hostelry just off the piazza. We had the most expensive room, and it was more expensive still because of the festival. It had a real bed, a great four-legged beast of carved wood stained black by years of touch. I was quite happy to share it with the Proctor, but as usual he marked out a place for himself on the floor, in the corner nearest the window.

I barely slept. The night seemed endless, and in the end I went out and walked through the streets in the company of cats and stars. The last crickets of the year were singing bravely from the brambles and hedges that lined the little gardens close to the wall. Something glowed in one of the hedges: it was a dog rose, months late. I thought of Santa Chiara of Assisi, who had made the roses bloom in winter, and picked it for a talisman, knowing that I was blessed.

When I got back to the inn I wrapped myself in my cloak

and slept for an hour on top of the bedcovers. Then I got up, buckled on my sword and dagger – I wanted to look dashing, after all – woke the Proctor and told him to wait for me, that I had paid for three days' use of our room but that I'd be back, God willing, that night. Have your horse ready, I told him. We might be riding through the night, and we might be pursued, but everything would be all right.

'A man of certainties,' he said, scratching his head furiously. 'A man . . . How old are you, Master of Winds?'

'Twenty-two,' I told him proudly. He crossed himself.

'I do not have your skills, your learning, your wellspring of knowledge. Your skills diagnostic, prognostic, paregoric. Your experience, hmm hmm? I am no adept of the arcane, I am master neither of caduceus or cook-pot. I cannot spice a civet nor bard a figpecker. I am a poor man, a wanderer, who has been robbed and reviled, cast out and cursed, purged and poisoned. But allow me to tell you, young – *very* young – Master Wind: things are never all right.'

'I know. But all that's changed now,' I said.

The road from Bevagna to Assisi was a spider's leg: long straight stretches that ran across the flat bottom of the valley, jointed on little villages whose names I'd learned from the innkeeper: Cantalupo, Cannara, Castelnuovo. I had a map, scribbled on a piece of bark. There was plenty of time: the stars were still alight, there was only the faintest glow in the east, and the waxing moon was falling towards the western mountains. I had time: and still I galloped. The Neapolitan hadn't had much fun on our journey so far, but now I gave him his head, and he sped down the dusty track, hooves thudding on packed chalk. Dust bloomed behind us, dark in the half-dawn, rising through the olive trees like squid ink through seaweed. A few men, going early to the fields with hoes on their shoulders, looked up slack-jawed as we passed them.

Light seemed to be growing behind every bush and tree, picking out the tiniest leaf, the merest twist of tendril, thorns, fruit. I was riding through the background of one of Filippo's paintings. Filippo, who had died somewhere near here, behind me where the dawn was breaking. He might have painted it just for his stubborn little nephew, so that he could finally take his uncle's advice and follow his heart. He would have cheered me on – God, he would have slapped my horse's rump to speed me on my way. I shouted his name, and the wind crammed the words back into my mouth. I held up my hand, feeling like the angel in one of the Annunciations I'd watched him paint: grasping the tall stalk of a lily like a knight's lance. I swear I heard Filippo's voice chuckling at all the things I called myself that morning: the Angel Gabriel, Tristano riding to his Isotta, Lancillotto to his Ginevra, Dante to his Beatrice.

The road was rising under the Neapolitan's hooves. We were in a narrow lane between high green banks, and just ahead, the gate of Assisi and its halberd-leaning guards.

35

I RODE UP INTO THE honey-coloured town. There were pilgrims sleeping in doorways, wrapped in cloaks and blankets, scattered beneath trees and colonnades. I was at the very eastern end of the town, and the gigantic basilica of the saint, more like a fortress than a church, with its buttresses like sandstone cliffs, dominated the western side.

There was a livery stable close to the gate I had come through, and I left the Neapolitan there. I also secured another horse for this evening, to be returned by the inn at Bevagna. I realized that I had no idea whether Tessina could ride, but then again, of course she could. Everything was going to be fine. I strolled up the hill, and before long I came to the long street, the Via San Francesco, that led to the basilica. Now I had to be careful. I was wearing my long riding cloak, which came down below my knees and hid my sword and dagger. It had a wide hood, and this I pulled up and draped so that my face would be in shadow.

It was a long street indeed, and lined on both sides with inns, hostelries, pilgrims' hospices, cook-shops, tavernas. Street sellers were laying out stalls of pious tat. Others were kindling grills and braziers. I decided that I had time to be thorough, so I walked into the first hostelry that the Proctor had mentioned and enquired after the Baroni family from Florence. Blank looks were my answer, so I crossed and re-crossed the street until I had threaded a cross-stitch of fruitless enquiry halfway along the Via San Francesco.

The sun was coming up and it was getting quite warm inside my cloak. People were starting to drift out into the streets and most of them turned towards the pale bulk of the basilica. Soon I was trying to ford a river of people, all streaming towards the shrine of Saint Francis like elvers swarming in a ditch: young and old, rich and almost destitute, the lame on crutches, the sick with sores bleeding through linen wrappings, noble ladies with handkerchiefs held to their noses. I jostled through the crowd, using my elbows as inoffensively as I could manage, and slipped through the open door of the Albergo del Gallo Verde, deciding that I would have a break after I'd questioned the innkeeper.

'Messer Bartolo Baroni and his wife?' repeated the man who met me in the hallway, a thin fellow with a melon-sized paunch jutting through his clean linen apron. 'Indeed. Of course. They have been here for two nights.'

'I . . . Ah.' I cleared my throat. 'Excellent.'

'Messer Bartolo Baroni of Florence . . . yes, I think they are still upstairs. Who shall I announce?'

'No! No need,' I said. For some strange reason I hadn't prepared for this moment, even though I'd gone over it in my head over and over again. I should have memorized an answer like I'd memorized the catechism as a little boy. But instead I was forming my tongue around words that were not there. I cleared my throat again, looked down at my boots. They looked expensive. 'My father . . .' I began. I was the son of someone who bought him expensive footwear. 'My father is a business colleague of Messer Bartolo. I said I'd pay my compliments, as we were both coming – from different directions – to the festival. But actually I'm just on my way to the shrine, and after that . . . Will they be dining here tonight?'

'Indeed! We keep the best table in Assisi. Shall you be joining us, Master . . . ?' He left the question hanging. I noticed that he was also looking admiringly at my boots. I bowed, stepped back into the doorway.

'Perhaps, perhaps!' I said airily. 'I have to worship, of course, or why would I have come all the way, you know, from Florence? And then there is some business, you understand, on behalf of my father. I'm sure you do understand. I'll . . . I'll send my man around with my compliments.'

Then I turned on my heel and all but threw myself into the twining, roiling rope of pilgrims in the street. This time I didn't fight them but let the crowd carry me along on a rough current of elbows and knees, breathing in the heavy fug of unwashed armpits and groins, rotten teeth, greasy hair, Hungary water, freshly laundered tunics and never-washed breech-clouts. Up the hill we went, blaring out prayers and hymns, and finally the street took a last turn and there was the great basilica, towering over us on a spur of hillside.

The shrine of Saint Francis hadn't actually been on my list of things to do in Assisi, strange as that might seem. My pilgrimage was to wherever Tessina might be. I hadn't forgotten, though, how the Proctor had clung to the saint's words in his delirium, the delirium I had induced with black hellebore. So I decided it would be appropriate – no, necessary – to offer up some prayers on behalf of my travelling companion, and to give thanks, myself, for keeping him safe from my amateur doctorings.

But it took an age to pass through the outer door of the basilica, even though I must have been at the forefront of that day's mass of pilgrims, and I felt like a pine nut being stuffed into a goose's neck and then roasted, because inside the basilica there was no escape from the hundreds upon hundreds of the faithful, and I was still wrapped in my heavy cloak. But there were things here that I'd wanted to see for years: the cycle of frescoes that Filippo had said were some of the finest paintings ever made. And there they were, all around me, Maestro Giotto's telling of the life of Saint Francis. I didn't really look at them, though. That is, I looked, but I didn't see.

My mind was somewhere else, as it was when I let myself be herded down into the Lower Basilica and up to the shrine of Francis himself.

After that I was completely exhausted, sweating like a man with a tertiary fever, and my feet were in agony from having been stepped on again and again by countless shuffling pilgrims. I'd all but given myself up for lost, deciding that I'd probably be digested down here in the guts of the basilica, when the mob sucked and heaved and spat me out into the sunlight.

I sat on some steps overlooking the plain, with my chin in my hands, gulping fresh air, trying to get the greasy film of other people's breath, of incense and candlewax, out of my lungs. The sun was past its zenith. Which was good: I'd killed more than half the day. I fought my way back through the throng until I'd got away from the busiest streets, and wandered down the alleys towards the wall. I found an abandoned garden with a dusty old palm tree and lay down beneath it. The rattling of its collar of dead fronds was soothing. I calmed down slowly and began to think more soberly about the evening to come. But before I'd managed to come up with any kind of plan, I fell asleep.

When I opened my eyes again, the sun had edged down a little further towards the horizon and there was a fairly large black scorpion dozing on the back of my hand. I jerked upright and threw him into the bushes. My mouth held the woolly, verdigris taste of a hangover and my shoulders were stiff from trying to hold my own in the crush of pilgrims, but apart from that I felt quite invigorated. There was a rather scabby, unpruned apple tree in a corner of the garden, its branches drooping under the weight of unwanted, un-claimed apples. I claimed a few and ate them under the palm. Good: I'd been hungry without knowing it.

Leaning back against the ridged trunk of the palm, I tried

to make sense of the day so far. It seemed obvious now, but up there in the packed, deafening basilica I might have been inches away from Tessina – or Bartolo Baroni for that matter. A possibility that hadn't occurred to me as I was being jostled and bustled, but which might very well have proved disastrous. I'd have to sharpen my wits. From now on I'd be careful. Up until this point I'd been acting as if Our Lady and the saints were going to put Tessina's hand in mine and hide our escape in some sort of divine fog, but that had been before the fact that Tessina was actually here, only a few minutes' walk from where I sat.

What was I going to do? In my fantasies – there had been hundreds upon hundreds of those by now, cooked up in my idle brain as I stood, bored rigid, behind the cardinal's chair at dinner, and as I jounced along the roads of Umbria – I strutted into wherever it was that Tessina was staying, reached out for her, pulled her to me. The two of us would stroll out into the night, leaving Baroni popping his lips like the impotent old carp that he was. I bit into another apple. It had hung for a little too long and there was a faint fizz, a tang of cider. What had the innkeeper said? Messer Bartolo Baroni and his wife. No mention of anyone else. There would be servants, of course – not worth telling me about. But if there were other Baronis, wouldn't the man have said *the Baroni party*, or something like that? Of course he would. Then why not just do exactly what I'd imagined? Wait until dinner, until old Baroni would have guzzled enough wine to make his ears red and his nose swell like a strawberry . . . I could picture the corpulent, liver-coloured old bastard, fat as a gorged tick, recognition blossoming in his veiny eyes as I strolled across the dining room; as I held out my hand to his wife. Perhaps he'd try and stop me. He'd try to rise, spluttering, but by then we would be gone.

I stretched like a happy dog, and the fronds of the date

palm rustled. Then I got up and went to find a pump or a fountain, somewhere I could rinse off the smell of pilgrim.

I walked right around the walls, taking my time, waiting for the sun to set. When it was dark I went back to the Via San Francesco. Across from the Gallo Verde, a friar was standing in the archway of an old portico, preaching to a crowd of country people, who were gathered around him in a tight half-moon, some of them eating their dinner, some of them holding cups of wine or ale. I slipped into the little crowd and stood with my back to a pillar, watching the door of the inn out of the corner of my eye. But an endless stream of people was flowing up and down the street, carrying torches and candles, and for minutes at a time I couldn't even see the inn. I waited and waited. Tessina and Baroni must have come back by now, surely . . . And if they had, I almost certainly wouldn't have seen them go in. So was this it, then? Was it time to walk in?

I crossed the street, but at the door I hesitated. Was this how it was going to be? It seemed messy, somehow – undignified. What if Tessina and Baroni weren't yet at table? I had visions of getting into some sort of argument, with the landlord perhaps, and Tessina looking up from her plate to see me, red-faced and flustered, being thrown out by the inn's servants. That wouldn't do. But then I had another idea. I'd send her a message.

It wasn't hard to find the service entrance. I stepped into the kitchen, which was working so hard that at first no one even glanced at me, and singled out the head cook, a startlingly small, completely bald man in a stained apron, whose hands, face and shiny, pointed scalp were sweating hard and as pink as boiled ham.

'Excuse me,' I said. 'I'd like to cook a dish for someone. It's a surprise.' The man whipped around and found himself staring at a stack of silver coins resting on my outstretched hand. Easily two weeks' wages for a man like him; his mouth opened, then shut again and his eyes narrowed. He was already weighing up a possible deal. I sweetened the pot a little more.

'I'm the personal cook to His Eminence Cardinal Federico Gonzaga,' I said. 'A great friend of my father's is out there in the dining room. He doesn't know I'm in Assisi, so I thought how hilarious it would be to surprise him with a dish I created for Lorenzo de' Medici.' I let the name slip casually. 'I'm happy to teach it to you.' The man's mouth tightened sceptically, but then his eyes, which had been looking me up and down, came to rest on my boots. They seemed to do the trick.

'What dish?' he croaked.

'Very, very simple. I just need a corner of that table over there to make it – in fact, I can put it together out in the yard. You have all the ingredients, I'm sure.'

'I . . . What ingredients?'

'Lean pork meat, some lard, salt, pepper, fennel seeds, parsley, thyme or marjoram. Oregano will do.' The cook was frowning, unconvinced. 'And a black truffle. Do you have one? From last year? A noble kitchen like this surely keeps a few to hand . . .'

'It'll cost you.'

'I will pay,' I said. He named an appalling figure. I just nodded.

'Fair enough. I have those things,' he grunted. The truffle must have convinced him that I was not a madman or a poisoner, because what assassin would be stupid enough to pay so much for last year's truffle? He held out his heat-swollen hand for the money. 'If this comes back to me in any way I'll kill you,' he hissed. 'I don't know who the *cazzo* you are, but I'll kill you.'

'Give me the ingredients first,' I said, closing my fist

around the silver and shaking it. I told him the amounts. 'And I'll need a chopping board and a thin spit.'

So far, none of the other men had paid me any attention, which was good. I retreated to the tiny yard at the back of the inn. It reminded me strongly of the Porco, right down to the filthy jakes. I found a barrel and pulled it over to the kitchen window so that some light fell across the top. The cook came out with a thick slice of pork, some metal skewers, a bundle of greenery, a heap of salt and a little jar of coriander seeds, all balanced on a slightly warped board.

'Knife?' he snapped. I drew my dagger. He retreated half a step. 'Where's my money, then?'

I gave him half, and told him he'd get the rest when the dish was cooked. That was a good part of my savings gone, but it didn't matter.

As soon as the man had stumped off, I set to work. The fennel I crushed against the board with the flat of my dagger. The pork – it was good: fresh-smelling and rosy – I cut into long strips which I pounded flat with the dagger's pommel before sprinkling them with salt and the ground fennel and mincing them together with the lard I took out my spice purse. From it I added cinnamon, cloves and pepper to the mixture. I rolled the pork strips herb-side in and threaded them onto a couple of the skewers.

By now my heart was knocking hard against my ribs and all my limbs seemed to want to travel in opposite directions. I told myself to calm down. Perhaps the Baronis weren't even in the house. I had to see for myself. I slipped back into the kitchen and followed a serving boy who was leaving with a platter held above his head. The dining room was down a short corridor. I waited for the servant to go in and then peered around the half-open door. The room was large, with a low ceiling of heavy oak beams and a fire burning in a wide hearth. The long tables were set out like a refectory. Feeling almost feverish I searched each table, but almost immediately I saw her.

She was seated at the top corner of the furthest table. I would have known her just by the fall of her hair, and indeed I couldn't see much more, because her head was turned away from me towards a big, shiny-faced old man at the table's head. He was slightly stooped, his sparse black hair no more than a ring around his bald and flaking scalp, plastered greasily against his skin. He had lips like a pair of chicken hearts and one eye was swollen almost shut by some kind of infection. With a shock I realized that I was looking at Bartolo Baroni. Christ, the man had aged. But Tessina . . . There was the curve of her nose, the smooth, round jut of her chin. I drank her in, drank and drank until I had to lean back against the wall. One last glimpse, and then I all but ran back to the yard where a stick-legged, bag-bellied cat was advancing on my skewers. I grabbed them, gave the cook the rest of his silver, and set the meat carefully to roast. Only then did the other cooks notice me, so I leered and winked and I suppose they took me for a rich young gentleman and, as such, someone above their notice, especially as their master was scowling at them with as much malice as he was directing at me. I picked up my knife and began to slice the truffle into papery black rounds.

The pork was done. I tasted the juices: perfect. But now I was shivering with nerves. I closed my eyes and pictured Our Lady and Santa Bibiana, glowing faintly, both of them smiling kindly, calmly. 'Dear Ladies,' I whispered. 'Help your servant Nino in his hour of greatest need. Help your servant Tessina and deliver her from servitude.'

A girl had just come into the kitchen with a pile of empty platters. I caught her arm, fished out a silver florin, put the steaming skewers of meat onto a clean pewter trencher. Taking great care, though my hands were beginning to shake, I dressed each skewer in a delicate black chemise of truffle. Then I picked up the platter and held it out to the girl together with the coin.

'Take this to Messer Bartolo Baroni and his wife,' I told her. 'In the far corner. He is old and apoplectic. She has fair hair and is . . . You'll know them. Say this comes with the compliments of a friend. Go now.'

The girl looked at me as if I'd just jumped down from the moon. But she took the coin and dropped it between her breasts. Then she took the plate. I bowed to the cook and to the other men who were doing their best not to stare at me, and followed her. I stopped her at the dining-room door, pointed to Baroni, then watched from the shadows as she walked across the room. It was like watching someone move through water, or through oil. Each footstep seemed to take an agonizing age. The noise of the diners was lost in the drumming of blood in my ears.

The girl was almost at the table. Bartolo Baroni lifted his cleft chin and his wattles quivered as the girl bowed and said something. Baroni frowned. The plate was set down in front of him. This was wrong. *Serve the lady first!* I hissed, though no one could hear me. Baroni was staring down at the plate. Tessina frowned as well, dislodged a truffle slice, dabbed a piece of the meat with her finger, licked it. And I knew. She understood. Her eyes lifted, found me, found me where I lurked beyond the door, as if she had known all along that I was there. And then she smiled.

I was walking across the floor of the dining room. Except, in a way, I was still watching from the door. No, I was here. My hip jarred against a diner's chair. Tessina had half risen. Though we were still half a room apart, I felt her: the tiny, coppery hairs on her arm that rose to attention when she was cold or aroused; the beautiful landscape of gooseflesh that was shivering across her skin beneath her robe; the flowery, powdery scent of that skin, as complicated as music. The faint freckles scattered across her cheeks and nose: I was falling into them, as though they were the starry summer sky.

Baroni tore off a piece of meat, shoved it into his mouth, chewed and nodded approvingly. He lifted his head to say something to Tessina, saw her staring, followed her gaze, saw me. His face went the colour of liver and he gave a choleric grunt. Was he, perhaps, choking on my pork roulade? There was an elegant detail I had left out of my plans, my dreams.

I barged another chair out of my way, raised my hand. And then a man sitting with his back to me, sitting opposite Tessina, a man I hadn't marked before because he had an ugly haircut and Tessina had seemed to be ignoring him, turned around. It was Marco Baroni. He was on his feet in a heartbeat, his chair clattering backwards, and the man next to him, tall, straw-haired . . . As in a waking dream I knew it had to be Corso Marucelli and of course it was, kicking his own chair over, opening his wound of a mouth to yell something I couldn't hear. I was watching Tessina's face. It was breaking apart, as if it had never been real. How could it be? I was waking up. I was back in Rome. I was back in Donna Velia's hut. I was back in Florence, on Via dei Benci, with the Baroni retainers drawing their swords. Then Tessina screamed.

'Nino!'

It was like a kiss, but it was like being struck as well. For a moment there was nothing, complete stillness. Tessina reached for me. If I stretched, if I took one more step, I would have her. But there was still so much between us. This floor, that table, those men, with their swords half drawn. Then Bartolo's hand came slamming down, knocking Tessina's arm, pinning her wrist to the table. She screamed again:

'Nino! Run!'

I did. Crashing back through the dining room, slamming a

boy with a plate full of roast fowl against the wall of the corridor, the birds flying – flying! Out through the kitchen, the cook's ham-pink face snarling, looming and then gone. Out into the yard, with its cats and its stink of shit – why had I not noticed that before? – and then down some steps and into the alleyway beyond, the hard, flat beat of shod feet clapping behind me. The alley sloped left, downhill, and I sprinted for the corner, turned into a wider street, sent an old man sprawling, scattered a knot of torch-bearing nuns. I shoved through, using my shoulders and my elbows, feeling my sword hilt catch in clothing, ignoring the curses and the blasphemies, burying myself in the crowd. It was still a river of flesh, surging towards the basilica, and I let it carry me along until I saw a tiny passageway on the right. I darted into it, ran up a steep, narrow flight of stairs, jumped over a low, tumbledown wall, stumbled through a bed of dead artichokes and a tent of bean poles, over another wall, into the sharp reek of chicken dung that sucked beneath my boots. Another wall and I was back in a street, this one empty. I fell into a deep doorway and fought for my breath.

Gone. She was gone. Of course she was. Hadn't I known it, as soon as I'd looked out into that dining room? We would never have touched, even if we'd reached for one another until our sinews snapped. I had been looking into another world. I'd never even come close to possessing her. These past months, I'd been sleeping in a nest of rags: curled up like a rat in the rafters, among the ragged scraps of dreams.

The street was still empty. I could hear the festival going full tilt just below. Marco couldn't have followed me. I'd have to get back to the livery stable, ride south. But then, I couldn't get that last vision out of my head: Tessina's lovely mouth, opened to scream; and Marco Baroni's thick black hair, cut in a straight line around his head. I couldn't leave Tessina with Marco. He would kill her – but perhaps that would be a kindness. His revenge – because he would take revenge, of that there was no doubt at all – might be something far, far worse.

The street sloped downhill towards the eastern edge of the city. If I went that way, doubled back, I would be at the inn while Marco and Corso were still out looking for me. I jogged down the stairways and steep, ramped alleys until I thought I recognized an old doorway with an unusual arch. The back of the Gallo Verde was up there, I was fairly sure. A bunched group of pilgrims turned into the street. They were singing holy songs, even though they were plainly a bit the worse for drink. When they had passed I slipped in behind them. But soon they turned off again. I was alone.

Someone had set up a small shrine on the next corner, a stone with a crude little painting of a saint, propped up against the wall. There were fresh flowers on the stone, and a candle, almost burned out and guttering. Another candle lay on the ground and, because the shrine had taken me by surprise and looked a little forlorn, I bent down, lit the fresh candle and stuck it into the wax of the old one. As I straightened up I heard a shuffling behind me.

I spun around just in time to see a man stepping out of the passageway. He was short, his mouth was twisting like a mastiff coming up under a bull's stomach, and he had a drawn sword in his hand. It was Marco Baroni. My hands found my sword and dagger and I wrenched them out, tasting burned candle grease in my throat. Another man appeared at Marco's shoulder, popping out of the darkness like a carnival puppeteer's crude trick. Taller, leaner: Corso Marucelli.

Marco hesitated for a heartbeat when he realized I'd seen him, but at once he took his sword in both hands, lifted it to eye level and charged. He was so near that I barely managed to duck out of the way of his blade. It flashed past my ear and hit the wall, showering me with crumbs of plaster, and as his arm jarred with the impact I brought my knee up between his legs and shoved him backwards. But he wasn't hurt and his blade came up like a scorpion's tail. His face was clenched and stiff with rage and he threw himself at me.

I just had time to glimpse Corso sidling around to my right, a blade in each hand, as Marco's sword sighed past my armpit. He let his weight carry him onto me, because he was inside the reach of my sword. Not my dagger, though: but I was holding it point down and before I could turn the point towards him it was crushed harmlessly between us. He was snarling into my neck – not words, but animal noise, pure fury. I stumbled back against the wall and his blade clattered against the stones again. I unlocked my left arm and smashed my knuckles into Marco's ear while he tried to wrench himself free. His heel came down on the bridge of my foot and I lurched forward. He was so much shorter than me, and so much stronger, that he had me off balance straight away. Like a ram, he battered me with his head until I fell sideways. I went down on one knee, still trying to twist the dagger into his chest, but he heaved again and I landed on my bum.

He should have had me then, but he paused and sighted along his blade at my chest. Perhaps he was savouring the moment, but whatever he thought he was doing, it was a mistake. I rolled and jumped up, changing my grip on the hilt of my dagger just as his perfectly aimed thrust should have had me through the liver. Whipping out my left hand I caught his sword arm at the wrist, shoving it wide and swinging him off balance. He spun, his foot caught against a step and he fell heavily into a doorway.

I would have run, but Corso was there in front of me, a wicked grin on his face. We raised our swords, and I tried to get into the middle of the street, away from Marco who was cursing and struggling to his feet. Corso was too quick. He lunged, and lunged again, and though I parried him easily, he was forcing me back towards his friend. I flicked my head towards Marco, and in a split second Corso's sword laid my doublet open from navel to left shoulder. I felt the tip of the blade burn against my skin, twisted, caught it with the hilt of my dagger. I stamped and lunged, running him through the shoulder pad of his own doublet. He laughed, jumped backwards to free himself.

Marco was up. His shoulders were hunched and the pommel of his sword, gripped in both hands, was against his breastbone. He thrust at me with all of his body behind the blade, just as Corso came in from the other side. Beyond panic, I swatted at Corso's sword with my dagger, knocked it down, but not far enough. It went into my upper thigh and passed cleanly through. My sword went past Marco's ear. Corso, still driving his sword into my leg, brought up his dagger and as he steadied himself to punch it into my face he stepped into the path of Marco's sword, which took him under his left armpit, the blade coming out under the other arm.

Corso screamed and twisted. He caught the bloody point where it jutted from his doublet in his fist and lunged towards me. Marco was trying to pull his blade from his friend's body and from his grasp, Corso was still trying to stab me. With a grunt I parried his dagger, deflecting it up and over my head, and without any thought or hesitation set my feet and put my own blade through his neck. For a moment he hung, pinned from each side. Marco tugged at his sword and Corso gave a throttled yelp. He tugged again, jerked it clear. Corso coughed up a great surge of blood and collapsed.

With a roar, Marco Baroni trod on his friend's back and swung his sword. His other arm was flung wide for balance and his chest was completely exposed. I was bent over, trying to understand what was happening, feeling the pain start to grow as Corso's blade, pulled by the jerking of his arm that still gripped the hilt with white knuckles, slid out of my thigh. All I could see in the dim light was the place where Marco's shirt had come open, revealing a pale V of skin. I seemed to have all the time in the world to raise the skewer of my sword and drive it cleanly into the pale target. Marco's legs went at once and he was falling towards me before I'd even got the blade out of him. Something unimaginably hard and sharp bit into my temple and the world went out in a pretty burst of silver petals.

I came to my senses, woken by a loud, shrill voice.

'Help!' For a moment I thought it was me that was screaming, high and out of control. 'Help! For God's sake, help! *Omicidio!*'

But it was someone leaning out of an open window. I was lying across Marco. His cheek was crushed against the ground, forcing his lip up to show a broken tooth. Something seemed to be drilling itself into my head, just above my left ear. I scrabbled, found wetness, pain, something hard. One of the quillons of his sword was tangled in a fat flap of my flesh and hair. I sat up, vomited. There was Corso, eyes open, his skin and clothes black with blood. The edge of his sword had caught beneath the edge of the rock that held the saint's shrine. We hadn't even put the candle out.

I tried to stand, but my leg wouldn't take the weight. It vanished from under me and all of a sudden I was sprawled in blood and sick. I managed to crawl back to Marco. Was he breathing? There was a lot of blood, more when I rolled him onto his back. I hadn't meant to kill him. I hadn't wanted any of this . . .

The woman − it was an old woman up there, screaming her head off − would not shut up. I lifted Marco's head and shoved a fold of his cloak under it. Then, above the screaming, I heard footsteps at the other end of the street, still quite far away. Fear got me upright again. I picked up my sword, found my dagger still in my left hand, got them into their scabbards and sliced into my right thumb as I struggled. Then I tried to run. My wounded leg felt as if a white-hot fire was being stoked right in its core, and I couldn't see out of my left eye, but I managed to slither and bounce my way along one wall of the street, going downhill, always downhill. I fainted again.

When I came to I was at the bottom of some steps. I must have fallen and rolled. There was just enough strength in my arms to drag the dead weight of my body a few more yards. There was a tree growing over the street, whose leaves and rotting fruit had made a rough carpet over the cobbles. I couldn't go any further, and let my head sink into the soft, crackling litter. There was a smell of honey and of vinegar. Oxymel: a suitable food for the dying.

36

I WOKE UP UNDER A tree, but it wasn't the same tree. At least, there was no smell of wasps and brown apple flesh. And the sun was shining through the leaves. It was an olive tree, and I was lying against one of its roots, a whorled limb that stuck up languidly from the mat of dried leaves. A horse was grazing a few feet away – no, two horses. My head was pulsing, blowing up and shrinking like a frog's throat. With each throb, a net of agony spread down the left side of my face, across the surface of my eyes – I couldn't see anything at all out of the left one – and along the roots of my teeth. My thigh was completely numb. The rest of me was one of those ice carvings which every rich man loves to buy for his feasts, and which are such a waste of money and time.

A shadow fell across me. Someone squatted down, settled onto the olive root. I couldn't see them: one eye blind, and I couldn't even turn my head. A gourd appeared in front of my face, tilted towards my lips. I opened them and let lukewarm water trickle into my mouth and down my throat. It tasted of metal and dried gourd flesh.

'Do you think you might be able to stand?'

The voice was familiar, but then again, it couldn't be. How interesting, though, that the Watch of Assisi were so polite. They hadn't even locked me up yet, but dragged me into some sort of garden. A black shape swooped down on me, clamped itself to the side of my head. Pain sparked, spat like gunpowder. Wetness seeped down my neck and into my shirt. Wet cloth dabbed at my closed eye. The lids ungummed, fluttered open. I found the Proctor studying me, a rag, dripping red and brown, in his fist.

'Did they get you as well?' I asked. My voice sounded like the wind blowing through the dead fronds of the date palm. I closed my eyes again, sank back into yesterday, under the palm, when all this had just been schemes – fantasy, and stupid schemes.

'*I* got *you*,' the Proctor's voice said, very precisely. I opened my eyes again, managed to lift my head enough to see further than my feet. We were in the country, in flat land, surrounded by olive trees and almonds. A line of half-bare willow bushes stretched away on the right, and beyond it, a mountain. 'We are near Brufa. Do you know where that is?' I shook my head. It was agonizing. 'No matter.'

'Not Assisi?'

'We are miles from Assisi.'

'How did I get here?'

'You rode,' said the Proctor, as if addressing the simplest man in Italy.

'But I don't remember.'

'Too much phlegm, I expect. Forgetfulness often comes with an excess of phlegm. I might administer a purge – calamus and Solomon's seal. You've been bled already.'

'I can't have ridden. I can't even walk.'

'You didn't ride your pretty Naples gelding, but you managed my sweet old mare well enough. That is, I arranged you on her back and you did not fall off.'

'You rode my horse?'

'I did. Thank you. He rides well, that Neapolitan. It is a pity we do not have far to go.'

'Go? Proctor, where could we possibly go?'

He bent down, dabbed at the side of my head with the rag. 'Have you ever been to Perugia?' he asked.

★

347

I do not remember getting back onto the gentle grey nag. From time to time I would find myself awake, with my face in her mane. When that happened my mind took me back to my first journey to Rome, and I wondered if Donna Velia was waiting for us in her little cottage. The Proctor had tied clean strips of linen – from my second-best shirt, as I'd discover later – around my head and thigh, but there were plenty of flies, slow, clumsy, living out their last days before winter, eager to investigate my wounds. I watched them travel from the horse's pink and black nostrils, her long-lashed eyes, to my face, and back again. Her hooves stamped steadily, resolutely, and my body answered with rhythmic stabs and clenches of pain. Sometimes I opened my eyes to find them moving over tracks of dusty chalk, over corn stubble, once over burned ground littered with bleached snail shells. I slept for a longer time, and woke to find that we were climbing a steep hill, on a busy road on which many people were passing up and down. Some of them looked at me curiously, but a damaged man on a horse didn't seem much of a novelty. I went to sleep again.

After that I woke and slept more frequently, though the sleep was deeper and the waking moments strange and murky. There was a ceiling, nicely coffered, painted and gilded. There were faces, every now and again, but the Proctor's was the only one I recognized. There was a pot into which I vomited, and salty liquid which I sipped but didn't taste. The liquids got thicker, burned. I vomited more often. My leg began to hurt, and my head hurt less. I had a fever, through which Tessina's face rippled like that of a drowned woman in a stream, while I floated above the water, helpless. At other times I saw nothing but Marco Baroni's mouth, caked with white dust and bubbles of dark blood.

When I finally came properly to my senses, when I opened

my eyes and found everything cool and focused, it was night. Faint sounds – footsteps, the creak of a window – were coming from somewhere, but around me everything was still, except for my breathing. I lay and listened to it for a while. I'd never really paid breathing very much attention, but what a miracle it was: air coming in, nourishing my body; going out again, taking with it the soot and smoke generated by the heat of my blood. I was alive. God and His Mother be praised: I was alive.

I finally dozed, and woke to find that bells were chiming somewhere nearby, and sunlight was coming in through a high window. I sat up to find I was in a kind of cell, with very plain limewashed walls and a simple black crucifix above my simple wooden bed. But as everything was spotlessly clean, I decided that I couldn't be in prison. My wounds, too, were clean, bound up with fresh linen. And in a few minutes the door opened to admit two long-faced, black-clad gentlemen and a short wall-eyed woman with curly brown hair forcing itself out from under a white coif. The woman carried a tray on which was a steaming bowl; some herbs, some vials of liquid and a cup. When they saw I was awake they put their heads together and whispered, very discreetly.

'Good morning!' I said. I was feeling almost chirpy, though I found that opening my mouth still involved a certain amount of pain. 'I'm afraid I don't know where I am.'

'You are in the Studium Generale of Perugia,' said the taller of the two gentlemen.

'The Università degli Studi,' said the other.

'The university?' They nodded. 'I've been here for days,' I went on. 'And you must have saved my life.'

'Days?' said the tall man. 'No, no. You came yesterday. And as to whether your life needed saving . . .'

'You are young and fit,' the shorter man said. 'And you

had been well taken care of, right from the time of your . . . your mishap.'

'Really? But it's just been me and the Proctor.'

Both men rolled their eyes at the same time, and came at me like a couple of ravens after a dead lamb's liver. One deftly unwound the bandage around my head, sniffed the wound, and painted on a little black fluid. It stung, and my teeth began to crackle with pain. Meanwhile, the other man was inspecting my leg.

'Will I walk again?' I asked through clenched, throbbing teeth.

'What? Of course you will. The blade went through the *vastus medialis*. Very neat, no tearing. A very sharp blade, plainly — and it carried none of your clothing into the wound. You may be thankful that your hose were made of silk. Long fibres, no little bits to fester.'

'It is your head that worries us,' said the shorter man. 'It appeared at first as if something had penetrated the vault of your skull. But instead, though the bone is bruised, there is no fracture.'

'How do you know?' I asked.

'There was a nice portion of skull exposed,' said the man brightly. He might have been saying *what lovely weather we had for the* calcio *game*. My hand flew to the side of my head, but he caught my wrist in time. 'Not quite ready for that yet,' he said. 'You have a few stitches. No one will ever know, though. You've been very, very lucky.'

'So you seem intent on telling me,' I said. 'Though, sirs and madam, allow me to confess that I'm not feeling especially lucky.'

'Dear me!' said the tall man. 'Pilgrims who meet the bandits of Monte Subasio do not usually survive. Had it not been for your companion . . .'

'Oh, my companion!' I exclaimed, thinking: *Bandits?*

'Where is he? Are you caring for him? He needs a special diet.'

'What? A diet?' The woman, who had been preparing strips of clean bandage, piped up indignantly.

'To address his . . . to address . . .' But whatever was being done to my head had brought on a wave of nausea. I leaned back against the pillow, letting them do their work, willing them to be done with it.

'Diet,' the woman was muttering irritably. She reminded me, somehow, of Carenza. And how Carenza would have laughed at that.

'Could you move your leg for me?' asked the taller man. I obliged, extremely slowly, and found that, apart from a deep ache and some tightness, I could move it quite easily. 'Excellent. Now – hmm. From your speech I think you are from Florence. I would not think of travelling home for the next week at least, and that is only if you continue to heal well.'

'I am a Florentine,' I said, 'but I live in Rome.'

'Unlucky, to be waylaid in Umbria, when the Holy City is, one hears, so much more dangerous.'

'Typical of my fortune,' I said, and tried to laugh, though I couldn't quite manage it. 'I'd like to go back to Florence. But I don't think I ever will.'

'You must do important work, if it keeps you from your home,' said the shorter man. 'From your clothes, we – that is, Donna Elena – thought you were a gentleman of substance.' He glanced at the woman, who beamed absently.

'Important? Not really,' I mumbled. 'Not at all.'

'You are treating none other than the personal dietary to His Eminence Cardinal Federico Gonzaga,' said a familiar voice. The Proctor was in the doorway. He approached the bed in his stiff-legged, angular way, bent, examined my head.

'What do you think, *dottore*?' asked the taller man.

'Very good. The stitches are just loose enough. If you had tightened them, as you wished to do . . .'

'Quite,' said the man.

'*Dottore?*' I asked. All three men turned to me. 'You called him *dottore*. But – I'm sorry, Proctor – neither of us are doctors. It is a jest between us. This is the man I was telling you about, who needs the special diet for his excess of black bile.'

'Yes? Is this true?' The taller man turned to the Proctor, looking amused.

'Of course it's true! Two months ago, this man was wandering around the Campo Vaccino, stark naked and raving about Perugia!'

'And now we are in Perugia,' said the Proctor gravely.

'I mean no offence, and plainly I owe you my life,' I told him. 'But, sirs,' I said to the doctors, 'he was a madman, no more or less, and he is not cured yet!'

'My dear young man,' said the shorter man kindly. 'This is Doctor Apollonio Ginori, late of this university.'

'Head of our medical faculty, and Proctor of the Catalan nation here,' said the taller. 'When I said you had received the best care possible for your wounds, I meant it most seriously.'

'You are very courtly, Ruggiero,' said the Proctor. 'I have not been a doctor for many years. But I remember . . .' He gave a twitch, shook his head. 'Yes, I remember some little things.'

'Proctor . . . So you really are a proctor?' I gaped at him.

Something in the corner of my mind was telling me that this must be a hallucination, what with a good portion of my skull having been exposed. But my travelling companion, whose eyes were closed as if he was listening to some internal dialogue of his own, nodded. He opened his eyes.

'I did tell you,' he said, without malice. 'I tried to tell a lot of people. I have spent years and years and years trying to tell them. But no one would listen. People do not listen, do they? They do not. You do not.' The taller man looked concerned and touched the Proctor's arm, but the other doctor shook his head and both men stepped back discreetly from the bed.

'So all my purges and diets – *Madonna*! You should have stopped me!'

'Why? You gave me food, you provided me with a bed, with clean clothes. Shaved and anointed . . .' He blinked, as if the words surprised him. 'Released me from the prison of my own stink, from the lice who were my close jailers. I felt a certain gratitude. And you were a doctor. One should listen to doctors.'

'No – *you* are the doctor!'

'Am I?' he asked, and looked around in surprise.

'Apollonio, you are still confused,' said the man called Ruggiero. He turned to me. 'We have not seen Doctor Ginori for almost nine years. He left here . . .'

'I did not leave,' said the Proctor firmly.

'You did, Apollonio,' said Ruggiero gently. He lowered his voice, bent down as if to adjust my bandage. 'Perugia is a volatile city. That is, we are subject to the arbitrary and violent whims of our rulers. Lately, that has meant the Baglionis and the Oddis. Being from Florence, you will have heard all about our troubles, I'm sure. Those two families are in the habit of conducting little wars inside the city walls, and in one such conflict, Apollonio lost his young wife and his two infant sons.' He glanced over his shoulder, but the Proctor was listening to the woman, who was holding up a glass vial of yellow liquid. 'He was grieving, of course, but we did not know that he was also grievously wounded, as it were, in his . . .' He lowered his voice even further. 'In his mind. We thought it was the normal reaction to his tragedy. When his confessor told him to go on a pilgrimage to Rome, the chancellor thought it would be an excellent idea. Nine years ago he left, and not a word of him did we hear until yesterday. Until he came riding in on a black horse, with a wounded man bleeding all over a grey one.'

'I am a fool,' I said. 'In everything I do: fool to my love, to my friends, and my enemies too. A cook, thinking he was curing a doctor . . .'

'I think he feels you *did* help him.'

'Then his politeness is – Christ! – a bitter, bitter purge. Did he tell you I gave him black hellebore? I know nothing of such things! Nothing! I am a cook, pure and simple. A cardinal's vanity made me a doctor and from the sickness of my own heart I chose to believe I was. Who is the madman? And in Assisi . . .'

'You should rest, Master Wind,' said the Proctor. 'Ruggiero and Alfonso are very pleased with your recovery, and Donna Elena is planning your luncheon, hmm, hmm?'

'Oh, God. Feed me the crassest food. Feed me horse oats. Teach me how to be a beggar, Proctor, and throw me out of doors. I don't deserve anything more.'

'You poor young thing,' said Donna Elena. 'I'm making you some boiled squab, some rice pudding and a *torta* of quinces.'

'And we will leave you to rest,' added the short man, who must be Doctor Alfonso.

It took a week before I could get out of bed. The good doctors of the Studium Generale looked after me so well that I could have imagined myself a saint or at least a prince, and not a murderer, which was what I most assuredly was. I suppose this ought to have caused me more anguish, but the truth was I was glad that it was Marco Baroni who was dead and not me. I would never be able to go back to Florence. I would die in exile. But at least Tessina would be safe, and that was all I cared about now. What else was there?

Marco had killed before. He had been quite convinced that he was going to kill me. Apart from his father, no one back home in Florence would be mourning him when the news came. The same went for Corso. I wasn't sorry they were dead; I might have wished, though, that their blood wasn't on my hands. Marco's blood, at least. I went over the fight again and again, and decided that Marco had killed his friend. His sword, with its wide blade, had gone right through Corso from left to right, through both lungs. Though I'd stabbed him in the neck, Corso had been as good as dead already. And Marco? He'd been trying to knock my head off. He'd been angrier than I had. I'd been luckier.

From the look of Bartolo Baroni, he would be following his son into the grave quite soon. No man could be so pumped up with blood and survive long. You didn't have to be a doctor, even a counterfeit one, to know that. Now, when Bartolo died, Tessina would be free. She would be a rich widow. There would be nothing to stop her joining me in Rome. How long would it be: a year, two? Even ten didn't seem like an eternity any more.

I'd never see Florence again, though. He was an important man, Bartolo Baroni. He might not have long to live, but I knew, as surely as I knew that lemon curdles milk, that he would use whatever time he had left to ruin me. My father would be safe: the Butchers' Guild would protect him. But not me. It would be easy for Baroni to get the Signoria to condemn me to death in absentia. He'd make sure that I would be hunted down if I ever set foot inside the republic, if I ever went further north than Pitigliano. I had condemned myself to Rome, or wherever Zohan went next. But Rome with Tessina would be paradise itself.

Would she have me, though? I was a murderer now.

Would she take me, knowing I had that shadow on my soul? I didn't have the answer to that. While I was still in bed, a priest had come to visit me – more of a scholar than a priest: a doctor of theology, or some such. He had heard that I was a pilgrim, a pious young man who had been robbed and left for dead outside the gates of Assisi; and this had been a most unjust reward not only for my piety but for my charity, seeing that I had saved the life of their lost colleague Apollonio.

I found myself playing the part he had ordained for me, though I'd have preferred to make confession, for Marco and Corso were weighing on my conscience. But instead I was forced to exaggerate my weakness and pain. I hid behind shallow breaths and bravely set teeth while the poor man praised me and even promised to have a mass said for me in the Duomo of Perugia. *I have killed two men*, I almost shouted, *and tried to cuckold another man and steal his wife. And I did it all while calling on the Virgin and the saints to guide me.* But I kept silent and let him kneel by my side and say a prayer to Our Lady.

He seemed satisfied with the state of my conscience, but I wasn't, and I had no idea how Tessina might be feeling. True, the man I'd killed had been her enemy. When I thought about what Tessina had written, of Marco threatening, wheedling, accusing; of my darling trapped in that house with that vile brute, it seemed, on the face of it, that she'd be grateful. But I hadn't rid her home of mice: I'd taken a human life. Would she want a man who had done that?

In eight days I was walking the clean, well-ordered corridors of the university. Another five, and I was climbing painfully onto the back of my Neapolitan. It was an overcast morning. The wind was from the north, and rags of cold mist were clinging to the roofs of Perugia. There is a moment, every year, when golden leaves and the last happy remains of the harvest vanish, to be replaced with bare branches and crows. That moment had come while I had been lying in bed. I was setting off on the road to Rome, and winter had come early.

Only Apollonio had come to see me leave. He led the horse by its bridle down the steep, cobbled street to the south gate. The Proctor had changed a great deal in the last two weeks. He had finally lost every hint of starvation, and his eyes no longer seemed like the empty sockets of a weathered stone mask. He looked, to all intents and purposes, like what he had once been and had become once more: a gentle, well-fed man who had the love and admiration of many friends.

I didn't know if he would ever teach medicine again. Sometimes he seemed to have the knowledge of Averroes himself, and at other times his shoulders would hunch and I would catch him staring intently into a corner of the room, or under the bed. But he would never be forced to wander again. And he had come home. The doctors had cautioned against seeing patterns in the Lord's work, but try as I might, I couldn't ignore the fact that the Proctor had found his home again, and I had lost mine for ever. In any case, we were both changed. It would be easy to say that the beggar had found increase, and the proud man had been diminished, and I suppose that was true, on the face of it. I was leaving Perugia almost penniless, with just my sword, my dagger and enough florins to get me back to Rome. I was even wearing the old clothes I had given the Proctor all that time ago, because the good doctors of the Studium had cut my blood-stiffened clothes from me and burned them. And I was alone, completely alone, while the erstwhile beggar was in the embrace of his loving friends.

As I rode down the slippery street I thought about how I'd almost killed him with my potions; about the man I really had murdered; the lie I'd told the priest, and all the other sins I had committed in my short life. A gust of wind blew the folds of my hood, already wet, around my neck, and I huddled. The Proctor bowed his head as well, but easily, resignedly. And suddenly I understood.

'Apollonio,' I said. 'The Virgin has been guiding me all along.'

'To Perugia?' he asked, blinking the mist from his eyelashes.

'Of course, to Perugia. But I meant, She brought me to Assisi to teach me a lesson. I thought she meant to give Tessina to me. But that was just stupidity and arrogance.'

'It was, perhaps, optimistic,' agreed the Proctor. 'The Lord and Our Lady have taught me lessons. Oh, many, many lessons. What did *you* learn, hmm?'

'I thought you were the madman, God forgive me,' I said. 'But Our Lady has ended up saving me from my own idiocy. And Tessina as well – she had to be saved from me – the man I was, don't you see? It was a *beffa*: another *beffa*. And I richly deserved it all.'

'Love's effect on the humours, and by extension the brain, is universally disastrous,' said the Proctor. 'Love, and grief. I have conducted my own experiments.' He looked up at me, but I couldn't read anything in his rain-streaked face to tell me whether or not he was serious. 'But I must be honest: I found your passion . . . admirable. Though I feared its conclusion.'

'You were right to fear,' I said.

'Never mind. You escaped.'

'We both escaped, Tessina and I. For which I give thanks to the Virgin. But, my friend, I don't understand how I could ever have believed that the world was just going to give my Tessina to me.'

'I am afraid I rather hoped your dreams would come true,' said the Proctor quietly, so quietly that his voice was almost drowned by the sound of hooves and the rain. 'I have found, in my life, that madmen are often filled with hope. Despair usually gets them in the end, but the hopes of a madman can shine like the sun.'

We had come to the gate. Below us, the land fell away to a wet, pewter-grey landscape, across which towering rags of mist were marching southward. I climbed painfully down from the horse and embraced the Proctor.

'So am I mad now, do you think?' I asked him, glad that the rain was hiding the tears that were starting to run.

'If you have gone beyond hope and despair, then no, you are not mad,' he replied.

'Despair? Yes, I have. But hope . . . The Lord commands us to hope,' I said, half to myself. The Proctor bowed his head, but whether or not he was agreeing I could not tell. 'I will miss our friendship,' I told him. 'As for Tessina, as for my love, I will put that part of me in the hands of the Blessed Virgin. I will put it beyond my own meddling. I will feel no more. I will not hope, or suffer. Best to be safe, Apollonio.'

'Then you are cured, Master Nino. Alas, you are indeed cured. And may God help you.'

⤙ 37 ⤚

Iᴛ ᴡᴀѕ ᴛʜᴇ ᴇɴᴅ ᴏғ November, and the weather had turned. It drizzled and misted for leagues and leagues, and my fine Neapolitan trudged through mud that often rose up beyond his fetlocks. It was a landscape of bruised purple hills and ploughed, half-drowned fields. That first day I arrived at a town just as the sun was going down. I don't remember the name – Torgiano? Deruta? – but there was an inn, and I had to sleep. Not even considering dinner, I was ushered, too tired to protest, into the little dining room which smelled of smoke from the green oak log smouldering in the fireplace. I was the only patron. The host apologized: they had nothing on hand except for *farro* and a nice fish his son had caught that day in the river. He'd been saving it for his own supper, but . . . I ordered the fish.

The host's wife brought me a heel of good, saltless bread, slightly dry and almost shockingly plain, the way we like it in Florence. There was a dish of their own olives, some stewed quinces. A dish of sausages arrived – 'Just *mazzafegati*,' said the woman apologetically, 'from our last pig. Your food will be out directly.'

The sausages – still leaking beads of hot fat – smelled tempting. I speared one, nibbled its end. I was thinking about Rome: what I was going to do for work, whether Cardinal Gonzaga would be back from Milan yet and if he'd take me on again. I wouldn't have anywhere to live, though I hoped that Leto might put me up until I found myself a job. But what if there was no work for me? I might end up like the

Proctor, stalking like a filthy heron around the Campo Vaccino, gibbering about Florence.

Then I noticed what I was eating. It was pigs' liver minced up with orange peel, pine nuts, raisins, black pepper, and sugar. The flavours were extraordinary: exactly that. Beyond the ordinary. Pigs' liver can be the most ordinary, depressing flavour in the world. It can taste like the smell of a busy jakes and take more chewing than sack-cloth. In short, the liver of the pig can stand in for everything that makes life almost intolerable: it is the rank fug of our bodies when they go wrong, the taste of all the things God in his wisdom saw fit to hide inside our skins. Cooked well, though – and in this as well, I suppose, it is like our lives – it smells like the farts of angels and takes the tongue skittering across the bed sheets of lovers, through forest floors thick with fungi, into fields of rich soil as the dew falls on them . . . These sausages did all that and more. As I lovingly addressed the last one on the plate, I realized that I hadn't tasted food since leaving Bevagna, hadn't properly savoured anything since that meal the Proctor and I had shared in Massa.

The last sensation I remembered on my tongue was blood: I had spat out a slimy, stringy mouthful when I had opened my eyes and found myself alive, sprawled over Marco's body. And the roulades I had cooked for Tessina? They might have been made of wax, for all I could remember of them. The only thing I did recall was the way her face had changed when she had dipped her finger, tasted. But that, after all, had been enough. I had that, in my eyes and in my heart. And, God and Mary forgive me, it had been worth it. We'd both been alive in that moment, alive in each other's skin.

At that point the woman of the house arrived with the fish. It was a good-sized trout, opened out, salted, pressed, floured and fried. The entrails had been cooked with some vinegar and mint, mashed up and spooned onto the plate as a sort of afterthought. It was delicious: simple and honest. I ate it all, and didn't give a single thought for what it might do to my humours. I sucked every bone, washed it down with some thick, spicy red wine – peasants' wine – from the hills above the town. I knew that I was tasting the place itself: the fish from the river I had crossed on my way into the town, the pig that had rooted in the woods I had ridden through, olives grown a short walk away. The pig had snuffled under the pine trees whose nuts had adorned its sausages. I had eaten the land. The town itself will always be nameless in my memory, but even now I can assemble it from its flavours, because I have never forgotten any of them. A meal of pigs' liver and fish, served with apologies.

After that I ate every meal with absolute attention, matching every ingredient to the land I had ridden through that day, asking questions, harassing bored or bewildered cooks, badgering innkeepers' wives for their secrets, for the things their grandmothers had passed down to them. Apollonio had been right. I was cured. I could feel again, but I was almost as I'd been as a little child: delighted and terrified by taste, by its possibilities and its dangers.

A few miles after Narni, at Orte, the way forks: west to Viterbo, south to Rome, north to Orvieto and, beyond it, Tuscany. How easy to turn the Neapolitan's head to the right, and start for home. The road unfolded in my mind like a freshly inked map, but drawn by an excitable cartographer, with giants standing astride the path. No, not giants: one figure only, vast and implacable. The great goddess Fortuna, one foot on Monte Amiata, the other on the hill of Montepulciano. I could never go that way again.

So I dropped down into the mournful, oppressive desert of the Roman *campagna*. Nothing but dejected cattle and piles of rubble, all but drowned in fig thickets, to show where buildings had once been. All the birds seemed to have flown away. The farmers I met on the road did not even raise their heads to look at me. On one such day, when the wind had started from the north-east, from the peak of Monte Terminillo, already white with snow, I came to the line of bare poplars and willows that marked the Tiber, and beyond the ancient bridge, the walls of Rome, ragged and black, like the broken jawbone of a skull dropped into the uneven plain.

Fortuna Turns Her Wheel A Fourth Time:
'Regnavi' — 'I Have Reigned'

⚜ 38 ⚜

Rome, December 1476

WHEN I'D GOT BACK FROM Assisi, still in pain, flat broke
and jobless, the first thing I'd done was to sell my fine
Neapolitan horse. I'd ridden through the Porta del Popolo,
straight to the dealer I'd bought him from. Of course I had
lost some money on the deal, but when the man started
trotting out his line, telling me I should be paying *him* to take
the poor beast off my hands, I suddenly became Roman, put
my hand on my sword, let my tongue loose. Then, with the
comforting weight of silver swinging against my hip, I'd
walked over to the palace at San Lorenzo in Damaso to ask
for my position back. But I had got as far as the back door
when I hesitated. Did I want to be a cardinal's dietary again? I
did not. Not one atom of my being desired such a thing. So
before any of the cardinal's staff noticed me I turned around,
limped to my bank, withdrew my savings, retrieved my few
belongings from the friars and paid a boy to carry them over
to a mid-rank hostelry behind Santa Maria Sopra Minerva.

The next morning, early, I went to call on Pomponio
Leto, but he was not at home. So I went for a walk in the
Campo Vaccino. The Proctor had been my usual companion
for such expeditions, and it was odd not to have him sidling
behind me, or flitting from pillar to roofless wall, both of us
pretending I had not seen him.

And I would have to eat my luncheon alone. There was a
place near the Teatro Marcello favoured by Rome's better
cooks. It was expensive, but I told myself that I would start

watching my florins after lunch. I ordered *pajata*, fried sweet-breads, roasted eels and some cardoons, because I was feeling the chill – both from the winter air and from my worries about my future – and I wanted their bitterness to warm me. I had just finished the last custardy little nugget of sweetbread and had speared a chunk of eel, when someone tapped me on the shoulder. In an instant I had twisted, risen halfway to my feet (my thigh screaming in protest), to find that my dagger, a black cylinder of eel impaled on its tip, was pointing at the throat of Luigino, my old lieutenant from the Gonzaga kitchens. We stood dead still, not even blinking, but I saw that his hands were empty, that he wasn't even armed.

'Eel?' I said, with a weak grin.

He took a deep breath, plucked the meat from the blade. I sat down, heavily, wondering if my thigh had opened again. Though scab had almost turned to scar, there was a greenish corner that was worrying me. I rubbed it to stop the twitchy pain that was rippling through the muscle. With my good leg I kicked another chair out from under the table and poured Luigino a cup of the excellent wine. He hesitated, then sat, picked up the wine and sniffed it. Then he seemed to relax. He drank and ate, leaned back.

'This is a good place,' he said, pulling a comb of eel spine from between his teeth. Leaning over, he filched a tube of *pajata*. Luigino was as Roman as the Tiber itself, so I couldn't help watching his face as he ate. 'I'd always heard it was good.' He licked his lips. 'And it is. Expensive, though.' He took another bit of *pajata*. 'So, *dottore*. It's good to see you. A relief, in fact. Bit jumpy, though, aren't you?'

'I had a bit of trouble on pilgrimage,' I said. 'And you don't need to call me *dottore*. I'm finished with that.'

'What happened to your leg?'

'Pilgrimage is dangerous.'

'I could've told you that. Next time, just go to Saint Peter's. Though fuck knows that's dangerous enough.'

'Very true. But what are you doing here?'

'Looking for you.'

'Dear God! Then here's a fine coincidence.'

'Not really. I saw you yesterday when you came to the door – thought you were a beggar at first. And you walked right past Pietro on your way here.'

'Pietro?'

'Was a pot-scrubber. Now promoted to vegetable-peeler.' He pushed up his lip with a finger.

'Ah. The hare-lipped boy. Didn't notice him. So don't tell me I've been missed.'

'Missed? Well, now . . . You hadn't heard, I suppose?'

'Heard what? I've only been in Rome since yesterday.'

'Maestro Zohan.' He paused, poured himself more wine.

'What about Zohan?'

'God rest his soul. He's dead. In Mantua.'

I had been ready with some rough joke, but my tongue froze in my mouth. 'A quartain fever,' Luigino was saying. 'Poor old man. Hardly a surprise though, was it? One big marsh, Mantua. By all accounts.'

'No, no . . . Maestro! My own maestro.' I pushed my plate away. The image of his squat, square bulk was hovering above the food, Zohan as I'd seen him that day in Florence, in the vile little courtyard of the Porco. 'He wasn't that old! I've never seen him ill. Never even a sniffle.'

'Comes for us all,' said Luigino, and crossed himself. Then he patted his doublet, pulled out a small, neatly folded piece of vellum. 'This came, along with His Eminence and the ill news. For you.'

I took it slowly, unfolded it expecting – hoping – to find Zohan's round, almost childish writing. Instead there was a neat stack of precisely scripted lines.

Whereas the gentleman who is called Zohan of Ferrara, who being sorely afflicted and awaiting the consoling rite of extreme unction has caused this to be recorded, and whereas the said Zohan of Ferrara has betaken his soul unto God and His blessed mother Mary, IT is his wish that these Instructions be set down and conveyed to the gentleman who is called Nino di Niccolaio Latini of the city and republic of Florence, to whit:

That the said gentleman who is called Nino di Niccolaio Latini be henceforth known, recognized and honoured with the title of Maestro, and that he assume the position of Head Cook to His Eminence Cardinal F. Gonzaga, this with the full approval of the said Cardinal F. Gonzaga, such position to be taken up at the earliest convenience of said Nino di Niccolaio Latini.

Dictated etc, etc. There were some witnessing signatures, a blob of red wax stamped with the imprint of my former employer's ring. The date, almost two months old. I had been riding into Assisi as Zohan lay on his deathbed. And at the bottom, a familiar thing at last: six words, large, thin and shaky, effort plain in every stroke. The hand was Zohan's.

GOD BLESS YOU MY DEAR SON

I followed Luigino back to San Lorenzo in Damaso, back to Zohan's kitchen. The staff fell silent as I walked in. They had been expecting me. I looked at all the familiar faces, all set into those masks that men put on when they don't know how they should feel. Even Luigino looked drawn, like a worried dog. He led me over to Zohan's chair. There was a bundle propped on the seat.

'The maestro . . . In his will. This is for you,' said Luigino.

I blinked the salty film from my eyes, fumbled with the knotted cord. The parcel held Zohan's best doublet, a gorgeous thing of red silk damascened with dragons and vines, which would have fitted me as a ten-year-old. The doublet was folded around a leather roll, which unfurled to reveal the maestro's knives: the big, broad-bladed one like a small falchion, with a turned ivory handle; a thin knife like a long stiletto; two fat-bellied ones; and a pair of delicate ones that looked like the tools of a surgeon. And in the last pocket of the roll, his spoon. I stood for a long time, turning it slowly in my hand. And when I looked around, every man in the kitchen bent their heads, the smallest of movements, but it was enough.

I rolled up the knives and spoon again, very carefully, and then saw that there was another package lying on the silk of the doublet. When I unwrapped it I found it was Zohan's book of recipes, ancient, greasy, scuffed and warped. I bent my own head, to hide my tears. And from the book there rose the smell of a cook's life: sweat, sweet spices. Flour and butter. Lard. Wine. The faint corpse-scent of spoiled blood. And onion juice draped over it all like the finest veil.

'Boys,' I said, when I thought I could keep my voice under control. 'I'm Master Cook now. Do we understand each other?'

'Yes, yes,' they said, every one – some with more enthusiasm than others, but they all nodded and agreed.

'Yes, *Maestro*,' Luigino corrected them.

'Yes, Maestro!'

The *credenziero*, Tranquillo Grazia, had been watching all this from the door of his own kitchen. It meant nothing to him, of course – we were both under the *scalco*, and though as head cook I was now his nominal superior, in practice we had nothing to do with each other's work – and we had always got on well together. He strolled over and offered his hand.

'You are now officially the thinnest cook in Rome,' he

said, looking me up and down. He was as well padded as ever. 'Have you been in prison, Nino?'

'He's been on pilgrimage,' said Luigino, affronted. 'Some Umbrian bastard sliced him open.'

'Dear, dear,' said Tranquillo, who always lived up to his name. 'Well, it's a joy to have you back.'

'So are you staying?' I said to Luigino.

'Of course, Maestro! Why wouldn't I?'

'Good. Then you're my lieutenant,' I told him. 'All right?'

'Thank you, Maestro!'

I didn't feel like myself. It was as though I were wearing Maestro Zohan like an ill-fitting costume. But of course, I *was* the maestro. 'You work for me now,' I told Luigino. 'Not His Eminence. Not the *scalco*. Me. Don't make your master ashamed.'

'I won't, Maestro.'

'Then all's as it should be.'

～ 39 ～

I WAS CARDINAL GONZAGA'S HEAD cook for a year and a half. A spell among the comforts of his northern home seemed to have completely cured my employer of his need for a dietary. He returned to his old habits, and the familiar dishes were required once more. I wondered if something had happened in Mantua, whether Zohan had managed to talk sense into the man. But in any case no new dietary was taken on, and the cardinal dealt with me as if he'd never given me his piss to taste, or begged me to analyse his fundamental eructations.

For eighteen months I ran his kitchen, eighteen months of the hardest work, first to learn, and then to keep hold of, my new powers and all the things that came with them. And there was power, because the *scalco*, old Orazio, was failing. He had been brushed by the tail of the fever that had killed Zohan, and it had turned his hair white and bent his spine as if he'd been a clay model in the hands of a clumsy child. The cardinal, a kind, sentimental man, kept him on for no reason other than loyalty, but his kindness meant that I sometimes did both Orazio's work and my own.

In a way it wasn't hard, because there are plenty of things a *scalco* does that a head cook can also do perfectly well, most particularly in the planning of the meals and banquets. If it had been a bigger household the work would probably have killed us both, but as it was, only one of us died. Orazio's fever returned in the late summer of 1476; he went into a deep sleep and did not wake up again. I mourned him, because I'd grown fond of the man and he, over time, had got over his aversion for my lowly birth – or maybe he'd just mastered it enough to hide it from me: either way, I appreciated the effort. For six weeks I was both cook and *scalco* while the new man rode down from Mantua. I knew, as I went about my business, exercising my skills and my power, that this was what my old master had intended for me. I wished I could tell him. And I wished that my father could see how his son had made good at last.

But since Assisi, no more letters had come from Florence, and I had sent none. I knew why no one had written. It was obvious that Bartolo Baroni had done as I had expected: had me sentenced to death in my absence and declared me an enemy of Florence. Anyone caught sending a letter to me, or carrying one written by me, would be a traitor. Tessina would have no freedom now. She wouldn't even be allowed pen and parchment, if I knew Baroni.

I imagined her in her cheerless room, praying, reading the pious books that ghastly old Aunt Maddalena would get for her. She'd be waiting for Baroni to die. Or perhaps that was just my own imagining: every morning, the possibility that the livid old boar wouldn't be waking up. That wasn't how I wanted Tessina to be spending her life. I didn't like the way I made her act in my mind, how she had turned cold and vengeful. It felt as if my own sin, my act of murder, had tainted her as well. So I imagined her safe and as content as she could be, and gave her a little hope as well, so she could share it with me.

There could have been other letters. I had disgraced my father, of course, and I prayed every day that he would forgive me before either of us died. But the right thing to do, according to the laws of *virtù*, was not to compound my disgrace by making my father complicit in any way. It was better for the Latini name, for now, if I was dead. I thought he would understand: he despised the Baronis, and he'd known love. And above all he understood *virtù*. But then, did he mourn me? Because he was just as dead to me, and I mourned him bitterly.

The thought of Carenza hurt even more keenly. I couldn't bring myself to think of her suffering on my behalf. Perhaps Father had told her some story – but no, she'd have heard all the gossip, and there would have been a lot of that. The Black Lion would have been singing about me like a barrel of cicadas. As for my friends, in a way I was glad that they were all such typical Florentines, practical and pragmatic. Of course they wouldn't write to me. They would know that I, as a fellow pragmatist, wouldn't expect them to. Sandro would be up to his eyes in commissions by now. Life was life, business was business. I didn't expect him to risk either for the sake of a little written gossip. Life went on. As the months passed, all these losses grew duller. I had mourned them all, as if plague had carried off everyone I loved, and left only me in the empty streets. But even mourning comes to an end.

Everything, indeed, comes to an end. As soon as he arrived I knew my time at San Lorenzo in Damaso was as good as over. Lodovigo de Lugo was as Mantuan an ingredient as could have been chosen to complete our household – unfortunately, the ingredients he resembled, so beloved of our mutual employer, were the tench and the heron. Messer Lodovigo was tall, angular, pop-eyed, thick-lipped, and his skin was pallid with a constant sheen of perspiration. Like a heron he darted and fished into everybody's affairs, and like the tench he would explore any depth, however silty, if it meant he might uncover something that would win him even the smallest advantage. He despised me from the moment we met: for my age, for the city of my birth, for my lack of title, or land, or inheritance; most of all, for my failure to show any awe for the majesty of his person.

He had opinions, our new *scalco*; many, many ideas of how things should be done. No, not ideas: marble-hard convictions. Where Orazio had run his affairs in an old-fashioned, apparently bewildered manner that was, in fact, perfectly calculated to create an air of intimate goodwill around all Cardinal Gonzaga's entertainments, de Lugo desired to demonstrate the status and pomp of the Gonzaga name to its fullest extent. That meant all the flummery and mummery, all the fake, feathered and furred spectacle, the ice carvings, the sugar cathedrals. In short, everything was to be in the eye and not the mouth. The food he ordered and supervised might have been made of plaster. As long as there was real gold leaf, as long as smoke issued from the stuffed boar's mouth and as long as the birds exploded in noisy terror from the flying pie, everything was in order.

Half of the cardinal's household came from Mantua, and on the whole they sided with the *scalco* in all things. The kitchen, though, was Roman to a man, except for two of us: myself, and the *spenditore*, the *palazzo*'s buyer, whose job it was to make the household purchases every day, to get the best price for the best produce, and if he found something particularly rare or sumptuous, to bring it back for me to cook. In theory the *spenditore* was my superior in rank, though I followed Zohan's tradition of making sure he answered to me and not the other way around. Things had been trundling along quite happily until the arrival of the new *scalco*. But over the course of the next month, I began to think that the *spenditore* was cheating his master. There was something not quite right in my ledgers: I couldn't tell exactly what, but something was wrong with the quality of ingredients we were using in relation to the price the *spenditore* was paying. The man had been in Gonzaga's employ for years. His name was Pietrobon, and it went without saying that he was one of the Mantuans.

On this particular day I had entered the receipts for a particularly expensive order of fish, though the fish that were waiting in the cool room to be cooked were average at best, and I would have to waste good spices to make them seem fresh. Pietrobon came in to ask me what we needed from the markets that day. I gave him my order, and he asked his usual questions. Perhaps I was looking for something to be wrong, or maybe I was just bored that morning (the cardinal was at the Lateran and would eat lunch and dinner with the Holy Father), but something in his voice or his eyes struck me the wrong way. He went out, trailing two boys who carried a pair of gigantic baskets each. But like the taste of a bad hazelnut, I couldn't get my suspicions to leave me alone. So I slipped out after him.

He made for the market at the bottom of the Campidoglio first. The order I had given him was small: eggs, veal, a cow's udder, some chickens, good herbs. He needed to top up our flour supply, and I'd also asked him to see what the market rate for sugar might be next week, as we needed more but Saracen raids in the Aegean Sea were making the prices go up and down wildly. He bought the eggs: all well and good. I knew the seller: she was honest, and her wares were fresh. On to the herbs. I wouldn't have chosen the man that Pietrobon bought from, but at that time of year, it was hard to go wrong.

Then I followed the buyer and his boys – still quite unburdened – over to Macel de' Corvi, where I almost lost them among the pungent curtains of deer and boar, the sides of beef, the sheep and goats with their bulging eyes and rictus grins. But there they were, examining the chickens at a highly reputable stall. Pietrobon seemed to be having a serious discussion with the proprietor, but then he moved out to the fringes of the market. There he haggled angrily with a fat, slit-eyed woman of the *campagna*, who grinned at him as if she found the whole thing quite hilarious. Apparently satisfied, Pietrobon handed over some coins and in return, one of the boys' baskets was loaded with a bundle of chickens. But they were already dead, and judging by the way the woman was handling them, they were as stiff as firewood. No one who cooked for anyone with any pretension to status, let alone a cardinal, ever bought chickens that had already been slaughtered.

I spat with fury, and was cursed by a man selling goat meat. I cursed him back. I was beside myself: the *spenditore* thought he could trick me in the most obvious way – the way any smelly little errand boy cheats his betters. Pietrobon had got the going rate from the decent seller, then bought these verminous birds for a quarter of the price, entered the high price and pocketed the difference. He did the same for the veal: haggled with a seller that every cook in Rome knew and trusted, then bought from a wheelbarrow crawling with bluebottles. The udder, at least, was fresh – hard to disguise a putrid udder.

So that was it. He would have one of my boys in his pocket, and he'd slip the wretch a few *soldi* to pluck the chickens and cover up any putrefaction. The boy would trim the veal as well, and if Luigino complained – if he even noticed, because I was beginning to have doubts about my lieutenant – the problem would be blamed on the markets.

I let Pietrobon and his sweating boys stagger back in the direction of San Lorenzo in Damaso. Then I went and talked to the poulterer, who confirmed that, yes, of course, the northern gentleman always bought from her if she was in the city.

Then another thought came to me. I ran through the market, and soon caught up with the buyer, who had sent the servants back to the *palazzo* and was striding confidently through the thronging streets. *Just wait, you thief*, I thought to myself. I trailed him along the empty river bank to a dingy warehouse where I watched him strike a deal for flour. I was under the impression that we bought our grain from the Altoviti warehouse near Piazza Navona.

He didn't waste any time, though, our *spenditore*. He scuttled further south, to a knot of houses within sight of the green hump of Monte Testaccio. From one of them a column of smoke was rising, and it was there that Pietrobon went. I was following from a safe distance, but the man was so caught up in his own affairs that he probably wouldn't have noticed me if I had picked his pocket. He knocked on the door, and when it opened, an almost naked woman stepped out and stood with her hands on her wide hips. Steam escaped from behind her. Pietrobon had led me to a bathhouse.

I watched as the buyer simpered and cringed like a naughty dog in front of the woman, who was wearing nothing but a bath sheet, plastered with sweat and steam to her body. It left little to be imagined. The woman's dark ringlets were sticking to her brow and neck. Her heavy breasts shifted as she adjusted her sheet with a deliberate tug. I could see the creases in her jutting stomach, the hair around her *fica* and the dimples of her arse. The *spenditore* bowed like a pagan in front of his idol. She took him gently by the ear and pulled him inside.

I was raging. Feeling like Saint Michael with his flaming sword, I went back to the warehouse and haggled for some flour myself: it was shockingly cheap, and when I tasted it, there was enough plaster dust mixed with the wheat to stucco my tongue. Then I stamped back into the centre of the city, until I found myself within sniffing distance of the fish market under the Portico d'Ottavia. Bloody Pietrobon. Robbing a cardinal just so he could dip his wick. And with a woman like that, a common *stufa* whore. Except that . . .

She hadn't been bad-looking. A bit old, but not bad. Not at all. I had the sudden vision of the damp sheet peeling away slowly from the pink skin of her belly, the steam coming up, those breasts, the weight . . .

It was as if someone had slapped me on the back of the head, and I had to sit down in the portico of Santa Maria in Cosmedin until I'd calmed down, both above and below. I thought of going inside to confess, but then again, what was there to confess anyway? I'd been chaste since Assisi – since before Assisi. After Tessina had opened her heart to me in her letters, I hadn't wanted to be with another woman. And now here I was, half stunned by a glimpse of a tart's bosom. It wouldn't do.

Having got things under control, I decided to do today's marketing myself. I would rather stab myself in the heart than feed His Eminence a rotten chicken. But he was always glad of fish, so I marched over to the Portico d'Ottavia to see what I could find. It wasn't far, but as I made my way, still bristling with righteous anger, I couldn't help noticing things. The girls seemed to be wearing their dresses very low in front this year. There was a brothel on the corner of Via dei Cerchi, and the women hanging out of the window looked as soft as bletted medlars, ready to dissolve at the touch of a finger. Everyone was looking at everyone else – speculating, evaluating, enquiring.

The crowd in the fish market was thinning out. By that time it was late in the buying day, and not much fresh stuff was left. I worked my way along the stalls, but found nothing. The narrower street beyond was starting to smell. All the guts and heads had caught the pleasant heat of a spring morning and made something foul of it. Scales were sequinning my shoes. I prodded some trout, decided their eyes were too faded. Some bream looked bright but their gills had gone a muddy brown. There were carp, tench, pike . . . No, I didn't like the look of them.

I strolled along, half listening to the filthy tongues of the fish sellers. Even the simplest question, the calmest statement, was dressed up in suggestion or insult. One woman with strands of grey in her hair held up a plump perch in one hand and squeezed her breast with the other. A man selling oysters was telling a story, but every other word was *cazzo, cazzo*: dick, dick. A younger woman was sitting on a step, her knees either side of a barrel of live eels. She was striking: high forehead, strong jaw, a wide, sensual mouth; big, dark eyes; oily tresses escaping from an old silk scarf wound like a Saracen's turban. She saw me staring at her and stared back. *Eels*, I thought, *His Eminence has been asking for eels*. And as if in reply the woman plunged her hand into the barrel and drew it out with a big fish flaring its gills above her finger and thumb, its thick, lead-coloured body curling around her bare, brown forearm. She grinned, dropped her eyes.

'Eels, is it, your honour?' A man with broken front teeth stepped in front of me. He wore a slime-streaked leather apron.

'How much?'

He named a price: quite reasonable. 'I'll take a basket,' I said.

'And take her as well,' he said. I stared at him, not sure I'd heard right. But he pointed straight at the woman. 'Take her. Round the back. You won't be sorry.'

'I beg your pardon?'

'Gentleman like you, doing his own shopping. You're having a *cazzo* of a day, sir. Am I right? Make it a little better. Cheer yourself up. You deserve it.'

'My good man, I—'

'She wants it,' he hissed. 'Look at her. Look how much she wants it.'

The woman stood up, swung her leg slowly over the barrel, looked down into it and back at me, and leered. There was eel slime on her wrist: it glinted as she took my arm, began to lead me away. And I let her.

We didn't take long. There was a sort of coffin-sized niche in the alley just behind her stall where an ancient wall hadn't quite met a new building. We fumbled – *I* fumbled, she had me out in a moment, slid me inside as she fell back against the wall. Her hands were on my bum, my face was against her neck, licking salt. She smelled of cheap ambergris: dark, dense, the mud of a perfumed river. Her skirt was bunched up in a thick roll of sticky, hairy cloth that was rubbing the skin from my bare stomach. She was slippery, urgent as I sought to still her with my hands. I was trying to possess all of her as brick dust trickled down the back of my doublet, but I knew, just as things all got too much, that I would never have more than this: her breath, suddenly catching in her throat; her hand in my hair; the sudden bright burst of her gold earring against my tongue.

'I'm not a tart,' she said as she briskly tucked me away. I was leaning against the wall now, wrung out, the cold tendrils of regret already forming, like frost ferns on a window pane. 'But if you don't give me a *scudo* my brother might . . . I don't properly know what he might do.'

I gave her the coin, a week's profit from any market stall. The brother – perhaps he was her brother, at that – had already packed up my eels when I came out of the alley, trying to look collected. The woman strolled back to her seat. She hitched up her skirt, paused as she swung her leg over the eels, turned back to me and winked. I paid for my writhing, reed-tied bundle and left the market as quickly as my unsteady legs could manage.

That afternoon I slipped off to the *stufa*, the place where the Proctor had been scrubbed and shorn. I'd thought that I needed to wash the woman off me, as if that would take care of the guilt as well – not guilt for my soul, but the feeling I'd let myself down – but as I sank into the water and her coarse musk rose up in the steam, I realized I felt more at ease than I had in a long time.

The next day I was waiting for Pietrobon on the steps of his own favourite bathhouse, the chickens – unplucked and beginning to reek – laid out beside me in a neat line. He halted four or five paces from me, and we stared at one another for almost a minute. Then he gave a brisk nod, turned on his heel and started back towards the city. I went inside and had a short bath – short, because I had work to do, but long enough to satisfy my curiosity about Pietrobon's woman. The *spenditore* never said another word to me, and his purchases, along with my accounts, returned to their proper state.

The events of those two days, happy, exciting diversions as they were, might have sent me off on a glutton's exploration of all matters relating to the *cazzo*. But Fortune decided that was not to be. My trouble with Pietrobon, though it was settled in the quietest way possible, brought me into conflict with the *scalco*. Lodovigo de Lugo was a Mantuan just like the *spenditore*. Whether Pietrobon had been sharing some of his swindled money with de Lugo I didn't know, and as I could never have proved it I kept the thought to myself. It might have been pure dislike that brought de Lugo down upon me, but whatever the cause, I had no time for women in all the rest of my stay in the Gonzaga household.

At first Messer Lodovigo just lorded it over me. He stuck his rank in my face as delicately as if it was the heel of his elegant boot that was being shoved under my nose. I had been accustomed, under Orazio, to make suggestions for each menu, but that came to an abrupt end. From the instructions he brought me every day, I could easily have decided that Cardinal Gonzaga had mysteriously lost his organs of taste. Worse, de Lugo made a deliberately insulting round of inspection every night, poking his long beak into every dish and pot, his expression as sour as if he'd been forced to sniff a battery of full chamber pots.

Even that would have been bearable – since coming back to Rome I had stopped giving myself airs, because if Zohan had managed to teach me anything, it was that the master's satisfaction is the true salary of a cook; and Gonzaga, if not excited by my food, was at least eating it without complaint – but de Lugo began to insist on such accurate reckonings, expecting every leaf and grain to be accounted for, that I was often bent over my ledgers until far into the night, especially if there had been a grand banquet. I could only dream of the dishes I wanted to cook, and I lived on the high table's leftovers, because although I was entitled to a generous ration of fresh food – meat, eggs (and fish in Lent and on Fridays), bread and five flasks of wine – de Lugo and Pietrobon contrived things so that my allowance was always in arrears. Thus I dined on the marshy food of Mantua, and yesterday's at that. I began to dread coming downstairs in the morning, in case today might be the day the *scalco* pushed me beyond endurance. But he never did, not quite. Like a heron, he was patient.

The end came because of a betrothal. Some cousin of Cardinal Gonzaga was getting married here in Rome, and His Eminence gave the couple a splendid banquet. It was weeks in the planning, but it was Tranquillo the *credenziero* who was getting all the orders: two gigantic sugar lions for the Gonzagas, a Moorish captive complete with gilded chains for the bride's family; sugar replicas of Saint Peter's, the Colosseum, various other Roman churches, the Duomo of Mantua, Trajan's Column, the Pantheon, the Castel Sant'Angelo. Tranquillo, always fond of a drink, spent his days in a sort of sugar-dusted delirium, and this confirmed what I had already suspected: that he was getting most of my wine allowance. As for Luigino and me, we had an endless list of things to cook, but all of them were dishes we had churned out again and again: the waterfowl, the fish of marsh and lake, sausages, rice, and squash: mountains of squash. It was unbearable. Luigino, blessed as he was with an ordered mind, didn't take it too hard, but for me it was like being broken on the wheel.

One day Tranquillo was gossiping loudly about a man he'd met in a tavern the night before, whose master, a merchant from Bari, had just returned from India and was in Rome to tell the Holy Father about his travels. This man, said Tranquillo, had told him of the wonderful store of treasures his master had brought back: statues of gold and ivory; silks; spices that no one in Christendom had ever seen before; and some rare drugs, among them some leaves that, if chewed, would rouse the most reluctant lover if . . . Tranquillo raised his clenched fist. If I knew what he meant.

I did. That luncheon, de Lugo strutted into my kitchen, speared his beak into my pots, as was his custom, and found fault with the dish of rice and meat that he had ordered. Too much cinnamon, too much pepper. Was I trying to rouse His

Eminence's grosser humours? Was I trying to heat him up like . . . like . . . I watched him grope for a metaphor that would not involve his ordained master in something carnal. *Like a bitch?* I almost put in. I didn't, but that night I sat down and began to design a few dishes that weren't on the *scalco*'s menu.

The next day I feigned a mild sickness, went off on the pretence of consulting a surgeon, and, using Tranquillo's directions, tracked down the man who had returned from India, and relieved him, for an exorbitant price, of his miraculous leaves. When he asked me who they were for, I told him I was buying them on behalf of Messer Lodovigo de Lugo, a fine gentleman who needed all the help he could get. If the worthy sir knew what I meant.

When the banquet came around I made sure that Luigino had the day off. Then I got the three best men together, all good Roman boys, ribald and up for anything, and gave them my alterations to de Lugo's menu. The cardinal's kitchen was big enough that a man inspecting dishes in one part wouldn't notice other dishes being hidden or disguised in another. Really, it was all too easy.

And childish. Perhaps I was trying for a *beffa*, but given the circumstances and the means at my disposal, there wasn't a hint of sophistication in what I did. Which, as if any patient soul reading this tale has not already divined it, was to cook the required dishes to as high a standard as could be achieved, but lay each one out in such a way that it conveyed what I might like to call a jovial invitation to the pursuits of marriage.

Thus a dish of tench and eel was arranged so that the pointed head of the eels, gills splayed, thrust through a sea of delicate yellow sauce (toasted breadcrumbs, red wine and vinegar, more red wine reduced to *defrutum*, long pepper, grains of paradise, cloves, all passed through a sieve and tinted with saffron) towards the gaping lips of the tench. A plate of grilled partridges was presented with the birds still spitted from arse to beak, the spits radiating out from a magnificent cockerel, skinned, roasted and recloaked in its feathers, tail and red-combed head; the whole arranged on an armature so that it raised one leg and crowed at the ceiling. Inside the hollow body of the cockerel I had arranged a small silver alembic, its narrow end, no wider than a stalk of grass (I had borrowed it from an alchemist I knew through the Academy) protruding from the beak, and below it a tiny spirit lamp, which I lit as the serving men were already taking the dish away. The alembic was filled with Greco wine tinted with the milk of almonds, and I calculated that the wine would boil more or less when the dish was set on the table, and jet from the proud cock, showering the skewered partridges in aromatic white sauce.

There were the ripest figs, all splitting, of course, served with boiled crayfish – as eager, these bright red fellows, to explore the figs as the eels had been curious about the tench – and *torte* of rucola and pine nuts, liberally spiced with garlic and cloves. The suggestive qualities of the cardinal's favourite gourds – hardly my fault – were not neglected. There were oysters, grilled sparrows . . .

I was cooking, in a way, like a naughty boy drawing *cazzi* on the wall of a public jakes. But though the sentiment was crude, I had put, into each dish, as much beauty as I could. The spice store had been robbed. The kitchen budget had been savaged. I had taken the inherent dullness of each dish and brightened every colour, heightened every sense. Everything I knew about delighting tongues, everything Zohan had taught me, had gone into this meal. But in case anybody missed the point, I had already shaved the dice against them.

Before a single dish had gone out, the guests had been served a special wine. I had persuaded Donnanzo the *bottigliero* that my Indian leaves, which rejoiced in the mysterious names of *betel* and *kannab* or *ganjika*, were a miraculous cure-all from the mountains of Cambay (was Cambay even in India? Did it have mountains? I didn't have a clue, but then again neither did Donnanzo) that I had bought from the Pope's own pharmacist.

I had investigated them, of course: the *betel* was a large, dry, almost black leaf smelling of black pepper that, when opened out, had the shape of a woman's parts, an excellent omen. The *kannab*, on the other hand, was long and gummy, like a pointed, double-edged saw. It smelled vaguely of hops. Donnanzo was intrigued, especially when I told him what the merchant had told me: apart from their effects on the organs of generation (that detail I kept from the *bottigliero*), they were a powerful stimulator of the appetite, and served to open the neck of the stomach. And when I asked if they might make an excellent infusion in, say, the fine Malvagia he was no doubt going to pour as the guests were being seated, he agreed. And so it came about. Was it my idea or Donnanzo's to have it poured by boys dressed in Eastern costumes? No matter. The party drank its fill, and continued to drink as the food came in.

I lost my job at the moment the cock crowed. I knew it had, because when Lodovigo de Lugo, heated up for once and red as an ibis, flew into the kitchen, his hand actually on the hilt of his sword, his beautiful black doublet was spattered with white. Alas, he was met with a gale of laughter from all quarters of the kitchen. Even Tranquillo was doubled over in the door of his *laboratorio*. There was nothing the *scalco* could do about the food. The banqueting hall was full, much wine had already been drunk, and the feast was already cooked and plated.

'Did they like the wine?' I enquired, safe on the other side of the wide central table. De Lugo's teeth were actually clattering together with rage.

'You animal!' he squealed. 'You filth! You heretic! You . . . you Florentine *bardassa!*'

'Is the food not perfect? Are the flavours not exquisite?'

'Fuck your flavours! A *cazzo* for flavour! I gave you orders, orders, do you hear me? Orders! And then that obscenity . . . that vile emission . . .'

'But we're celebrating a betrothal!' I protested, edging nearer to Zohan's falchion, which I had just cleaned. 'Surely the bride- and groom-to-be will have appreciated a few little pointers for the joys to come?'

One of the turnspits howled and banged his head on the table. I thought Tranquillo was about to succumb to an apoplexy. But Pietro, the hare-lipped boy, thoughtfully nudged the falchion close enough for me to take hold of, gently but deliberately. The laughter went on, but there was a sudden air of expectation in the kitchen. A little bead of spittle was sliding down the *scalco's* chin.

'You've ruined me, you—'

'Oh, no. I can't let you take any credit for this masterpiece of a banquet, Messer Lodovigo. I'm much too proud for that. Are they enjoying it, the honoured guests? I thought you'd approve of the cock, or do you only care for real ones? Of course the esteemed company of Messers Pietrobon and Lodovigo would have served up stinking meat with garnish of maggot, in plaster sauce, wouldn't they?'

'I don't know what you mean.' The *scalco* darted his heron eyes around the kitchen but found no friends there. 'You are plainly a madman, like all cooks, and as such your employment here is at an end.'

'Excellent. Perhaps, seeing as I have no further duties here, I'll come and drink a toast to the happy couple. By the by, *scalco*: did you try the Malvagia? I'll warrant that you did.'

'Leave this house!'

'Boys, if any of you are virgins, which I doubt, give Messer

Lodovigo a wide berth tonight,' I said. 'If I know his habits, he's had at least a pint of the magic wine.'

There were giggles. I picked up the falchion, reached for my knife roll, began putting things away. De Lugo stood for a full minute, bobbing faintly on his long shanks. Then he raked us all with a blistering look, and left. I turned to my staff.

'Luigino is head cook now,' I said. 'Anyway, until they appoint some heron-boiler from up north. Do what Luigino says. Don't give him any shit. And don't ever, *ever*, do what I've done tonight: make a total *culo* of yourself and your employer. That's my speciality, you little *cazzi*.'

Tranquillo would see to my things – he told me not to worry. I wasn't worrying then, but in a few minutes, when I was wandering through the noise and smell of a busy evening in the Campus Martius, knocking shoulders with black-toothed street sweepers, with empty-breasted old women who slept in the ruins and lived off celery ends and turnip tops they found in the gutter, I didn't feel so cocky. I was expecting some little taste of satisfaction, but it was all depressingly familiar. My pride had jumped up and knocked me into the mud yet again.

My wanderings led me up the Viminal Hill, very late in the evening, with the full moon lighting up the country beyond the walls, as far as the mountains above Tivoli. The world went on and on, further than the sea, to Africa, to India. Creation was so vast, and I was such a little *cazzo*. I sat down on the corpse of an old olive tree and pulled my cloak around me. It was going to be a long, cold night.

The next morning I went straight to the hostelry behind Santa Maria Sopra Minerva. They had a decent room for not too many *soldi*, and I took it. Their runner was sent to the Palazzo Gonzaga with strict instructions to ask for no one except the *credenziero*. While I waited for my things to arrive

– *if* they arrived, because it certainly wouldn't be above the *scalco* to try and confiscate them – I tried to work out what I was going to do next.

The question that kept snipping its way to the front of my brain was whether I was really a cook. Here I was, in the twenty-sixth year of my life, and already I had pissed away not one but two chances to grope Lady Fortuna, chances that most men would hardly even dream about. My pride had got me banished from Florence, and it had put an end to my life in Rome, because surely no one would employ me here again. So what next?

I thought of Florence, of course. But what was the point? Bartolo Baroni was still alive. I heard enough of the news and gossip from the Florentine quarter – second-hand, though, because I dared not show my face there after what had happened in Assisi. Baroni was closer to Messer Lorenzo than ever these days, so far as I could gather from the wisps of conversation I overheard. Nothing else about the man, though: the death of his son, the health of his wife – all of it less than newsworthy.

People were more interested in the bad air that was growing between Messer Lorenzo and the Pazzi family. Something about an archbishop of Pisa, as far as I could make out: the Pope had appointed one Francesco Salviati, a close friend of the Pazzis, but Messer Lorenzo had been furious. Messer Lorenzo and His Holiness had not been seeing eye to eye for some time, and after the Imola affair, the Medicis had been shutting the Pazzis out of Florentine life wherever they could.

Things had been going from bad to worse. Lorenzo had refused Archbishop Salviati entrance to Pisa, but the Holy Father had threatened to excommunicate him. Now Salviati was in Pisa, and the Pope had taken away the Medici's alum-mining monopoly – worth a fortune – and given it to the

Pazzis. I could picture how the mood in Florence must be: people splitting into parties, fights in the piazzas, poisonous graffiti on the walls . . . Not – and this was very clear to me – a good time to be an enemy of Bartolo Baroni.

So, south to Naples, perhaps? King Ferrante was known to like his food, and that meant his court would always need good cooks. Or Milan? France, as I'd once planned? But then it would all happen again. I'd never be satisfied, not until I was someone like Zohan. But even Zohan had bridled against the men who paid him. I'd have to be God himself before I was satisfied.

Well, I could always paint. I knew how to do that. Not well, but I could always learn. Filippo would approve, wouldn't he? I could stare at lovely women all day long and play with them all night.

My baggage arrived from San Lorenzo in Damaso. The men who brought it were chattering about the cardinal's banquet.

'What's all this about?' I asked one of the men innocently, as I paid him.

'Cardinal Gonzaga gave a feast for his nephew or cousin or whatever,' said the man. 'Now I've seen His Eminence often enough – from a distance, mind – and a good, mild-mannered fellow he seems to be. But last night he gave this nephew, and his bride – who's as plain as a paving stone, by all accounts – a love feast the like of which Nero himself would have been proud.' He crossed himself at the mention of Nero, as many Romans did, afraid that the emperor's evil shade still prowled through the city. 'Lifelike cock and balls on the table, so I hear, smoke and steam coming out of the end. And every sort of thing to get a man and a woman going. Richo here says the nephew made His Eminence do the wedding right there, so that he could roger the bride on the table!'

'That's what Gilio told me,' muttered Richo. 'Don't know if it's true. The cock part's true, though, sir. I swear it.'

Tranquillo himself turned up at that point and I sent the carriers away as quickly as I could. 'It's not true, is it?' I demanded.

We were sitting with a jug of cheap wine, and both of us were drinking it like medicine. Tranquillo had his wet feet propped up on the hearth.

'No, no. Nothing like that. No rogering.'

'Thank God.'

'Only just, mind you. When I went in with the sugar pieces, it was like a bloody cage full of stoats. Everyone had these big cow's eyes' – he bulged his own eyes and stuck the tip of his tongue obscenely from the corner of his mouth, like a hanged man – 'all looking as if they were about to start licking each other and not the sugar. And all of them red and sweating. It was a sight, I can assure you. Not that they weren't all having the time of their lives. I swear His Eminence looked like a stallion in a field full of brood mares. Never seen anything like it.'

'And this morning?'

'There must be some thick heads around. Bloody de Lugo has been shut up with His Eminence for an hour or so. One of the maids said it isn't pretty.'

'I shouldn't feel sorry for him, but in a way I do.'

'What the *cazzo*? The bastard's never put on a decent banquet in his life. He should have been a preaching friar, not a *scalco*. He's an embarrassment to the Gonzagas. But you, on the other hand. I've never seen food like you sent out last night. I loved the old maestro, but you, my boy . . .'

'It was meant to be a joke,' I muttered. 'Pretty simple stuff, really.'

'Simple? I had some of the leftovers – there weren't many – and dear God, they were good.'

'What did you have?' I asked, despite myself.

'A couple of sparrows – wouldn't normally touch them, of course.' He lifted his arm, fist clenched, and quivered it graphically. 'Fantastic. What did you put in them?'

'I can't remember. Long pepper, grains of paradise . . . Just whatever would bring out the bird, if you know what I mean. It's delicate meat, but it has a taste and I wanted to honour it.'

'Honouring tastes? You sound like a pagan, my boy.'

'But why else be a cook? Why eat anything except bread, if not to taste what you're eating? What's the point, Tranquillo?'

'I thought the point was to get paid.'

'So does everybody. Except me, apparently. Anyway, I'm not planning to disturb anyone else in Rome. I'm going to Naples.'

'Bloody good idea. You could start a brothel. "The Mantuan Cock".'

'Ha! No, no. I'm done with cooking. I'm going to paint.'

'Oh, Jesus and Mary. Have another drink, man. So you're an artist now, are you?'

But I didn't get to explain myself, because at that moment two men-at-arms walked into the hostelry. They wore exquisite blue and white livery which, alas, was wringing wet. Another man walked behind them, a slight man dressed in clothes that were at once drab and exquisitely expensive. He shook himself like a cat, scanned the room, which in any case was almost empty, and whispered something to the soldiers. I wasn't surprised at all when he made straight for our table.

'Would one of you gentlemen be Maestro Nino?' he asked. His voice was calm, gentle, even, but he was plainly accustomed to complete obedience.

'*He* is,' Tranquillo piped up, before I'd even opened my mouth.

'Is this so?' said the man. He sounded like a patient priest, but then again, he had two soldiers with him.

'It is,' I said, standing up. 'What is your business with me?' I eyed the men-at-arms, waiting for them to stroll over and grab me, but they were more interested in the wine barrel that was being broached by the landlord.

'I am Domenicho Pagholini. Have you heard of me?'

I told him that I hadn't, which was true. He didn't seem put out.

'And you are the master cook? Cook and perhaps alchemist?'

'As I said before. If you've come to arrest me, will you let me settle my bill here first?'

'Arrest you?' Pagholini frowned. 'Have I given you that impression? In that case I must apologize. I've come to invite you to luncheon.'

'That's very kind of you, Messer Domenicho. But if you're not taking me off to the Castel Sant'Angelo, I have to be leaving. Ordinarily I would be honoured to dine with you, but circumstances—'

'Ah. No. You see, the invitation is from someone who attended Cardinal Gonzaga's banquet last night.'

'I'd better be going,' said Tranquillo abruptly. He stood up, kissed me briskly on both cheeks and left, with a last worried look at the soldiers, one of whom was now bouncing the end of his pikestaff against the floor.

'Stop that!' ordered Pagholini. The soldier came to attention, looking embarrassed.

'I apologize – obviously – if your friend, colleague, acquaintance, whoever he might be, did not enjoy his meal,' I said. 'Please know that I chose all the ingredients personally. Everything was fresh and wholesome, and quite ordinary.'

'On the contrary. The person of whom I speak enjoyed his meal very much. Very much indeed. Will you come? He will be disappointed if you don't – and so, if I may say so, will you.'

That sounded like a threat, but Pagholini was anything but threatening. His soldiers, on the other hand . . . I had run out of choices, yet again.

'If it is understood that I'm leaving for Naples directly afterwards,' I said gruffly.

'Excellent. Shall we go now? It isn't far.'

'Very well. But you haven't told me who I'm dining with.'

'You're right. How remiss of me. It's the man I serve. Cardinal Rodrigo de Borgia. And he's *very* anxious to meet you.'

❧ 41 ❧

STRANGE TO REMEMBER THE LIVING man who has become such a famous corpse. I know – everyone knows – the end that Fortune painted for Rodrigo Borgia, or Pope Alexander VI as he had become. Little boys make their sisters squirm and retch with the vile embroideries the story has gathered: the foaming mouth, the blackened tongue, the blasts of pestilent wind from the dead man's fundament, the pauper's coffin too small for the monstrous, swollen carcass. A pitiless end, too vile for pity, too wretched, almost, for human compassion. For what man makes such a corpse, unless he has stored up corruption inside him like black and dripping honeycomb?

Perhaps it's all true. So what? Death is a joke played principally upon the living: the dead care very little whether they disgrace themselves. I do not for one minute believe that Rodrigo Borgia enjoyed the manner of his passing, but I think he would greatly have enjoyed what came after. Not that he would have laughed, because that was not his way. But if such things as ghosts exist on this earth, and the ghost of Rodrigo Borgia was standing in a corner of his chamber, watching while his little German secretary sat on the lid of his coffin, trying to close it enough to set the nails while he rocked and swayed on the billow of deliquescent flesh, the Holy Father, no longer imprisoned in that flesh, would have nodded, quietly, and let his lips purse into a faint, almost secret smile. *Oh, dear*, he would murmur. *How interesting. How very, very interesting.*

I don't believe the stories of Borgia's death. They hinge on the self-righteous assumption that a grossly undignified man was paid out by divine justice with an undignified end. But the man waiting for me in his offices inside the Vatican palace seemed to radiate dignity. He was tall, much taller than me. My first thought, strangely enough, was that here was a man I wouldn't want to find on the other team at a game of *calcio*. The cardinal, even in his shapeless robes of office, had the build of one of the Roman warriors who trudge through perpetuity up the spiral of Trajan's Column. He had broad shoulders, well-turned calves, long elegant hands, one of which was being offered to me. I knelt and kissed the great gold ring of office. The cardinal offered a chair, a beautifully carved thing with a back of red leather tooled with gold. I sat, right on the edge. Borgia noticed, gave a small, almost imperceptible smile. Curiously, it put me at my ease straight away. As the cardinal turned to speak to Pagholini, and to the servant who was hovering expectantly, I settled back into the chair and examined my host.

He would have been in the middle of his fortieth decade then, but he looked perhaps ten years younger. His face was remarkably unlined, his black hair hardly touched by grey. All the planes and angles of his face were still sharp: the noble chin, the long peregrine's beak of a nose. His eyes were large, dark and slightly hooded. Though he seemed in complete control of his body, the eyes were busy, darting towards every movement, every distraction. But he himself was not distracted. I found out later that he had been a lawyer before entering the priesthood, and I have always wondered whether he learned the habits of careful examination, of consideration; or whether they were the grain of the man himself. I had an impression of extraordinary focus, and that focus was directed almost entirely at me.

The servant came back with a silver jug and silver cups. The jug held an exquisite pale Malvagia, not flavoured or watered. The cardinal took a careful sip and waited until I had done the same.

'Is it good?' he asked. I realized he was talking to me. His voice was very deep and rich – foreign, of course, with a deeply buried sharpness. The Saracens make a thick syrup from sour pomegranates, and that was what I thought of whenever I heard Borgia speak: dark, seductive, with the sudden ambush of tartness.

'It is excellent, Your Eminence,' I stammered.

'I've never really understood the enthusiasm for putting things in wine,' he said. The hooded eyes flicked from my cup to his own. I took another very cautious sip, ran the wine across my tongue – but no. Just grape and the giddy breath of spirits.

'I'm of the same opinion,' I said, into the silence that Borgia had left for me to fill. 'But as you say, Your Eminence, it's an enthusiasm. Or a fashion.'

'And it can have such amusing consequences.'

'Well . . .' I looked from Borgia to Pagholini, and saw nothing but interest. Still, I chose my words very carefully. 'I believe it is a cook's duty to experiment. And a new ingredient . . . It is a temptation.'

'Temptation.' Borgia rolled the word like a golden pebble around his mouth. 'Rather appropriate.'

'If Your Eminence suffered in any way . . .'

'No, no, no! My good maestro, I found it all quite diverting. What was in the wine? It was the wine, wasn't it?'

'*Betel* and *kannab*. From India.'

'Hmm. And you knew their properties?'

I winced inside. This was the moment, then. A handful of glib replies, lies and excuses offered themselves, but I knew, as surely as I knew anything, that lying to the man in front of me would be utterly useless.

'Yes, Your Eminence.'

There was a long pause. I felt myself shrink inside my clothes. Then the cardinal laughed. It was a proper laugh, musical and warm.

'I had almost none of the wine,' he said. 'But a great deal of your food. Excellent, all of it. The proud cockerel: very interesting. Very ingenious. I wonder, though, if by that time anyone else was paying attention?' I opened my mouth to reply, but Borgia held up his cup, tilted it this way and that. I saw a faint reflection from its surface play across his face. 'It was a most appropriate betrothal feast,' he said. 'I have no doubt at all that young Gonzaga's marriage will be blessed, and that his bed will be . . .' He paused, glanced at Pagholini.

'Rumpled,' said the steward, his face expressionless.

'Exactly so,' said Borgia. 'So, Maestro. The question must be, what now for you?'

'I'm going to Naples, Your Eminence.'

'To cook?'

'I think not. I have a desire to paint.'

'Of course, you must have a strong desire, Nino di Niccolaio Latini. Your uncle was Fra Filippo Lippi, isn't that true?'

'Your Eminence . . .' I swallowed, hard. 'Yes,' I said. *Yes* to all of it. Best to own up now, whatever was coming.

'And did you inherit his genius?' Thankfully, he gave me no chance to reply, because I wouldn't have been able to. 'You didn't, at least not entirely. I will not denigrate your artistic talents, Maestro, because I have no right to, not having seen your work. But it seems to me that your genius lies in the spoon and not the brush. You might make a good alchemist, as Pagholini believes. But there again, the cook is a little like an alchemist – as is the painter. Taking coarse matter and transmuting it into something ineffable.'

I was an alchemical genius all right, I thought to myself: I had managed, again and again, to turn gold into lead. 'Your

Eminence is kind,' I said out loud, 'but I really don't think I'm the man you're looking for.'

'Ah, but *I* do. I need a *scalco*, Maestro. Someone with the palate of Lucullus, the probity of Cicero, the poetry of Virgil and the sensuality of . . .'

'Nero,' finished Pagholini.

'With the greatest regret, Your Eminence, after last night I don't think I'll be a free man for very long if I stay in Rome. Cardinal Gonzaga . . .'

'Leave Gonzaga to me,' said Borgia. 'Leave everything to me.'

'But there's more,' I said.

'We know,' said Pagholini. 'A confession is not sought.'

'Wait – what do you know?'

'Everything that is necessary.'

'I wouldn't presume to treat His Eminence like a common confessor, however much it would help my soul,' I said. 'It's that I've made my world a very small place, a very dangerous place. As you seem to know everything about me, you'll have heard what I did in Assisi?'

Both men nodded. It has occurred to me many times since that if I had just confirmed what it was exactly that they knew, I would have saved myself a good deal of trouble. But I was far too ashamed and nervous for that. 'Then you'll know that I'm certainly notorious in Florence and possibly a listed traitor.' The cardinal steepled his fingers and nodded. 'And unfortunately, your palace is just a few steps from the Florentine quarter.'

'Well now, my son: when were you last in Florence?'

'Almost six years ago.'

'If you please, Domenicho?' Borgia signalled to his steward.

Pagholini nodded, took the silver jug off the tray and set it down on the table, picked up the tray, polished it with his sleeve. Then, with a flourish, the silver disc appeared in front

of my face. And in it, another face entirely. He was handsome, this man, though as I stared, I noticed that his cheeks
were puffy and his jaw was losing its line. His hair looked as if
a gardener had pruned it with dull shears, and a swathe of
grey striped from his left temple, out of a ragged, star-shaped
scar, its arms radiating towards his left eye, up onto his brow
and almost into his ear. There were little pinpricks of grey,
too, in the three days' stubble on the man's chin and lips. The
green eyes stared back at me, slightly truculent, slightly lost.

'I'm old!' I gasped.

'Don't tell me that Gonzaga's master cook does not have
the use of a mirror?' asked Borgia. He sounded like a lawyer,
then: fortunately, I seemed to be his client, not his adversary.

'I don't . . . In my profession, particularly in my last
position, there isn't really much need,' I said distractedly,
running my hand across the place where Marco Baroni's
sword hilt had laid my head open to the bone. I knew it
much better by touch than by sight. 'I've seen myself often
enough. But I haven't actually looked.' I went closer,
pinched the loosening skin of my cheek. 'Now I know
why.' Pagholini held the tray still, his eyes exploring something up on the ceiling.

'And is this the man who left Florence five years ago?' said
Borgia.

'No.' I held up my hand and Pagholini took the tray back
to its place. 'I don't know who he is.'

'Well, then. Maestro Nino is not Messer Nino. Will you
accept my offer?'

'I'm not suited, Your Eminence! I bridle at authority. The
food that I'm required to cook I find ridiculous. People say
they want to eat, but what they really want is spectacle. My
cockerel was a dirty joke and I regret it, but if it had been a
peacock, and fire had come out of its mouth, they would
have called it genius. Genius – I've heard them say it: and all

for a weak jest. So I should have done a peacock, but I'd have regretted that as well.'

'But you enjoyed making the cockerel. It was very obvious. And hilarious – absolutely hilarious. I think your anger is pretence. You went to some pains to give offence, and I submit that you enjoyed it.'

'My lord, I'm afraid I did. And I will pay for that.'

'So. You scorn artifice for its own sake but revel in it for the purposes of mockery. You think food should be art, but in the taste, not the appearance.'

'It *could* be art, Your Eminence.'

'Then let us have both. The Lord has ordained you to be a great cook, Maestro – or perhaps it is Fortune, or whatever pagan being presides over the kitchen. Now, I am rather fond of jests, but like you I prefer them to have a little more, shall we say, spirit. So I shall pay you for both: the flavours you command, and the artifice I require. We shall serve up the most flavoursome jests Rome has ever seen. Will you accept my offer?'

I touched my scar again: Fortune's fingerprint. She was offering her hand once more, in spite of everything. And you don't turn Her down.

'What are your terms?' I said.

That evening, as I was walking back to Santa Maria Sopra Minerva through the Florentine quarter, I felt strangely invisible. It wasn't a particularly nice feeling, wandering like a ghost through my own people, but it was better than the alternative. Because this was going to be my home from now on. Rodrigo Borgia's terms had been excellent. Lady Fortune had not only taken my hand again: she had guided it up her skirts. The pay alone was staggering. And then there were the perks: my own chambers, as much firewood as I needed, three pounds of meat a day, plus a capon, four pounds of bread, as much wine as I thought necessary, the pick of the day's leftovers . . . It was a goldmine, because I could sell most of it out of the back door, as was expected, and save the money . . . If Tessina came to join me, I'd be a rich man in my own right.

I stopped outside the Palazzo della Cancelleria, Cardinal Borgia's palace. Now, when even the deaf-mute beggar has heard fables of Borgia and his wickedness, it is hard to credit that I felt no anxiety for my immortal soul as I stood there in the street. But in those days, Rodrigo Borgia's reputation was for largesse, nobility, generosity of spirit and of purse – especially of the latter. The cardinal opened his purse for friends, for the needy. But if there was an advantage to be bought, he would empty it. In those days, the Spanish cardinal was well loved by the people of Rome, and those who did not love him still jostled for a sniff of his money.

He was also known, then as now, for his love of women, but when I lived in Rome it was a city that provided a living to seven thousand prostitutes, and no one gave a cardinal's mistress very much thought. Like everyone else, the Pope included, I knew about the lady Vannozza, who lived in a palace just below San Pietro in Vincoli, and who had just borne the cardinal a new son, his second. But Borgia was reckoned to be a good husband in all ways a man can be whose marriage cannot be sanctified by Mother Church. No: in those days, the worst that could be said of Cardinal Borgia was that he liked to dance, perhaps rather more than a cardinal should.

Should I go in and introduce myself to the kitchen? I walked around the walls, wondering about the dim lights behind the windows, what sort of a world they might be illuminating, because that was my world now. I found the service door, which was guarded by a portly old man in a greasy blue and yellow tunic. I announced that I needed to talk to someone in the kitchen and stepped past him. He made no effort to stop me.

I had grown used to the kitchens in the Palazzo Gonzaga. Those were magnificent, created to satisfy the desires of the greatest epicure of the age. But the palace in San Lorenzo in Damaso was old, and the Palazzo della Cancelleria had only been standing a few years. The kitchen I walked into, waddling in my best butcher's fashion, on legs that ought to be stiff from years of lugging sides of meat, was vast and almost shockingly modern. A succession of tables with thick oak tops marched down the middle towards two enormous hearths, one with a bread oven let into its side, both fitted with complicated arrangements of spits that looked like the workings of a clock. On one side of the room was a long range, seven or eight fires under a stone counter, each burning in its own domed compartment, the flames licking through iron grates set into the stone. Copper pots were steaming away over some of these, and at others men were frying and searing. On the other side, two stone troughs on carved legs stood side by side under a row of bronze spigots, each with a tap in the shape of a dolphin, which jutted from the wall. Next to them, shelves from which legions of pans hung from iron hooks; and cupboards, some of them open to reveal glimmering innards of jars, canisters and metal dishes. Great metal frames hung from the ceiling, some holding cauldrons, roasting pans, spits, baking paddles, bunches of dried herbs, festoons of sausages; others hung with metal cages as big as a man, each with its own padlock, in which expensive meats were locked. There were doors leading off to storerooms, to what I guessed was the *credenza*, and no doubt to a pastry room, a brew house and a laundry.

No one noticed me. I leaned in the doorway and watched the spectacle. A red-faced man was examining a tray of pies while a younger man looked on, biting his thumbnail absent-mindedly. Two boys were struggling to fix a spit loaded with trussed pheasants into the machinery in one hearth, and another boy was mopping some thick, reddish marinade over the carcass of a small deer that was revolving slowly over the coals of the other fire. A woman and a younger girl were standing side by side at the trough, scrubbing pans, while a grey-haired, jowled man leaned on the table behind them, staring at their bottoms and gutting sardines. Someone was weighing out spices on a set of goldsmiths' scales and handing them on to another cook who was being watched, out of one eye, by the fat man with the pies. I guessed that the maestro was in after all.

The air was thick with fragrant steam from the ranges, mixed with smoke from the fires beneath. This steam met a second column billowing up from the washing troughs, which was heavy and slightly rank. Beneath the steam, the familiar kitchen smells of hot lard, frying onions, fat and meat drippings splashing into fire, pepper dust, spilled cloves, burned sugar, crushed mint and thyme, blood, fish guts and men's armpits. I breathed it in, feeling the spices catch in my throat, and my body shuddered with the rightness of it. Could I really have thought I'd be able to turn my back on all of this?

I watched with approval as one of the cooks touched up the edge on his knife and took out a tall wooden box from one of the cupboards. He opened it, revealing a row of other knives stuck blade down into a bed of flour-like lime powder, and stuck his own blade in among them. Someone dropped an egg, and someone else cursed him floridly.

I turned and left. Out in the wet street I could still feel the spices burning faintly in my throat, and the rain, as it soaked my cloak, brought the kitchen smells to life again. There was a good taverna nearby and I was starving.

⁓ 42 ⁓

IT HAD BEEN RAINING FOR ALMOST TWO WEEKS. A ceiling of heavy clouds, as thick and grey as the belly of a wild goose, hung suspended over the city, and the water came down in curtains, in blankets, in sheets, in winding-cloths, in shrouds. The river came up and sniffed at its banks, hesitated, then boiled over. Rome went to bed on Monday night and woke up on Tuesday morning to find two feet of water in the streets. Every one had become a brown, turgid brook, upon which dense fleets of rubbish manoeuvred and clashed.

I wanted to head for higher ground, but instead I was wading towards the Tiber, a big leather bag with all my possessions slung over my shoulder. I'd planned to have it delivered, but the man had never turned up – caught, no doubt, in his own damp crisis. Just ahead was the palace of my latest employer, dark and forbidding in the half-light. I shivered, pulled my wet cloak around me, and trudged up to the back door of the Palazzo Borgia.

I had the best job in Rome: *scalco* to Cardinal Rodrigo Borgia. *Maestro Nino steps in shit and it turns to sugar.* So everyone was saying. Perhaps they were right. I'd only been working here for a week, and most of that time had been spent forcing my staff to do what they were told. The same old ritual: the lead-swingers, the men passed over again and again for advancement, the head cook who believed he should have got my job, the lippy pot-boys. All of them had to be dealt with. I had ordered them to clean the kitchen from top to bottom, to scrape the inch or so of fetid grease off the floor beneath the tables and in the washing troughs; to scour the pots until they shone. They all hated me, and I didn't care. Nothing was new. The same words, making sure they knew I didn't give a dick if they were happy, if they loved me or hated me, if they were dying, just as long as the patron's food was perfect. It had to be perfect. And perfect meant the way I wanted it. Was that simple enough? If it wasn't, they could fuck off now. I could replace them all in an hour. Most of them had stayed.

When I walked in, already changed into clean, dry clothes, they were all huddled together over one of the tables, and when they saw me they scattered, like black beetles in a dark room when you strike a light. I made sure they had work to do and went and sat in a corner with my ledgers.

There was nothing important happening that day, or for the rest of the week. The floods had sent the cardinal up to higher ground, to his mistress's *palazzo*. But today was when I was finally moving in to my new quarters. A rather haughty young servant, one of the cardinal's cousins, perhaps, or the *maestro di casa*'s son, because they had the same air of self-entitlement, led me up flights of stairs and along corridors to my door. Although I was aware that my new position carried proper rank, I was still surprised – though I took care to hide it from the gimlet-eyed servant – to find that my rooms were not in the service quarter of the palace but would have been perfectly acceptable to a guest of middling importance. It was two rooms with well-made furniture, including a writing desk, a large bed that had all the weight and gloomy presence of a papal tomb, and a grand fireplace. I was about to make a fire, to drive out the damp and to dry my boots, but saw the young servant hovering in the doorway. I set him to work on the fire, told him to unpack my things, and sat down at my new desk. I'd never had my own desk before. It even had a drawer. I opened it, and there was a piece of good Venetian paper and a broken quill. The paper was just the right size for a letter. But I didn't write letters.

'Don't touch that!'

The boy was holding up my little leather valise, which I'd wrapped in a cloak to keep it from the wet. I could tell he'd been about to peep inside the flap from the way he jumped. I knew guilt when I saw it. Stalking over, I took it from him and carried it into the bedchamber. Looking around, I saw a small, carved and painted wooden altar with doors folded shut, on a stand in one corner. I opened it, took out Sandro's drawings – of the Madonna, and, most precious, of Tessina – propped them inside and shut the doors.

'What's your name?' I asked the boy, who was sullenly laying out my clothes in the oak press.

'Alonso Ruyz de Bisimbre,' he said. A faint sneer was playing around his lips, and it had found its way into his voice as well. I'd been right: a little nobleman.

'The fire isn't catching. See to it,' I said.

So this was success: you got your own rooms, but they came with a supercilious little snob to keep you in your place. If he thought he was going to lord it over me, though, he'd made a terrible mistake. And – a long time ago, it seemed now, but really, not that long – I had been a superior little bastard myself.

'Do you know who I am?' I asked. He had his back to me, squatting on his haunches in front of the fire, blowing some smouldering oak splinters into life. He turned, studiedly, as if I was bothering him.

'You're His Eminence's new cook.' His lips were almost puckering with disgust.

'I am His Eminence's *scalco*. You will be aware of what exactly that means. And *what* are you, Alfonso Ruyz de Bisimbre?'

'I am a gentleman. I will be a cardinal one day.'

He really was like me, this little bastard. So young and so convinced that lovely Fortune had him firmly by the hand. Just wait until you're a bit older, a little taller, I wanted to tell him. Then you'll see that Fortune is leading you down a narrow path between two infinite cesspits. So far I'd kept my footing, but only just.

When I went back downstairs, the kitchen was full. The head cook greeted me with a solemn bow and we went into my room to go over the day's requirements. His name was Teverino, appropriately enough, as he was as Roman as the Tiber that was making its presence felt outside. As I had guessed, he was the ginger-haired man with the impressive pot belly I had spied on two weeks ago.

To my relief, he wasn't going to cause me any trouble. He'd heard of me – about the betrothal feast, of course, or the Feast of Gonzaga's Cock, as it had become known throughout the kitchens of Rome. That wasn't a good start as far as I was concerned. But as it turned out, he had been an acquaintance of Maestro Zohan, which told me that Teverino must be worth something, because my dear old master hadn't ever wasted a moment of his time on people for whom he had no admiration. He was shrewd, was Teverino, and instead of wasting his energy hating me for my youth and my luck, he saw me as an opportunity. He was an excellent cook – old-fashioned, but diligent, energetic – and imaginative enough, which he had to be, working for Borgia. But he was getting on: forty or so, though he looked ten years older. And if he was ever going to be *scalco*, he would have to make a powerful alliance. And who better to have on your side than a young man with Fortuna hanging on his arm? It suited me very well, but I wanted to tell the poor bastard that I was the last person he should put his trust in.

Meanwhile, there was a lot of work. Cardinal Gonzaga kept a good table, but compared to Borgia, my erstwhile master was an ascetic. Here, we were required to serve the food of Spain as well as that of Rome, Florence, Naples, Milan, and if the cardinal had a distinguished guest from somewhere else, we would have to give him the food of his home as well. Borgia didn't care what he spent, and with the right ingredients a kitchen should be able to do anything.

So far, I'd arranged three small banquets – nothing elaborate, in fact rather plain. Borgia had a staggering collection of plate – silver, gold-plated, even solid gold – and he was most particular that I should show it off to its best advantage. I hadn't used the gold, not yet, but the cheaper silver services, of a quality that would have made a Medici clear his throat, were used every day. It was completely meaningless as far as flavour went, but I was forced to admit that, when my dishes were arranged on the shining metal, the food seemed to assume another level of *desirability*. There was something almost indecent about what certain trenchers could do to an ordinary dish of, say, grilled squab. My job was to take everything just a minute degree further: to push the senses a little more than they were accustomed to. It was exciting. For the first time since I'd left Florence, my work was starting to feel like the calling I'd once believed in. I had my vocation back.

As *scalco* I was in charge of anything that related to food in the palace: that is, I did everything except get my fingernails dirty. The palace itself was run by Messer Domenicho, who was part steward, part *maestro di casa*, and part *condottiere*. I found myself liking him more and more, though he was a mystery to me. He seemed to do nothing at all, and yet everything was done. The household appeared to neither love nor hate him, in fact, he was almost invisible. Pagholini never raised his voice, but all over the great house people were following orders that he seemed to have issued silently, whereas I spent my life bellowing at everyone in my little kingdom.

So I was rather surprised, that wet day, when Pagholini glided into the kitchen and politely requested my company.

'Do you have a horse?' he asked, as I followed him into his office.

'I don't,' I said reluctantly.

'No matter. We'll find you one. We aren't going far, but I think it might be best to ride.'

We went out to the guardroom – flooded, of course; we walked on boards set up on bricks – where Pagholini ordered two horses to be saddled. We helped ourselves to heavy riding cloaks, and soon we were splashing through the turbid water in the courtyard.

'Where are we going, by the way?' I asked casually, as we headed west towards the Capitoline, barely visible in the distance.

'It just occurred to me that I should introduce you to one of your . . . hmm. Suppliers.'

'Thank you, Messer Domenicho. But there's really no need. I have the pick of the markets,' I said, slightly peeved. I wouldn't presume to tell him where to buy furniture polish, after all.

'Of course you do. But I am making the assumption – you will tell me, of course, if I'm mistaken and I will offer my most abject apologies – that His Eminence Cardinal Gonzaga did not require you to furnish this particular commodity.'

To say that the morning caught me off guard would be a hilarious understatement, because the building proved to be a very expensive brothel. We weren't there as customers, I hasten to add, at least not in the ordinary way. I followed Pagholini into the main room where he was greeted by a jolly, round-faced woman wearing an unadorned black tunic. She looked like someone's favourite aunt, except that when you caught her eyes they bored into you. They were doing that while Pagholini introduced me as the new Borgia *scalco*. I thought she was going to pinch my cheek, but instead she curtsied, giggling coyly. At that point I still thought Pagholini had brought me to meet his family, because I couldn't for the life of me imagine why else we were in this homely place. Then the girls came in.

Ten young women – where had they been hiding? It did not seem like a big house – came in through a low door in the far corner of the room. They walked gravely, their heads up, each slippered foot placed carefully before the other. They were all dressed alike, in long, simply cut dresses made from the finest material. They were so demure that my mind was still telling me these must be Pagholini's cousins as they lined up before us and struck subtle, languid poses. All were perfectly beautiful. I was just wondering how the steward could have relatives from all the corners of Italy when he inclined his head towards me.

'For the Sforza ambassador's banquet on Friday,' he said. 'I'm inclined to take all ten, but the decision's yours, and will be from now on, of course.'

'To serve?' I said, confused.

'Serve?'

'Food.'

'Ah. I do apologize. We haven't had one of these particular banquets since you joined us.'

'Messer Domenicho, I'm not following you.'

'No, no. The fault is mine. Friday, then.'

'Duke Galeazzo Maria Sforza's ambassador and his retinue,' I said. 'In fact, I would have been working things out now, but . . .' I nodded towards the women, who were still standing like a row of unbroken statues.

'Good, good. Now then, you know those Milanesi. The ambassador is said to be a very close companion to the duke,

413

and we must, of course, entertain him in a manner which will summon up the comforts of home.'

The Duke of Milan was known all through the lands of Italy for one thing alone: untrammelled debauchery. Anyone – woman or man, mother, daughter or son – who caught his eye would end up in his bed whether they wanted to or not; and apparently, the less they wanted to, the more the duke enjoyed himself. So I said that yes, I had heard a few things about the Milanese court.

'Excellent. So you'll be envisioning something like your masterpiece for Cardinal Gonzaga's nephew, I expect, with – no doubt – certain embellishments.'

'As for embellishments, I . . .' But at that moment I saw that the women had all pulled up their tunics and were standing stark naked from the neck downwards.

'Really, a very nice selection,' said Pagholini. 'They would look rather splendid dressed as Poor Clares. Do you think? Or ancient Vestals, perhaps. Or too obvious?' He was waiting for me to answer, and the girls were revolving slowly, their tunics still up over their heads. At that moment, everything – professionally, at least – became clear.

I took a deep breath, feeling slightly queasy. 'Thank you, my dears,' I said to the girls. 'Please cover yourselves. Don't catch cold on our account.' The girls dropped their tunics and I felt oddly relieved. They stood still, watching us with rapt indifference. 'So . . . Hmm. His Eminence will be there, of course?'

'Naturally. And he likes to lead the sport, as you will have noticed.'

'I suppose I had.' In the few banquets I had already managed, Borgia had been a careful and perfectly proper host, expertly leading his guests into conversation and merriment while seeming to maintain a calm, solicitous distance. But what had he said about the Gonzaga betrothal? *Interesting . . .*

hilarious. 'The girls, all ten, dressed as . . . dressed as Sabine women,' I said. Pagholini nodded, waiting. 'Umm . . . the guests, men of Ancient Rome, perhaps?' The steward raised his eyebrows encouragingly. 'His Eminence could be . . .' I cleared my throat. 'Would he perhaps play Romulus?'

'Aha. Yes. Excellent.'

'Now, His Eminence . . .'

'Do you see him in ancient garb?'

'Would he? Yes, if he so desired. *Someone* should be the leader of the Sabines.' I wished I had paid more attention when Leto had told me the story. 'Ersilia, I think her name was.'

'Yes, indeed! We could get another girl, but . . . Would *you*, perhaps? That way you could keep an eye on things and . . .' He nodded matter-of-factly towards the girls, one of whom clearly needed to visit the jakes, as she was shifting surreptitiously from foot to foot.

'Can I just ask what my predecessor would have done?'

'He wasn't a great one for joining in. The man had many talents, but he didn't seem to take much pleasure in his work.' He watched the girls leave the room, still expressionless, the woman I had taken for Pagholini's aunt muttering endearments or threats in their ears as they went through the door. 'Do you like serving food you wouldn't eat yourself?'

'No, absolutely not.'

'Quite right. Our loyalty – yours and mine, as heads of His Eminence's household – are to our master's comforts and delights. We have no self. Our master's pleasures are our own, something your predecessor just could not grasp. But ultimately he was rather a small person, while you, Messer Nino, you see possibilities. You see potential. I'll ask the good madam here about an older girl to play Ersilia, but I think you'd rather the part was yours – am I right?'

★

415

Which was how I found myself, on Friday night, dressed in the primitive drapes of a Sabine woman, the whiskery cloth chafing my naked skin as I led my troupe of ten sisters in a solemn procession around Cardinal Borgia's dining table, swinging, God forgive me, an ancient silver censer that billowed with the suggestive smoke of ambergris and frankincense. The Milanese ambassador, a long-faced, pouch-eyed fellow, was roaring with laughter and bouncing up and down in his chair like a little boy on his birthday. His retinue, most of them young men, had finally relaxed and were making grabs at the girls as they swayed past. I dared a glance at the cardinal himself. He was leaning back in his chair, a contented smile on his countenance, but I noticed that he was watching his guests, not the women, with intense concentration. His manner was so relaxed, though, and the expression on his face so carefully maintained, that none of the men sitting at the table would have felt themselves under scrutiny.

'Ersilia needs a shave!' yelled one of the Milanesi.

'Where are your manners?' I quavered, in a horrible, cracked attempt at a female voice.

I had tried to plan this part of the evening – in fact, I'd barely slept for the last three nights, so anxious had it made me – but the truth was that I had no idea what to do until the girls had arrived, cloaked and hooded and chaperoned by the aunt-like woman. The food had been easy: a couple of off-colour puns involving poultry, shellfish, wire and a small amount of gunpowder; the usual aids to virility such as sparrows, eels and garlic; a big sugar Sforza serpent from the *credenziero*; and of course a liberal dose of my Indian leaves.

As the girls were getting changed, which they did in front of me with no sign of modesty or shame, I offered them some food and wine. As they were picking at the tray of morsels, one of them had asked me what I wanted them to do. *Do?* I still had no idea.

'Have you been to one of these banquets before?' I had asked. She nodded, much more interested in the *tomacelli* she was eating. 'And what . . .' I'd cleared my throat. 'What is usually required?'

'Usually? Well, we've never done Sabines before. I'm better at nuns. But we mostly . . .'

Swinging my censer like a madwoman, I got the girls lined up in front of the table. I signalled to the musicians – Borgia employed four of the best players in the city – and they struck up a grave, ancient air on three viols and a lute. The girls stood to attention, hands folded in prayer, ten pairs of eyes lifted heavenwards, pleading for mercy from Jove, or whoever Sabines might pray to. I bowed to the cardinal.

'Great Romulus, spare us,' I simpered, trying to conjure up a twittering old prioress who had taught me my letters as a boy. I'd been planning a long, pompous speech full of puns and double meanings, but a quick look at my audience told me to get to the point as quickly as possible. The Milanese ambassador was shaking like a greyhound. 'Spare us, I say!'

The cardinal leaned forward and rested an elbow on the table, the great gold ring of office like an ember in the candlelight. He pondered, seriously, weightily.

'No,' he said, softly. The ambassador, unable to restrain himself any longer, let out a strangled cheer.

The musicians switched to a *bassadanza* and in an instant the girls had shrugged off their togas. At the sight of ten stark-naked women, the men at table set up a racket of the sort that apes might make in dark forests after they have gorged themselves on fermented fruit. My work was done. I flounced over to His Eminence and planted a kiss on his proffered ring. Then I bowed and backed out of the room.

I shuffled into the antechamber under the eyes of the serving boys and girls, who to my relief paid no attention to me, and indeed seemed utterly bored by the entire evening. I changed back into my own clothes as quickly as I could, then went to the kitchen and made sure everything was running properly. I knew what was going on in the dining hall: the girls would dance and then the guests would be invited to join in. If things went any further, that was up to the guests themselves: His Eminence had paid for the girls until to-morrow morning, his palace was furnished with many beds and his staff was utterly discreet. With the amount of *kannab* I had put in their wine, I had no doubt that things would go much, much further. I had a quick drink with Teverino and went back to the banqueting hall, not sure what I was going to find.

The Milanese ambassador was gone, and so were half of his retinue. There were three girls left, now completely naked. The table was in disarray, the sugar serpent in pieces all over the floor. And Borgia was still in his chair, deep in conversation with a soberly dressed man, one of the ambassador's company, neither of them paying any attention to the rest of the party, who were playing a drinking game with the other two girls.

'There will be one left, I think,' said a little voice at my side. It was the grey-haired madam. 'I'm usually right, and if I am, will you take her?'

'Me?'

'The *scalco*'s prerogative. Though the last *scalco* was a sodomite,' she added, without a hint of judgement. 'If you are as well – begging Your Honour's pardon – I'll take her home.'

'I'm sorry – if I'm what?'

'A sodomite. No offence, Your Honour, but Messer Domenicho tells me you come from Florence. And you did make a lovely Sabine.'

'I . . . Thank you.'

And so I ended my first week in the Palazzo Borgia with a whore called Roma, which I doubt was her real name. She was from Reggio, with dark skin that smelled of olive wood, and after we were finished, she told me her grandmother's recipe for *maccheroni* with wild hyacinth bulbs, and smiled for the first time that evening.

43

WHENEVER I HAD SOME FREE time, which had always been a rare commodity but was now even more scarce, I was in the habit of walking up the Quirinal Hill to visit Pomponio Leto. On this particular day – one of those days in autumn when the sky seems to be clear all the way up to the gates of Heaven – I met him coming down the track, carrying a spade and a lantern and a coil of rope.

'Nino!' He trotted up to me and we embraced, the lantern banging rather painfully against the small of my back. 'I've found a cave on the Esquiline! Absolutely fascinating. Will you come?'

I agreed very willingly. Leto had taken me on a couple of these expeditions before, but they had been to catacombs that were already partly explored, down on the Appian Way. I'd always enjoyed Leto's enthusiasm and the sheer joy he found in poking around in what were, to me, holes filled with spiders and rubble; besides, I always learned something, and it couldn't be further from my everyday life. So we went back to his house to fetch another lantern, then made our way over to the Esquiline Hill, which overlooks the Colosseum from the north, a place of gentle slopes, ruins, olives and goats. Leto headed for the curved wall of the Baths of Trajan and stopped a few dozen yards away from it, among a clump of old olive trees.

'Now then,' he said, fiddling with flint and tinder. 'You know I make it a habit to pester all the shepherds and goat-herds for any bits of old stuff they may find. Well . . .' he paused, and lit the lamps, 'yesterday a young goatherd of my acquaintance came to my house, very excited – and very eager for a few *scudi*, needless to say. He'd fallen through a crack in the earth, so he said, into a vast grotto. And he brought me . . . Here.' He picked up his shovel and marched over to where one huge and ancient olive tree had fallen onto its side. 'I didn't have a lantern yesterday, but now, *fiat lux*, eh? Come along, Nino!'

He put down lantern and spade, shrugged off the rope and threw himself down full length on the ground. At first I thought he was playing a trick on me, but then his arms, his head and finally his shoulders vanished into the earth, only to reappear moments later, cobwebs and leaves sticking to his grey hair like a mournful victor's crown.

'The lantern, the lantern!' he said excitedly.

I knelt down and handed him one of the lights. Now I could see that he was lying on the edge of what was indeed a crack in the earth, or rather a hole between two regular-looking blocks of stone which had been exposed by the fall of the old tree. 'Good. Now, take the rope and tie one end to the tree.'

I did as I was told, and threw the other end into the hole. The coils unravelled and vanished into the pitch-darkness. It looked less than inviting down there, but Leto had already taken hold of the rope and was letting himself down, the handle of his lantern hooked over his ankle. The crack devoured him until just his long face was visible. 'Nothing underfoot yet!' he announced cheerfully. Then with a few gasps and grunts – he was remarkably fit for a man of his age – he disappeared altogether. The rope jerked and swung, jerked and quivered. Then it went slack.

'Come on, Nino! Hurry!'

My friend sounded quite agitated, and very far away, so – swallowing my misgivings – I swung my legs over the edge and hooked my own lantern onto my ankle. Then I let myself down, hand over hand. It was not as easy as Leto had made it look. I was in a narrow shaft, and the lantern was casting mad shadows on the walls. Above, a rapidly shrinking slot of daylight, and below me, absolutely nothing. Then I felt a hand grab my leg and take the lantern. Another few heaves and I was down.

I was standing on a solid, level floor in a cave. No, not a cave, because the high, regular space had not been carved out of rock. I was looking at walls of frescoed plaster. Leto handed me a lantern and I held it up, struck dumb. Because the frescoes were as bright as if the plaster had just dried.

A woman was looking at me, draped in a thin, coral-coloured toga, one hand holding a bundle of bay twigs, the other dangling languidly. She had black, lustrous hair held in place by a golden circlet, and huge, dark eyes. In the wavering lamplight, the effect was so unnerving that I stepped backwards, nearly tripping over a fallen stone beam. Then I pulled myself together and had another look.

The woman was standing inside a sort of painted frame made up of elaborately scrolled flowers, vines, fruit, cornstalks and strange, half-animal, half-human faces, some with the horns of sheep or goats, others with long, curling tongues. In fact, the whole wall was divided into such frames, and in each space stood another figure: here was a man, tall and thick-necked, looking down at me with quiet self-satisfaction. And here was a half man, half goat. A naked woman, a warrior, all painted as if from life. I shook my head, hardly able to take it all in.

'What is this place?' I said.

'No idea,' said Leto. 'But isn't it . . . fabulous?'

He was pacing excitedly from one wall to the other, criss-crossing the space impatiently. Then he vanished. It seemed as if he had just stepped into one of the paintings, but then I saw that what I had thought was another frame was in fact a doorway. I followed, and found myself in another room, almost identical to the last, except that here the walls were a maze of patterns, ropes of tangled foliage dividing the wall into squares and ovals, the spaces between a startling yellow, and in those spaces elaborate processions of men, women and demons danced.

'There's more,' said Leto. He was standing next to another doorway. We both peered inside. This chamber was round, or perhaps octagonal, though it was difficult to tell as part of the roof had collapsed and there were piles of rubble heaped up against the walls. Beyond, other doors opened onto other rooms.

'The lamps are burning down,' I said at last.

How long had we been here? I was lost in a strange half-dream of faces and flowers, but now the lights were smoking and growing feeble. Like sleepwalkers, we made our way back through the halls to where the rope hung down through a small crack in another delicately painted vault, through which the sun was shining like a crude, grinning mouth. I held the rope while Leto dragged himself up it, far more slowly than he had come down, and then I came up too. After that we just sat on the old tree trunk, listening to the thrushes cracking snails against the stones of Trajan's Baths.

From then on my responsibilities began to devour what was left of my freedom, and I never went on another of Leto's investigations, though the sunken halls began to appear in my dreams and I thought about them often.

Cardinal Borgia looked up from a purple-bound book. I had been summoned to his Vatican chambers, which was not unusual, but I was surprised to find Pagholini standing in a corner of the study, another book in his hand. I had the impression that neither of the men had been reading but simply waiting for me, as a certain something passed between them as I walked in: a flick of the brows or a barely perceptible nod of my employer's head.

'Nino.' The cardinal leaned back in his chair and folded his hands slowly and carefully over the edge of the desk. 'It seems I was right in my opinion of you, though something has happened to make me a trifle – yes, it must be said – a trifle jealous. Your talents have come to the ears of someone else.'

'How very flattering,' I said. 'But I work only for you, Your Eminence.'

'Of course, of course. But how would you feel if I said you were . . . Hmm. On loan?'

'If Your Eminence requires it.'

'Bravo, Nino. Bravo. I thank you for your loyalty, but of course it has never been in doubt. And in case you doubt *my* loyalty—'

'Absolutely not, Your Eminence!'

'In case, sir, you imagine I've lent you to a friend like a common slave,' he went on, swatting my words away, 'I am reluctantly parting with you for one banquet, and only because the one who asked this favour of me cannot, really, be refused.'

'Very well,' I said. This was meant to be something significant, plainly, but I had long since stopped anticipating any of my master's wishes: it was best not to think at all, just to do. Pagholini coughed discreetly.

'Your discretion is admirable, *scalco*,' he said. 'And I will be plain: it is your discretion as much as your skill that has brought this rather delicate matter to your door.'

'That is correct,' said Borgia. 'The thing is, it's the Holy Father himself who has asked for you.'

'Oh,' I said. Now that was surprising. 'I am very flattered. Extremely.' To myself I was thinking, *Dear God, what sort of thing am I required to be* discreet *about? Does the Pope get up to all this nonsense as well?*

'And you should be. A great honour – a very great honour. Which reflects well on us, of course, which will not be forgotten. But that's another matter. To the one in hand: His Holiness wishes to give a small banquet for some intimates. To be honest with you, the details are a trifle . . .' The hand fluttered. Borgia himself looked genuinely discomfited. 'Yes, a trifle mysterious. But I do not ask the Holy Father his business. I would not presume.'

'I understand, Your Eminence.'

'Do you? Well, I don't. But never mind that. His Holiness has heard about your discretion, of course, but also your reputation for flights of fancy – for your imagination. Now, the thing of it is, this banquet is to be a simple affair: simple food . . .'

'Simple entertainment?' I ventured.

'No entertainment at all,' said Borgia, looking more puzzled than ever. 'His Holiness would like a decidedly classical feel to the proceedings – you know he is a great admirer of the ancients – but above all, the setting is to be completely secret.'

'Secret, Your Eminence? In what way? As a theme, as it were, for the evening? Intrigue, and so on?'

'No, actually secret,' said Pagholini. 'And undiscoverable. Away, one gets the impression, from prying eyes. For effect, one imagines.'

'Well, Nino? May I tell His Holiness that you accept?' Borgia leaned back, knowing what my answer had to be.

'Of course, Your Eminence.'

'Excellent. Pagholini will tell you all about it. I'm afraid you will not get to meet His Holiness, as he will be in Castel Gandolfo until the day of the banquet. And one last thing, Nino. Your discretion is indispensable to me. But I should not like you to think that I insist on your being discreet with me. I should be happy to think that you will feel able to tell me anything, *scalco*. You understand? Do not let His Holiness's affairs burden you. I shall be happy to share the weight of your discretion.'

'As you say, Your Eminence.'

I allowed myself to be dismissed, and left the cardinal's chambers with Pagholini, who told me what to plan for: no more than ten people, including His Holiness; security a priority – there would be papal soldiers at my disposal. No staff other than the Pope's own servants of the body. The cook? Why, that would be me, and me alone. I would be required to swear an oath of secrecy – such a thing not to apply, naturally, if things happened to come up in conversation with His Eminence the cardinal, who as a prince of the Church . . . I understood? I did.

I decided, almost immediately, to use Pomponio Leto's sunken halls. What better place? There was one entrance to guard, if the Holy Father and his guests were willing to climb down a ladder. No: they could be winched down, using one of those pulleys that builders used to hoist stones. The second hall could easily be swept clean, and lit with torches. Trestle tables, folding chairs . . . Cooking would be a problem, because lighting a proper fire down there would stifle everyone. But perhaps I could set up a small field kitchen above. There wouldn't be anyone hanging around on the Esquiline at night, and if the soldiers put some sort of cordon, if that was what it was called . . . It would work.

And work it did. I arranged my little kitchen in the lee of Trajan's Baths, no more than two fires, an iron stand borrowed from the papal guard which allowed me to hang two cauldrons and a number of roasting spits, and a trivet for pots and pans. That was adequate for my menu, which I had cobbled together from the few pages of Apicius I had copied out from Leto's manuscript. I'd been excited about resurrecting these ancient foods, but in the event it was all rather baffling: the old ones had been completely ruled, it seemed to me, by various manias: for lovage (it was in everything – why?), for *defrutum* and *garum*. And as a result it all tasted more or less the same. Still, perhaps down in the grotto it would make better sense.

I had spent the best part of two days under the earth, decorating. First, the floor had been swept. Under a thick coat of dust, the guardsmen I had enlisted – sworn to secrecy and paid handsomely for it – had found a rich mosaic floor, more or less intact, the equal of any I had seen in the churches of Rome. I had draped the doorways with curtains and set up as many candelabra as I could get my hands on. The candles gave off less smoke and stench than torches, and made the colours on the walls and ceiling glow. How strange that no light had touched them for a thousand years or more . . . A trestle table was arranged in the middle of the floor, with the best folding chairs from Cardinal Borgia's palace, and silk cushions, a red damask tablecloth and a set of silver plate made by a goldsmith who often worked for the cardinal, and who had recently modelled a complete service on some dishes and cups found while workers were digging a foundation. I'd hired them for a huge sum and an even bigger deposit – he'd wanted me to buy them, but perhaps he'd get a papal commission out of the deal. Not that I'd told him what I needed his service for. I'd told no one.

When His Holiness, a man of not insignificant presence, not to mention heft and girth, was lowered in a basket through the narrow crack – barely wide enough for the basket – while a company of soldiers strained at the pulley above him, all of them muttering strangled prayers under their breath, I was standing at the head of a small phalanx of servants. Every one of them was dressed in the same thing: a plain white linen toga, a metal circlet around the head, sandals. But as the Holy Father descended, he would have seen fourteen identical faces staring up at him; knowing that secrecy was as much a theme of this party as Ancient Rome, I had made masks for all of us. There was a man I had discovered, an old fellow with a workshop built into the side of the Temple of Hadrian, who made masks for carnival. I'd thought this would be a great and costly task, but the old man had knocked them out in a couple of days: identical, bland white faces with empty almond eyes and Cupid's-bow lips. Maybe the young man who had modelled for the original sculptor had walked through these very chambers.

Pope Sixtus looked like the Ligurian fisherman's son he had once been: a heavy, muscled body gone to fat, big hands, a thick neck and a wide, jowled face let down by a sharply hooked nose. He didn't seem, from a distance, as if he was the sort of man who would appreciate anything more complicated than a furze roof, and yet this was the pope who had set out to restore Rome to the greatness it had cast off many long centuries ago, and whose interest in the writers and artists of the past was exceeded only by his desire to make his family the most powerful in Italy.

The Pope sat straight away and the party got started on the food without ceremony. One man was tall and rather handsome in a pampered, slightly effeminate way. The Holy Father called him 'nephew', and there was a resemblance. Two of the others were Florentine: a man in late middle age, wearing the robes of an archbishop and a much younger man who looked vaguely familiar. There was an older man, Signore Montesecco, who had the straight back of a soldier, and whom I overheard the Pope addressing familiarly as 'Giovanbattista'. One of the other men, with a strong Urbinese accent, might have been called Ortona.

None of them looked particularly bothered by the lovage

or the *defrutum* – they fell to with a good appetite, though they seemed more interested in the wine, an excellent Greco, flavoured with peach leaves. I had set up a small battery of charcoal braziers in the furthest room, where there seemed to be a draught to move the fumes around, and there the food was being kept warm. And because I was *scalco*, *bottigliero* and *trinciante* on top of being the head cook, I spent most of the evening hurrying backwards and forwards, plating up the food, darting ahead of the servers to be ready with my knives when the meats and fishes arrived, and making sure that there were no spiders in the wine. I would have liked to study Pope Sixtus, to make myself useful to him, because here I was, a butcher's son from the Black Lion, cooking and serving a meal for the Holy Father himself, but there was no time. It was surprisingly hot down in the grotto, and the candles and braziers weren't helping. I was sweating in my toga.

I was in the back chamber, arranging, predictably, lovage around the stuffed piglet, when one of the guards called me out to announce the arrival of our late guests. I hurried into the dining hall, pulling my mask down over my face, just in time to see the basket inching the last few feet towards the mosaic floor. The wicker was bulging and the rope was creaking in protest, because it was bearing the massive bulk of a bald man in a tent-like crimson robe, who was cursing the soldiers above. The basket jerked and fell a good foot, twisted in my direction. The man's face swung into the candlelight. It was Bartolo Baroni.

He barked at me, beckoned me over with a swollen, impatiently hooked finger. It took me an interminable, befuddled moment of horror before I remembered that I was wearing a mask. I forced my limbs to march, with drugged deliberation, over to where Baroni was pulling himself up-right. I grabbed the rim of the basket, steadied it. Baroni stuck out his red, bloated hand and I helped him puff and grunt his way onto the floor. The younger Florentine was hurrying over to greet him.

'Francesco!' grunted Baroni, and they embraced warmly. The basket was hurtling upwards behind us. Keeping silent, praying that my mask was securely tied onto my head, I showed Baroni to his seat. Then, amidst another barrage of oaths, creakings, falling pebbles and dust, the basket began to descend once more. Making sure that Baroni's cup was filled and that one of my masked troupe was serving him, I turned in time to see the basket nearing the grotto floor. A scowling man swung his short legs over the edge while it was still coming down and dropped the last few feet. It was Marco Baroni.

A dead man, in this place of ghosts. I felt all the blood rush from my face, and the scar on my temple began to throb and sting. *You are not real*, I whispered. But Marco, far too much blood flushing his own mastiff face for him to be any kind of phantom, paused, dusted off his knees, and marched over to the one empty chair, sat down and immediately fell into a hushed debate with the man called Francesco.

He looked as he had that night in Assisi, two years ago more or less to the day. His hair was still thick and hacked into shape, giving his hard face its usual brutish look. Perhaps his brow was more furrowed, set into a perpetual scowl. *Don't make that face*, Carenza had told me again and again when I was little. *The cock will crow, and you'll stay that way for ever*. Well, the cock seemed to have crowed for Marco, though he showed no sign that I'd ever spitted him clean through the breastbone. His chest still swelled like a bantam, and he leaned on his elbow and glared at everyone, masked and unmasked alike, as if he was just waiting to be let off the leash so that he could tear us all to pieces.

I slipped away, back to my braziers, where I retied the cords of my mask and tried to warm my shivering body. Marco was alive and more horrible than ever. And that meant Tessina had, in one instant, been cut out of my future. Fortuna had sliced her away from me like a conjoined twin separated from its sibling. Baroni – he looked healthy enough too, in his own fashion – would die sooner or later, but Marco would never let Tessina go. It was gone: Florence too, as if the map had been torn and Rome moved to the other side of the world.

It occurred to me that I could just turn and walk into the dark tunnels that led away into the hillside until I had lost myself for ever. But even then, I wouldn't be any more lost than I was already.

A servant ran in. Marco was calling loudly, boorishly, for meat, so I came out again and picked up my *trinciante*'s knife, a long, thin-bladed thing with a handle made from a piece of narwhal's horn, and began, with all the usual flourishes, to carve slices from the piglet. I juggled one piece expertly in the way I'd seen Horlandino, Borgia's expert *trinciante*, do a thousand times, and placed it delicately on Marco's plate. He scoffed and called me a vile name in the language of the Florentine streets: *buggerone e poppatore*. Bugger and cocksucker.

It would have been so easy to raise the slim blade, as slender and pointed as an iris leaf, and slip it into his throat, into the dip below the Adam's apple; or into one of his little, red-rimmed eyes. Much harder was what I did instead, that is to say, cut another perfect slice of pork, dance the circle for a moment on the flat of the knife, displaying its layers – the golden circlet of skin, the pale meat and the dark, pine-nut-studded roundel of stuffing – letting the steam with its delicate, savoury aroma curl seductively beneath Marco's nose, before setting it down as reverently as a consecrated Host onto the plate. Then I did the same for his father.

After that the evening became more terrifying, more inescapable than the worst nightmare I had ever suffered. And all the terror and despair was trapped behind the cold, expressionless mask that I kept binding ever tighter against my face. It made me strut and skip around the table, carving and serving with ever more exquisite flourishes. It made me search every word I spoke for the merest speck of Florence. It made me pray to God, to the Virgin and, by the end, to whatever devils might live in this grotto – the ones, perhaps, who leered from every wall – that I might be invisible. And I was too terrified to realize that, of course, I was.

But suddenly it was over. The Pope heaved himself upright and beckoned me over.

'Dismiss your people,' he said curtly.

'Was everything to Your Holiness's satisfaction?' I stammered.

'What? Yes, yes. Very nice.' He had a surprisingly thick Genoese accent, and his jowls seemed even more pendulous than they had at the start of the meal. 'But you will send your people . . .' He stabbed a finger skyward, a remarkably vivid gesture considering who was making it.

'Very good, Your Holiness. And will you be requiring me?'

'No,' he snapped. 'You may wait for us above.'

I called for the guards to lower the scaling ladders they had brought along – we servants had gone up and down on these narrow, rickety structures but I had judged them too undignified for guests – the captain of the guard descended and my masked company climbed, one by one, up towards the faintly moonlit slot in the roof. I was about to join them when I remembered the braziers. It wouldn't do to leave them burning, because there were some powder-dry wooden beams lying nearby and besides, I suddenly needed to empty my bowels quite desperately.

The Pope and his guests were standing in a knot, their backs to me. Assuming they were waiting for the captain of the guard to arrange the basket for their ascent, I slipped past them, made sure the braziers were more or less cold, then cast about for a place to squat. There were three doors, each leading off into utter darkness, but there was enough light from the bank of candles I had set up around my cooking area to throw a weak glow past the frescoed pillars of the nearest one. I peered inside: nothing except the impression of a vast emptiness rising all around me. I went in, stepping carefully in case there were any fallen blocks or beams to trip me, and when I was far enough away, completely enveloped in silence and night, I pulled down my *mutande* and squatted.

Thank God that the strain of the night, all the fear and the running about, had dried up my guts. I had the sensation of needing to relieve myself, but no relief came. So I squatted, silent, straining to no effect. Nothing issued forth: no droppings, not even a rasp of fundamental wind. And while I squatted, I heard voices in the next room. The Pope was standing next to the braziers, perfectly framed in a little rectangle of orange light. Then the young Florentine appeared, then Bartolo Baroni, the archbishop, and finally the Pope's nephew and the soldier.

'I understand, Girolamo,' the Pope said impatiently to his nephew. 'No man on earth wishes this matter resolved more than I. But such things cannot be countenanced.'

'We do not intend to spill blood,' said the nephew. 'But if we should—'

'I will not have it, Girolamo!' The Pope's voice cracked and echoed around the walls. I squatted on all fours, not daring to pull up my underclothes, hardly daring to breathe.

'Holy Father, it would be more or less impossible to affect the result without the deaths of, at the very least, Lorenzo and his brother.' It was the soldier who had spoken. He sounded patient and sensible, and faintly disapproving, though of his subject or its audience I could not tell.

'It may be unavoidable, Uncle,' said Girolamo.

'In God's name, nephew! Have you taken leave of your senses? We have often discussed how fortunate it would be if something – revolution, say, or happy accident – were to rid Florence of that villainous Lorenzo. Without the Medici family, the republic would be our friend . . .'

'Of course, of course,' said the archbishop smoothly. 'We are in control, Holy Father. Nothing will happen if you do not wish it.'

'Salviati.' The Pope heaved a sigh: he was obviously rather drunk. 'Do not misunderstand me. The results of . . . of what I have just laid out would be very pleasing to me. But I will not – cannot – countenance any loss of life.'

'Then we are done here,' said Montesecco the soldier, with obvious relief.

'You must trust us, Your Holiness!' The younger Florentine had been shifting from foot to foot, and now he clasped his hands in entreaty. It was plain, though, that he was angry. Bartolo Baroni nudged him hard in the ribs.

'Pazzi. The Holy Father is tired,' he said firmly. 'We must thank him for a . . . a diverting evening. No more of this. I came because of my son and certain interests I share with the archbishop. But Lorenzo de' Medici is a man of reason. I am sure Your Holiness has gentler means of persuasion than this . . . This . . .'

'Your humanity does you credit, my son,' said the Pope. 'But I would wish these others to share your patience.'

'Can we at least speak again?' asked Girolamo, exchanging a glance with Pazzi – Pazzi: of course I would have seen him before. Christ, if this was Francesco Pazzi, and he was the right age, I'd played *calcio* against him more than once.

'Messer Bartolo is right,' said Pazzi. 'We cannot countenance a death, no matter whose it might be. I'm sure that Lorenzo's own wickedness will bring him to grief before long. And then we shall be ready.'

'That is sense, young man,' said the Pope. 'Now, we must to our beds. I am too old to sleep in a cave.'

They left. Only after their voices had died away, and I had heard the basket rise and fall and rise again eight times, did I dare to stand; and the popping of my knee joints whispered around the unseen walls. Now other voices sounded: soldiers and servants coming back to start clearing up. I took off my mask, straightened my toga and went out into the light where I started collecting my things.

I climbed the ladder and stood at the edge of the hole, staring around me at the dim glow of the cooking fires, at the servants sitting on the fallen tree, drinking the leftover wine. It all seemed terribly ordinary after the strangeness of the grotto and the awful, dreamlike things that had happened. I'd seen a dead man come back to life and steal my future. I'd seen dumb statues serve dinner to a pope. I'd heard men speak longingly of the deaths of men I knew. But what had come of it all, really? Some foolishness, a game of angry drunkards, that the Pope would never allow to happen. My own story was finished, though. I had never felt more alone than I did at that moment, listening to the crackle of the fire and the servants' low banter.

44

I GOT TO KNOW THE girls of the grey-haired madam – she was called Donna Eufemia – very well in the next few weeks. Sometimes all ten would come to the Palazzo Borgia and dance, as they always called it; and at other times, only three or four were required. The little redhead, Magalda, was a gift from Heaven, or perhaps from the other place, because she gave me the details of every other dance she had taken part in, what the last *scalco* had required, what the cardinal seemed to like – *like*, she said, not *enjoy*, for apparently my employer seemed to take more pleasure in his guests' pleasure than his own. He'd never taken a girl for himself, for instance. Thanks to Magalda, I was able to put each banquet together as if I'd been doing it my whole life, as if my father had been a brothel-keeper and not a butcher, because as the days went past I found myself drifting further and further away from the kitchen. I was many things now – as *scalco* I had to be a politician, a dance-master, a stage manager, a pimp perhaps most of all – but hardly ever a cook. I spent more time in brothels and the houses of courtesans than I did in the food markets, for it was not just Donna Eufemia who supplied girls for the Palazzo Borgia but two dozen others as well.

Sometimes genteel women were needed, courtesans, as the convention has it, whose treasure lay in their wit, their reading and how well they knew the latest dances from Florence or Naples. At other times I was forced to recruit street whores from the city's most unsavoury quarters, whores of either sex. It all depended on the guests around whom each particular banquet was planned. Pagholini would brief me, in his measured, unemotional way, about the predilections and peccadilloes of each guest of honour.

For one evening I was forced to prepare the thing I hated most of all: a flying pie. Except that this one was to be filled with girls. They had to be small, so I recruited Magalda and then scoured the brothels and streets for the shortest whores I could find. I was already gaining a reputation as a veritable prince of debauchery, and there were parts of Rome I couldn't set foot in without a score of women asking me to choose them for whatever I had in mind. So I had no difficulty finding six tiny women of passable appearance who didn't mind the thought of being painted with honey, stuck with feathers and crammed into a large wooden vat beneath a roof of pastry tiles.

For that evening, the guests, men and women, were required to come dressed as cats, and when the cardinal cut into the pie with a wooden sword and the girls jumped out, the cats hunted the birds around the chairs and under the tables. I doubt any of the cats remembered a single taste from that evening save the sweat of hot, scared women mixed with honey and crushed chicken feathers.

Some banquet nights I spent alone, but not many. Whether I had used Donna Eufemia or one of the other madams or whoremasters, they always seemed to have a girl left over for me. At first I felt uncomfortable with this arrangement: I found the banquets and the so-called dancing tawdry and vulgar, and I was just conducting them: so I imagined the girls felt even worse. But as the months went by I slowly let go of my old life as a cook and began to relish the challenge of putting on one marvellous, memorable party after another – the challenge only, mind: I convinced myself it was all about making the impossible a reality, and that in a way I was still an artist, just one with many more colours at his disposal. My *scalco*'s prerogative became something I felt I deserved. And why not? I knew I would never love again. Fortuna could do nothing worse to me than she had already.

As the madams came to know my likes and dislikes, so the girls would be more desirable, more willing, more cunning with their minds and bodies. And I expected that. I came to require it. The men of the household all envied me now. They studied me as I came downstairs in the morning, all of them wondering what I'd got up to the night before, and how they could ever aspire to such luck and such virility. It was a young man's dream come true in every possible way, to have a woman in my bed whenever I wanted one, and to be admired by everyone. A lucky man – might they all be blessed with such luck. I wasn't lucky, though. I was merely empty.

As time went on these pleasures began to have a strange effect on me. Instead of coming into my own, I seemed to have become an actor. Having lost everything I cared about, the only thing I feared was seeing displeasure or disappointment on His Eminence's face, or on the faces of the whores I took to bed.

I had every pleasure I could require, but there was a price. The madams and whoremasters were testing me: I was their master now, but things could turn in a single night and plenty of *scalcos* ended up as the corrupted puppets of their own greedy suppliers, which had been the downfall of my predecessor. I had the best job in Rome: everybody else wanted to be me, or to control me. And to make sure that never happened, I began to take my own Indian leaves. The *betel* had no effect, so far as I could judge, save for a numbing of the tongue. But the *kannab*, steeped in wine, made my whole body sing like a bell. There were other things too: wild poppy brought calm and gave me quite alarming stamina in bed. A girl from one of the brothels, who had been bought by slavers from the Guinea Coast as a child, introduced me to a sweet purple nut she called *kola*, which if you chewed enough of it made you wake up and set your head buzzing like a wasp's nest. The harder I worked, the more I took; and the more I dosed myself, the more I worried about failure. But that was all in private. Outwardly, I became more like Pagholini with every passing day. Nothing surprised me, no desire was too great to satisfy. I had no self. I lived to delight Rodrigo Borgia.

His Eminence, though: what did he live for? Power, obviously, because you could feel it trembling in the walls of the Palazzo Borgia. But unlike other great men I had known, Borgia, though he held onto power with a mercilessly tight grip, let that power lie on him very lightly. I never heard him say a cruel word or do anything to hurt another man or woman. His son Cesare had just been born and with the baby, and with his older son Giovanni, a sweet little boy of three years, he was gentle and patient.

At first, I almost believed that the banquets and dances were all the creation of Domenicho Pagholini and that the cardinal just went along with them. But the more I watched him, and the more he trusted me, the stranger he became. Because it was Borgia who knew every secret, every buried shame, every need and desire of his friends, enemies, colleagues, neighbours, household and family. It was as if he had a hidden window into all the bedchambers in Italy, and all the counting houses too, because while every one of his guests was treated according to the honour of their station, above all it was money which decreed whether you enjoyed the lascivious delights of His Eminence's table.

He seemed to have few desires of his own. He enjoyed the food he ate with an ordinary savour. He drank neither too little nor too much. Though the most beautiful women in Rome passed through his chambers in a more or less unending procession, he appeared entirely faithful to Donna

Vannozza. And at his banquets, he watched. There are men who will pay to watch a whore do it with another man, or who will sneak around to find an open window, or a chink in the wall of the women's bathhouse. The cardinal was not one of those men. As the whores danced and the courtesans beguiled, Borgia observed, not for his own arousal, but – so it seemed to me – to learn. He was a philosopher, in his way; perhaps one of the greatest of his age. And his study was humanity: the ways of men, their motives, and above all their weaknesses.

It was the fourth week after Easter in the year 1478. I was in my office going over the endless accounts when I received a summons from His Eminence.

'I was speaking to His Holiness yesterday,' he said. Giovanni was playing in the corner of the cardinal's study, and Borgia was paying more attention to his son than to me. 'About painters. I mentioned to him that you were the nephew of Filippo Lippi, God rest his soul, and that you have many friends among the artists of Florence.'

'*Had*, Your Eminence. It's been a long time since I heard from any of them.'

'A shame. By the way, who do you think is the best painter in Rome?'

'Melozzo da Forlí,' I said at once. 'There's no one better in the city. He'd even be hailed in Florence, I think.'

'Hmm. Well – Giovanni, don't rip that up, my angel – the Holy Father is, as you know, rather interested in classical statuary. He was showing me a piece just dug up out of the Campo Vaccino, the Forum, as he insists on calling it. Quite extraordinary: the artistry was good enough to confuse the eye. One could almost believe that the stone was a mere skin over flesh and blood. Which brought us to the subject of anatomy. The ancients, apparently, thought nothing of cutting up the dead to see exactly how things worked – no doubt why their statues are so exquisitely accurate.'

'I've heard that said, Your Eminence.'

'Which set me to thinking: what lies within?'

'Within, Your Eminence?'

'Yes. Within *us*. Why do we breathe? Why the various offices of excretion? Where – and this must have occurred to you, as a cook – where does the food go, eh?'

'I have a rough idea, Your Eminence . . .'

'I'd like you to get a better idea. Because I'm giving a banquet for His Holiness next week, and I thought, given our conversation and his interests, what better subject than "what lies within"?'

'Fascinating, Your Eminence. Do you have a particular wish?'

'No, not at all. Up to you as usual, dear Nino. I've no doubt that you will delight His Holiness.' He turned back to Giovanni, picked up his son, kissed his nose. I turned to leave.

'Oh, yes! This will help you, Nino. Your Melozzo da Forlí. He's conducting a dissection tomorrow.'

'A dissection?' I turned, frowning. 'But surely the Church forbids such things?'

'It does, it does, at least for now. Though it was His Holiness who told me about it. He's given his blessing: he thinks it's a small price to pay for giving our modern artists the knowledge that the ancient ones took for granted. Anyway, perhaps you'd like to attend.'

'I don't think . . .' But I knew Borgia well enough by then to know when a suggestion was an order. 'That is, I'm sure it will be fascinating and, well, useful,' I lied.

'Excellent. Pagholini has the details.'

'As to cost?'

'My dear Nino. Don't give it a thought.'

⚓ 45 ⚓

AT THAT TIME, THE *BOTTEGA* of Melozzo da Forlí was the most famous in all of Rome – indeed, it was the only proper *bottega* south of Perugia. This morning the front was closed up, and when I knocked, a peephole opened. A moment later, the lock clicked and I was admitted.

The *bottega* was a long, vaulted space stretching the whole length of the building, cluttered with all the usual flotsam of the artist's profession, not to mention the maestro's collection of Roman marble. Maestro Melozzo lived upstairs. A boy had let us in, one of Melozzo's minor assistants, dressed in threadbare hand-me-downs, holding a lamp. He looked scared, but not of us. He pointed to the far end of the *bottega*, which was lit by a high window and a great array of lamps and candles. There were a lot of shadows looming all the way up to the vaults of the roof, and muted voices.

There were about twelve people – it was hard to tell in the trembling candlelight, but I recognized some of them: a decent artist called Antoniazzo; Melozzo's pupil Marco, and one of Pomponio's friends, a doctor called Leonardi – gathered around a plain wooden table, and on the table lay the corpse. Strangely, it filled the room, larger and more real than the half-seen paintings, the statues. Just the fact of it: a dead man. Death: the one certain thing in life . . . and all the other obvious statements that the sight of a corpse always seem to dredge up. The trouble is, they're all true. The naked man – he was quite short, in his late twenties, with thin blond curls and sparse yellow hair on his chest and in his groin – had made himself the centre of everything in the *bottega*, just by virtue of being dead. I could feel someone squirming next to me, and I understood how he felt. That wasn't a cow lying there, an array of knives, probes and saws lined up next to him. That was me, more or less. I thanked the Virgin that I'd taken the trouble to treat myself with *kannab* this morning, a good dose, washed down with a big pinch of nutmeg in *acqua vitae*.

I saw Maestro Melozzo on the other side of the table, and waved. It seemed an inappropriately lavish gesture, and I dropped my hand quickly.

'Maestro!' I called in a loud whisper – a church voice. 'How are you?'

Melozzo leaned across the corpse towards me. The strange light made him look like a tomb carving come to life, cutting his long face, his great, bent nose and bald, domed forehead, into planes of white and black.

'Delighted to see you, *Scalco*. I hope you have an empty stomach.'

'My family are butchers,' I said without thinking. 'So my stomach is quite strong.'

'Butchers? Well, well.' Rumour had it that Melozzo's own family were rich and disapproved of his career. 'So you already have some knowledge of what goes on under the skin. It's not much different whether you're talking about a man or a . . . a donkey. Muscles, tendons, bone.'

'Yes. An armature of bone, the rest sculpted in . . . well, as a butcher would see it, in meat. Though there are people who would call that blasphemy.'

'His Holiness doesn't believe that God approves of ignorance, and nor do I. Do you?' said Melozzo.

'No,' I said. 'I don't. Knowledge leads us to God, not away from Him.'

'Exactly. Now, that's Antonio Benivieni,' said the artist, pointing to a man in his late twenties, with wide-set, friendly eyes. 'A Florentine, like you. Well-known surgeon. He will be helping me. And now, we shall begin.'

Antonio Benivieni picked up a thin, slightly curved knife and made a long cut down the length of the dead man's arm There was no blood. With everyone else, I craned forward the better to see and stared as Benivieni peeled back the skin to reveal the dark red meat, criss-crossed with white tendons and patches of yellow fat. Melozzo began to pick apart the rope of muscles while Benivieni named them: *flexor carpi radialis, palmaris longus, flexor carpi ulnaris, pronator teres* . . . My mind went back to a day long ago, when I'd watched my father butcher a pork leg, separating the light from the dark, the tender from the tough. *This does this* – and with knife and pointer the two men demonstrated. *And this does that.* The bones of the hand, the colour of buttermilk, were fanned out on the table top in abject surrender. Skin pulled back, the secrets of the shoulder, then the neck, then the chest exposed. Someone turned noisily on their heel and slipped away into the shadows.

The two men rolled the corpse onto its front and went back to work. The great fan of the trapezius, and beneath it, *rhomboideus major* and *minor*. See how the *splenius capitis* holds up the head! Look at the sweep of the *latissimus dorsi*. Down to the thigh goes Benivieni and his knife, to meat I recognize. Not much difference, after all, between a beast and a man, between a butcher and a surgeon. Then the body is rolled back, wetly, only half human, because like some bizarre Venetian fashion, the corpse is clad in waxy skin on his right side, and in ragged, picked-through meat on his left. And at the centre of it all, the dead man's face, unchanging. Had I perhaps expected it to flinch? Or to sit up and howl the outrage of its desecration at us? But this was death, and even when Melozzo slit the waxy torso and pulled back the wide flaps of skin and muscle to show the glistening organs and the pallid coil of guts, the dead man suffered his dismemberment in silence.

It was all familiar to me. Twice familiar, you might say. It didn't bother me, really, which made me feel uneasy. But then Benivieni went to work with his pincers, snipping the ribcage down each side with a sound like old vines being pruned, and with Melozzo lifted off the inverted basket of bone to expose the pinkish lungs. Suddenly a wave of sadness washed over me. Useless now, all these things: lungs, heart, liver. That was the man, it seemed to me. That was myself. Whoever he'd been, this poor bastard, whatever it was that had made him alive, made him *himself*, had lurked in and among the soft cobbling of viscera that Melozzo was now lifting out like eggs from a nest.

Benivieni pointed out the liver, the kidneys, thymus glands, pancreas – sweetbreads, as I knew them – and the red, webbed sac of the stomach. There was the *pylorus*, which had caused Cardinal Gonzaga so much worry. But where was the fire that ought to sit below the vessel of concoction? There was nothing but a great coil of guts. I wanted to ask, but Melozzo was holding up the heart with its crown of severed arteries and veins, while Benivieni named each part: *vena arterialis, arteria renalis*. Galen tells us that this performs such and such an office. Here air from the lungs enters, and here in the left ventricle it is transformed into the vital spirit. The heart is muscle and if wounded can beat on, as those who fight duels have found to their cost, but cut these – delicate blue and pink vessels branching like precious coral – and death is instantaneous, for the vital spirit cannot circulate. How many times I had cut through hearts – hearts of pigs, of sheep and oxen – and made a wreck of all this alchemy, this frail machinery.

I watched it all, even when Benivieni showed us the muscles of the face, even when Melozzo took out an eye so that the glistening string of nerve quivered between the white orb and the empty socket. Even when they sawed off the top of the skull and lifted out the brain, proving that it was nothing more extraordinary than a ridged, puckered turnip. The place had begun to stink like a shambles. People had begun to drift away, alone or in pairs, until at the very end, when the man on the table had ceased to be anything very much other than the leavings of some savage beast, only a few of us were left. Some hadn't lasted beyond the snipping of the ribs.

'*Puttana!* I'm in need of wine,' It was Antoniazzo. He had taken off his cap and was mopping his brow. The air in the *bottega* was stifling, and the smell of meat and the contents of stomach and intestines was becoming overwhelmingly strong. He bowed with dignity to Melozzo and the surgeon, who were washing their hands in a bowl held in the unsteady hands of the apprentice who had let us in, his face now the colour of an eel's belly. 'My friends, we thank you for revealing to us these mysteries, for shining light into the darkness of this sacred form, and for advancing our craft. But I am afraid we can't help you tidy up. Are you coming, *scalco?*'

'No – but thank you. I think I shall go to the *stufa.*'

I said a short but fervent prayer for the soul of the poor, dismembered wretch whom the apprentices were bundling into a sheet of old canvas, and left on my own, wondering how in God's name I was going to turn the morbid destruction I had just witnessed into a banquet fit for a pope.

I WENT TO A METALWORKER who had made things for me before, a man with a *bottega* not far from the fish market, and explained what I needed: six gilt salvers in the shape of a man's head, trunk, arms and legs, with covers to match. Base metal would do, because we'd melt it all down afterwards. The craftsman, a pug-nosed fellow with skin cured black by the smoke and fumes from his fires, thought he knew what I meant, but he didn't. I wanted the dishes life-size, and made so that when they were laid out on the table with the covers on, it would seem to the guests as if a man's golden body lay there. He hummed and mumbled, before drawing me something crude on the back of a piece of wood.

I had woken early that morning with one of Donna Eufemia's girls in my bed, and I'd given myself a little pick-me-up of wine and *kannab*, so my head was still full of ideas. I subjected him to a few, and because my commissions were worth a lot to him the poor bastard put up with me, but then I asked him whether he could take sheets of copper and beat them over an old statue. He thought he could, and so I took him to a place near the Pantheon where workers were digging the foundations of a new *palazzo*. There was a small pile of marble torsos and limbs stacked up like pallid firewood. None of them were worth much and the workers were happy for me to slip them a few coins in return for the pieces of my choice. I had them carted back to the *bottega* and left the man to it.

The days before the Pope's banquet are more or less lost to me. A whoremonger, the owner of a large and expensive brothel near San Clemente in Rione Monti, was getting very keen for me to use his girls and boys for dances, and had taken to sending me a different whore every night except on Saturdays, a rather unnecessary dab of piety on his part, because I doubted he took his flock to mass. I worried that my manhood was being tested – was this reason on my part, or the preparations I was starting to find so useful? – so I dug ever deeper into my bags of herbs, not to mention various unguents and potions from the cardinal's apothecary (very discreet and very, very expensive). I would wake up, drink a glass containing a raw egg, cloves and the dried and powdered vulva of a doe, and while that unimaginably foul liquor was percolating down through my innards towards my *membrum virile* (the exhausted organ safely encased in a fashionably padded *braghetto* and anointed with an unguent made from crushed-up flying ants, elm bark, musk, amber and quails' balls), I would go downstairs to whatever problems needed sorting out in the kitchen. Luncheon would be my pick of last night's meal, which often meant some handily aphrodisiac treats such as cuttlefish cooked with pine nuts, truffles, and more quail, washed down with wine into which I'd put dragonmouth leaves or nettle seeds. A quick visit to the metalworks, a look around the markets to make sure the *spenditore* was being honest; perhaps some haggling with a supplier. Then back, to begin putting together the night's revelries.

That meant chasing musicians, threatening and if necessary bribing them (and all too often trying to sober them up); barking at the kitchen; barking at the servants as they laid His Eminence's table; standing through the meal itself; co-ordinating whatever festivities I had planned for it; making sure Horlandino the *trinciante* did not cut someone's nose off with one of his whirling knives; escorting each guest to the door or to their bed, with or without company; seeing that the kitchen was cleaned, the spices locked away and the meats hoisted out of rat reach; that everyone had been paid, if necessary; that Teverino was happy; that his lieutenant was happy; that the girls who washed the dishes were happy; that Messer Domenicho was happy; and that His Eminence was satisfied with the night's proceedings.

I would eat my own dinner, usually a flask of wine, a heel of bread and whatever Teverino had put aside for me — hopefully something pure and easy to digest, like a bit of boiled capon or some fish cheeks. Some Indian leaves in the wine, perhaps something else for the *membrum*, such as roasted dragon arum root. Then, and only then, would I be able to lurch back to my chambers, to find whatever girl was waiting for me there. With any luck she'd have made the fire, because otherwise little Alonso Ruyz de Bisimbre would have to be summoned, and then I'd have to get rid of him because he'd be busy sneering at me and leering at my woman.

But my toils weren't over, not by a long shot. Because now I had to prove to my companion, who by now I always suspected had been carefully briefed to watch my every move (however implausible that fear seems when held up to the light of day), that I was a man — more than a man. Much more: a bull, a charger, inexhaustible in appetite and energy; that I was a *condottiere* whom any man would be insane to cross, because Rome seemed to be strangely full of men who wished to best me, to usurp me, to trick me into committing some fatal *brutta figura*. Only when I was satisfied that I had brought satisfaction, by whatever means that was being measured; only when I was convinced that I had not lost face, that my reputation was intact for another day, would I allow myself to fall into a shallow, fretted sleep.

★

I've set the things out on the table in front of me. I couldn't sleep: the banquet less than a day away, too much medicine, the girl in my bed sobbing quietly in her sleep. So I have come down to the kitchen to do something. I have what I need: bowls for the powders – orange, white, black, yellow, red. Eggs. There's a brush somewhere about. And my knife. The board is untreated. No gesso here. But it will have to do. I break an egg, separate the yolk, burst the sagging golden ball and let the treasure fall into a saucer. Some pigment on the tip of my knife, cut it in slowly. It's bad, ground too coarse, but I drip some vinegar onto the ugly paste, mix it again. Let's try the yellow. Better. The black is good, just charcoal from the cold hearth.

The wood is smooth from years of work and sanding down. I'll do a quick sketch, and then the paint. Yellow hair, pink skin, green gown. Figures, taking shape, rising up past the knots and the join in the boards. A boy, holding out his hand. A girl . . . what did she even look like? I remember her hair, all those springy curls, and the delicate swoop of her nose. What a funny thing to have stuck in my mind. I screw up my eyes, try to recall something else: a smell, a taste. Tessina . . .

'Maestro!'

There are footsteps on the tiles. I have time to throw a wet rag over the table and sweep it all away.

'Maestro! Is that you?' It is Bardi, the night watchman. 'What are you doing?'

'Nothing, Bardi! Just getting things in order. The feast tomorrow . . . Some meat needs trimming. My father used to be a butcher, you know.'

But he isn't listening. He's already gone. I tap the bowls and let the spices settle. I search the air for something: a memory, another ghost. She's not there. I slap the wet, crimson meat down and bend to my work.

*

Everything was ready for the banquet on the seventeenth day of April. All was exactly as I had imagined it. As Pope Sixtus walked past me into the Palazzo Borgia, he gave me a small nod – we had met before, though he'd never seen my face. Nor had his nephew, Count Girolamo Riario, who glided along behind the Holy Father. The count, though, ignored me, staring down his long nose at his exquisite shoes. I led the guests – none of the others were familiar to me: three noblemen and their wives, a French cardinal – into the dining hall, and though the Holy Father hadn't actually gasped – others had – I noted with some satisfaction that his heavy gait had faltered for a moment when he'd seen what was awaiting him on the table.

Because it looked for all the world as if a naked, golden man was laid out on his back, or rather a corpse, because the metalworker had proved his worth and made the face with slightly open eyes and bared teeth. Everything was true to life, from the veins bulging through the muscles of the arms to the foreskin on the *membrum virile*. I had set candles at his head and feet, and instead of cutlery I had provided Borgia's guests with surgical instruments.

The guests sat. Two of the women were blushing furiously and fanning themselves, repulsed or excited, though their husbands were nudging them and pointing out details, lingering – naturally – on the *membrum*; and Horlandino began his usual dance around the table, plucking off lids and flourishing knives and forks of all possible shapes and sizes. As each cover was removed, I was relieved to see the guests lean forward and laugh – with excitement, not disgust – because I wasn't exactly sure how well I'd judged my audience. I was standing at one end of the room, quivering slightly. I had felt so furiously overworked, earlier in the afternoon, that I'd taken a tincture of wild poppy – quite a strong tincture, and quite a lot of it. I breathed a deep and ragged sigh as the head was lifted off to reveal a small mound of perfectly fried lamb's brains, a poached veal tongue, two jellied pig's ears on either side, and two eyes made of the tongues of unborn lambs rolled around boiled, halved quail's eggs.

It required two serving men to lift the cover from the golden man's trunk. And then I got a proper gasp from the table. Two standing racks of roast mutton stood erect, the ribs meeting in the middle. At the throat, a selection of sweetbreads: fried; in *torte*; mixed, in the ancient style, with rose petals. I had fashioned a heart from red-cabbage leaves wrapped around a stuffing of lean pork, ham, veal udders, pine nuts, garlic, saffron and good spices, the whole thing boiled in cloth like a dumpling. The lungs were the poached wings of a giant skate. Below, a mix of fried liver and kidneys, and below that, a great coil of steaming blood sausage. Finally, a beautiful lamprey, complete with its blunt head (from which I'd carefully pulled back the skin to reveal the perfect circle of its tooth-crammed mouth), lolled between two wine-poached, sugar-crusted figs. One of the women pointed and screamed.

By now the party was calling loudly for the other covers to be lifted, so I gave the signal. There were more exclamations, and I thought I even saw a rare smile flit across Borgia's usually impassive face as his guests pointed out each ingredient in turn. In one arm was a roasted conger eel, with fried anchovies as the fingers; and in the other, a line of stuffed goose necks. The thighs were haunches of roebuck, and the shins were boned, stuffed and roasted hares, while each foot was a lobster in its shell.

Horlandino was no surgeon. It was unnerving to see him strut and twirl, his yellow curls flouncing, as he atomized my edible corpse: flaying the eel, its dark, bluish skin peeled back, the white flesh steaming. The ribs, parted with a short knife, the heart sliced into thin circles. It didn't take long before the body was as ruined as the poor fellow I'd seen cut up at Melozzo's *bottega*. The Holy Father, having put away two of the brains, was being helped to a second serving of mutton ribs and a length of sausage. His nephew was working his way up the eel-arm. Cardinal Borgia turned and rewarded me with another secret smile.

It was an evening without dancing, though the cardinal's musicians sawed and blew their way through the latest pieces, and so I wasn't required to do very much – a blessing, as I could barely keep myself upright, and spent as much time as I could manage propped against the wall. The *credenziero* sent in sugar sculptures of the della Rovere oak tree, the crossed keys of the papacy, and – I had insisted on this, even provided him with a model – a regrettably crude human skeleton, half-size, seated in a sugar chair and holding a sugar knife against its own arm. There were more shrieks, and then the snapping of sugar bones and the sloshing of wine into cups.

The Holy Father's banquet went on until late, and afterwards, the Pope, his nephew and Cardinal Borgia withdrew to the cardinal's inner chambers while the other guests went home. There was no further need for my services, but there was more to do. I sucked down some more *kola* nuts, which sharpened me up just enough. I made sure that the kitchen was locked up, the dining hall cleared, the plate shut away. I ate a couple of leftover brains, though they had gone cold and their custardy innards were slick and tasted slightly of wet dog. By the time I sat down to examine the day's accounts, my eyes were sore and throbbing, and there were disturbing lights flashing in the corner of my vision. A vein was throbbing in my neck and my hair felt as if it was trying to jump out of my scalp.

And still my day wasn't over. There was a girl waiting for me upstairs, I knew, sent by that bastard from Rione Monti.

He had scented a weakness, because the other night I had gone a bit soft; temporarily, of course, and everything was sorted out by a quick rub of nutmeg, which stung like hell but brought the *membrum* back to attention. After that there were no more problems, but since that night the whoremaster had been laying siege to me in earnest. Any more failures and he would be angling for exclusivity, for introductions and patronage. Or else my reputation would be encouraged to rot, like an unbought mackerel on the steps of the Portico d'Ottavia. My hand was shaking as I prepared myself a small tonic from the locked apothecary's box under my desk: *kannab*, saffron, tincture of woundwort, honey, cloves and galangal. Any one of those would probably have done, but why take chances? I added a bit more *kannab*, just to be on the safe side.

The girl, rather heavy, with a tangle of oiled and curled hair done up in gold ribbons, was dozing when I came in, which suited me fine. But as I shut the door behind me, she propped herself up woozily on an elbow. She was wearing a loose muslin shift, and one large, freckled breast had fallen out. I bowed, ridiculously, and tottered over to the fire, knelt down, picked up a log . . . Suddenly my face was very close to the hearth. How had that happened? I shook my head, threw the log onto the embers, poked at it carefully. Very carefully. The embers glowed, each one a door into a lovely, molten world. I bent closer. Were there people in that coal, or birds? Flowers snaked up around the smouldering log.

'Are you coming to bed?' The girl had a sleepy, rough voice, but she'd failed to keep the boredom out of it.

'Right now, my beautiful one,' I said, standing up and feeling my head soar almost to the ceiling. 'Where are you from?' I asked, to buy myself some time.

'Velletri,' she said. 'I've come all the way here just to fuck you.'

'Velletri? Don't you mean Monti?'

'Hurry up, love,' she muttered patiently.

I had to concentrate very hard on my stays and ties, because my fingers couldn't quite do what they were told. But as soon as my doublet was off, thrown into a corner of the room, and I had unpicked one of the stays that held up my hose, the girl – a woman, really, of around my age – heaved herself off the bed with a resigned sigh and finished undressing me.

'What would you like?' she whispered into my ear. I felt the lobe flinch away from her lips like an oyster when the lemon juice hits it. Feeling more and more bewildered, I reached into her gown for those breasts. There was something I could understand, at least.

'Show yourself to me,' I said, and she obediently slipped the gown from her shoulders and lay back on the bed, legs spread languidly, hands brushing her breasts. *Madonna* . . . I was confused. What was going on, exactly? She changed, worryingly, into the golden man, the man of dishes, and then back to flesh. As if to prompt me, her hand trailed down between her legs and rather impatiently showed me what I was supposed to be concentrating on. Good. That was better. I went over, laid my hands on her nice round belly. Still my mind could do no more than compile a blurry catalogue of sensations. I needed to feel something: anything at all. She raised her hand from her *fica* and rubbed it across my mouth and under my nose. Now I understood. My body quickened and I felt the stirrings of . . . not desire, but blunt, stupid lust.

As it usually did, the old dance of flesh against flesh restored me somewhat to my senses. And everything was working where that mattered. Except time kept stretching and jerking back on itself. But never mind. I was the master. I was made of iron. Time stretched, and I lost myself quite happily in the lines of the plaster on the wall.

And then I was present again, everything in crystalline focus. The woman had a long, freckled back upon which beads of sweat were glistening. I was thrusting into her, had been thrusting away for God knew how long, looking down at the oval, slightly corrugated cheeks of her arse, at my hands pressing into the ample flesh around her waist. She'd told me her name, hadn't she? What was her name?'

'Fortuna?' I said, tentatively.

She had her face pushed deep into the pillow, and she might have been asleep, because she was quite still and her breath under my hands was slow and regular. Suddenly I was looking down on the two of us from high above, at the supine whore and the skinny, sweating man banging away like a mechanical hammer in a forge.

'Oh, Jesus!' I yelled in despair and fell backwards, overwhelmed by the tawdriness of it all. The girl lifted her head drowsily.

'Mmm. Well done,' she mumbled, rolled over and went back to sleep.

I was sprawled on the floor next to the bed, my arse sticking to the Saracen carpet, a corner of sheet across my lap, which was still straining at the leash, though everything was completely numb, when there was a knock at the door. I ignored it, but then it came again, and the door opened a crack. A head peered in: one of the senior house servants, and he looked upset.

'What do you mean by this?' I slurred, tucking myself away in the sheet but failing to hide the ridiculous, pointless tumescence.

'I'm truly sorry to disturb your . . . your rest, Messer Nino,' he hissed. 'But I didn't know what else to do. One of the master's guests is in a terrible state.'

'Get Pagholini,' I grunted.

'Messer Domenicho is out,' said the man. 'I wouldn't

dream of bothering you, but . . . It's His Holiness's nephew as well.'

'And?'

'Drunk and raving. He already punched Arturo. We can't throw him out: he's a count, God help him.'

'Fuck.' I scratched my head: my nails felt like a lion's claws. 'And the Pope's bloody nephew. All right. All bloody right.'

Putting my clothes back on was a trial, but it went more smoothly than the undressing, though my hose were hanging down behind my arse and my doublet was buttoned unevenly. The servant was waiting for me in the hall. Whatever he thought of me, of what he had just seen, he kept it to himself. 'His Holiness went home,' he was saying, 'but Count Girolamo wanted to try one of the *bottigliere*'s special wines, and after he'd had one cup he wanted another and another. Started calling for a woman. Said . . .' He lowered his voice. 'Said he knew what sort of things went on here. All sorts of disgusting . . . begging your pardon, sir.'

'We all exist to serve Cardinal Borgia,' I reminded him biliously. My insides felt like an ants' nest, and my head was filled with dying coals. 'I don't question. You certainly shouldn't.'

I followed him downstairs, and to my surprise he led me to the kitchen. There was Girolamo Riario, seated on Teverino's favourite stool, his face ghostly white. I noticed that his tunic was spotted with grease and wine, and there was a lump of mutton fat embedded in his magnificent gold chain. He saw me and sat up, flailing for a moment to keep balance.

'Ah! Good brothel-keeper!' he called, pointing a wavering hand at me. 'I want to fuck.'

'I'm sorry, Your Grace,' I said. 'I cannot accommodate you, I'm afraid. This is the house of a cardinal, you see.

Perhaps I could have one of our staff escort you to a reputable . . . a house of entertainment?'

'How dare you. How fucking dare you!'

Riario lurched to his feet. Thinking he was about to fall over, and deciding that it was better if the Pope's nephew didn't crack his skull on the cardinal's flagstones, I rushed over to him, none too steady on my own feet, and caught him around the chest. Immediately he swung his arm and punched me in the face. Luckily for me there was no power behind his fist, and it glanced off my ear. I managed to catch hold of his wrist and forced it down.

'It is dreadfully late, Your Grace,' I said through gritted teeth. 'I'm sure you would hate to wake Cardinal Borgia. I'm sure you'd like to go home now.'

'I . . . want . . . a WOMAN!' he yelled, and struggled against me. I managed to turn him and push him face down onto the table, where to my surprise he went limp.

'I've sent for your horse,' I said, hoping I sounded professional, though I was actually wondering which one of us was likely to vomit first. 'Our most reliable men will see to it that you get home safe and sound.'

'Florence,' said the count.

'I beg your pardon, Your Grace?'

'Florence. You're from Florence. You sound like you have a cat turd in your mouth, as do all men from your bloody little town. Lorenzo Medici most of all. Well, listen to me, Florence. Your Lorenzo is a dead man.'

'I don't think so, Your Grace,' I said. The words I had heard in the grotto came back to me very clearly. 'You'll feel a lot better about everything tomorrow morning.'

'I mean he is dead! My uncle is the Pope – the bloody Pope, you Florentine turd! He will sweep the Medici away like . . . like . . .' He peered up at me, perhaps hoping I'd supply his simile.

'We'll forget about it,' I said soothingly; tempted, a little, to grab his golden locks and slam his head a few times against the table top.

'You won't. You'll never forget. Francesco Pazzi, who is worth more than a host of Medici, will see to that. He's already done it . . . what day is today? No, not quite done it. But soon, Florence. Very soon.'

'Done what?'

'Killed Lorenzo. He won't see May come in, that prick who thought he'd defy my uncle. Who defied me, a bloody Riario!' He twisted his head and yelled it at the ceiling: 'RIARIO! Bastard Medici, who showed his arse to Archbishop Salviati! Good as showed his arse to him, did you know that? Good men. Good, good men. Willing to do what must be done.'

'When?' I asked. The world was very cold, all of a sudden, and everything had stopped jumping around. My body belonged to me again, at least for a moment. 'Who? Who are you talking about, Your Grace?' I spoke gently, patiently.

'Pazzi. Salviati. Montesecco. Old Baroni's son – Marco's a Florentine, you know, a *dirty* little bugger, like all of you . . . Married his mother-in-law.'

'What? What about Marco Baroni? Who did he marry?' I wasn't patient any longer. I discovered my fist, locked around a pretty bunch of Riario's hair.

'Ow! Old Bartolo, old Blood Sausage . . . His wife. His *widow*. What was he doing with that dirty little bitch, eh? Fucked him to death, so I believe. Eh? And Marco . . . In like a ferret. Good man, Marco. He'll do it.'

'Marco married Tessina Baroni?' I shook his hair, and he tried to push me away.

'What of it? What of whores – *whores*, Florentine bloody *whores*, when we're talking about the death of princes? Eh? Pazzi, Salviati, Montesecco: they'll do it. All of them, invited to Medici's bloody villa. I sent them, to make friends. Aha. They'll make friends, believe me. Soon, soon.'

'Before May Day?'

'Oh, long before. Twenty-sixth day of April. That's the day. The day . . . RIARIO!' He yelled again, and started to cough, violently. I gave him a shake, not a gentle one. His forehead bounced off the wood and he shut up.

I let him go, walked backwards out of the kitchen, keeping my eyes on the shambles on the table. 'I want a fucking woman!' he bellowed into the table. The servant was waiting for me just beyond the door.

'Begging your pardon, Messer Nino – and I would never say such a thing under ordinary . . .' He tugged at his fingers and bit his lip. 'You *do* have a . . . that is to say, a woman. Upstairs. Forgive me, but she *is* a prostitute.'

I had the sudden urge to cry. Instead I patted him shakily on the arm.

'I'll see what can be done. Meanwhile, give him all he wants. With any luck, he'll pass out. Either way, put him to bed. And I'll . . . arrange things.'

'Are you sure?'

'I'll take all responsibility.'

He nodded, reluctantly, but I was already striding back to my chambers. It was true that my feet seemed to be gliding just above the floor, and my strides seemed to be unusually long, but I knew what I was doing. At last, I knew exactly what I was doing.

Fortuna Turns Her Wheel A Fifth Time:
'Regnabo' – 'I Shall Reign'

⁂ 47 ⁂

THE DRUNKARD WAS STILL ROARING down below as I slipped back into my quarters, bellowing out the names of great men, delighting in murder to come, or already committed. I cared for none of them: Salviati, Pazzi, Medici – that, perhaps, least of all. All I could hear was Tessina's name on the man's foul, spittle-flecked lips.

Without waking the snoring woman in my bed, I got dressed properly in a plain grey tunic, doublet and hose, pulled on my travelling boots. It took a long time, and every ribbon and lace that had to be tied was a task fit to be tackled by Maestro Brunelleschi, but finally it was done. I shoved some *mutande* and my best doublet into the leather bag I had taken to Assisi. Zohan's knives and his wooden spoon in their roll; my knives as well. Zohan's book of recipes, and my own stained, hasty notes. Then I took Sandro's drawings from their place in the old wooden shrine. The Virgin I tucked into the bag. Tessina I folded in a few sheets of stiff vellum from my writing desk and slid her into my doublet, over my heart. There was a bag of gold and silver hidden under a floorboard I had prised up months ago, which was where I had been throwing my wages. I'd never really had time to spend much of it, and the bag was much heavier than I expected. I looked over at the woman.

'Wake up,' I said, shaking her gently. She looked up blearily. 'Get dressed.'

'You aren't throwing me out?' she rasped. 'It's the middle of the bloody night.'

'You can't stay here.'

She rubbed the sleep from her eyes, blinked, saw I was dressed, and the sword and dagger hanging from my belt. That was something she could understand, apparently. Without another word she rolled off the bed and began pulling on her tunic and stockings. As she fastened her long, featureless cloak with a cheap brooch I rummaged in my bag and selected a good handful of coins. Five ducats — more than a month's wages for me — and some loose silver and copper. I took her wrist and poured the money into her palm.

'Go back to Velletri,' I said.

'Don't be soft,' she said, looking wide-eyed at the money.

'Or somewhere else. Just stop doing this.'

'I'll do what I want.'

'Of course you will.'

I hung the purse around my neck, put on my riding cloak, and left the room. The woman trailed me, looking around her distractedly. As I'd hoped, everyone who was awake was in the kitchen, dealing with Count Riario. We slipped out through the service door, past the snoring guard, and into the street. The livery stable was north of us, towards the Piazza del Popolo. I took the woman's hands and squeezed them, hard.

'I'm sorry,' I said. 'I'm terribly, terribly sorry.'

Then I ran. I didn't stop to see where she went: east, back to Monti and the whoremaster; somewhere better; perhaps, or somewhere worse. I just ran, the bag knocking into my back, my sword rattling. And after that I rode. At some point after sunrise I reined in the horse. I was alone on the silent road. I looked back, but Rome had already sunk into the haze, and all I saw were empty fields and flowering trees: purple for the Judas, white for the almond.

I rode a little further, but the jogging of my horse was throwing my insides into confusion. I should take something for that, some tincture of poppy, but . . . I rummaged in my bag, as if seeing it for the first time. Nothing. No tinctures, no leaves, no little vials of powder. I thought I'd brought them. I must have! But where were they? I rummaged. Nothing. Not even any wine. How could I have come away with no wine? No *kannab*? How in the name of Christ was I going to ride to Florence with no *kola*? My stomach lurched and I stopped the horse, slid down and, bent double, puked into the dusty sage scrub beside the road.

And there I stayed, on my knees, until the horse put her soft, moist nose against my ear and nudged me, gently but insistently. By the time I had hauled myself back into the saddle it was as if I had my nose very close to a brightly frescoed wall. The countryside, the trees, the ruined huts, the rooks: it was all very bright and throbbing with colour, but entirely flat and unreal. The harder I stared, the less real it became, and if the horse had not decided to get on with things, I would probably have stayed there until nightfall. As it was, she started to walk north, and as soon as I was sure I could control my stomach, I let her trot, because, though my limbs were barely working, I did have the sense that I ought to hurry.

The wine I'd drunk, the *kannab*, the poppy and all the other things I'd prescribed myself had leached away. Of course: that was the natural order of things. But I would, under normal circumstances, simply have topped myself up. After a hectic night like the cardinal's Feast of the Body, I would have made sure that I was as armoured against the day's possibilities with all the arts that alchemist and apothecary could contrive. But now it was wearing off – had worn off, in fact. I hadn't let that happen in months.

And how sensible I'd been! Because the world around me was strangely not as I remembered it. The wind was buffeting my face, filling up my nose and making me retch. The cries of birds, the beat of horse hooves, the chatter and laughter of others on the road clanged into my head as if my eardrums were made of copper. My skin was being flailed by extremes of hot and cold, my hair felt like metal wires pinned into my scalp.

When at last I came to a spring, a little marble column with water pouring from an iron spigot, I gulped from my cupped hands, and it burned my throat and hurt my teeth. Still I gulped, lapping like a mastiff until I was soaked all down the front of my clothes. Strange: it revived me, though the liquid seethed agonizingly in my stomach like molten tin.

By the time I got to a decent-sized village my head felt as if an invisible spike had been inserted at the point where the three plates of my skull met. There were hot thumbs behind my eyes forcing them outwards. My throat burned and my teeth felt like splinters of ice. My stomach roiled, my limbs ached, my skin was streaming with sweat even though it was rippling with gooseflesh. Without the thought of Tessina somewhere ahead of me, Tessina in danger, I would have rolled myself into a ball under a tree and waited for the end. Because that was the one thought that I had managed to keep in my head since last night. Tessina married to Marco Baroni. Marco, in his mad arrogance, allied with the Pazzis and moving against Lorenzo. If he succeeded . . . But how could he? And if he failed, Tessina would be stained with his treason. She wouldn't escape the Medicis. Did I care about Lorenzo and his family? Hardly at all. The picture that had scored itself into my brain was of bodies dangling from the windows of the Signoria. To look up, in the middle of a baying crowd, and see Tessina hanging there . . .

After endless miles, I found an inn and persuaded the owner to sell me a wineskin, which I filled with good white wine, there being no guarantee of more springs nearby. I sampled a cup as well, and though it burned like the fires of Hell, it did at least stop some of the banging and battering around my skull, and my flesh stopped creeping and settled into a kind of sullen rawness.

Horse fed and watered, I pressed on through the empty land. As the false confidence of the drugs ebbed away, guilt rushed in to fill the void, along with one vile realization after another: all the stains I'd made on my soul, all the selfishness, all the pride and greed.

I decided to ride through the night, for speed's sake, and because sleep was doubtful; and if I did sleep, what dreams would come? But just before the sun had touched the horizon, I found myself on a stretch of road that seemed familiar. At first I thought it was the hallucinatory workings of my tortured system, but I knew that rock, that high hedge of rushes. And there, just ahead, was the little path that led to . . . I tried to remember. An old woman, a sweet, kind old woman. Donna Velia. I turned the horse's head and we left the road.

The valley was as I remembered it: the reed thicket, the walls, the goat-stripped, stony fields. And there was the little stone house. 'Donna Velia!' I called, so as not to frighten her. There was no light showing, and no smoke coming from the chimney, but I had a recollection of her staying out late, in the higher fields, and so I urged the horse on, right up to the door. I tied her to an old peach tree and knocked. Knocked again. Tried the latch. It stuck, then gave. When I pushed the door open, the hinges dragged and I could feel the nails shift and give in the wood. I stepped in.

The hearth was cold. The heap of charcoal and ash didn't even smell of fire. And then I saw that the place was abandoned. The rafters of the ceiling were beginning to sag, the old cupboard was open and its shelves were falling in on each other. The table where Donna Velia had fed me was scattered with twigs and crumbs of plaster. The bracken on the bed had dried into nothing more than thin brown hay.

I went back outside and sat down on the stone lintel that had been Velia's bench. As the sun went down behind the low, round-topped hill, the fields faded and became ghostly. Where had she gone? Surely her daughters would be here, if she'd died? Because the house and the land were deserted, I found a way to tell myself that the daughters had taken their mother somewhere else, somewhere more comfortable, more dignified.

It was quite silent apart from the scraping of crickets. I took my bag inside, wrapped myself up in the musty folds of my cloak and lay down on the bed. My head began to spin, and shapes danced up into the musty gloom. A flayed man, a man of golden dishes, festoons of guts; jiggling, jouncing sacks of lung and liver and stomach. The eyes of fish, of deer, rams, boar, boiled and filmy or roasted and blistered. I turned over and sobbed into the crumbling bracken.

I fell asleep at last, or passed out, only to wake again in utter darkness. I remembered Donna Velia, sitting beside me as I lay in this bed, feeding me white ricotta from an old earthenware bowl. *You were empty as a blown egg*, she had said.

'I never came back, *donna*,' I whispered into the darkness. 'I never made your soup for the Holy Father. I never came back to build you a proper house when I made some money. I had enough, Velia: for you, for your goats. I never repaid you.'

Repaying kindness? Is that some Florentine thing, like selling food to buy food?

The voice came from my memory, but even so she was there beside me, with a spoon of ricotta, the milk from her goats, the honey from a wild nest in the chestnut forest. I knew she was dead then, buried somewhere in the fields, or just lying out in the woods. But that was all right: that was how it should be. Velia had lived her whole life here, with her goats, with the sun and the rain, far away from money, and pride, and vanity. Had she been happy? I imagined her laughing at me for that thought. So she fed me again, there in the thick dark of the house she had left, and I told her about Tessina, and Marco Baroni, and Riario's plot to kill Messer Lorenzo. I could taste goat's milk and honey on my tongue. I would never repay her for this last kindness, but she fed me anyway.

The next day, about noon, I rode into a village with an inn, and bought some food. It was overpriced and poor in quality, because the place itself was poor and they made their living from gulling the foreigners who passed through in ignorant droves. Saltless bread, pecorino that was on the knife-edge of rancid, some dried figs. I ate, I tasted, I felt the nourishment soak through me. I fed myself like a peasant, not like a cardinal's *scalco*. The fuel to keep riding was all I needed. My body still felt bad but at least it belonged to me again, and the world was just the world, full of bad food and men who stared with bored suspicion.

'Any news from Florence?' I asked the host, but he shrugged and shook his head.

So I took to the road again, praying that there wouldn't be any news, that it had all been the ravings of a drunken swine, or some dream from my apothecary's chest that had set me off on this madness. Madness or not, I was in it now. No going back to Cardinal Borgia, or the whoremasters, or the apothecaries. I had no idea what I would do if there was no plot, whether I cared, really, if Messer Lorenzo was killed. I tried to imagine how I would steal Tessina from Marco Baroni; or if, when it came to it, she'd have me. Why would she, indeed? I didn't deserve her – she had no idea how little I deserved her love.

My horse went lame outside San Quirico and I had to buy another mare to carry me on the last stretch of my journey.

Coming down into the low hills of the Arno valley, every-thing looked calm enough in Florence. By which I mean nothing big seemed to be on fire, there were no armies out here beyond the walls, and the sheep in the fields were all minding their own business. I had just passed through Galluzzo and my horse was still cantering along nicely when the peasants stepped out of the vines on either side of the road and levelled their scythes and hoes at me.

'What's amiss, my friends?' I asked, reining in hurriedly.

'You tell us! What's the word?' said the tallest. He was holding an ancient two-handed sword and looked both scared and elated, not a safe combination. His friends were edging forward to outflank me, eyeing the sword and dagger I was wearing. I could probably escape quite easily, but then, I'd come this far with only two words in my head. The first, the secret word was *Tessina*. I stood up in the stirrups and yelled the second:

'*Palle!*'

'*Palle! Palle!*' they shouted.

'My father is Niccolaio di Niccolaio Latini from the Black Lion, and we're Medici through and through,' I told them, banging my breastbone with my fist.

'He's all right!' said one of the men, and the others nodded. The one with the sword hesitated, then rested the rusty blade on his shoulder and stepped out of the way. I rode up to him and stopped when he was beside me.

'What are you doing here?' I asked.

'Haven't you heard?'

'I was in Greve yesterday. A messenger came . . .' I couldn't tell them the truth, could I? 'Come on, brothers! I've been riding all night! Messer Lorenzo. Is he safe?'

'Yes, yes, he is,' the men chorused. 'But those bastard dogs of Pazzi, those *bardasse*, those *carnaiuole* . . .' They all started shouting at once. I heard 'Killing all the traitors', 'Pope's soldiers from Bologna', but I'd already started galloping on towards the gate. I could see men on the battlements and soldiers milling around in the road. As I came up they met me with lowered pikes. This wasn't a time for subtlety.

'I've come to kill the Pazzis!' I bellowed in my dirtiest Black Lion accent. 'Let me through, you *cagne*, you bitches! *Palle!*'

Let me through they did, without much fuss. And why not? If I was a friend, well and good. And if I was an enemy, I'd just been let into the shambles and there were plenty of willing slaughtermen. Because as soon as I'd ridden through the Porta Romana and into the narrow streets of Oltrarno, it was clear that things were very wrong in Florence.

A mob was kicking at the door of a new *palazzo* in the Via della Chiesa. That was the first thing I saw, because the streets had been completely empty from here to the gate. I rode past, shouting '*Palle!*' along with them. More angry men and women in Piazza Santo Spirito: they had two young men up against the wall of the church and were hitting them with sticks. Another woman was bustling across the square, holding a heavy wooden pestle. I didn't wait to see what happened next, but trotted on through the Dragon neighbourhood.

What had begun as unease in Galluzzo was growing into cold terror – not for myself, but for Tessina. She was Marco Baroni's wife, and Marco was a traitor. I kept passing houses with their doors smashed, thickening blood on their steps. A man's corpse, well dressed but barefoot, was lying in the gutter halfway down Via Maggio. Small groups of men were running, crossing the street in front of me. I yelled '*Palle!*' every time someone noticed me. I was late. Two days earlier and I might have stopped all this, but then again, I hadn't really believed that *coglione* Riario, had I? I'd come to save

Tessina from Marco, not from . . . A window smashed above me, and a man's face appeared for a moment, streaked in blood, glass falling away from him. Another man's fingers were clamped to his cheek. Then it vanished. If I had come to save her from this, I couldn't. Surely, nothing could.

I kicked the horse into a canter and rushed, in a clatter of iron on stone, down Via de' Guicciardini. But after seven years of flitting in and out of warped, tangled dream-maps of my own city I was taken completely by surprise as the first buildings on the Ponte Vecchio appeared in front of me. I was galloping now, something you could never do in Florence, and it made the city even less real, because what was Florence without her rules? And what was a Florentine, if he wasn't bound by them? There were more people here, thin crowds milling about, some of them shouting, others just angry and strangely lost. I kept yelling '*Palle!*' I would have crashed on over the bridge, but there, ahead on the left, was the shop. The shop. It had broken into my dreams more often than my own house, and now here it was, unchanged. I saw, with a shock that almost stopped my heart, that the sign still read *LATINI E FIGLIO*. And below it stood Giovanni, feet set wide in front of the boarded-up door, the big cleaver – *our* cleaver – cradled in his crossed arms.

I heaved on the reins, and the horse reared and danced sideways across the cobbles. She was sweating and rolling her eyes, but I got her turned around.

'Giovanni!' I called, swinging down out of the saddle. 'Giovanni! It's me!'

Giovanni didn't laugh in disbelief, or call my name. Instead he swung the cleaver in a low arc and held it up at arm's length in front of him. Without thinking, I had my sword half out of its scabbard. People were looking, starting to come towards us. '*Palle!*' I screamed at him. '*Palle*, for fuck's sake!'

'Get off the bridge, you bloody *pippione*,' he growled, raising the cleaver for emphasis.

'No! It's me, Giovanni! Nino! Nino Latini! Don't you know me?'

'Fuck off! I mean it!' His knuckles were white on the handle of the cleaver. I knew that wood so well: wax-smooth and warm in the hand.

'It's Nino! I've been in Rome . . . Look!' I pushed my sword back into its home and held up my arms. 'Look at me!'

He narrowed his eyes, and the dull grey-blue slab of steel hung, unwavering, between us. Then it went down.

'*Dio merda*,' he breathed. 'It's Nino.'

'Giovanni, what the fuck is happening?'

'Happening? Those *pompinari* of Pazzis have murdered little Giuliano, that's what's happening!'

'Giuliano . . .'

'De' Medici! For Christ's sake, Nino! They've hanged Archbishop Salviati, and Pazzi, and . . . The Signoria looks like a ratcatcher's pole, there's so many bodies dangling from it.'

'And Baroni?'

'Marco Baroni? No idea. I heard he was in the cathedral with Pazzi, though.'

'In the cathedral?'

'It happened in the *duomo*! Those heretics, those Judases . . .'

'My God.' I staggered towards Giovanni, who dropped his weapon with a clang and enveloped me.

'If only your father were here,' he said thickly into my neck. I twisted around, stared at him, my sweat frozen against my skin.

'What do you mean? Where is my father?'

'At the Guild palace, of course! The Beccai.'

'*Dio*. Yes, of course. Giovanni, I have to go.'

'Do what you have to do, little Nino. Nothing's right today. Everything's on its head. The good are struck down, and now the dead come back to life.'

'What do you mean?' I paused, halfway into the saddle.

'You're dead, Nino. Marco Baroni killed you.'

'Me?'

'Yes, little one. Marco murdered you, but not before you spitted him and killed that *bardassuole* Corso Marucelli. Everyone knows about it. We were all proud of you.'

'I thought I'd been declared a traitor.'

'Traitor? No! Bartolo . . .' He paused, and spat copiously. 'He'd already started to stir things up against the *Palle*. And he got ill soon after he got back, which made it easy for Messer Lorenzo to squeeze him out of the Signoria. That's why the Baronis became the Pazzis' *carnaiuole*.'

'So all this time . . . And Papá?'

'Niccolaio mourned you for a year. He never believed all that shit, you know, from before. You see?' He pointed to the sign. 'If you're not a ghost, God speed you. And Nino: too bad you didn't finish off that *fica* Baroni, eh? There's not a soul in the Black Lion who wouldn't take a minute to kick that goblin-faced bastard's corpse.'

'God keep you safe, Giovanni – I've got to go now.'

North of the bridge I had to walk the horse through crowds that parted reluctantly, angrily, for her. If I hadn't kept bellowing the Medici watchword, I would have been pulled down, because there was a sea of enraged faces, and I was something out of the ordinary on a day when that might be fatal. It took an age to push my way into the Piazza della Signoria. It was thronged, of course, and above the crowd rose a strange sound, a disjointed, not quite human noise, something between the screeching of cicadas and the clatter of tiles coming off an old roof in a gale. The other times I'd seen the square this full – when some poor bastard was being executed – the crowd had been still or sluggish, but today it swirled and ebbed, lapping at the walls of the Signoria itself. And over all the people: the dead. There they hung, twenty or more, dangling from every upper window, their faces, their bound hands, already swollen and purple. Above the crowd, heads were bobbing, stuck on the ends of pikes, boar spears, even a pitchfork – and not just heads, but legs, half a torso with the arm waving, stiff and crooked. I was almost at the other side of the square when someone pushed a dead face into mine. For a moment I stared into filmed, yellow eyes, at blood crusted on stubble below the nose. I didn't recognize the man. Should I? *'Palle!'* I bellowed into the bruised ear, and the head wavered and moved on.

The Borgo de' Greci was like a flooded river and I had to beat against the current of angry bodies. It might have been an hour before I reached Via de' Benci. I was home now, in the Black Lion, but as Giovanni had said, the city was all wrong. Florence hadn't changed so much in seven years, surely? I was thinking of one thing, and one alone: to get to the Palazzo Baroni. But still, my senses were vibrant, alive, all of me seeking out the familiar, the marks of my city: her smells, sounds, the colour of her stone. The stone was still here, but the smells weren't right. Where I should have been riding through wafts of *battuta*, of frying lard and grilling beef, I could smell nothing but cold hearths and spilled, souring wine. With the roar of the crowd, the rage and confusion thickening the air, Florence was more like herself than I remembered, and less. Something nagged at me: what if I'd done something to ruin my city, the one I carried around inside me? What if all the *kannab*, the *betel*, all the wine and the seeping, tarry embrace of lust had broken it for ever? What if this was an entirely different city? Otherwise, how could I be here, and not here? But then, what was my city without food being cooked? In all my dreams, in all my fevers and hazes and wanderings, I could never have imagined such a thing. I was riding through streets I knew, and the voices were real, the corners were real, the saints in their shrines were real. But there was no cooking

A gap appeared in the crowd and I spurred my horse into it. Suddenly a thicker press of men and women surged out of a side street. I let them carry us along. A man was being led through the crowd, his face bruised almost black, his eyes swollen shut, a rope around his neck. People were leaning over their fellows to land a blow on his bowed head and sagging shoulders. *Palle! Palle!* The noise was deafening.

At last, Via de' Rustici appeared on the right. I forced a way through the crowd and into the wider street. Palazzo Baroni was just beyond the church. The street was almost empty and I managed to get the horse into a sort of canter. But at the corner of Piazza San Remigio three pikemen stepped into my path. They were wearing hastily improvised Medici tabards over their clothes, but their pikes looked official enough. Before they had time to lower them I put my head to the horse's neck and set my spurs. We bowled past them, and I could almost smell the grease on the pike blades as they flashed on either side of my head. They were yelling at me, but I was already pulling at the reins, because in front of me the road was blocked by broken furniture, and there were people standing on the barricade, yelling up at other people I couldn't see. It took me a moment to realize that this was the Palazzo Baroni. I looked up. A white object appeared in one of the upper windows, and burst into the air as if a goose had somehow found its way into the house and was escaping, but which turned into a bolster that plummeted into the arms of a pock-marked woman standing just in front of me. She held it up and whooped, and so did everybody else. I jumped down, dropped the reins over a wooden bench that was upended against the wall. The pikemen were running down the street towards me but I ignored them, shoved past the woman celebrating her looted bolster, and stopped in the entrance to Bartolo Baroni's house.

The Palazzo Baroni had an arched gateway opening onto a small courtyard. The gates were lying twisted in the street. When I'd last been inside, there had been a beautiful bronze statue in the centre, with clipped orange trees arranged in embossed lead tubs around it. The statue was still there but the trees were in ruins, shattered and trampled, and over one of them was slumped a body dressed in bloodstained white, face down, the back of its head a shapeless pulp. I yelled and threw myself through the people blocking my way, lashing out with fists and elbows. The courtyard was echoing with shouts and laughter. Things kept falling from above: tumbling books, their pages fanning; cups, plates . . . Something hit my shoulder but I kept running. I almost slid in the blood that had leaked away from the body, caught myself and dropped to my knees beside it. Almost choked with horror, I turned it over.

It was a man's face, tongue out, eyes slitted. I didn't recognize him. His body had been slashed and stabbed so many times that his nightshirt was no more than a rag. There was a roar behind me. The pikemen were standing in the archway. I stood up and faced them.

'Where is she?' I yelled.

'Stick him! Stick the *fica*!' someone was screaming. The pikemen were grinning with rage. Their pikes were down and levelled at me. Something snapped in my head: perhaps the thought that Tessina might be lying dead just out of my sight; perhaps the madness that had corrupted the entire city. I pulled out my sword and my dagger.

'Answer me!' I could feel the veins in my neck straining. The pikemen took a step forward, and another. 'Where is she?' The blades were almost an arm's length from my chest. 'Come on then, you *buggerone!*'

'That's Nino Latini!' said a voice above me. 'It is! Fuck me! Nino's come looking to finish the job!'

At once, people swarmed around the pikemen – who plainly were not from the Black Lion – pushing up their spears. I found myself surrounded. And at last there were faces I knew: Nardo Chomi, was it, the pork butcher? And Papi, the bricklayer from Via Torta, and Agnolo di Giunta; Salviano di Scecho, and Marino Buonaccorsi, the dyer's son . . .

'Where is she?' I demanded. 'Where is she?'

'Where is who?' they asked.

Hands were reaching for me, my hair was being tugged and ruffled, my back pummelled. *Palle! Latini and the Black Lion! You're alive! You're back for the fun! You're looking for that* puto *Marco, true? We don't know where he is, or the* fica *would be hanging in the piazza . . . We'll find him; we'll find him and we'll make him bark, the filthy dog . . .*

'Donna Tessina!' I shouted into each deaf, uncomprehending face. 'Madonna *strega*, where is Tessina?'

Don't know . . . No one knows where Marco is . . .

I pushed past them. Out in the street, someone was about to steal my horse, but seeing the blades in my fists they faded into the crowd. I sheathed my weapons and mounted, men pawing at my boots.

'Nino!'

I looked down. It was Marino. I'd known him my whole life, from fights, from *calcio*, from church . . . Wine had started to thicken his face, and his hands were bluish-black. So he'd become a dyer like his father.

'Marco's gone – he never came back here. The *donna . . .*' Marino blinked. He had known Tessina back then. We'd all played dice just around the corner. 'She wasn't here either, but then, I don't think she would have been.'

I was about to ask him what he meant when the others grabbed the reins and started making a loud fuss of the horse.

'You've got to come with us!' said Nardo Chomi.

Yes! Come, come! They pulled the horse's head around and began to lead her up the street. There was nothing I could do. The crowd was alongside us, behind us, people streaming out of the Palazzo Baroni, out of their own houses. The pikemen had shouldered their pikes and were marching along in front.

'Where are we going?' I asked. *Not far! Not far!*

It was a short procession, because we only got as far as the church of San Remigio. There were men in the doorway, and when they saw us they started up with '*Palle! Palle!*' I thought we were going to pass by, but instead the men leading my horse stopped. Everyone started pushing through the doors of the church. Hands were already taking my feet from the stirrups and helping me down.

I was being bustled along, trapped inside a knot of gabbling, chattering men and women. The mood had changed. Now it seemed like carnival. Inside the church, under the high, cool, pointed arches, it was the same. The crowd was up in front of the altar. Marino took me by the arm, as if we were strolling through the piazza on a summer day.

'Wait! Wait, boys! Look who's here! It's Nino Latini!'

'He's dead,' someone piped up.

'Proves that Marco Baroni is a bastard liar along with everything else,' said Salviano.

The city was all wrong. Men like Salviano di Scecho didn't swear in church. I closed my eyes for a moment. If only Marino wasn't holding on to me . . . Just there, there to the left, was the plain white slab of Carrara stone, and beneath it, my mother. I wanted, very badly, to walk over, kneel and put my palms onto the stone, but there was no silence, no space. No time. And now Papi was pushing past me, a pickaxe and a crowbar in his huge, knotted hands. The crowd parted, and I found myself standing in front of a tomb I didn't recognize. It was a serene marble frieze of a young Virgin kneeling in prayer, very simple, very beautiful. I recognized the hand of Andrea Verrocchio straight away. Below the Virgin, the inscription read: *This is the one I esteem, he who is humble and contrite in spirit, and trembles at my word*. Just as I was wondering why exactly we were wasting our time on the least humble and contrite man I had ever known, Papi's crowbar smashed into the marble rectangle set into the floor below the inscription, and then the pickaxe, in the hands of a man who looked as if he pulled the heads off pigs for a living, came down next to it. Again and again, metal against stone, sparks and sugary marble chips flying. The slab cracked across the middle in a jagged line. Papi grunted, bent down, shoved the bar into the crack and levered one half up. Instantly, ten or more hands grabbed it, threw it aside, then stooped and wrenched up the other piece. I peered – every soul in the church craned forward, peered down into the neat slot in the floor.

A dusty plank of wood. Papi and the other man knelt, reached down . . . 'What the dick are you doing?' I said into the sudden hush. Nobody paid me any attention. All eyes were on the two straining men. There was a splintering, a creaking.

'The rope! Give me the rope!' demanded Papi. Someone handed him a coil of thick builders' rope. He bent again. I was suddenly conscious of a savage reek in the air, a sweet, meaty foulness. 'Let's have you, you traitorous old wineskin,' muttered Papi. Then he stood up, wiped his hands on his hose. He threw the rope into the crowd. Hands reached, fought for it. The rope went tight, and then, up from the grave, a shape rose, bound tightly in yellowed, stained linen. Up and up it came, the dreadful thing, sliding up into the light, a long, supple slug. The outline of crossed arms, the sunken hollow below it, dreadfully marked with dark fluids; and the head, earless in its wrappings, without a nose, the linen tight across open lips.

'*Palle!*' someone called, then everyone was yelling and crowing. Someone darted out of the crowd and kicked the corpse. Then we were all running down the aisle, the body hissing across the smooth floor, jouncing when it struck a crooked flagstone. Out into the square we burst, the corpse hurtling over the three shallow steps. The linen split and an arm, black but still plump, with a leathery sheen, came free and began to flop and flap. Now everybody was rushing forward to kick, to thrash with sticks, stones, flowerpots. The shroud peeled back, and I caught a last glimpse of Bartolo Baroni's face before the crowd ran out of the little square, leaving me alone with the shivering horse. Baroni, dead and rotting, had looked almost exactly as he had in Assisi when he'd seen me across the crowded dining room: dark with blood, shocked and furious. I was sick against the wall of the church.

Then I went back to the *palazzo*. It was quiet now. Someone had left a crude yellow and red Medici scarf on the ground. I tied it around my neck, secured the horse in the courtyard away from the dead man, and went in through the front door. It had been ransacked. Not a hanging remained on the walls, not a scrap of curtain, not one cushion. The portable furniture had gone, the heavy pieces – linen presses, cabinets – prised open. A pool of wine covered the floor. I went upstairs. A woman was cutting down curtains with a butcher's knife, ripping along seams calmly and deliberately. She saw my scarf and went back to work as if it was the most natural thing in the world. Tessina's room – second floor, left-hand side – was bare. The bed was stripped, the drawers empty. I sniffed. The air was quite empty too: none of the smells of a person's chamber were there: yesterday's clothes, the pisspot, slept-in bed linen, candlewax. The other bedchambers had been lived in. Marco's room – I decided it must be his from the hideous black-oak bed and heraldic nonsense painted all over the wall by a talentless hand in the most expensive golds, blues and reds – reeked of copulation, of stale wine and piss. The window was shut. I opened it carefully and left.

The palace of the Butchers' Guild is just across from Orsanmichele. Not very far, on an ordinary day, from the Piazza San Remigio, but on a day like today I rode in a fat loop around the Piazza della Signoria, into parts of Florence I barely knew. How strange, to return from exile, and find your city gone mad, forcing you into alien neighbourhoods: the Wheel, the Ox. Crossing the Via Ghibellina, I glanced east towards Verrocchio's *bottega*. Was he out in the streets? Where was Sandro? Leonardo? The pie shop was shut up, all the cook-shops were closed. The only blood scent in the air was the blood of men. I trotted west, struck a loud, agitated mob close to the *duomo*, yelled '*Palle!*' until I could taste my own blood in the back of my throat. At last, there was the Palazzo dell'Arte dei Beccai, square and functional, as a butcher's palace should be.

The Guild brothers were in the courtyard, gathered around a fire on which a big black pot was steaming. I saw him straight away: my father was holding a dripping lump of boiled beef on the end of a toasting fork and arguing about it with someone. I pushed through the men – some I recognized, some I half knew; but I understood them all – and then Father noticed me. He stopped talking, and rather carefully put the meat back in the pot. He stood for a moment, as if there was something very important going on down there in the *bollito*. When he looked up again . . . *Madonna!* We were both crying, in the middle of all those bull-necked butchers. I took my father in my arms and wept like a little child.

He took my shoulders and held me at arm's length, staring. Why should it have surprised me that he was crying as well? Tears were running down the furrows of his cheeks, furrows that I didn't remember. All the time that had passed was chiselled and planed into his face, so that, in a strange way, he looked like someone else's idea of my father, as if he'd become a sculpture of himself. He lifted his hand and touched the scar on my temple, pinched the strand of grey between his fingers.

'It's you,' he muttered. 'If you were a ghost, you wouldn't look this bad.' Turning his head away, he pulled me to him again.

'It's all right, Papá,' I said.

'I know. I know.' He sniffed, wiped his face gruffly on his sleeve. 'They told me that Bartolo Baroni's son killed you in Assisi.'

'He tried. But he's a liar. What about you? How are you, Papá?'

'As you see me.' He picked up his fork and started prodding at the *bollito*. Then he looked up and almost grinned. 'So he's a liar, eh? Well, well. We held a mass for you, Nino. At San Remigio. That way, I thought you'd be near your mother.' He winced. There were butchers all around us, and they'd suddenly stopped barking and guffawing. Papá winced again. Then he threw the fork into the pot.

'My son's come home,' he announced simply.

We were enveloped in a hot, loud, sweaty maul of Guild members who surrounded us, pounding shoulders as only butchers can, cheering and – it didn't escape my notice – carefully fishing the fork out of the *bollito* pot and making

483

sure all was in order down there. I was trying to tell Papá everything that had happened to me since I'd disappeared. He was nodding, frowning, though perhaps he couldn't even hear me, because everyone was talking at once, demanding to know what had happened to me, where I'd been, about that *frocio* Baroni, about Assisi, about Rome, about the *beffa*, my original sin. In one way I might never have left, in another I really had come back from the dead. It turned out that my father had just finished a two-month term as prior in the government. He was high up in the Arte now. Messer Lorenzo was good to him after you . . . *fucked up*, I saw in their eyes, but it wasn't ill meant. Time had made the pathetic dupe I'd been back then into a lucky rogue. I'd returned to Florence with La Fortuna hanging off my arm.

Loaves of bread were being torn up and bits dipped into the steaming broth. 'Papá, is Carenza . . .'

'Carenza? She's well. Slightly blind in one eye. You should go and see her.'

I was about to reply when a man who'd bounced me on his knee when I was a baby, now quite bald and with a gap where his front teeth had been, grabbed my cheek and pinched it hard, and at the same time shoved a knuckle-sized, gravy-drenched piece of bread into my mouth. I chewed automatically.

There were the subtle malts and brans of the crust and the pallid no-taste of good old Florentine bread. The snaking sour-sweet of the beef, like a slab of porphyry shot through with crystalline onion sugars, salt and soil-rolled toffee carrots; sparks of bitter thyme and mint oils; the velvet honeycomb of fat; and under it all . . .

'*Battuta!*' I said.

'*Battuta?* Why wouldn't there be *battuta*?' The man shook his head, baffled. But the city was . . . It was there. It wasn't broken at all. It had just been punched down, like risen dough, and now it was rising again, all around me. Or perhaps it wasn't the city. Perhaps it was just life. But something was rushing back into me. I took the fork, pulled out a bit of beef, took off a corner.

'This isn't yours, Papá,' I said, chewing. 'It's Federighi's.'

'It's not – it's Spicchio's,' said somebody.

'Yes, but Spicchio gets his steers from the man Federighi used to use.' Spicchio agreed that this was the case. It turned out that Federighi was, alas, dead. So were many others. Half the people I'd known as a boy seemed to have gone . . . But that could all wait.

'Where is Tessina Albizzi? That is, Tessina Baroni? Is it true she married Marco?' I said, to anybody who caught my eye.

She's gone. Left Florence. That beast, that dog, that swine . . . Finished, the Baronis and all their kind . . . Don't know what happened to Donna Tessina. Poor girl. What a fool you made of yourself, Nino, eh, remember? But she'd have done better with you after all . . .

'Do people remember that . . . that thing? Messer Lorenzo's *beffa*?' I asked my father when I'd managed to fight my way back to his side.

'They sing songs about it,' he said, and his mouth puckered as if he'd just bitten into a lemon. 'But it's been the making of you. You're a man.'

'I cooked a banquet for the Holy Father,' I said. 'Twice. I thought of Mamma. I think it would have pleased her.'

'It would have.' He nodded. 'But you left Rome. Did something happen?' he added bluntly.

'No. I mean, not like that. I came back for Tessina. I'm a fool. But I didn't think I had anybody. I thought I was alone, Papá.'

'And I thought *I* was alone. I *was* alone, these past seven years. We were both wrong.' He crossed himself. 'What are you going to do?'

'I must find her!' I said. 'The Baroni house is being looted. It's empty – Marco's gone. Is he dead?'

'We'd have heard,' said Spicchio, and spat, venomously, behind him. 'He was one of the bastards in the *duomo*. One of the ones that killed poor Francesco Nori.'

'Who?' I said, confused.

'Nori. Head of the Medici bank here in Florence.'

'And Giuliano?' I thought of the young man – a boy, really – I used to see in the Palazzo de' Medici.

'Dead. Butchered. By that . . .' There were no words, plainly. He groaned, and shook his head. 'By Pazzi. Lorenzo got a wound in his neck, but he's all right. At the palace. We all saw him on the balcony. Christ, it was mad! They rang the *Vacca*.' The *Vacca*, the Cow, was the great warning bell in the tower of the Signoria. 'Those *carnaiuoli* of Pazzis went riding around, yelling "*Popolo e Libertà*" . . . Francesco Pazzi went home to bed, the *fica*. Killed beautiful Giuliano, then went to bed. When they dropped him out of the window . . .'

'He was smiling, the prick,' said someone else.

'But Marco?' I tried again.

'He went home as well, God knows why – thick as pigshit, these bastards. I suppose he thought it was done and to-morrow he'd be *gonfaloniere*. Then he changed his mind – he was just slipping out the back door when the crowd saw him. They caught him too, for a moment.'

'Beat the tripe out of him,' said an old man called Benci. He must have been eighty at least, but he was waving his bony fists like a prizefighter. 'Stabbed him!'

'But he got hold of someone's sword, killed two good men and ran away. He won't escape, though. He's already a dead man.'

'They dug up Bartolo,' I told them. 'I saw it. I think they've hung his corpse from the Signoria.'

'Too late. He died in his bed,' muttered Papá.

'Listen, friends! Where's Tessina?' I demanded.

'No one's seen her,' said Spicchio. 'There was a marriage – Marco marched her into Santa Croce and there were vows said – but after that, nothing.'

'*Dio* . . . Is she . . . is she dead?'

'He might have killed her,' someone said. Someone else agreed with him but disagreement was louder. 'No, she's gone,' they chorused. 'Old Diamante had that *castello* in Greve – perhaps she went there.' *No, no, we'd have heard, he'd have fetched her back, the dirty beast* . . . 'There wasn't a door in Florence that wouldn't have been open to her,' added Spicchio. 'Everybody knew that little runt forced her to the altar.'

I noticed that my father was trying to catch my eye. He slipped out of the crowd, and I shouldered through men who were arguing about everything, it seemed, that had ever happened in Florence. Papá was waiting for me in the little bit of cloister that the Guild had been meaning to demolish for years.

'What are you going to do with your money?' He tapped the jingling bag at my waist. 'Thieves will be shouting *Palle* too, you know.'

I was back. Back in practical Florence, city of banks. 'Can I leave it here? In the strong room?' He nodded and I handed it over, seeing with a squeeze of pride how his brows went up as he hefted its weight.

'Are you going to leave again?' he said abruptly.

I shook my head.

'I mean, if you find Marco's wife.'

'It's Tessina, Papá. Tessina Albizzi. She's never been anybody's wife.'

'Now, Nino . . .'

'It's true. I know it, Papá.'

'Still. She's a traitor's wife.'

'Only on paper. And not for long, if I'm not mistaken. Marco will be hanging in the square before nightfall, if he isn't already. That's why I have to find Tessina.'

'And then what? What will you do next, Nino? It's just that I fear you never know. There will always be something else, until you die. Consequences always happen. Perhaps not to you, but they happen.'

'I'm sorry, Papá. I've tried to do the right thing, always, but sometimes I'm not good at knowing what that is.'

'Being right is one thing,' he said. 'Believing that you are right is quite another.'

A runner had just come into the courtyard, and whatever news he'd brought made the butchers roar and cheer. 'Tessina is in the Convent of Santa Bibiana,' he said. 'She joined the day she wed Bartolo's son.'

'Then I've lost her.' I slumped against a column. Papá touched my arm.

'That was six months ago,' he said softly. 'She isn't a nun yet. She's taken no vows. Perhaps she will. Perhaps . . . I'm not a priest, Nino. I'm a butcher. I know about ox hearts, not human ones. Nor do I know what God intends.' Then he brightened. 'Still, it didn't stop your uncle Filippo, did it?'

'No! No, it didn't.'

'And you always took after Filippo. Which pleased your mother, God rest her soul. So . . .'

'So?'

He gripped my shoulder gently. 'I miss your mother,' he said. 'If she was alive, you know what she'd say. And I would disagree with her. But she's gone, and the dead . . . You cannot deny them.'

'Thank you, Papá.'

'I'll be at home.'

'I'll see you there.' I kissed his cheek quickly and went to find my horse.

48

Tʜᴇʀᴇ ᴡᴇʀᴇ ᴅᴇɴsᴇ, ᴀɴɢʀʏ ᴄʀᴏᴡᴅs jamming the Via dei Calzaiuoli, so I headed back across the river. I rode as fast as the crowd would let me, eyes fixed, mind also fixed on a single point. The streets were hardly more real than drawings on a map. I passed the alley that led to the garden wall I'd climbed so eagerly, so long ago; turned the corner, and there was the Convent of Santa Bibiana.

I hesitated . . . But why hesitate? What had the past years been but rough hands shoving me here to this very moment? My fist sounded hollowly against the worm-eaten oak. I banged again, and again, not quite believing that there was anyone, anything beyond the door. But at last there was a grinding of rusty iron, the handle jerked and turned, and the door swung inwards to reveal a small nun. She had cheeks as white and puckered as two poached eggs, and she was standing in a small entrance room with a crucifix as its only decoration. We both stood, staring at each other in consternation.

'Sister,' I said. 'I've come for . . . that is, I've come to see Donna Tessina Albizzi. Or Baroni, as she must be.'

'Who?' The sister sounded absolutely terrified.

'Tessina Baroni. Widow of Bartolo Baroni. She's a novice here.'

'She's not!' The nun took a step back into the shadows. Without thinking I stepped over the threshold towards her. She gave a pitiful little cry and held up her hands. 'No! You can't come in here! This is a house of the Lord! Go away – go *away!*' She stamped her foot in sudden defiance but to my horror I saw that she was crying.

'No, no, sister!' I remembered the blue and yellow scarf on my arm, and the sword hanging against my leg. 'I haven't come because of . . . for the *Palle*, or anything like that. But I have to see her. She knows me. Don't be scared. I'm not one of those men out there.' I wasn't entirely sure what I meant by that, but the little nun seemed to understand. Or perhaps she knew that she couldn't stop me even if she tried. So she waved her hand furiously.

'Shut the door, then! Shut the door! And be quiet!' I did what she told me, as she glowered, a white finger pressed to her lips. Then she turned and bellowed into the passageway that opened into the far wall. 'Mother Abbess! Mother *Abbess*!'

There was a tapping of feet on stone floors, and three more sisters appeared in the doorway. The oldest had a silver cross around her neck, strung on a hempen cord, and had once been beautiful. She regarded me very carefully, the other two sisters twittering behind her skirts.

'Who are you, my son?' she said at last.

'Nino di Niccolaio Latini, Mother Abbess,' I said. 'I'm a friend . . . I used to be a friend of Tessina Albizzi, as she was then. Tessina Baroni. My father told me she came here six months ago. It's very important that I see her.'

'Why? Why so important, that you come here and disturb our peace?'

I wanted to tell her that it was the little sister who had disturbed the peace, but I didn't. Because the Mother Abbess had asked a question which I wasn't sure how to answer, at least not to the satisfaction of an abbess. I had to say something, though.

'I've heard that Donna Tessina came to this place because she needed to be safe from her husband. Donna Tessina does not need to be kept safe from me. There is no man in this wide world who desires her peace and happiness more than I.'

'Latini? The butcher's son?' one of the sisters whispered. There was some muffled twittering and perhaps a giggle.

'Mother Abbess, is Tessina Baroni a novice here or not?' I said, unable to bear this any longer.

'No.' The abbess touched her thumbs together gently and looked down at her feet. Then she put a hand to her cross.

'Tessina isn't a novice,' she said. 'She is a postulant. You may see her. If you leave your sword with Sister Abbondanza.' The little nun who had opened the door stepped forward and narrowed her eyes at me. I shrugged, and unbuckled my sword. When I passed it to her it seemed ridiculously large in her hands.

'She's with Sister Beatrice. Follow me.'

I was led down a corridor to the back of the building, past the kitchens and laundry room. Sister Beatrice, though: surely she had been dying six years ago . . . We stepped through an archway into a long, low-ceilinged room that was clean but obviously disused, like most of the convent.

I opened the door. There was barely space for the bed that took up most of the floor. On the bed was a tiny, shrunken woman with a blindingly white sheet pulled up to her chin, wearing a white coif and her head resting on a pillow of bleached linen. At her side, sitting on a three-legged stool, was Tessina. She was wearing an old grey tunic and her hair was bound up in a white coif like that of Sister Beatrice, tied under her chin. I hesitated. Was it her, after all? This woman had dismal shadows under her eyes, which looked tired and resigned. But I recognized the amused shape of her mouth, the curve of her nose. She was holding the old nun's tiny hand, and the two of them had obviously been deep in conversation, because they both turned towards the door, looking startled, as I closed it behind me.

No one said anything. I stood in the doorway, as the nun and Tessina regarded me. I knew I looked bad, of course: I'd slept in my clothes for more than a week, I hadn't shaved since God knew when. I had grey hair and a scar.

'This must be Nino.' It was the nun who had spoken. Her voice was as tiny as she was, high and almost insubstantial. I realized that she was staring at me and then she smiled. 'I'm right,' she said. 'Am I, dearest? Is this the one?'

'It can't be him,' said Tessina, very quietly.

I couldn't speak, so I held up my hand, stupidly. The nun raised hers, no bigger than a blackbird's skeleton, and beckoned to me.

'Come and sit,' she said. 'I am sorry if I upset you. God has chosen one thing for my body and quite another for my mind. I find it peaceful, but it scares the young. All except for my lily here,' she added, and patted Tessina's hand.

She had unlocked my tongue. 'You don't alarm me at all, Sister,' I said, and sat down carefully next to her. The room was so small that my knees were almost touching Tessina's thigh. I looked at her and she blushed, her lower lip caught behind her teeth.

'Talk to him, then, girl!' The nun batted Tessina's hand like a kitten with its plaything. 'He isn't dead. He weighs too much for a ghost. Look at my sheets.'

'It's not Nino Latini, Sister Beatrice,' said Tessina. 'It isn't. It's some man about the . . . about the troubles.'

'Tessina, it's me. I didn't die. I can't have, can I? I'm here.'

'Talk to him,' said Sister Beatrice loudly.

Tessina took a deep breath. 'Hello, Nino,' she said. 'If it is you?'

'I came to find you. From Rome,' I said.

493

'From Rome.' She took a sharp, shallow breath. 'But I thought . . . Marco said . . .'

'That he'd killed me. Everyone believed him, didn't they? The whole city.'

'Nino, I saw Marco when they carried him back to that inn. He could barely speak. I thought he was dying – and then Corso really was dead – but the only thing he said was that he'd done for you. I believed him!'

'Just because Marco said so?'

'Because Marco has killed men! And Nino never – you never hurt anyone!'

'But where was my body?' I pressed.

'Bartolo said the Assisi magistrates had taken you and thrown you into a pit.' She let go of the old nun's hand and stood up so suddenly that her stool fell. She slumped against the wall, her face in her hands. 'It wasn't my fault!' She began to sob bitterly. 'None of it was my fault!'

'Oh, Tessina! Of course it wasn't! I never—'

'You're dead! You're dead, you bastard!'

'For heaven's sake, girl.' Sister Beatrice's voice, tiny though it was, still managed to silence us. 'If you can't believe a man can rise from the grave, you've no business in a place like this, my dear.'

'Sister Beatrice, I'm sorry! But what's happening? Why is everything so terrible?'

'Terrible? You were waiting for him, and now he's come!' She waved her hand in my direction. 'Ignore me. I'm dying, you know.'

'I've been waiting . . .' said Tessina. She turned. 'Yes. I have. Nino . . .'

No matter what had passed, no matter what I had dreamed, wished, prayed, conjured, pleaded for; all the things I had expected and imagined: it wasn't like that. I took her in my arms and she was tiny, her bones a shock beneath my hands, her warmth, the cheapness of her nun's tunic. But when she looked up at me, it was Tessina. Not the woman I'd seen in Assisi, whose face was painted onto every wall of my mind, but the Tessina of this moment. I undid the ends of her coif and pulled it from her head, releasing ropes of gold, tangled, matted, but enough to stop my heart. I took her face in my hands, hardly daring to touch it, and kissed her.

'You taste the same,' I said, in wonder.

'So this strange gentleman is your dear one after all?' said the nun, as if nothing extraordinary was happening.

'Yes,' said Tessina. 'I think it is.' I could barely breathe. 'I think it is,' she repeated. 'He's . . . He's a bit dirty, though. He didn't always look like this.'

'He isn't quite how I'd imagined him,' piped the old lady.

'What?' I looked at Tessina, shocked. 'You've been talking about me? About *you* and me?'

'Oh, yes,' she answered. 'Sister Beatrice has heard so much about you. More or less everything, in fact.' The nun was chuckling silently to herself.

'Then you'll know that we did something wrong,' I told her.

'A kiss is wrong? A thought is wrong?' The old woman shook her head, but she was smiling.

'It must have been, because God has punished me for it, and I deserved it. But you have to understand, Sister, that I've always loved her. Always. It isn't just love, it's . . . It has no value in the calculations of men, as I've come to understand them. But it is everything.' I stopped, thinking I'd gone too far, but Tessina laid her head against my chest and closed her eyes.

'You're mistaken about the Lord, Nino,' said Sister Beatrice. 'He sees love. He values it.'

'That's not what the Church says.'

'Isn't it? I am a nun, yes. And a virtuous one. But I do not believe that the Lord wants us all to renounce the body. He does nothing in vain, and if He gave us flesh that can feel the ecstasies of pleasure as well as suffering, we should embrace his gift.'

'Does anybody else know that?'

'About me? Oh, of course! Why do you think they have exiled me to this cold corner? And why do you think that they approve of the ministrations of this chaste and virtuous young woman? For the good of my soul! And it does me so much good, my dear. It truly does.' She took Tessina's hand in both of her own. 'Like attracts like, they say. I never thought this girl should lock herself away in a place like this. But when she fled here from that brute, that brother-in-law husband, when she said she wanted to join our order, I thought that perhaps, if I had served my Lord faithfully all these years, and still chose not to renounce the pleasures He invested in it – not to indulge them, but also not to call them sinful or deny them their reality – then Tessina could do the same. But my dear child, I am so glad you have arrived to save her. It's too late for me. But not for you. Be happy for all time. Love is everything.'

'But you're married, Tessina.'

'That means nothing to me.' There was an anger in her voice that I'd never heard before. 'Do you love me, Nino? Do you still love me?'

'I would die, now, if you couldn't be mine. Nothing else matters any more.'

'I should take her away, if I were you,' said Sister Beatrice. 'No vows broken. No harm done. Leave, my sweet ones. And may God rain his blessings upon you.'

Tessina knelt by the bed and kissed the old woman gently on the brow. I took one of her almost weightless hands and kissed it. Her skin had no more body than the ghosts of burned paper you find in cold hearths, that crumble to the touch. Tessina picked up a linen satchel that had been under her chair, took my hand and led me out of the little room. I expected the nuns to be clustered, eavesdropping, outside the door. I guessed they had been, because my sword was propped against the wall. But the passageway was empty.

'Come with me,' said Tessina, and took my hand again. I grabbed my sword and followed her up a corridor to a narrow door. She opened it and there outside was the garden, even less tended than it had been. We had to pick our way through tangled snares of bramble and thorn seedlings. And there, beyond the vines, was the hermit's cell.

'It's still there,' I said, amazed. 'I thought it would have fallen down by now.'

'Nino, we'll go away, to wherever you want to take me. But my love, there's something I have to do first. You have to trust me.'

'I trust you.'

'Then you need to put everything behind you. Everything.' Her eyes were pleading. 'Do you still trust me?'

'Always.'

'Then come.'

The door of the hermitage was barely attached to its hinges. Tessina pushed it open gently and stepped inside and I followed. The smell − dry wood, spiders − was the same. And there, in the corner . . .

Tessina took hold of my wrist and held it, hard. 'Nino . . .' she said. And then I saw him.

Marco Baroni was hunched against the disintegrating plaster. I knew it was him because of the thick, chopped-off crown of hair. There was no one else in Florence with such ugly hair. My hand was around the hilt of my sword and I was already drawing it when Tessina threw herself on me.

'Don't, Nino! Don't! Stop. Look at him.'

497

I kept my hand on the hilt but I stopped. And forced myself to look. Marco was completely still except for the rise and fall of his chest. He was curled into a ball, his arms hiding his face. He had dressed in his finest clothes yesterday to go out and murder, but now they were torn almost to pieces and stained with blood and gutter filth. One foot was bare and the leg as well, up to the knee, a mass of bruises and welts. His arms, too, were bruised and bandaged, now soaked through with blood.

'What is he doing here? What does this mean?' I hissed.

'Do you still trust me?'

'Yes.' I let go of my sword.

'He came here yesterday night. To find me, I suppose. God in his mercy knows, but I don't. The Mother Abbess took him in.'

'Why?'

'Out of duty. It's her vow, not to turn away the needy. I think he came to speak to me, but he couldn't say anything. We've hidden him out here. He's terribly hurt.'

'He tried to kill Messer Lorenzo!'

'And now he's dying.'

She fell silent and we both stood, staring at the man on the floor. There was a tiny sound in the room and I realized that it was Marco's breath, scraping in and out. Tessina squatted down next to him. Very gently she pulled his hand away from his face. He looked at her in terror, then at me, and pressed himself even further into the corner, sitting in a pool of blood, some of it clotted, some of it fresh. Tessina rummaged in her satchel and took out a cloth and a stoppered flask. She opened it, poured out water onto the cloth and wiped Marco's face. He tried, feebly, to push her away, muttering something. Tessina bent her head.

'Food . . .' he said hoarsely. But the effort was too much.

His legs came out from under him and he slid down the wall until he was lying in his own blood.

'Marco? Marco, listen to me! I'm coming back, with food. I'll be a moment.' She stood up and whispered in my ear: 'Nino, stay with him. I have to get Mother Abbess. He's going to die.' She grabbed my hands and held them up to her face for a moment. Then she was gone.

I stood in the doorway, feeling the weight of the sword on my belt, remembering . . . Marco stirred, tried to lift his head. It fell back onto the stone. How small he was. How alone. I found myself kneeling beside him, next to the broken bed. He was grimacing with pain, his brutal face barely human. He groaned. I reached out, reluctantly, and took his hand. His fingers tensed and then he gripped mine weakly.

'It's all right,' I muttered. 'It's all right.'

There was a sound behind me and I turned to find Tessina, alone. She was holding a cup and something wrapped in a clean white napkin.

'I couldn't find Mother Abbess,' she said. 'So I took these.' She held out the cup. It had red wine in it.

'The Host,' she said. 'Left over from yesterday. Mass was interrupted by . . . by . . .'

'Tessina,' I said. 'We shouldn't do this, should we? There has to be a priest.'

'I don't think it's even been blessed,' she whispered, uncertainly. 'But even if he just thinks – surely?'

'Perhaps,' I said. 'You'd better do it, then.'

She knelt, reached for the cup, drew back her hand. 'I can't,' she said. 'I thought I'd be able to but I can't.'

I was still holding Marco's hand, but it was barely grasping mine, and the pulse ticking at the base of his thumb had gone very faint. 'Let me,' I said.

It was strange to touch the Host with anything other than

my lips. I took the milk-white disc and broke off a small piece. Marco's lips were slightly open. I dipped the bread into the wine and put it between his teeth. His eyes fluttered, opened, flickered from side to side and alighted on me.

'Eat, Marco,' I whispered. 'It's good. Just take a little bit.'

He tried to chew. I cupped my hand under his head, lifted it and poured a tiny trickle of wine into his mouth. He swallowed, stared into my face. *What does it taste like?* I wondered. *What is taste, to the dying? Is it food, or something to carry you away?*

'The body of Christ,' I said softly. He licked his lips, still staring at me, and smiled. His eyelids started to flutter.

'May the Lord protect you and lead you into life eternal,' I said into his ear.

'He's dead, Nino,' said Tessina.

I opened my eyes. Marco's face had surrendered some of its rage, at last. I crossed myself and wiped a drop of wine from his chin.

'Please come away with me now,' I said to Tessina.

'I can. Oh God.' She buried her face in her sleeve and her shoulders began to shake. 'God. Now I can.'

We went over the wall. I showed Tessina where to put her feet, how the old fig was a crooked ladder. I jumped down into the dark, fetid alley and swung her to the ground. Then we ran, hand in hand, to the corner, past the step where the crone had always sat, empty now, and round to the next corner.

The house across from the convent was blazing, flame roaring from its windows. Men were running around with buckets. My horse was nearby in a group of other terrified beasts, and a tall red-haired boy was stroking his nose. I ran over, gave him a *scudo* and told him to bring the horse to the Palazzo Latini in Borgo Santa Croce. He nodded, persuaded by my *Palle* token. Then Tessina and I walked to the river, across the Porta Santa Trinità, through the *mercato* to the Piazza della Signoria, where all Florentines end up sooner or later. As we walked across, heading for the streets of the Black Lion, I looked up at the wall of the Signoria. The bodies were hanging quite still. Marco would end up there too, as soon as he was found. There weren't as many people in the square. People had set up stalls and meat was grilling, soup was steaming. At the corner of the palace a large man stood, looking up, looking down. His thick yellow curls shook whenever his head moved.

'Sandro!' said Tessina.

He turned. 'Good Lord!' he shouted. 'Tessina Baroni! And . . . *Madonna mia*! Nino?' He grabbed me and almost cracked my ribs with his embrace. 'I thought . . .'

'I'm not dead,' I told him. 'I shall have to have it announced.'

'And the lady! You've been hidden from me, dearest one. Locked away from your Sandro. My art has turned to shit since you left me.'

'Nonsense. You're the richest painter in Florence,' she said.

'An indication of the debased tastes of my patrons, not my withered talents,' he said. 'Look what I've been reduced to.' He held out his notebook. It was filled with sketches of the hanging dead. 'An instant commission from Il Magnifico. I'm going to paint these brutes on the wall there,' he said, pointing to the wall of the *dogana*. 'Look up there: how Salviati bites Pazzi's corpse.'

There were the faces I had last seen in the grotto on the Colle Oppio. Salviati, still in his archbishop's robes, hung next to the naked body of Francesco Pazzi, his teeth fixed in Pazzi's left breast.

'Is that my husband?' said Tessina queasily. 'I never

thought I'd see him again in this life. Nino, can you take me away from here?'

'Go, go,' said Sandro. 'I'll paint you. Of course I'll paint everyone, living and dead. But you, Donna Tessina, I shall *paint*! What are you going to do in the meantime?'

'We're going to get married,' I said.

'As soon as we can,' said Tessina.

'Really?' I said.

'Don't you want to?'

'But I haven't asked you properly!'

It was Tessina again, the Tessina from long ago, from the hermit's hut, from the market, holding out stolen fruit for me to taste.

'Properly?' she said. 'I've lost a husband today, another has risen from the grave, and you weren't dead at all. My life has become a *beffa*! I think you'd better act fast, Nino, before something even stranger happens.'

'Tomorrow, then.'

'Good. And no trumpeters.'

'I swear it.'

We kissed then, properly. Nobody noticed except for Sandro Botticelli, and he didn't see things the way other men did. A man kissing a nun in the middle of the Piazza della Signoria, under a pergola of dead men. It could never happen again, not in a thousand lifetimes. Florence spread away around us: the walls, the towers, the flags. The hot lard, the onions, parsley, beet leaves, the *battuta*: because Florence had begun to cook its dinner. It had all gone on too long, this nonsense. Time to go home, or to a taverna, or to a cook-shop, and eat. And then, tomorrow, life would begin again. And there would be a wedding in the church of San Remigio, where hopefully a hole in the floor would have been mended. But tonight the bride and groom would be eating in the kitchen of an old palace on the Borgo Santa

Croce. There would be things to learn, things to tell. Tastes, missed for so long, to be rediscovered. But for now, there was the nun and the cook, and the rest was just noise.

49

THAT EVENING, MARCO BARONI'S CORPSE was taken from the Convent of Santa Bibiana, dragged through Oltrarno and over the Ponte Vecchio to the rope that was waiting for it in the Piazza della Signoria. When it dropped, so they say, all the crows that had been swarming over the other bodies screamed and flew away, and didn't return to the feast for a day afterwards. It wasn't true, but what did that matter? The city needed monsters, and Marco Baroni was a better one than most. Sandro painted Marco's body on the wall of the *dogana* along with the rest of the traitors, so that Tessina was forced to walk past her first two husbands whenever she went up the Via dei Gondi — until, that is, they were painted over in the year the French emperor entered our city. And because Sandro had painted them, they might have been the dead flesh itself, preserved by some necromancy, so that they haunted the city. You could smell them, almost, though they were nothing but pigment and plaster. So they passed into the city's memory, and so they will always be. Better, I say, to remember than to be remembered.

The priest of San Remigio wouldn't marry us until Marco was buried, and it was a week before they took down what was left of him and threw it into the Arno, which was good enough for the priest, though not for the children of San Frediano, who found him washed up on the bank and dragged him around the streets on the end of a rope until their fathers made the Signoria bury him again in a ditch far outside the walls. By then, though, Bartolo's empty grave had been repaired and filled with someone else, and Andrea

Verrocchio had sent his men to chisel the old brute's monument from the wall. It was a small wedding: Papá, Carenza, Maddalena Albizzi – Diamante having died a few months before Bartolo – my uncle Terino and his wife; Sandro Botticelli, Leonardo from Vinci, Andrea Verrocchio. Leonardo had wanted to design a special carriage for us to sit in, 'Some sort of crawling wagon with feet,' as Sandro had explained it.

'Dogs' feet?' I'd wondered, remembering how carefully he'd once drawn his little dog in Andrea's studio.

'No. Swan, I think. Said something about traction. Amazing drawings, but honestly . . . He needs to calm down, that one.'

There was no white horse this time, no golden cloak. No trumpets. Until it was over, though, until the ring was on Tessina's hand and the priest was saying the last words of the rite, I half expected for Tessina to pull off her mask and reveal herself as Lorenzo de' Medici or for Bartolo to bob up from under the floor. But nothing happened, and when we stepped outside into the little square, the Black Lion was going about its business as always. We ate a banquet at my father's house, which would be our home now. Tessina should, by rights, have been rich, but the Signoria had seized everything that could be traced to the Baroni family. The palace, the estates in the Mugello and Chianti: it was all in the hands of the republic. Even her father's castle in Greve was gone. Tessina herself, though, was quite safe. The Gonfaloniere di Giustizia had even published an edict that exonerated Donna Tessina from any of the crimes of her husbands. In fact, to the people of the Black Lion and even further afield, she was much admired. Everybody seemed to know that neither of her husbands had ever had their way with her, and that she'd maintained her virginity in spite of being under constant assault from two such monsters . . . So it was that I married a famous virgin.

Tessina's fame had all but wiped away the memory of my humiliation, the *beffa* of Helen and Paris. The *beffa* itself was remembered fondly, but the truth seemed to have remoulded itself. Now it was recalled as a master stroke of Messer Lorenzo against his arch-enemy Baroni. Bartolo had been the victim of the joke, it was explained, and to most people my part became as important as that of the actor wearing Lorenzo's armour: a prop – a good one, to be sure – but no more than that. One person remembered, though. Waiting for us at home after the wedding was a beautiful carved and painted chest, and when we opened it we found a carefully folded golden cloak and a necklace of gold and jewels: interlocking leaves of gold and gemstone grapes, and hanging from them, a swan of gold, enamelled all over with black and studded with pearls. And lying beneath the necklace, the deed to the Palazzo Baroni, now called Palazzo Latini-Albizzi, made over to Tessina and authorized by the careful, elegant signature of Laurentis Medicea, Lorenzo Il Magnifico.

I don't remember the banquet itself: through some caprice of memory not one single taste remains. I know it must have been good, because Carenza oversaw the cooking of it: dear Carenza, who had grown a little larger, a little softer, but still as sharp-tongued as ever, who, when she saw me walk into the kitchen, had dropped her knife into the pile of onions she was slicing, pushed her scarf up and off her forehead, revealing hair now shot through with white, and said, quite calmly:

'*Madonna* . . . And I was just talking to your dear mother about you.'

'Talking with Mamma?' I asked, standing, open-mouthed, in the kitchen door.

'Not *with* her, *pazzo*! What do you take me for? And

506

besides, who doesn't talk to the dead? I talk to you often enough.'

'But I'm alive, Carenza!' I'd run over and pulled her against me, and she was exactly as she always had been.

'I knew it. I always knew it,' she'd said again and again, as she covered my face with kisses that were hard enough to hurt. 'They told me, and I said, no, that boy's too mad to die.'

Perhaps I don't remember the banquet dishes because I don't have to. I see silver, and flowers, and fruit, and steam. I see the wine falling from jug into cup, and hear the chink of knives against plates. I see my father, smiling; I see Carenza, a cataract beginning to film one eye, sitting with us as an honoured guest and not a servant. I see Tessina's hand on the white tablecloth, skin almost as white. I can touch it whenever I want, reach out a fingertip and touch. I didn't need anything else then, and I've never needed more since. Wanted, yes, and received, *grazie a Dio*! But needed? What more could a man dare to require? In this world it is not the usual lot of broken things to be made whole again, but I was. So perhaps I don't remember the feast because I sat down to it without hunger. Appetite must have a moment when it is sated, or it becomes a kind of madness. It becomes ruin.

I do remember a taste from those days after I came home, though. I woke alone, because Tessina had slipped downstairs some time between midnight and dawn to the room Carenza had prepared for her. We had both agreed that Carenza was the one person in Florence we could not cross, no matter what sacrifices that might demand. But before we satisfied convention we satisfied ourselves, in my bed, in the room that my father had left untouched since the day I'd fled from the *beffa*. And the next day I dragged Tessina out into the city, because there was one thing above all else that I needed to do.

The *mercato* was the same as it had ever been. Perhaps there was more pigeon shit on Dovizia's gilded shoulders, but there were the stalls, with their keepers shouting out familiar words; there were the whores in the windows of the Malvagia, the *bardasse* heading for Baldracca in the hopes of an early-morning dalliance. Spring vegetables were piled up in shades of brightest green. It was too early for fruit, but there were wrinkled morels, tiny yellow carrots, shoots of every possible kind. I led Tessina along the rows towards the far south-western corner of the square, but we were still only part way across when I stopped.

'Where is he?' I said, half to myself.

'Where's who?' asked Tessina.

'Ugolino!' I said.

'Tripe? At this hour? What did they do to you in Rome?'

'Not tripe. Ugolino's tripe. Where is he?'

'Look, there's a fellow over there selling beef tendon. Have some of that.'

'It has to be Ugolino,' I said, shaking my head. 'I wonder where he is? He's always here. Always. Come on.'

I pulled the sceptical Tessina along with me, over to the place where Ugolino's stall had always been, as permanent as Dovizia's column. His tall figure, long spoon in hand, had stood here in all weathers, and I half expected his shadow to be visible on the dirty cobbles. But instead there was another stall, a man selling roasted chickpeas.

'Listen,' I demanded. 'Where's Ugolino moved to?'

'Who?' said the man rudely, enough of an expert to know that we weren't about to buy any of his chickpeas – which did, however, smell good: of earth, hazelnuts, last year's sunshine.

'Ugolino. Ugolino the tripe seller. You're on his pitch.'

'What, *bastardo*? This is my pitch.'

'Mind your tongue!'

Things might have taken an unfortunate turn at that point, but just then a wide-hipped woman in a bloodstained apron bustled over, a dead partridge dangling from one large hand.

'Ugolino? Where've you been, sir? He's been gone a year.'

'Gone? What do you mean, gone?' I snapped.

'I mean dead. He died right there.' The game seller pointed to where the chickpea seller was puffing out his chest, and he stepped back hurriedly, looking down at the ground as if there might still be a corpse under his stall.

'Jesus!' I let my hands drop to my sides. My eyes were burning and my throat was tight.

'What's the matter, Nino? We can get tripe!' said Tessina, stroking my arm gently. 'You're back in Florence! There's tripe everywhere!'

'I know, I know . . . But he *was* Florence, Tessina! I've tried to make his *trippa* so many times, and I've never managed it. I was going to come back here and finally – *finally* – see if I could get his secret from him. Or just have a bowl. That would have been enough. I don't need to make it myself now, I just need to taste it!'

'What a lot of fuss!' said the game seller. 'Over poor old Ugolino. Did he have a secret? Was he hiding something?'

'His recipe.'

'*Pazzo* . . . go to Remigio over there! What's wrong with his? Best in the city!'

'The signora's right, Nino,' said Tessina. 'I'm sorry about your friend, though.'

'The trouble is that he wasn't my friend, dear one. He was more than that. And he's gone. I can't believe it. I wanted to tell him something. It was really . . . it was important to me.'

'You could tell his wife, I suppose,' said the game seller.

'He had a wife?' said Tessina, curious.

'*Madonna!* Yes, he had a wife! I thought you knew him? Dear God . . .'

'Where does she live?' said Tessina, ignoring her.

'Ulivetta? She lives just beyond Santa Maria Novella.'

'I should go and see her,' I mumbled.

'Why not? She'd be glad of the company, poor old thing. It's been hard on her, Ugolino dying like that.'

'What was wrong with him?'

'Nothing but age and standing here every day for half a century. Go and see Ulivetta. Past the church, down the weavers' street until you come to the end. There's a big old oak tree, and a house next to it. That's where Ugolino lived.'

West of Santa Maria Novella, the city is hardly a city at all. The people who had lived there, once upon a time, had all died in the *peste nera*, and now it was fields and gardens, but mostly the ground was fallow and deserted, home to a few horses and cattle, a lot of goats and to hundreds of pigs who fed on all the rubbish the city threw into the waste spaces. It wasn't somewhere I'd ever really gone, because there was no reason to; and besides, the boys of the Unicorn neighbourhood didn't like us easterners. So I was feeling as nervous as I might have done as an eighteen-year-old as I walked, arm in arm with Tessina, down the shabby street of the weavers.

'I know I'm acting like a madman,' I said to her. 'But after I . . . After I had to leave, it was as if I hadn't completely gone from here.'

'What do you mean?' Tessina asked.

'Well, my heart was with you.'

'I know. I kept it hidden in my linen chest.'

'Thank you for looking after it so well. The rest of me, though . . . When you went to Assisi, did it feel strange to leave here? To leave Florence?'

'It did. Very strange. I didn't really feel comfortable from the start. Or safe . . . I was adrift.'

We left the houses and made our way along a rutted lane to the oak tree, which was certainly much older than the *peste nera*. There beside it was a tiny house built out of scavenged stone, almost as old as the tree. A gnarled grape vine, its trunk as thick as Tessina's waist, rose up next to the door and spread its many fingers out over a rickety frame of wooden poles. We ducked under the veil of leaves and I knocked. There was a shuffling from inside and the door opened a crack, revealing the smoke-streaked, red-eyed face of a woman in the last years of her middle age.

'Donna Ulivetta? We've come from the market,' I said. 'Can we come in?'

She looked us up and down. We were dressed as gentle-woman and gentleman, and I suppose we looked good enough, at least for her. She opened the door, and fanned the air apologetically with her hands.

'Apologies to you, fine lady and sir. I can't seem to get the fire to stop smoking today. It's the chimney, I suppose. When my husband was alive . . .'

'We heard about your husband,' said Tessina. 'We're very sorry.'

'Sorry? For old Ugolino?' She looked surprised, and were there tears in her eyes, or was that just the smoke?

'I've been away for a long time,' I said. 'And all the time I was away, I thought of your husband's food. I've cooked for cardinals and dukes, signora. I've cooked for His Holiness, and . . .'

'God save us!' She crossed herself vigorously. 'The Holy Father?'

'I did. But I would have served His Holiness your husband's *trippa* if I could.'

'What's your name, sir?'

'Nino Latini. I used to be cook at the Taverna Porco. My father is Latini of Latini *e figlio* on the bridge.'

'Latini . . . The Porco, was it? Really? I know you, sir!'

'I don't think so, signora.'

'No, I do! My husband talked about you.'

'About me?' I stared at her. The smoke was starting to sting my eyes too.

'Of course, sir! The butcher's son who ate his *trippa* and his *lampredotto* as if it was – he used to say, "as if it was the elixir of life". It made him happy, sir.'

Happy . . . Tessina was holding my hand and I squeezed it, hard. I'd never thought of Ugolino being happy or sad. Or cold, or hot, come to that. I'd thought of him as a genius, but not as a man.

'Signora, this is a strange request, but do you have the recipe for Maestro Ugolino's *trippa*?' I said tremulously.

'Maestro?' The woman was aghast. 'He was a market tripe seller!'

'But he was as great a maestro as any I've known.'

'Dear God . . . How he'd have loved to speak to you. You must know the recipe, if you've cooked for His Holiness.'

'To my sorrow, I don't.'

'It's just *trippa*, sir! Tripes, which we washed out in front, at the well. A ham bone – but you know that. A boiling hen, three calf's feet. White wine—'

'Which you made from the vine outside?' I interrupted, eagerly.

'Mercy, sir! That old thing barely kept us in wine. No, from whoever had the best price. Saffron, a little tiny bit. And then nothing but long pepper, sage and mint, and salt.'

'It's the mint!' I burst out. 'What mint, signora? What kind of mint?'

'*Nipitella* from the market,' she said patiently. 'Just food, sir. Just plain food.' Then she brightened. 'Ugolino would have been so happy to tell you this himself, sir,' she said. 'But would you like something, to remember him by?' She didn't wait for an answer, but went over to the set of plank shelves leaning on the wall next to the smoking fireplace and reached up on tiptoe, scrabbling for something on the top shelf.

'Got you, you old thing,' she muttered. When she turned, she was holding Ugolino's long, slightly bent spoon of olive wood.

'He'd have been proud for a proper maestro to have this,' she said. 'If you'll use it?'

'I will,' I said, taking it in my hands as if it were the leg bone of a saint. 'If you don't mind?'

'No, no. Take it. To tell you the truth, it makes me a little sad. He'd be so happy.'

Poor Tessina. Having dragged her out into the pig-churned fields of Santa Maria Novella, I dragged her back to the market, bought tripe, already boiled, from a man I'd bought from many times before but who didn't give a flicker of recognition as I paid him; a ham, an old hen, calves' feet, white wine, *nipitella* – the first I came across – and *salvia*. All the while I gripped Ugolino's spoon as a drowning man might clutch a drifting oar. It was smooth as amber and the colour of buckwheat honey, so soaked with oil that the wood seemed to be turning into something else, bone, perhaps. Then back to Borgo Santa Croce, where she stood next to Carenza, looking concerned, as I scrubbed and scrubbed at the tripe, making the whole kitchen smell of it. Then I did as Donna Ulivetta had said.

'Where did you get that monster?' said Carenza, watching me stir the big pot with the long spoon. I felt I should use it, for this at least. Then what? Perhaps I'd put it in a reliquary. It deserved no less.

When the *trippa* was done, it was late afternoon. I ladled out three bowls and Tessina, Carenza and I sat together and sniffed. I had sprinkled cheese and sweet spices on top, as Ugolino would have done.

'It smells good, at least,' said Carenza. 'You fool, did you come all the way back to Florence to cook peasant food?'

Tessina dipped her spoon first. 'It's really good,' she said. 'Perfect *trippa*. You should open a stall, Nino.' She grinned to show she was joking, and sucked up another meaty ribbon. 'Fit for the Pope,' she added.

'It's just tripe!' protested Carenza. 'You've cooked for the Pope himself! Dear God! Is this why they kicked you out of the Vatican?'

'Tripe fit for the Pope,' mumbled Tessina. 'You could call it that. Or Holy Tripe. But, Nino, am I to understand that this is going to be a regular feature of our life together?'

'My poor girl,' said Carenza. 'I'm afraid he's completely off his head. And he always has been.'

But I wasn't listening. Because the taste unfolding on my tongue was Ugolino's *trippa alla Fiorentina*, everything: the meats, the spices were there, of course. I'd put them together a thousand times. But there was something else, not just the sum of mundane ingredients: a spirit. A ghost? More like the animating spirit that makes the meat of our bodies into living beings. It was perfect. If God put down his hand, took up Florence and squeezed it like an orange, the juice would taste like the food in my bowl.

'I don't understand,' I said. 'I've got to go back.'

'Nino, what's the matter?' asked Tessina. She pushed her bowl away. 'Isn't it what you wanted? This is what you've been trying to make. I know you don't taste things like I do, but you've done it now, my love. You're home. You don't need to chase any more ghosts.'

'But I've got to know, Tessina,' I said. 'It's the one thing I need to find out. The rest of it . . . It's true: Ugolino could have cooked for the Pope, or my cardinals, or any one of those people. There's nothing to this: but it's perfect. It shouldn't be perfect. I promise, just this and then *basta*. But I've got to find out.'

'I'll come, then,' said Tessina.

'Don't encourage the idiot!' Carenza protested.

'But I love him,' said Tessina. 'And this is the part I loved first of all.'

'Madonna *cagna*,' sighed Carenza. 'I love him too. So I am the idiot, eh? Go! Go. But come back this time.'

We all but ran back across the city. There was proper smoke coming from the chimney now, and when Donna Ulivetta opened the door to us, the room behind her was a little more airy.

'But what can be wrong?' she asked, looking almost frightened.

'Nothing's wrong,' I assured her. 'But there's something I don't understand. Perhaps you can tell me. Something about your husband's cooking.'

'There's very little a maestro like you wouldn't understand, I'm afraid.' She thought for a moment. 'Good people, are you hungry? I've made a little nettle pottage.'

We could not refuse her hospitality. She seated us at the stained cypress-wood table, bustled, set down little bowls of fragrant, muddy green soup in front of us.

'Please, Donna Ulivetta: I don't understand. I've made your husband's tripe, and it was perfect! I've done it more times than I can count, exactly that way, but it's always been ordinary until today!'

'It is ordinary!' she said, sitting down stiffly. '*Trippa!* What could be more ordinary? He put the things in a pot and stirred them with his spoon. That's what he did every day, and that's what he was doing when he died. Stirring! There is nothing more ordinary, surely?'

'That's what you do, Nino,' said Tessina. 'It's his life as well, Donna Ulivetta,' she said to the puzzled woman. 'And do you know, I've known him all my life, and I never saw him cook until today. Stirring a big pot, with your dear husband's lovely spoon.'

'*Dio* . . . Yes! Tessina . . .' I stood up. 'The spoon! He must have put something on the spoon! Donna Ulivetta, did Ugolino rub anything onto the spoon? A spice? A herb? Something from your garden?'

'Nothing, nothing! It was just our old spoon. He used it in the day, I used it at night. I would have known if there was anything funny about it.'

'Wait – you used it as well?'

'Of course.' She shrugged, calmer now, no doubt realizing that I wasn't the dangerous sort of madman, just the persistent kind.

'But what did you cook with it?'

'Cook? What would I cook? The usual things. Plain food. *Our* food.'

'But it could be anything, the flavour! Anything. Why, signora, did he let you use his spoon?'

'Why? We only had one. When he died, I bought another spoon, because . . . I don't know. It reminded me too much of him. But when he was alive we had one spoon, like most people. Because we were poor.' She paused and raised a sooty hand to wipe away the tear that was creeping down her cheek. 'Because we were poor, and because he loved me,' she said. 'He stood behind those pots every day, and when he gave me the spoon, I could feel where his hand had been. His fingers had grown old around the wood, you see. When he came home, I had to rub them, just to get them straight. That's what I could do for him. He worked all day, stirring pots, because he loved me.'

And then I understood: only then, sipping nettle soup, tasting the green shoots, the force of life itself that had pushed the young nettles up through paving stones, cobbles, packed mud. Ugolino had flavoured his dishes with this. With everything: *our* food. The steam that drifted, invisible, through the streets. The recipes, written in books or whispered on deathbeds. The pots people stirred every day of their lives: tripe, *ribollita*, *peposo*, *spezzatino*, *bollito*. Making circles with a spoon, painting suns and moons and stars in broth, in *battuta*. Writing, even those who don't know their letters, a lifelong song of love.

Tessina dipped her spoon, sipped, dipped again. I would never taste what she was tasting: the alchemy of the soil, the ants which had wandered across the leaves as they pushed up towards the sun; salt and pepper, nettles; or just soup: good, ordinary soup.

And I don't know what she is tasting now, as the great dome of the cathedral turns a deeper red, as she takes the peach from my hand and steals a bite. Does she taste the same sweetness I do? The vinegar pinpricks of wasps' feet, the amber, oozing in golden beads, fading into warm brown, as brown as Maestro Brunelleschi's tiles? I don't know now; I didn't then. But there was one thing we both tasted in that good, plain soup, though I would never have found it on my tongue, not as long as I lived. It had no flavour, but it was there: given by the slow dance of the spoon and the hand which held it. And it was love.

ᐖPPETITE
Reading Group Notes

The Story Behind *Appetite*

Appetite began as pure escapism, a way to write myself out of a time and place I wasn't particularly enjoying: New England in winter just as the banking crisis was about to hit. The central idea first came to me as I was making sausages in an unheated workroom looking out onto a frozen river in Vermont. My wife and I owned a restaurant, the economy was tanking and our business was on the skids. I was making Tuscan *salsicce* with a hand-cranked machine and thinking about how much I'd rather be in Florence and buying these sausages from a stall in the Mercato Centrale than grinding them out here in sub-zero New England with bankruptcy hanging over my head. We'd last been in Florence a couple of years earlier and the meals we'd eaten there, along with the all-encompassing passion that goes along with Italian food, had been the main inspiration for our restaurant. That day I was using a very simple recipe: just pork, salt, pepper, a little ground ginger and grated orange zest, which is almost perfect; so as I cranked the handle my mind wandered off on a ramble about Tuscan cooking, the creativity of food in general and the artistry of the best chefs (I'm a writer, not a trained chef, hence the lack of mental discipline – the *salsicce*, by the way, turned out fine).

The next day I started doing some research – I think I was actually looking up sausage recipes, not book ideas – and stumbled across the fact that Fra Filippo Lippi, the great Florentine painter, was the son of a butcher. *Appetite*, in a sense, emerged right then and there. I began to wonder: what had it been like to be an artist growing up in a world of food? If you look at the self-portraits of Fra Filippo, he doesn't look at all like the beautiful, glowing figures with which he peoples his art. He's short, stocky, blunt. He looks like everybody's idea of a butcher. Incongruous – but why not? The Italian Renaissance was more than a rebirth of science and classical learning. The first real cookbooks were written in the fifteenth century. The first celebrity chef, Maestro Martino of Como, died sometime in the 1450s. So I pondered: you have the man destined to be a butcher, who became a painter instead. What if you reverse things? What if you have a cook with the eyes and the soul of a painter? And so Nino arrived.

Shortly after that, the restaurant closed and things got extremely chaotic. Then we had to put a lot of pieces back together. I had another book to finish. We ended up moving home to England, and I wrote *Appetite* – appropriately enough – on the dining table of our tiny cottage, with meals being set out around me, children playing under my chair, building work going on, Lego pieces falling onto my keyboard through a crack in the ceiling. But this was what I was writing about: to cook is to bring order out of chaos, to some extent, and food brings us together on so many different levels. I realized that writing about food kept putting me in touch with universal aspects of life: family, love, hunger, creativity, greed, revulsion, joy. I found myself communing with the memory of my grandmother, who came from Northern Greece: how I'd watched her cook as a child, her plump hands stirring egg yolks into flour for a cake, or spicing a dish of stuffed cabbage. Standing on a chair and watching my mother cook. Wandering through Florence as a teenager and realizing that incredible cooking smells were wafting through every window, then walking into a museum and being confronted by the most sublime art. I was immersed in a character, Nino, who lives entirely through his senses and although Nino certainly isn't me, I found the whole experience very revealing. I learned a lot from writing *Appetite*.

Philip Kazan, 2014

For Discussion

⚘ How do the epigraphs set up your expectations for the novel to come?

⚘ Why is remembering in Florence so difficult?

⚘ Why does Arrigo see the world 'as the saints must see it', and Nino approach 'God as the layman that I am'?

⚘ 'You really are like your mother. She couldn't take care of herself, only other people.' Why is Nino like this, do you think?

⚘ How far is *Appetite* about perception?

⚘ Are there coincidences in Florence?

⚘ 'But then my elders were always telling me that life had nothing to do with fairness, that a man took what he wanted, that respect was earned by setting your foot on the faces of your enemies.' Do you agree with Nino's elders?

⚘ How has the author contrasted Rome with Florence?

⚘ What do you understand by *virtù*?

♣ 'Consequences always happen. Perhaps not to you, but they happen.' To what extent are consequences a theme of the novel?

♣ '"Being right is one thing," he said. "Believing that you are right is quite another."' What is the difference?

In Conversation with Philip Kazan

QUESTION

'The kitchen would become more important to me than church.' Do you share Nino's passion?

ANSWER

I do, absolutely. Religion tells us how, why, where and when to communicate with the mystery of existence, but really we're doing that all the time, directly, through the medium of our senses, and cooking engages most of them. There's extraordinary magic in the everyday.

QUESTION

'"Some people think that life is a field strewn with peach blossom," said Carenza. "While some see things as they really are – that we live through every trial the Lord sends us, just to get to the next one."' Which are you?

ANSWER

I tend to be on the gloomy end of the spectrum, but even when things are going badly wrong I try to notice the blossom, as well. Life is both, after all: you can't have the peach tree without the dung.

QUESTION

'I would have done the same thing. I'd have to have known.' Would you have tasted the apple like Eve?

ANSWER

I'm afraid so.

QUESTION

'You always need onions.' Do you agree?

ANSWER

'Always' might be stretching it, but I do tend to get anxious when the onion bin is empty.

QUESTION

'The best art is a record of things seen, firm and solid, in some place between dreams and the everyday.' Do you agree?

ANSWER

Yes. I believe that the greatest art allows us to rest, even it's only for a moment, somewhere just outside our normal reality. And great art will always do that, if we let it.

QUESTION

Do you love kitchens when they are full or empty?

ANSWER

Cooking in a busy kitchen can be fun, but fun isn't usually the objective. I love the escapism of cooking on my own. And, of course, I'm free to make as much mess as I like.

QUESTION

'Things are never all right.' Is the Proctor correct?

ANSWER

No. Things are often quite bearable.

QUESTION

'What had the past years been but rough hands shoving me here to this very moment?' Do you believe in fate?

ANSWER

Not at all. We make our own destinies according to our actions.

QUESTION

'Better, I say, to remember than to be remembered.' True?

ANSWER

Completely.

QUESTION

'Appetite must have a moment when it is sated, or it becomes a kind of madness. It becomes ruin.' How far is this the theme of the novel?

ANSWER

To a certain degree. It's a lesson Nino has to learn the hard way. There's a fine line between appetite and greed. I think we're still trying, as we were in the fifteenth century, to tell the difference between the two, and we need to get it right. But really, I think the main theme of the book is the joy – often well-hidden – that exists in the simple fact of being alive.

Suggested Further Reading

The Birth of Venus by Sarah Dunant

The Medici by Paul Strathern

Chocolat by Joanne Harris

Girl with a Pearl Earring by Tracy Chevalier

The House of Borgia by Christopher Hibbert

The Botticelli Secret by Marina Fiorato